THE INHERITANCE

Other Novels by Tamera Alexander Include:

Fountain Creek Chronicles

Rekindled

Revealed

Remembered

Timber Ridge Reflections

From a Distance

Beyond this Moment

THE INHERITANCE

The Inheritance

Tamera
Alexander

Thomas Nelson
Since 1798

NASHVILLE DALLAS MEXICO CITY RIO DE JANEIRO BEIJING

THE INHERITANCE

Published in Nashville, Tennessee, by Thomas Nelson. Thomas Nelson is a registered trademark of Thomas Nelson, Inc.

Thomas Nelson, Inc., titles may be purchased in bulk for educational, business, fund-raising, or sales promotional use. For information, please e-mail SpecialMarkets@ThomasNelson.com.

ISBN-13: 978-1-60751-880-8

Printed in the United States of America

To Kurt
A true hero,
in the most godly sense of the word.
Go bravely wherever He leads,
and your mother's heart will trust His hand.

It was by faith that Abraham obeyed when God called him to leave home and go to another land that God would give him as his inheritance.

He went without knowing where he was going.

—Hebrews 11:8 NLT

ONE

Copper Creek, Colorado, Rocky Mountains

Tuesday, June 5, 1877

McKenna Ashford climbed down from the wagon, holding firm to the belief that she'd made the right decision in coming West—as if her brother's behavior back in Missouri had given her a choice. She surveyed the not-so-quaint-looking mountain town of Copper Creek and found it to be rougher than she'd envisioned from her cousin's descriptions in her letters. The town was more rustic with its clapboard buildings, some slightly leaning and arthritic in appearance, their cracked windows staring out like dazed, bloodshot eyes on unsuspecting passersby. But the mountains . . .

Tilting back her head, McKenna traced a visual path across the craggy range that stood sentinel over Copper Creek. And lingering on their highest snowcapped peaks, feeling both awed and humbled, she knew Janie was right—a person couldn't see these mountains and not be changed.

"So this is it? *This* is what we left home for?"

McKenna stared up at Robert, still seated on the wagon

bench, and read familiar disdain in her brother's smirk. Only fourteen—nine years her junior—Robert stood a head taller than her and sported muscles most men would be proud to claim. "All I'm asking, Robert, is that you take the wagon and go on to Vince and Janie's so they'll know we've arrived." Exhausted and hungry, she worked to keep the frustration from her tone, and failed. Again. "It's only a half mile or so from town." She gestured to the envelope on the bench seat beside him, knowing the letter's contents by heart. "The directions are in her letter. I'll get a horse from the livery and meet you there shortly."

Robert didn't move. "I don't see why I can't go on with you to the livery." He gave the letter a cursory glance. "I've never even met these people."

"Yes, you have. I've told you before, they knew you when—" She caught herself, realizing it was no use, considering the stubborn set of his jaw. "You don't remember Vince and Janie because you were too young. But they'll remember you. Though they won't recognize you, that's for sure." Patience teetering, she managed a smile. "Just tell them who you are. They're expecting us."

"I still don't see why I can't just—"

"Robert!" She exhaled. "Please . . . simply do as I've asked. I'll work out the details with the livery owner and join you shortly."

He narrowed his eyes. Using more force than necessary, he released the brake on the wagon. "You're probably right, sis. It's best you go on without me. We both know *you're* the one he's hired anyway. Whether he knows it yet or not." He gave the reins a hard whip.

The wagon jolted forward and McKenna jumped back, the wheel narrowly missing her boot. Her patience threadbare, she watched him go. How could she love that boy so much and still want to throttle him?

Seeing Robert's natural ability in the way he managed the heavy rig, she felt a twinge of envy. They'd purchased the horses and wagon in Denver, and she'd wondered how he would manage over the steep mountain passes. But there wasn't a rig Robert couldn't handle—or build, for that matter. Saddlery equipment and supplies they'd brought from home weighed down the wagon bed—tools of their father's trade she hadn't been able to part with. No matter how destitute their father's untimely passing had left them. In so many ways . . .

Wagons cluttered the main thoroughfare, but Robert maneuvered his way around them without a hitch. Lengthy hours spent alone with him on the two-week journey from Missouri to Colorado had been made even more so by his repeated sullen sighs. Constant reminders of his not wanting to be here. As if she could forget.

She held her breath as he cut close corners on two freighters—twice. Intentionally, no doubt, judging by the smart tip of his hat to the drivers as he passed. Each driver threw him a dark look, and both were large enough to break Robert in two. Not an easy task with her brother's broad build.

Her eyes narrowed. Part of her prayed Robert wouldn't do anything to further provoke the men, while the rest of her wondered if a good thrashing might do him some good. Her own hand at disciplining him had never been a strong one, but then again she hadn't sought the role of mother that God had thrust upon her at such a young age. *Please don't let him do here what he did back home.* This move was their chance to start over again, and they wouldn't get another one. She couldn't afford for this attempt at a new beginning to fail.

She arched her back and stretched the taut muscles in her shoulders and neck, weary from the day's travel from Denver. A surprisingly cool breeze swept down from the snow-drifted mountains, granting reprieve from the afternoon heat.

The air here—she took a deep breath and her lungs tingled—tasted like God had breathed it fresh from heaven's storehouse that very morning. Surely this was a sign.

Since stepping off the train in Denver, she'd felt a sense of homecoming. It sounded silly, even to her, and she'd be hard-pressed to explain it—coming home to a place she'd never been before. Not one usually given to romanticisms, she couldn't help but wonder if perhaps this move to Copper Creek was by God's design after all. Perhaps this was the inheritance He'd been storing up for her. The inheritance her father had failed to provide.

Grasping her skirt with one hand, she made for the boardwalk, working to avoid numerous deposits left from animals who had passed that way. People occupying the planked walkway and those milling about the entry to the mercantile nodded when their eyes met hers. She returned their smiles when offered. Maybe she and Robert really could start over here.

Maybe Copper Creek could become home. A place where no one knew about their past.

Her spirits lightening, she stepped inside the mercantile. She'd meant to purchase a little something for Janie's five-year-old daughter, Emma, before now, but hadn't. Just a small gift, a token of appreciation for Emma's willingness to share her room—only until McKenna arranged for another place for her and Robert to live. She thought of Emma's drawings tucked safely inside her satchel. Sweetly penciled renditions of a cabin and barn that Janie had included with a recent letter. She could hardly wait to meet the little artist.

McKenna met an older couple coming down the main aisle of the mercantile and scooted aside to allow them room to pass. Catching a good-natured wink that the elderly gentleman tossed in her direction, she couldn't miss the attentiveness he showered on the woman beside him. The way he held her steady at the elbow, his other hand cradling the small of her back. The way he anticipated the placement of her feet as she started down the boardwalk stairs. So caring. So gentle.

Watching them, McKenna found herself smiling. How long

had they been together? What manner of time and experience had fostered such closeness? A closeness so inherently personal, so endearing, it was nearly tangible. The questions nudged at a memory better left buried, and her smile faded.

There had been someone special in her life. Once. Someone she'd thought she might grow old with. But Michael's love of honor and justice ended up taking him away from her. Honor was an attractive thing in a man. Until it crowded you out of his heart.

Unsettled by the memories, McKenna swallowed against the tightness in her throat and pulled her attention back to the task at hand.

After browsing for several moments, she finally settled on the perfect gift for Emma—a wooden toy consisting of a little cup with a ball attached by a string. She'd had something similar when she was about Emma's age and had loved it. She paid for the item while eyeing a package of what looked to be homemade cookies on the counter. From where she stood, she smelled the sugar and spice. Her favorite.

"Would you like some cookies, ma'am? I bake them myself. Fresh every day."

McKenna looked up at the woman behind the counter and then discreetly counted the dwindling coins in her change purse. "I'd better not today, thank you. It's so close to dinner. But they do smell delicious."

The compliment earned her a smile, but McKenna felt her cheeks burning all the same, sensing the woman knew her real reason for refusing. Thanking her, McKenna quickly exited the store, consoling her hunger with the knowledge that Janie would have dinner warming on the stove and a pan of her delicious buttermilk biscuits in the oven. It had been seven years, but McKenna still remembered the taste of Janie's biscuits, along with the honey butter she served alongside.

Realizing she'd failed to ask the woman in the mercantile

where the livery was, McKenna approached a gentleman on the street and made an inquiry.

"Which livery you want, ma'am? We got us three."

Three? She hoped Janie's advice about which livery to contact had been sound. She needed the livery that would provide the most business for her and Robert. After the cost of traveling here, and then purchasing the horses and wagon, their funds were nearly depleted. "I'm referring to the livery owned by a Mr. Casey Trenton."

He pointed. "Trenton's place is on the other side of town, toward the mining camps." The man—short of stature but with a wealth of heft about his middle to compensate—pursed his lips and eyed her up and down with improper leisure. "You just get off the stage, miss?"

McKenna caught the hint of onions on his breath and something untoward in his manner. "If you'll excuse me." She moved past him down the uneven walkway, ignoring his repeated attempts to pursue the conversation.

She headed in the direction he'd indicated, glancing behind her to make sure he wasn't following. He was, but only with his eyes. She took the nearest side street. As a rule, for all their boast and swagger, men were an easily read gender consisting of too few chapters and all too common a subject.

It felt good to walk. She lengthened her stride, eager to conduct her business with Mr. Trenton, the livery owner, and find her way out to Vince and Janie's before sunset. Which might be sooner than she expected with Copper Creek nestled so close between the mountains. "*A supply depot to nearby mining towns*" is what Janie had called Copper Creek, which McKenna hoped boded well for the use of both her and Robert's talents.

She passed structures made of hand-hewn pine, closely spaced, as though still huddled together from the harsh winter this territory was known for. And yet, already, a liking for this place was growing inside her. She preferred it to the big-city feel of St. Joseph that she and Robert had left behind.

It would be good to see Janie again after all these years, Vince too. Janie was a cousin by blood, but more of a sister in heart. The sister McKenna had always wanted. Janie could well have had their second baby by now. She was due any day. The last letter McKenna had received had been dated two months ago, but spring was a busy time on a new ranch, not to mention when one had a five-year-old running underfoot. How well she remembered Robert at that age.

"Good afternoon, ma'am." A young woman smiled as she passed on the boardwalk, a little boy situated on one hip and a slightly older one clutching her skirt, trailing behind.

"Good day." McKenna grinned seeing the older boy's short legs pumping to keep up, his smile saying he enjoyed the challenge. Robert had beamed that very same way as a toddler too, holding tight to her skirt as they'd gone to the mercantile together. She sighed. All that seemed like forever ago now. So much had changed.

She lifted her gaze to where the sun crept steadily toward the snowcapped peaks, lustering the mountains a burnished gold. Some days, admittedly, she'd wondered if she'd only been grasping at the last proverbial straw in coming to Copper Creek. But she'd prayed long and hard about it, investing many sleepless nights until finally . . . she'd felt a nudge inside. So it was gratifying to feel this deepening certainty settle inside her. Finally, a well-made decision.

She peered into shop windows as she passed—a women's clothier and a cobbler's shop, a bakery where the door stood propped open. The aroma of freshly baked bread and something sweet drifted through the portal and caused her pace to slow. Her stomach tightened in hunger. But she consoled herself again with thoughts of Janie waiting dinner on her, and continued on.

Cooking was a talent she possessed in fair amount, but baking was not. As a young boy, Robert had let her know that her leftover biscuits made excellent fodder for his slingshot. And he'd been right. But a woman couldn't be good at everything.

Best to learn early on what your strengths were and make the most of them. She'd been forced to learn her strengths early enough, and her weaknesses too, which were plenty.

She reached the end of the boardwalk and stepped down to the street. Some people might say she'd been forced to learn them at too young an age, but at least she'd—

Pounding hooves portended the rider only seconds before he was upon her.

McKenna dove from his path—narrowly escaping the horse's hooves—and hit the boardwalk stairs with a thud. Searing pain shot through her shoulder and down into her left hand. The man *had* to have seen her, yet he'd made no effort to stop!

Blinking, disoriented, she finally managed to stand—only to hear the answering pursuit.

TWO

McKenna scrambled to move from the second rider's path. But unlike the first man, this rider reined his mount sharp to the left to avoid her. Bits of gravel went flying as they rounded the corner. In one fluid motion, he swept aside his long black duster and retrieved the rifle sheathed on his saddle before cutting down an alleyway.

McKenna stared in the direction he'd disappeared, feeling an unpleasant pulsing in her left hand. Looking down, she discovered her left palm bloodied from a small gash at the base of her thumb. So much blood for so tiny a wound. But the cut went deep. Wincing, she reached inside her reticule for her handker—

She flinched at the sound of the gunshot.

The rifle's report ricocheted off the mountains and reverberated in waves back across the town.

She paused, waiting, her pulse ticking off the seconds. But no more gunfire sounded.

Using the handkerchief, she stemmed the flow of blood and wrapped the delicate lace-edged cloth around the wound. Her mother's initials, embroidered into the ivory material, quickly turned a deep crimson. She was certain of two things—the cut would need sutures to ensure proper healing. And the bloodstains would never wash clean from the treasured heirloom.

Steps on the boardwalk drew her attention, and she became aware of people who had filtered out from shops and buildings onto the walkway. They searched up and down the street. A shuffling noise behind her brought her gaze up.

A petite woman, dark hair drawn straight back from her face and fastened in a knot at the nape of her neck, loomed above her on the boardwalk. "You hurt, miss?" Thin, black brows arched behind a razor-straight fringe of hair.

Her almond-shaped eyes were dark and probing, and McKenna's first thought when looking into them was . . . *she's familiar with pain.*

The woman gestured. "You hurt!" The inflection in her soft voice changed. She rose and turned, and with tiny mincing steps, she disappeared through a shop doorway and returned seconds later, clean cloth in hand.

McKenna couldn't help but notice the woman's gait and her shoes—blue slippers made of embroidered silk. Exquisite. So small. And so pointed.

Wordless, the woman stooped and reached for her hand. With motions that bespoke experience, she gently removed the handkerchief and rewrapped the injury with the fresh cloth, looping the material between McKenna's thumb and forefinger, then around her wrist, with the practiced care of a physician.

Grateful, McKenna watched as she worked.

Delicate described her best, as did *graceful*, and when the woman leaned down to tear the end of the soft cloth with her white teeth, McKenna got a whiff of something pleasant in her black hair. Her slim fingers worked quickly, tying the two ends of the makeshift bandage into a loose knot. Then she smiled and spoke in a language McKenna didn't understand.

As if realizing what she'd just done, the woman quickly bowed her head and squinted as though searching for the words. "Better . . . now?"

McKenna glanced at the bandage. "Yes, much better now . . . thank you." She tried moving her shoulder and grimaced. It wasn't dislocated. Thanks to a spirited stallion a couple of years earlier, she knew what that felt like. Still, the joint would be sore for several days, not to mention bruised.

A man appeared in the doorway from which the woman had come, his countenance stern. He was shorter in stature, yet there was nothing weak-looking about him. The hair on the front of his head was shaved off above the temples, and he wore the rest in a tight braid extending down his back to his waist.

He addressed the woman in a sharp tone, and though McKenna couldn't understand what he was saying, she got the gist of it—he wasn't pleased.

The woman reacted immediately, grabbing the bloodied handkerchief as she rose. Instinctively, McKenna reached for it. "No, please, I—"

"I take," the woman whispered. "I wash." Her smile lived only a second before her expression smoothed into an unreadable mask. With hurried, stuttered steps, she moved to stand, head bowed, before the man who shared her distinctive features and clothing. She wore gray trousers, similar to his, though not as full, with a knee-length tunic of rich blue that mimicked the style of his outer coat.

Was this her husband, perhaps? He appeared too close in age to be her father, but McKenna would be hard-pressed to guess the woman's exact age. Or his, for that matter. In appearance, she looked younger—but her manner contradicted that. Regardless, something about her inspired kinship. And trust.

Head still bowed, the woman folded her hands demurely at her waistline, clutching the stained handkerchief. McKenna opened her mouth to say something, but a sharp look from the man kept her from it. She'd carried that handkerchief with her every day of the past fourteen years, since the day of Robert's birth—and their mother's death.

The man spoke again, his voice softer this time, and only then did the woman lift her gaze. She nodded and hurried inside without a backward glance. His focus shifted to McKenna. Though she'd seen Chinese men and women before, she had never made their acquaintance. He said nothing, but McKenna sensed an unspoken question. She nodded once and brushed the dirt from her skirt, indicating she would be fine. He walked inside and closed the door behind him.

Her focus rested there, on the door, and she wondered what it would be like to be subservient to a man in that fashion. She couldn't imagine.

With her hand throbbing and shoulder aching, McKenna climbed the stairs to the boardwalk, no longer interested in seeking out the livery this afternoon. She only wanted to get to Vince and Janie's home before dark. Surely Janie would have salve for the wound. She would seek a doctor's care first thing in the morning.

One by one, the shopkeepers and patrons who'd been staring—some white, most Chinese—began retreating inside, and she walked in the direction of Vince and Janie's. Before rounding the corner, she looked back to read the shingle above the door where the man and woman had entered, and smiled.

Laundry.

"I take. I wash." The woman's comment made more sense now and renewed McKenna's hope of seeing the kerchief again, though not of the stains coming clean. Nodding to lingering onlookers, she retraced the path to the mercantile. Janie's instructions on how to get to their home had used that store as a reference point, so best to begin there and follow the directions she had memorized from Janie's letter.

Two streets over, McKenna spotted a carved wooden shingle bearing the name *Dr. Clive Foster*. Instinctively, she glanced at her bandaged left hand. The gash was small, but already the blood had soaked through the bandage, and she changed her mind about waiting to see the doctor until tomorrow. Having it sewn up tonight would mean getting a jump on healing and less chance for infection. She could also get a poultice from the doctor that would help with the pain and swelling. She couldn't risk not having full use of both hands, not with the current state of their finances.

Decision made, she knocked on the physician's door, peering through the front window. Waning sunlight illumined the interior of the office. But she saw no one within. She knocked again, louder this time, wondering if the doctor was in the back of the building, beyond the closed door on the far side of the room.

When tested, the knob gave without argument. She stepped inside. "Dr. Foster? Hello?"

Bottles of various curatives lined two shelves, clearly marked in neat legible script, all with labels facing out at the same angle. Lidded glass jars bearing names of herbs she recognized sat on nearby shelves, arranged with similar care. Dr. Foster's organization boded well for his attention to details. She only hoped that same quality would describe his suturing abilities.

"Is anyone here?"

No answer.

Turning to leave, she spotted labels she recognized—*willow bark* and *burdock root*. During her father's lengthy illness, she'd learned a fair amount about mixing poultices and had gleaned a basic knowledge from their physician about which herbs cured certain diseases or helped relieve symptoms. She'd even experimented with using poultices on leg injuries for horses in the livery back home and had witnessed significant improvement.

Without her handkerchief, she had nothing in which to wrap the herbs. She scanned the office and spotted a stack of apothecary papers tucked on a side table. With painstaking effort, her left hand throbbing, she managed to fold a paper to form a makeshift envelope and sprinkled enough bark and burdock root for two poultices, then withdrew two coins from her reticule. Surely Dr. Clive Foster wouldn't mind parting with some herbs in exchange for remuneration.

Finding paper and quill on his desk, she penned a note to the doctor explaining what she'd done and declaring her intention to return on the morrow for him to suture her hand; then she signed her name, thankful that the injury wasn't on her dominant hand. If she needed to pay him more, she would, or perhaps he would be open to bartering. After all, doctors rode horses and horses needed saddles.

She situated the note and coins on his patient table, then thought better of it and placed them on his desk. He'd be sure to see them there. By the time she finished, her hand was aching. She retrieved her reticule and turned to go when the door to the clinic burst open.

It slammed off the back wall and would have closed again had a powerfully built man not stepped across the threshold, more than filling the doorway. Sunlight at his back obscured his face, and she couldn't make out his features.

But the long black duster told her who he was, as did the lifeless body slung over his shoulder.

THREE

The man in the doorway shifted. His breath came heavy as he dumped the body unceremoniously onto the examining table.

The patient, if he was still alive, was unconscious, and McKenna winced at the dull thud of his head hitting the wooden surface. Blood stained the front of his shirt—stemming from a gunshot wound, she presumed—and his left arm dangled from the table at an unnatural angle.

"You're not the doctor." Irritating certainty undergirded the man's voice as sunlight played off his hardened features. He removed his hat and ran a hand through his dark hair. "If you are, then this'll be a first for me."

His boots and trousers were covered in dirt, and the long duster hid the precise definition of his frame, but one thing was certain—he was impressive in stature and rivaled the height McKenna imagined Robert would eventually reach.

"No, I'm not the doctor," she answered, attempting to match his confidence—and sarcasm. "Sorry to disappoint."

His brow lifted slightly. "Who said anything about being

disappointed?" Hinting at a smile, he laid his hat aside. "Is he here?"

Understanding who he meant, she shook her head. "I called out. No one answered." His gaze slid to the door behind her, and she guessed at his thoughts. "Those are likely his private quarters. I don't think we should—"

He opened the door without knocking. "Dr. Foster? You back there, sir?" Seconds passed. He turned around. "Doesn't look like he's in." His eyes narrowed. "You ever sewn up a man?"

Glancing back at the bloodstained shirt, McKenna didn't answer. Her thoughts raced, trying to form a response that would skirt the truth without being a lie so she could be on her way. The subtle change in his expression told her the delay had been a mistake.

"I'll assume that to be a yes." A wry smile tipped his mouth. "And I'd wager you're good with a needle too."

She stood a little taller. "Actually, you're mistaken in your assumption." He was right on the second count, but no need to volunteer that. "I've sewn up animals before, but never a pers—"

"That'll do." He gave a humorless laugh. "Especially in this case." He gestured to her bandaged hand. "You get hurt back there? When he tried to run you down?"

"So he *did* see me?" Her instincts had been right.

"Sure he did."

"But why would he—"

"Because he knew that if I caught him, he'd be tried—and hanged—for murder, which he will be. If he ran you down, then I would've had to stop and see to you. So I'm much obliged for you being so quick on your feet, ma'am." He motioned to her hand again. "Is that his doing?"

She fingered the edge of the bandage. "Yes, but it's not serious. It just needs a few stitches"—she arched a brow—"which is why I'm here."

He watched her, saying nothing. She got the feeling he was

the type who could read people well, whether they wanted to be read or not. Being of the "not" persuasion, she looked away.

Infusing her tone with a sweetness that didn't come naturally, she moved toward the door. "I appreciate your concern, sir, but if you'll excuse me . . . I need to be on my—"

The gleam in his eyes brought her up short and said he hadn't found her feigned gentility convincing. The smile edging up one side of his mouth hinted that he wasn't the least bit insulted either. Quite the opposite, in fact. He seemed amused.

Her hand tightened on the door latch and, unbidden, an image came to mind—that of him rounding the corner earlier and reining to one side to avoid her. She looked at him, then to the injured man stirring on the table. He would be conscious soon if they didn't do something. At the earlier mention of murder, her compassion for the prisoner had all but vanished. *He'd be tried and hanged*, or so his captor said. Cautious of both men, she weighed the cost of helping.

Remembering the kindness of the Chinese woman didn't help her decision. Finally McKenna sighed, her sense of duty winning out. She deposited her reticule on the desk. "We'll need the ether." She gestured. "It's on the shelf behind you, in a bottle."

"Which one?"

"The one labeled *Ether*." Silence punctuated the curtness of her reply, lending an edge to the response that she hadn't intended but didn't entirely regret. Not with the way he'd coerced her into helping.

He turned, bottle in hand. "You can check me, ma'am, but I think this is the right one." His expression proclaimed victory and an invitation for sparring, if she was willing.

She wasn't.

Ignoring him, McKenna found a clean cloth in the third drawer she checked, as well as supplies for suturing.

"I appreciate your assistance, Mrs. . . ."

She huffed softly, thinking him coy, then noticed that the bandage on her left hand did indeed cover part of her ring finger. Not that a person could always tell by that. Wedding rings were expensive. "It's Miss, actually. Miss McKenna Ashford."

He smiled again, but this time it was different somehow, as though he found her answer pleasing. "Marshal Wyatt Caradon," he offered quietly. "Pleased to make your acquaintance, Miss Ashford. I appreciate your willingness to help."

His sincerity was unexpected and his politeness, disarming. Nodding, McKenna turned back to her preparations but snuck glances when he wasn't looking.

A razor hadn't touched his face in at least a week, maybe longer. But it was the badge on his vest that drew the bulk of her attention. Even in the dim light, she read the lettering clear enough—*U.S. Marshal*—and her stomach knotted. She was especially glad now that she'd followed her instincts and sent Robert on ahead.

Marshal Caradon shrugged out of his black duster, draped it across a chair, and began rolling up his sleeves. She unbuttoned her suit jacket and laid it aside, then edged up the sleeves of her shirtwaist, mindful of her bandage. He hadn't asked her if she was left- or right-handed. Apparently he assumed right. Uncertain whether or not she was glad she'd stayed to help, she was here now, and no good would come from getting on the wrong side of local authorities. Not again.

She poured the anesthetic on the rag and held it to the patient's nose and mouth, familiar with this procedure and praying Dr. Foster would return any minute. She'd seen her share of wounds, both on animals and humans, so it wasn't the blood that bothered her. She'd just never had to worry about leaving a scar before. "I'll do what I can, but I can't promise the stitches will be comely."

"Comely doesn't count for much with him. This only has to hold him until he hangs."

She stilled, disquieted by the marshal's response and by his steady, unrepentant stare. She located matches and lit the oil lamp, then poured water from the pitcher into the washbasin and set it on a nearby table. "I'll need your help taking off his shirt."

Caradon assisted, tossing the bloodied shirt on the floor. "You have someplace to be, Miss Ashford? Something I'm keeping you from?"

McKenna gently probed beneath the injured man's right shoulder, aware of Caradon's close proximity. "Would you please hold the lamp so I can see better?"

He reached for the lamp and held it steady above her head. "There's no bullet in him. It went clean through."

Sure enough, she felt the exit wound. "Was that by chance or by design, Marshal?"

"By design." He gave a faint shrug. "I can shoot fairly well."

"Fairly well?" She laughed softly. "Your aim was perfect." Right between the man's upper chest muscles and his collar bone. Straight through. "Were you riding when you shot him?"

"Yes, ma'am."

Even more impressive. "Fairly well" didn't come close to describing this man's ability to shoot. Something handy in his line of work, no doubt. His tone was noticeably absent of pride too, as though anyone could do such a thing. "Let's roll him onto his side, please."

Caradon did and held him there as she cleaned the wound in the man's back. She managed ten sutures, an eleventh to be sure it would hold, then tied the stitch and bandaged it. Caradon eased him back down. The man on the table began to stir, and she held the cloth over his nose and mouth. His breathing quickly evened.

"You live here in Copper Creek, Miss Ashford?"

She dipped a fresh cloth in the water and washed the bullet wound in the patient's shoulder as best she could. "I do now. We arrived today." She paused and straightened, the muscles in her back in spasms from bending over the table, and from too much riding on trains and coaches and wagons.

She thought of Janie waiting at home, watching for her, and hoped she wasn't worrying. Robert's only concern would be that she'd left him overlong with people he didn't know. He hated making chitchat. She just hoped he wasn't acting sullen and stone-faced with Vince, Janie, and Emma, like he so often did with her.

Hearing a clock ticking somewhere behind her, she rethreaded the needle and focused again on her task. Suturing a man was different from suturing a horse, and very definitely different from sewing saddles. Yet something about the repetition of the act felt similar, which made her wonder if she was doing it right.

"We?"

Finishing the third suture in the man's shoulder, she peered up at Caradon, the needle poised between her right thumb and forefinger. "I beg your pardon?"

"You said 'we arrived today.'"

Not wanting to talk, she tied off a fourth suture, and a fifth, aware of him watching her. "My brother and I."

"Where did you move from?"

She raised her head to find him leaning close, their faces inches apart. "If you don't mind, Marshal Caradon, could we . . . not talk right now?"

The tanned lines at the corners of his eyes tightened ever so slightly. "Not much on that, are you, ma'am? Talking, I mean."

Though his expression denied it, she heard a smile in his voice, yet she held back from responding to it. Outwardly anyway. Someone like Wyatt Caradon was the last person she, or Robert, needed in their lives right now. "I don't mind talking, Marshal. When I'm not exhausted, famished, and stitching up a gunshot wound."

Catching his grin before she looked away, she finished suturing and bandaging the wound. The man's left forearm was badly sprained, though not broken, and she did her best to wrap and secure it against his chest in a makeshift sling. Dr. Foster would have to see to the rest, if Caradon allowed him to.

By the time she washed up, gathered the dirty rags, and put the doctor's office aright, her patient was waking again. She reached for the ether, but Caradon stopped her.

"I carried him in here, but he's walking to jail on his own."

When they left the doctor's office minutes later, dusk had fallen. Two lamplighters made their way down the street on wooden stilts, torches in hand, lighting the coal lamps that sat atop poles in front of each building.

Aware of the prisoner's continued stare, McKenna made certain not to look directly at him. He was about Caradon's height and build, and had a surprisingly boyish quality about him—that ended abruptly whenever he opened his mouth.

"I about ran you over this afternoon, didn't I, ma'am?"

McKenna ignored the man's comment and fell back a couple of steps.

"That's enough, Slater," Caradon warned, his hand resting on the gun at his hip. "Keep walking and keep quiet."

"Wished I'd been awake when you was sewin' me up, miss. Maybe I'd've gotten me a better look at them—"

Caradon shoved him hard in the back, right in the wound. Slater moaned and stumbled forward, cursing him through gritted teeth.

Tired and eager to be on her way, McKenna paused at the edge of the boardwalk. She'd planned on arriving at Janie's well before nightfall, and she'd also hoped to get a horse from the livery. But nothing had gone as planned . . . Debating her options, she patted her right coat pocket and felt the Derringer tucked safely inside. Her decision was made. "I think I'll find my own way from here, Marshal Caradon."

Slater started to say something, but one look from Caradon silenced him.

"The jail's just ahead, ma'am. If you'll walk with me there, I'd like to see you home. Or to wherever it is you're going."

"That's most kind of you, Marshal, but not necessary. I'm sure I'll be able to protec—"

"*Thank you* for agreeing to let me do this." His tone held finality, and he gave her a look she couldn't quite interpret. "It's the least I can do, after your kindness."

She stared, wondering if he'd misunderstood her. But the faint challenge in his eyes said he hadn't. He'd overruled her—nicely—but he'd still overruled her. And she didn't like it, nor was she accustomed to it. "Again, sir . . . your offer is generous, but I'm perfectly comfortable with—"

"I won't be long." He touched the brim of his hat. "Thank you, ma'am."

Slater snickered. "I think the lady's trying to tell you to—"

Caradon gripped the man's upper arm, and Slater fell silent again. They started down the darkened street. After a few paces, Caradon glanced back.

McKenna hadn't moved.

"Please, ma'am." His tone held an entreating quality it hadn't before. "I'd appreciate the opportunity to see you home. Safely," he added, gesturing discreetly toward Slater, whose back was turned.

Not understanding how someone who was going to jail could possibly be of harm to her, she opened her mouth to protest again when Caradon raised a forefinger to his lips.

Reluctantly, she followed him, feeling foolish for doing so and angry at herself for relenting. She didn't know Wyatt Caradon any better than she knew the other man. Though, granted, the U.S. Marshal's badge must offer some reference for his character. Still, she preferred not to be told what to do.

Caradon stepped inside the sheriff's office with the prisoner, and she moved down the boardwalk a ways, intentionally not wanting to be in the same spot where he'd left her when he returned.

FOUR

Flames flickered yellow-orange behind the sooty glass of the streetlamp, making the darkness beyond the halo of light seem darker still. McKenna glanced back at the door of the jail. What was she doing standing here, waiting for this man? She didn't even know him. But she also didn't know this town. A wave of fatigue hit her again, and she wished for home. Wherever home was now. For the time being, it would be with Vince and Janie, until she and Robert could afford a place of their own.

Before leaving St. Joseph, she'd sold her great-grandparents' house. The house where her father had been born, and where her mother had given birth to her and Robert. The sale of the house, the land, and the livery had brought a goodly sum, but little remained after paying outstanding debts and the fines the sheriff had levied against Robert. Barely enough for the cost of the trip and the horses and wagon once they arrived.

The homestead and livery had been in the Ashford family for three generations, and despite her father's last wishes, she'd lost it all. Robert's poor judgment had exacted a costly blow. But at the root, she was to blame, and she knew it.

The door to the Copper Creek sheriff's office opened, and Caradon emerged. Another man followed. She took a step from the haloed light of the streetlamp deeper into the shadows.

"Thanks for keeping him locked up, Sheriff Dunn." Caradon shook the man's hand while searching the street. McKenna knew the precise moment he spotted her by his almost imperceptible nod. "I'll wire Denver in the morning. He may be with you for a night or two. Then we'll transport him back to Denver to stand trial."

"You can leave him here as long as you need. I'll assign two deputies to guard him. Got any leads on the others?"

"Not yet. But I will . . . soon."

"I'll be sure and have Thompson put a notice in the paper telling folks to be on their guard. It's good to see you again, Caradon. Been a long time since you've been through here." Dunn reached for the door. "You be sure and tell them over at Ming's that I said to treat you right while you're in town. And to feed you some of those dumplings. They don't get any better."

"I'll do that, sir. Thank you kindly."

Caradon made his way toward her, confidence in his gait.

A little *too* much confidence, in her opinion. And the closer he got, the more it grated on her. Perhaps it was the weariness from the long trip, or the culmination of everything that had gone wrong before they'd left St. Joseph, but her final smidgen of patience evaporated. As did her fear of getting off on the wrong foot with "local authorities." Caradon wasn't local. He didn't even live here. He was just passing through.

"For a second there, I wasn't sure you'd waited for me, Miss Ashford. I appreci—"

"I don't altogether know why I did, Marshal Caradon." She stepped into the light so he was sure to see her expression. "I'm certain you meant well, but I don't appreciate being spoken to—or coerced—in such a manner. Nor am I accustomed to it. Now, if you'll excuse me, I'm going to find my own way. Good evening, sir." She turned and began to walk down the dimly lit boardwalk.

"Ma'am," the marshal said, loud enough for her to hear, "you should know something."

McKenna stopped midstep but kept her back to the man.

"Ben Slater, the prisoner"—she could hear Caradon walking closer as he lowered his voice—"has accomplices. They're still out there, fairly close by is my thinking. And they've . . . violated women before—"

McKenna closed her eyes.

"—on more than one occasion. That was the reason for my request. I didn't want to say anything in front of Slater. He thinks I was only sent for him, and I'd rather him keep on thinking that, just in case."

Slowly, McKenna turned, head bowed, glad her face was shadowed. "I didn't . . ." She swallowed, making herself look at him. "Obviously, I . . ."

The subtlest emotion moved across his face, not a smile, not anything she could name exactly, but it was there. And it told her he didn't hold anything against her. Still, he said nothing. Her face felt like it was on fire, but it was her pride—what little was left—that bore the brunt of her misunderstanding.

"I spoke out of turn, Marshal Caradon. I–I apologize."

"No need for that. All I wanted was the chance to explain my actions, so you wouldn't jump to any conclusions."

The way he said it made her smile. But only briefly.

He took a step closer. "That said, I'd still appreciate the chance to see you home, if you're willing."

Feeling considerably less comfortable in her surroundings than moments before, she nodded. "That would be most kind, thank you."

When they reached his horse tethered two streets over, he assisted her into the saddle. Caradon's horse was a beauty of a mare—chestnut with a black mane. As Marshal Caradon untied the reins, McKenna scooted back so she'd be riding behind him instead of afore. Her preference. But not his apparently, telling by his short-lived frown.

He climbed into the saddle and guided the horse down the street. "Not much room back there."

She balanced easily enough, having ridden this way with her father when she was a girl. Though that seemed like another lifetime ago. She was accustomed to having her own mount these days. "I'm fine. I'm an experienced rider."

"With a hand that needs stitching."

She glanced at the bandage. "I'll hold on. If the situation arises."

He gently urged the mare to a faster pace, as though challenging that statement. Sensing his test, McKenna smiled and held on to the cantle, with no fear of falling, but mindful of the close proximity of her hand to Caradon's backside.

He slowed the mare's pace.

"Can't blame me for trying," he spoke over his shoulder, grinning.

"Marshaling must be lonelier work than I thought, Marshal Caradon." She heard his soft laugh and was reminded again of who he was. Best to keep some distance between them, and not only in proximity. She spotted the mercantile ahead, where she'd asked for him to take her. "We need to go two streets from here, and then to the left."

He did as she bade.

The majority of businesses were closed, but people still milled about on the boardwalk. Mostly men, congregated in small groups, their lit cigarettes standing out against the dark. When they rode past a crowded gaming hall near the edge of town, she couldn't help but wonder if Robert had slowed the wagon when he came to this place. If only he could learn from his mistakes . . .

A man stumbled through the hall's open doors, near legless

with liquor, and proceeded to relieve himself in the middle of the street. McKenna turned away, grateful again for Caradon's offer to provide escort.

In general, the vulgarities of men rarely surprised her anymore. Being raised around a livery had seen to that. The stranger called out to her, but Caradon rode on. And even though the circumstance warranted an "I told you so" from him, he kept silent, and her estimation of him rose by the tiniest bit.

Something occurred to her. "What happened to your prisoner's horse?"

Caradon glanced to one side. "It threw a shoe. Slater had whipped him hard, and not just today. I left the gelding with a livery here in town." Having taken the left on the road she'd directed, he reined in.

The lights of Copper Creek were a good distance behind them now, and the road ahead rose at an incline. "Where to now?" he said.

"We go about a quarter mile on this road, then there should be a turnoff, to the left, that leads to my cousin's house."

"Your cousin?"

"Yes. My cousin and her husband live here. My brother and I will be staying with them for a while."

As they rode on and took the turnoff, the lack of food and rest caught up with her, and McKenna fought to keep her eyes open. Caradon's chestnut mare was well-tempered and had a smooth, even gait. Especially for being so large. The animal was well trained, too. Obeyed Caradon's commands with hardly a nudge from him. Almost as if it read his mind.

Up ahead, the lights from a cabin shone through the night, and anticipation of seeing Janie caused McKenna to sit up a little straighter. She'd been close to other girls when she was younger, but in recent years friends had been scarce. Decisions she'd made—and those God had made for her—had seen to that. There'd always been Janie though. They'd been close since they were little, and when Janie left seven years ago to go West with her husband, it felt as if half of who McKenna was had been ripped from her.

And now . . . after all these years and so many letters exchanged, the two parts were about to be made whole again.

Caradon helped her down from the horse, and she glanced at the darkened porch. Proper manners dictated she invite him inside, at the very least to meet her relatives. But she knew what Robert's reaction would be at meeting a U.S. Marshal, and she didn't want Vince and Janie to be biased against her brother at the outset. She'd written to Janie about Robert having become "more of a challenge" recently and had shared some mild examples, while withholding the greater details.

"Marshal Caradon, I appreciate you escorting me out here, and—"

The door to the cabin opened, and Robert stepped out. A man followed him. Even in the dim light from the cabin, she could tell it wasn't Vince. Vince stood a good foot taller than this man and was a good deal younger.

Robert took the porch steps in twos and brushed past her. "I told you moving here was a mistake."

McKenna reached for him, but he jerked his arm away. "Robert, come back!"

He strode around the side of the cabin and into the darkness.

Embarrassed, and very much aware of Marshal Caradon behind her, she faced the man on the porch again, wondering what Robert had already said or done in her absence. "I'm Miss McKenna Ashford, Janie Talbot's cousin from Missouri." She glanced in the direction Robert had gone. "I apologize for my brother's behavior. The trip here was a long one, and I think he's a bit overtired right now."

"There's no cause for you to apologize for your brother, ma'am." The gentleman walked as far as the top stair and paused.

"He's young yet, and the situation here isn't what he expected. I'm Dr. Foster, Copper Creek's physician. And I'm sorry, Miss Ashford, but . . . I fear it's not what you were expecting either."

FIVE

The woman in the bed was a shadow of what Janie had once been and looked as though she were approaching the winter of her life, instead of the summer. McKenna stood near the footboard, unable to move. It didn't seem real. It couldn't be. And yet—the gauntness of her cousin's features told her it was.

She moved to the bedside and eased onto the mattress. Sweat beaded Janie's forehead. Her hand was hot to the touch.

Dr. Foster rinsed a cloth in a bowl of water on a table by the bedside and laid it across Janie's brow. "The fever set in four days ago." His voice was hushed. "Shortly after she delivered the baby."

Only then did McKenna notice the absence of the expected swell around Janie's middle. She glanced around the bedroom looking for the cradle.

"I'm sorry, Miss Ashford, but . . . the baby died shortly following his birth. He had trouble breathing. I cleared his air passage, did everything I could. But his little body just wasn't strong enough."

Aching, confused, McKenna looked back at her cousin and willed her to waken. Tears she'd managed to contain until now slipped past her defenses. "Did she have a chance to hold him?"

"Oh yes, she was very much aware of her surroundings during that time. She and little Emma hugged and loved on the boy real well . . . before he passed." He motioned toward the next room. "Emma's already asleep in her room."

It struck McKenna then that he hadn't mentioned Janie's husband. "Where is Vince?"

Regret shadowed the doctor's expression. "This will be difficult, I realize, but cholera swept through the town about a month ago. We've lifted the quarantine, so it's safe for you and your brother, and the marshal . . ."

He nodded toward the door, and she turned to see Marshal Caradon leaned forward in a chair at the kitchen table, elbows on his knees, his head bowed. She'd thought he'd already left.

The doctor's movements drew her back. "I regret to tell you, Miss Ashford, that . . . Vince was one of the first to succumb to the disease."

Still seated on the bed, McKenna couldn't shake the sensation that she was falling. As if the wooden floor beneath her had opened wide to swallow her whole. It was strange, this downward spiraling inside herself, and something she remembered from a long time ago. Fourteen years to be exact. Except the last time she'd felt this way, the baby boy hadn't died. But his mother—*their* mother—had.

She rested her head in her hands, aware of each of Janie's ragged breaths, and of the uneven rise and fall of the blanket covering her chest. The weight of this news and the burden of past weeks pressed hard. She held her breath and gave herself until the count of ten. Then exhaled. Long ago she'd learned that facing reality was inevitable. She could skulk about, trying to avoid it or pretending it wasn't there. But in the end, reality always found her. And its *finding* her seemed a harsher blow than if she'd faced the situation straight on from the very start.

A noise came from the kitchen, and she glanced up to see if Robert had returned. It was only Wyatt Caradon. He looked in her direction, but the vagueness in his eyes made her think it wasn't her he was seeing.

She wiped her tears and reached for Janie's hand again. The flame from the lantern on the bedside table danced and swayed, casting shadowy pirouettes on the plastered walls. "When was the last time she was lucid, doctor?"

"Late yesterday afternoon. When she came to, she recognized me. And asked for Aaron. The baby," he added softly.

"What did you tell her?"

"I told her he was sleeping."

"Good." She sniffed. "That was good. No need to add to her pain."

"That was my thinking too. But she knew, Miss Ashford. It took her a moment, but she remembered."

Her eyes burned as she imagined the scene. "Do you think . . ." Her voice broke and she cleared her throat before trying to speak again. "Do you think she'll get better?"

The doctor's silence answered before he did, and in that space without words, each mile of her journey to Copper Creek seemed to stretch out like a ribbon before her. As she'd been coming steadily closer, Janie had been slipping farther away. And she hadn't known. Surely she should have *felt* something. Some kind of tug on her heart. But . . . nothing.

"There's always a chance that Janie will improve, ma'am. Some mothers do, in these instances. But it's going to take more than my skills to make that happen. Janie's going to have to fight. She's going to have to want to live. Right now her body is exhausted. The labor was long and difficult. And she and Vince have been putting everything they had into this ranch, trying to make a go of it."

"She wrote me when they bought cattle last fall."

Dr. Foster nodded. "Vince was so proud of this place, of all they'd accomplished together."

McKenna rinsed the cloth again and smoothed it over Janie's cheeks and brow. Janie had always been the more delicate of the two of them, and the one with a sweeter disposition. From childhood, her tender nature had contrasted McKenna's more stubborn one. She leaned closer. "Wake up, Janie," she whispered, squeezing her hand again. "It's Kenny. Please, wake up!"

But the fever held its grip.

McKenna pushed up and walked to the open window. A cool breeze met the dampness on her face, and she breathed its heady scent. Lavender. Planted outside the bedroom window, just as Janie had written. A knot of emotions tightened her stomach, and she wondered if she was going to be sick. Doubtful, with nothing in her stomach.

"I buried the baby beside his father."

She glanced back to see Dr. Foster placing a stethoscope to Janie's chest, his movements measured and tender. He was older—she guessed him to be well into his fifties—and he had a calm, assuring manner she found herself wanting to trust.

"I buried him," he continued, "on the hill, just behind the cabin. It overlooks the valley."

The valley where Emma took her first steps on a picnic. McKenna could picture it through the descriptions in Janie's faithful exchanges. *Oh God* . . . It hurt so much inside. She looked for the hill behind the cabin but couldn't make it out. It was so dark, being this far out from town. Living in a city the size of St. Joseph, she'd forgotten how dark the night could be, and what it felt like at times like this. When the darkness slipped inside and threatened to suffocate the slightest flicker of hope.

Yet even in such moments she didn't doubt that God existed. She just sometimes wondered whether He remembered that *she* did.

"Janie!"

She turned to see Dr. Foster bent over the bed—and Janie's body shaking. Violently. She raced to the bedside.

Still in the throes of fever, Janie arched her back, then her head, and made a gurgling sound.

"Is she choking?"

"No, she's having a seizure," Dr. Foster said with surprising calm, filling a syringe. "This happened twice yesterday. Try to hold her still."

McKenna worked to subdue her, amazed that Janie's body still commanded such strength.

She became aware of Wyatt Caradon's presence beside her. He took hold of Janie's wrists and gently, but firmly, held her down.

Dr. Foster was about to slip the needle into the pale flesh of her arm when she suddenly stilled. Janie opened her eyes and blinked. Her breaths came staggered.

McKenna leaned closer and brushed back the limp blonde hair from her temples. "Janie, can you hear me?"

It took her a moment to focus. "Kenny?" she finally whispered.

"Yes." McKenna gasped softly, part laugh, part cry. "It's me. I'm here."

"You came . . ." Janie's hand moved over the covers, seeking hers.

McKenna clasped it and brought it to her cheek. "Yes, I came. I'm here. It's going to be all right, Janie. I'll take care of you."

Janie squinted, as though trying to see beyond the temporal. "Vince . . ." Her face crumpled. "Our baby . . ."

The hopelessness in her eyes told McKenna there was no use trying to mislead her about the child. "We'll get through this. I'll help you. We'll be together just like we were when we were younger."

Janie's eyes slipped closed again. "I'm just so tired."

"Look at me, Janie. Look at me!"

Janie did as she asked, but already there was something different about her gaze.

McKenna's throat tightened, and the dark hole inside her yawned wide. She cradled Janie's cheek in her palm. "We'll have the ranch we dreamed about when we were little girls. Do you remember that? What we used to talk about?"

Janie squeezed her hand. "I remember . . ." A smile ghosted her parched lips. "I'm glad . . . you're here." Her breath caught and she winced.

"Are you in pain? Dr. Foster's with us. He can give you something."

"No . . . I'm—I don't . . . feel much." Slowly, Janie's attention moved around the bed and settled near the footboard. The smile that barely touched her mouth seconds ago somehow found new strength and bloomed. "Thank you," she whispered.

Frowning, McKenna looked to see where Janie was staring, and something inside her gave way. No one was there.

"Where's Emma?" Janie whispered, trying to raise her head.

"Emma's asleep in her bed." Dr. Foster urged her back down. "Don't you worry about her. Emma's fine."

Janie sank back in to the pillow. "You've always . . . been strong."

It took McKenna a moment to realize Janie was speaking to her. She shook her head, sensing what Janie was doing, and couldn't stem the tears. "You're going to be all right."

"Emma's . . . just like you, Kenny. When we were young."

Her breath caught again, and McKenna could almost see the strings binding her cousin to this earth loosening, bit by bit.

"Take Emma . . . and make her your own."

It wasn't a question. And the request wasn't something McKenna could deny, even if she'd wanted to. But surely Janie was forgetting about the letters telling her about Robert. McKenna leaned closer, wishing they were alone, and very much aware of Marshal Cardon beside her, listening. "Janie, I—I don't know if I'm the best choice. Things haven't turned out very well with Rob—"

"*Please*, Kenny."

McKenna felt herself nodding and forced the words past the lump in her throat and the fear in her heart. "I will. I'll take care of her."

"The ranch . . ." Janie's voice faltered. "Everything . . . is yours."

McKenna bit back a refusal. She didn't want it. Any of it. "Janie, I only want you here," she whispered. She wanted this precious woman to live. The beseeching in Janie's eyes finally won out, and McKenna nodded again.

Slowly, Janie's gaze shifted to Dr. Foster, whose expression was gentle.

"I understand," he whispered. "I'll serve as witness to your last wishes, Janie. Don't you worry about a thing. We'll see it all done."

Janie blinked, and tears slipped down her temples into her hairline. "Bury me . . . with my son."

"We will." Dr. Foster smoothed a hand over her hair. "We'll bury you right beside him."

With a soft cry, Janie shook her head. "No. I want Aaron . . . in my arms."

Dr. Foster shot McKenna a look. "But he's already buried. Beside Vince."

Tears slipped from the corners of Janie's eyes into her hairline, and McKenna shivered when Janie aimed the request at her.

"Promise me, Kenny?"

She couldn't respond. Exhuming a body was sacrilege. And judging by Dr. Foster's disturbed expression, he agreed. "Janie, what you're asking is—"

"I don't want him . . . to be alone." Janie's fingers tightened around hers.

"He's not alone, Janie," McKenna reassured her. "He's in heaven, with Vince."

"Please, Kenny. Promise me . . ."

McKenna heard the struggle in her voice, saw it in her eyes, and a thought came . . . Perhaps this was what Janie needed to pull her through, to survive. The *fight* that Dr. Foster had been refer—

"I'll do it, ma'am." Wyatt Caradon leaned closer.

McKenna caught his gaze and shook her head. "No," she mouthed. He clearly saw her and understood. She was sure of it.

Yet the marshal still took hold of Janie's hand. "Don't you worry about your little boy, Mrs. Talbot. I'll make sure he's safe in your arms." He took a quick breath. His jaw flexed hard. "I give you my oath."

Janie sighed, and peace gradually erased the anxiety from her features. But it was a peace McKenna neither welcomed nor shared. Not with the cost it would exact.

As the night hours crept by and Janie's breathing grew more shallow and raspy, McKenna stayed by her side, helpless to watch, as snippets from their childhood splashed in watercolor hues across her memory. Two little girls, opposites in so many ways, yet equally kindred, skipping hand-in-hand down a wooded path toward their favorite swimming hole, dreaming of all they would be once they grew up. Their only certainty . . . that they'd be together.

Hot tears slipped down McKenna's cheeks, and she struggled against the ache in her chest as she realized they were again walking a shadowed path. Together. Only this time, Janie was walking on ahead. And no matter how much she wanted to, she couldn't catch up. She couldn't follow.

Not now. Not yet.

SIX

Dawn's first light spilled through an open bedroom window and gave Mrs. Talbot's sallow blonde hair the appearance of spun gold against the dingy white pillow. Her breathing stopped—only for a second—but Wyatt sensed what was coming and slowly rose from his chair at the kitchen table.

He drew nearer to the bedroom, but stopped short of going inside.

The hush of morning lay gentle inside the small bedroom, yet from the way Doc Foster and Miss Ashford both leaned toward the bed, they too sensed the impending change. No doubt the physician had experienced this more times than he could remember.

As Wyatt watched the scene from outside the doorway, his heart settled on one memory alone. And an ache—one he'd thought long healed—rose again inside him. The weight of the memory threatened to drag him under, and he drew a needed breath. Felt the cool mountain air in his lungs. And within a slice of a pendulum's swing—it happened.

The rasp of Mrs. Talbot's breathing faded. Where seconds before there had been three people in the bedroom, now there were only two. The twitter of sparrows drifted in through the open window, punctuating the silence as the young mother's soul passed from this world to the next.

Miss Ashford struggled to her feet, and for a moment, she stood motionless. Wyatt recalled the way she'd reacted last night when he'd made the pledge to her cousin, after neither Miss Ashford nor the doctor would. Clearly Miss Ashford hadn't approved, but he hadn't made the promise lightly and was determined to carry out Janie Talbot's wishes.

Miss Ashford bent and pressed a lingering kiss to her cousin's forehead, then sank down beside the bed and rested her head on the mattress. Her shoulders shook, gently at first, until a sob finally broke through. He started to go to her but stopped himself, doubting comfort from him would be welcome at the moment.

Dr. Foster had asked him to stay through the night and had left for a short time to check on two other patients—both turned out to be faring well. But he hadn't wanted to leave Miss Ashford alone with her cousin, and Wyatt understood. He had nothing waiting on him except a cold boardinghouse bed, so he'd stayed to help in whatever way he could.

Despite his repeated offers of sustenance, Miss Ashford hadn't eaten much of anything and had barely touched the coffee he'd made. She'd refused to leave Janie Talbot's side for any reason, and even now she clung to the woman's hand.

Watching her, he wondered if she was aware of the irony of the two journeys occurring in this moment—a beginning and an end brought together precisely in a splinter of time. If a person believed in the Creator, one might think He hadn't wanted Miss Ashford to lose her cousin in the darkest hour of the night. Rather, He desired she be surrounded by the warmth of His light when that dreaded moment came. Yet Wyatt doubted Miss Ashford could see that now. Neither had he, in his moment of greatest grief.

It took distance to view loss with such perspective. And though seven years had passed for him, there were still days he questioned the why of it all. No telling how many petitions he'd piled at the foot of heaven's throne—most of which remained unanswered. But answers didn't always bring peace. He'd learned that along the way.

Dr. Foster walked from the bedroom and pulled the door closed. Sighing, he ran a hand through his thinning hair. "I appreciate you staying the night, Marshal." Fatigue weighed his voice.

"It was the least I could do, sir. Especially after what Miss Ashford did for my prisoner."

Foster poured himself another cup of coffee. "I'd have to agree with you there. Not many a woman—or man—would have attempted that." He eased his frame into a kitchen chair and stared at the closed bedroom door. "For a while there"—he took a sip—"I thought she might pull through."

Hearing sincerity in the statement, Wyatt also thought he'd read something different in the man's demeanor last night. "But that was *before* Miss Ashford and I arrived. Wasn't it, sir?"

The doctor's attention crept back to him. "Yes . . . it was. But I see no reason in thieving a person's hope. I've been wrong before . . . guessing what the Almighty might—or might not—do." He rubbed his eyes. "The longer I live, Marshal, the more I learn about God's character, and the more I trust Him. Yet oddly enough"—his gaze clouded—"the less I understand His ways. A childless widow of sixty-two recovers, while a young mother dies and leaves behind a daughter who, at such a young age, will likely not remember her. Or her papa."

Doubt and assurance met in the doctor's expression, and Wyatt shared them both. He gave a faint nod, choosing to leave the silence between them undisturbed.

"I delivered Emma in the same bed where Janie's lying now." Dr. Foster bowed his head. "Vince and Janie Talbot made me feel more like family than anyone else in Copper Creek. My wife died twenty-two years ago. I've been alone since. The Talbots used to have me out for Sunday dinner after church. Janie made the best biscuits you've ever put in your mouth, and she always sent me home with the extras."

Wyatt hadn't considered how personal a loss this might be to the older man. He moved closer and briefly laid a hand on his shoulder, unable to find the right words.

After a moment, Dr. Foster pushed to standing. He sniffed and wiped his eyes. "I'm going to go wash up outside. Then I need to head into town to look in on my patients again. I'll check your prisoner while I'm there. Ben Slater, was it?"

Wyatt nodded.

"I told Miss Ashford I'd be gone for a while." Foster paused by the front door. "Would you remind her to rub some of the salve I left on the bedside table onto her hand this morning? The sutures will be sore at first, but that will help."

"Will do, sir. And thank you for going by the jail."

"Any chance of you still being here when I get back?"

Wyatt detected a hint. "I'd planned on heading back into town myself, sir. But . . . how does my staying around for a while work for you?"

"Works well, and I'm much obliged to you, Marshal Caradon. I'd prefer she not be alone right now. Not with being so new to town, and not knowing anybody." He paused, looking behind him. "Emma should be waking up soon enough. Miss Ashford made it clear to me she wants to be the one to tell Emma about . . . what's happened." He gestured out the door. "Did the boy ever come back?"

"He did. He bedded down in the barn. I checked on him about an hour ago. He was sound asleep."

"Guess he was tired from the long trip."

Wyatt suspected the soundness of the boy's slumber stemmed from something more than exhaustion, but he kept the thought to himself.

Dr. Foster glanced back at the closed bedroom door. "I'm afraid Miss Ashford's welcome to Copper Creek hasn't been a very good one." With a last look that didn't call for words, he closed the door behind him.

Wyatt finished his coffee and dumped the grounds from the pot outside, then washed the pot and cups and put them back in the cupboard. He figured Miss Ashford's brother to be around sixteen or seventeen, and he didn't have to wonder long at the tone of their relationship. From his brief encounter with Robert Ashford, he'd best describe the young man as *surly*. Not uncommon for a fellow his age, but not a good trait to wear so openly in a town like Copper Creek. A chip on a man's shoulder was an awfully tempting thing to take a shot at. Especially a chip as large as Robert's.

Wyatt glanced at the closed bedroom door, tempted to check on Miss Ashford. But the better part of him knew to leave her be, give her space. For now anyway. After all, too much space could be as bad as not enough.

A creaking hinge drew his attention, and he turned to see a little girl peeking at him through a slightly opened door.

He went as far as the sofa and paused, not wanting to frighten her. He half-expected her to shut the door fast against him. But she didn't. She only watched, eyes wide and speculative. And he couldn't help but think of the heartache that awaited the precious girl in days ahead.

He took a tentative step toward the door and knelt to be closer to her height. "Are you Emma?"

She nodded, squinting. "Does Mama know you're here?"

He smiled, hearing her true question. "Yes, she does. I'm Wyatt." It wasn't exactly proper to give only his first name, but *Marshal Caradon* seemed too much for the moment, and for one so tiny. "Your mama and I are friends. Is that your room?" He indicated past her.

She opened the door wider. "Yes. But I haven't made my bed yet." A petite frown knit her pretty brow. "I do that after breakfast. Is my mama awake yet?"

Remembering what Dr. Foster had said, Wyatt shook his head and quickly changed the subject. "Are you hungry?"

She nodded again and briefly pursed her lips. "I like pancakes best."

"I like them too. But I'm not sure we have what we need to make pancakes. You want to help me check?" He held out his hand.

She toddled out in her nightgown, looking decidedly younger than her vocabulary had led him to believe.

"How old are you, Emma?"

She held up five fingers. "Mama keeps the maple syrup in the cupboard. But I can't reach it." She climbed up into a kitchen chair and tucked her legs beneath her.

Emma was a mirror image of her mother—blonde hair and delicate features, big blue eyes. To say the child was pretty was an understatement. But she had an air about her, even at so young an age, that didn't quite fit with the Janie Talbot he'd met, however briefly. And he couldn't quite decide what it was.

A quick search turned up little in the way of pancake fixings, so he turned to his backup plan. "Let's head outside and see if those chickens have laid us some eggs. We'll have those instead."

Emma didn't budge. "But you said we'd have pancakes."

He eyed her and caught a spark of challenge in the tilt of her diminutive chin. Which spoke volumes. "I said we'd *see* if we could make pancakes. I didn't say we *would*. Now . . ." He leveled a friendly stare. "Let's go check on those chickens."

With a coy smile he didn't buy for a second, she hopped down. *Cute little scamp.*

It was warm enough outside, so he didn't go looking for her

shoes. Judging from the dirt between her toes, she'd already been going without them for a few days. They reached the porch steps, and he swung her up on his shoulders. She giggled, the sound impulsive and pleasant, yet he felt almost traitorous in a way. As if he were misleading her about what awaited her.

But the time for knowing her mother's fate would come soon enough, and she'd have a lifetime to live with the loss.

A while later, he was doling out scrambled eggs when the bedroom door opened. Miss Ashford stepped out, her eyes swollen and red-rimmed. She saw him and frowned. Apparently, she hadn't expected him to still be here. Her gaze fell to Emma, who was seated at the table, fork in hand, and the many emotions accompanying the moment were easily read in her face.

Fear, dread, hurt, and exhaustion all left their mark as she saw Vince and Janie Talbot's daughter—*her* daughter now—for the very first time.

SEVEN

E*mma looks just like Janie.* Exactly as McKenna remembered Janie as a little girl—all sweetness and goodness. The realization twisted the knife already lodged in her gut. Would Emma remember Janie? Even the least bit? Of course, Robert carried no personal memories of their mother since she'd died at his birth, but McKenna had made sure he knew about her. Everything she could recall.

McKenna determined to capture every detail of Janie that she could. She'd write them all down, starting today. Every memory, every funny moment, every dream Janie had had, and she would share them all with Emma so Janie's daughter would never forget who her mother was. And she'd do the same for Vince, though she hadn't known him nearly as well.

"I made some eggs, Miss Ashford . . . if you're hungry."

She'd hoped the deep voice she'd heard moments earlier through the door belonged to Dr. Foster. Or even Robert, assuming he'd come back, which he always did, eventually. And that Marshal Caradon would have already been on his way. When she looked at him, she couldn't help but think of how differently things might have turned out if he hadn't been here last night. If he hadn't made that unreasonable promise to Janie. Something told her that her cousin might still be alive. And she'd sensed the same hope from Dr. Foster. She'd made it clear to Caradon that she hadn't approved of his promise, and yet he'd made it anyway.

"I'm not hungry, Marshal Caradon," she lied. "But thank you." She glanced around. "Has Dr. Foster gone to town?"

He nodded. "It would do you good to eat, ma'am. You're going to need your strength." Kindness touched his mouth, something compassionate and gentle. Something unwelcome from him at the moment.

"Have you"—she glanced at Emma—"explained the situation yet?"

"No, ma'am. I was told you wanted to do that."

That didn't stop you from interfering last night. McKenna started to say as much but held her tongue, knowing it wouldn't change anything. She needed to stay in this man's good graces, if only for Robert's sake.

He tousled Emma's hair. "Emma here helped with breakfast by making the toast."

"But not by myself . . ." Her slender shoulders slumped. She looked up at Caradon, a pout forming. "*You* wouldn't let me."

Eager to encourage the child, as well as introduce herself, McKenna went and knelt before her. "I'm sure you did a fine job, Emma. I bet you're a wonderful little cook." She took Emma's hand in hers, grateful to see a shy smile. "My name is McKenna. I'm your mama's cousin. The one you drew those pretty pictures for, which I'm still enjoying very much." She brushed a wisp of hair from the child's forehead, wondering how often Janie had done that very thing. "Your mama told you I was coming, remember?" Emma nodded. "Your mama and I were—" McKenna caught herself. "She and I are more like sisters than cousins. I love her very much, and therefore . . . I love you very much too." She forced a smile she didn't feel.

Emma shook her head. "I don't have a sister. I had a brother, but he died."

Surprised by her bluntness, McKenna seized the opportunity, suddenly feeling ages older than her twenty-three years. "Do you know what that means, Emma? To die?"

"It means you go to heaven. And that you're not sick anymore."

How well she could imagine Janie using those same words to explain Vince's death. "Yes, that's exactly right. You're a very smart little girl." Preferring to continue this conversation when they didn't have an audience, McKenna stood and smoothed her skirt. "Marshal, when did Dr. Foster say he would return?"

"He didn't say exactly, ma'am. But he left well over an hour ago." His tone seemed to have shed a layer of warmth. "He should be back shortly."

"Very well." She took a seat at the table. "The toast you made looks delicious, Emma." She kept her voice light, and noticed the girl sitting a little taller beneath the praise.

"I like pancakes better. Wyatt said we could have those, but then he—"

"Marshal Caradon, you mean." McKenna caressed the girl's arm. "Let's address him as *Marshal Caradon.*"

From the corner of her eye, McKenna saw Caradon begin to speak before falling silent. Emma repeated the name but pulled her arm away. And whatever hint of a smile had been there seconds before quickly faded.

McKenna took a bite of eggs to be polite, then another because they were delicious. A U.S. Marshal who could cook. Now there was something. Realizing just how hungry she was, she finished the eggs on her plate as well as a piece of toast. Chewing, she noticed the satisfaction creeping across Marshal Caradon's face. Yet he said nothing, and neither did she.

The front door opened and Robert strode inside, looking disheveled and perturbed. His scowl held warning, and the dark hair curling at his temples was still wet from where he'd washed, but the redness around his eyes betrayed emotion McKenna knew he would rather have kept hidden. He looked nearly as tired as she felt.

He spotted Wyatt Caradon, and his steps slowed. McKenna trailed her brother's focus to the badge on Caradon's vest and she rose from her seat, only then seeing the empty place setting at the table and the extra eggs left in the pan. Marshal Caradon had anticipated Robert joining them.

"Robert," she said, gesturing. "I don't believe you've had the opportunity to meet Marshal Caradon. The marshal and I met last night in town, quite by chance. He was kind enough to escort me home, then he stayed in case we needed any help." She glanced behind her. "Marshal Caradon, this is my younger brother, Robert."

Courtesy dictated that Robert speak first, but a cool stare was his only response.

Caradon nodded. "Nice to meet you, Robert. Though I wish it were under different circumstances."

"Yeah, me too," Robert finally grumbled. He glanced at the bedroom door, then back at McKenna. His eyes narrowed. "So did she d—"

"Robert!" McKenna intentionally softened her voice and inclined her head in Emma's direction. Emma seemed watchful, wary. "If we could speak about this later, that would be better."

His jaw went rigid. "So she did."

McKenna glanced at Emma, who showed no sign of understanding. "Yes," she said softly. "At daybreak."

"So does this mean we'll go back now?"

McKenna stared. "No, it certainly does not. I told you before that our going back isn't a—" Catching herself, she smiled at

Emma, then at Marshal Caradon. "If you'll excuse us for a moment, please."

Caradon rose from his chair, his attention fixed on Robert. "Take all the time you need, ma'am."

With effort, she guided her brother out the door, mindful of the open windows. They walked a short distance before she spoke. "Janie died this morning, Robert. But before she did, she . . ." Emotion tightened her throat. "She left me—*us*," she added quickly, "all of this. Their home, their ranch . . . everything."

Robert looked around. "Doesn't look like much to me."

Trying to view, through a stranger's eyes, the rustic homestead and barn with the few head of cattle dotting the field, McKenna understood his assessment but couldn't share it. Not knowing how much it had meant to Janie.

"What about the kid?"

McKenna bowed her head.

Robert gave a harsh laugh. "Don't tell me . . ."

"Janie asked me to take care of her, and I'm going to. What else was I supposed to do? I loved Janie like the—"

"Sister you never had. Believe me, I know." He scoffed and raked a hand through his hair, looking for all the world like their father. Robert had never known William Ashford. Not really. He'd only known the man whose wife had died while giving birth to him. And that William Ashford had shared little resemblance to the father she'd known before.

"There's nothing for us to return to in St. Joseph, Robert. You know that. Don't forget the trail you left behind."

"How could I forget, Kenny?" His smile was cruel. "You won't let me."

Regret soured her stomach as he walked away. She'd done her best with him. The best she knew to do, but it hadn't been good enough. Her thoughts went to Emma, and she sighed. "Oh Janie," she whispered, half hoping heaven would hear. "Are you certain you made the right choice?"

Rubbing her temples, she walked back toward the house and spotted Dr. Foster standing around the corner of the barn, tethering his horse to a post. She hadn't heard him ride up, and realized he must have been there the entire time. His back was to her, and his simple task was taking far longer than it should have.

When she drew closer, his head came up. "Miss Ashford . . ."

She briefly looked at him, and away. "You're kind to pretend you didn't overhear that conversation."

Sheepishness crept over his features. "I hear all sorts of things in my profession, ma'am. And for what it's worth, I still remember what it was like to be a young man, eager to be on my own, with an older sister doing her best to look out for me."

"Robert's hardly a man, Dr. Foster. He's only fourteen."

He glanced at Robert again, mild surprise showing. "Still, he's a lot closer to being a man than a boy, ma'am. Fourteen or not." He reached for his medical bag looped around the saddle horn. "I brought what we need to prepare Janie's body. I figured I'd do that here at the house, since you said you wanted to help."

Sobered by the waiting task, McKenna nodded and walked with him to the cabin.

"I spoke with the preacher while I was in town just now. The funeral will be tomorrow morning. He'll let people know."

"So soon?"

He paused. "Is there a reason to wait, Miss Ashford?" The question was gentle but straightforward.

"No . . . I guess not." She studied the hill rising up behind the cabin where Janie would be buried. "Tomorrow will be fine."

"By the way, you're mighty good with a needle. I was impressed."

She stared up at him.

"Marshal Caradon's prisoner. I checked on him at the jail this morning. I'm guessing your talent is going to make some ladies of this town mighty happy. Though Mrs. Claremore at the dress shop will be none too happy about the competition."

"I assure you, Mrs. Claremore needn't worry about competition from me, Dr. Foster. I much prefer working with leather than lace."

Footsteps on the porch drew their attention.

"You're back, Doc." Marshal Caradon and Emma walked out.

McKenna noticed he was wearing his coat and hat, which could only mean . . .

"I'll be heading back into town." Caradon glanced her way. "I've got some things I need to tend to."

Dr. Foster distracted Emma with a lollipop and discreetly relayed the information about the funeral to Wyatt. "Pastor Vickery said he'd be out here about ten o'clock tomorrow. So Marshal, we'll need your *pledge* to Mrs. Talbot fulfilled before then."

"Not a problem, sir. I'll see it done."

McKenna cringed, thinking about the prospect.

Dr. Foster walked inside, patting Caradon's shoulder as he passed. Emma shadowed the doctor's steps, doing her best to peer into his bag, presumably looking for more treats even as she slurped on the hard candy he'd given her.

A warm breeze rustled through a stand of trees close to the house, quaking the leaves and sounding like a thousand tiny bells. McKenna stared up at them, mesmerized.

"Those are aspens," Caradon said, answering her unasked question. "They're common to this area. You should see them come fall. That's when they're the prettiest." He took the porch stairs by twos. "Emma's asking about her mother again, ma'am. A moment ago. Just thought you should know." He brushed the rim of his Stetson. "Good day to you, Miss Ashford."

McKenna took a breath, gathering her nerve. "Marshal Caradon, may I have a word with you, please?"

He turned. "Yes, ma'am?"

"Last night, when Janie requested that her son be buried with her, I don't think she realized what she was asking. With the fever and medicine, and her having been ill for so long, and the stress of recent weeks—I think all of that combined was simply too much for her. She was . . . confused when she made that request." She searched his eyes. "Do you understand what I'm saying to you?"

He didn't answer right off. "Yes, ma'am. I think I do."

Relieved, she sighed. "Good. I felt you would, once we talked."

He closed the distance between them. "I understand that you don't like the idea of a body being dug up after it's already in the earth. You might even hold that it's a sacrilege. To be honest, it's not something I ever thought I'd do." Pausing, he nodded toward the cabin. "Do you think your cousin was *confused* when she asked you to take care of her daughter, Miss Ashford? Or when she left everything she and her husband had spent their lives building together . . . to you?"

Heat flooded McKenna's body. She knew from his tone, his manner, and the steel in his eyes that Caradon meant for the questions to be rhetorical. Still, she wished she could think of something to say in response, find some weakness in his argument. But she couldn't.

"I don't think so either, ma'am. I think she spoke from her heart. So I'm going to see to it that Janie Talbot's little boy is in her arms tomorrow when that casket is lowered, because I gave her my word. On her deathbed, just like you did."

EIGHT

Is my mama awake yet?" Emma asked for the tenth time that same day.

Sitting in a chair on the porch, McKenna pulled a brush through the little girl's blonde hair. She'd dreaded this moment and had been putting it off, letting Emma play outside after breakfast while she pondered what to tell the child. The truth, most certainly . . . But how? She snagged a tangle.

"*Oowie*!"

"I'm sorry, sweetie." She rubbed the tender spot on Emma's head. "I didn't mean to hurt you." But she was about to do exactly that—regardless of how gently she tried to phrase what needed to be said.

She turned Emma to face her and stared into eyes the same brilliant blue as Janie's had been. She prayed for the right words and the wisdom not to say anything that would frighten the child—like some of the things that had been said to her when her own mother had died.

She took Emma's hands in hers. "Emma . . . your mama didn't

just go to sleep. Her body was sick, and she didn't have the strength to get better." McKenna spoke slowly, as tenderly as she could, and watched for the slightest sign of comprehension in Emma's expression. "Your mama . . . passed away early this morning. She's in heaven now with Jesus and your papa, and with your baby brother, Aaron."

The light in Emma's eyes flickered. She squinted, and McKenna could see her young mind working to keep up. *Oh God, help me to be what I need to be for her.*

"It's hard to understand this, Emma, I know . . . But the last time you saw your mama was when she had a fever. Do you remember that?"

A slow nod. "I helped Doc Foster get her water 'cause she was thirsty."

McKenna somehow found a smile. "You're a very brave girl." She leaned closer. "Your mama's body is still in her bed inside, and we're going to go see her together in just a minute."

"But you said she was with Jesus . . ."

"She is, sweetie. But her body is still here." How to explain this to one so young? She briefly looked beyond Emma across the sea of field grass bowing in the breeze to the mountains rising stony and gray in the distance. "When you see your mama, you may feel . . . different inside, and that's okay. I did, too, when I first saw my mama's body after she'd died."

Subtle suspicion slipped into Emma's gaze. Children were much more perceptive than most adults gave them credit for. Robert always had been.

The warble of a songbird drifted close and brought an idea with it. "Have you ever seen a bird's nest when it's full of eggs?" McKenna asked, already knowing the answer.

"My papa showed me one in the barn. It had babies in it." Emma scrunched her face. "But we can't touch them."

The sparkle in those precious eyes caused a pang in McKenna's chest. "Do you remember what the nest looked like after the babies had grown up and flown away? When it was empty?"

Emma nodded again.

"In a way, that's what your mama is going to look like when you see her. It's still your mama's body, but she won't be inside of it anymore. She's with God now." Images of long-ago days brushed up against her thoughts—images of her mother lying still and lifeless in death. As soon as she'd walked into the front parlor—only four years older than Emma now—she'd known. And a part of her had been frightened. Not of her mother, never of her. But of the *absence* of her mother while still having the shell of her still there.

For a long time, she'd stood in the doorway, staring at the woman who'd rocked her at night when she'd awakened from bad dreams, who nursed her when she was sick, who'd stayed up late mending her skirt when McKenna had once gotten too close to the livery's forge. But the woman lying across the room in the pinewood box had not been her mother. Not anymore.

McKenna cradled Emma's cheek. Looking at a loved one who had passed away changed a person. And she wondered how it would change Emma, especially being so young. Yet not allowing Emma to see her mother a last time, denying her that chance to say good-bye—however a five-year-old could—wasn't something she felt right doing either.

She reached for Emma's hand, and the child took hold without hesitation.

Dr. Foster was inside the cabin, mixing salves and spices to prepare Janie's body for burial. When he looked up, then looked at Emma, he seemed to understand.

McKenna inclined her head toward the bedroom. "You're welcome to come with us, if you'd like, Dr. Foster." She secretly hoped he would, in case Emma had questions she couldn't answer.

He led the way and pushed open the door.

McKenna had unlatched a window earlier to air out the room. Sunshine poured inside, layering the small space with the sweet fragrance of lavender and crowding out the stale reminders of death.

Emma held back, and McKenna hoped she hadn't frightened her by what she'd said moments earlier.

"It's all right, Emma. We can take our time in saying good-bye." McKenna looked at Janie's body on the bed and tears rose to her eyes as she recalled what it had felt like to kiss her mother for the very last time, how her heart had pounded in her ears, and how foreign her mother's cheek had felt to her in that moment.

She guided Emma to the bedside, and Emma raised her little chin to peer into her mother's face. Janie's expression was smooth and serene, though gaunt from illness. Gone were the flushes of fever, and her freshly brushed hair lay spread across the pillowcase, a duller mirror image of her daughter's.

Emma reached out, then quickly pulled her hand back.

"It's okay. You can touch her . . . if you want to." McKenna brushed her fingers across Janie's hand.

Emboldened, Emma did the same. "Mama?"

Only silence answered, and McKenna's throat tightened.

Emma leaned closer, touching her mama's arm. "Mama?" she whispered, her voice going higher. She peered up at McKenna, her blue eyes pooling. Her bottom lip shook.

Tears slipped down both their cheeks, and suddenly all the things McKenna wished someone had said to her in a similar moment years ago, came rushing back. She knelt beside her. "Your mama still loves you very much, Emma," she whispered. "Her love for you hasn't ended simply because she's not able to be with you anymore. She's thinking about you right this minute, in heaven, and she'll watch over you until you're together again. And you *will be* together again . . . someday. I promise you that."

Emma's breath stuttered beneath the weight of her tears. "But . . . I-I don't want my . . . mama in heaven."

"I know you don't, sweetheart. I don't want her there either. I want her here with us. But that's not possible anymore." She attempted to brush away Emma's tears, but the child shrank back. Surprised at the reaction, McKenna sought to comfort her with words. "Before your mama passed away, she asked me to take care of you. And I promised her I would. I'm here now, and I'm not going to let anything happen to you. We're going to live together in this house you love, that your papa built. And I'll be here whenever you need anything, okay?"

She reached out to hug her, but Emma's tearful scowl told her the affection wasn't welcome.

Dr. Foster came around to their side of the bed and leaned down to pick up Emma. She went to him willingly, which stung. McKenna tried her best not to show it. Emma was only a child, after all. But when Emma laid her head on Dr. Foster's shoulder, McKenna couldn't mask the hurt.

He cradled Emma's head. "Don't let this upset you, Miss Ashford. I delivered Emma. She's known me her entire life. Vince and Janie used to have me out for Sunday lunch after church, too, so we've gotten to know each other real well. Give it time. She'll come around to you."

As if on cue, Emma looped her thin arms around his neck and gave McKenna a look that said quite the opposite.

A familiar dread clawed its way up the back of McKenna's throat. "Of course," she forced out, nodding. "I understand." And she did. She was a stranger to the girl.

But understanding didn't remove the sting of rejection, and she wondered again if Janie had made the right choice. And if *she'd* made the right choice in coming West to begin with. Maybe if she hadn't been here, Janie would have struggled harder to live. McKenna felt a sinking inside. Maybe her own arrival to Copper Creek had been the deciding factor, and she hadn't realized it. Until now.

Following a dinner of beans and cornbread, McKenna enlisted Robert's help in watching Emma, already bracing herself for his refusal. Judging from the scowl on his face, his mood hadn't improved much since earlier that day. "I only need you to watch her for an hour. So I can help Dr. Foster with"—she lowered her voice—"preparing Janie's body for the funeral tomorrow."

Frowning, Robert glanced behind him where Emma sat at the table, her head bowed. "What do you want me to do with her?"

"Take her for a walk. Ask her to show you the barn. Anything to occupy her for a little while, so I can help Dr. Foster. Please, Robert. I would really appreciate it."

He sighed and turned away, running a hand through his hair. Then he looked back. "Hey . . . Emma!"

Cringing at the casualness of his tone, McKenna saw Emma's head come up.

"I'm wondering if you've got any cows around here." Robert peered out the kitchen window, as though not seeing the cattle in the adjacent field. "Sure would like to see me some. If you know where any are."

Emma's tear-rimmed eyes widened. She nodded, shyly.

The unlikely pair went outside and walked down the road together. As she watched them, McKenna prayed for them both, then joined Dr. Foster back inside. They worked in silence, a late summer sun casting a golden glow over the room. She washed and arranged Janie's hair and chose Janie's best dress from the chiffarobe, all while memories of better days long past pressed especially close.

Later, after Dr. Foster had gone and Emma was finally asleep, McKenna sat on the front porch steps as darkness swiftly approached, sifting through the decisions facing her now. Faint light from the barn told her of Robert's whereabouts, as did the sound of crates being moved. He was unpacking the wagon as she'd asked him to do—and without having to be told twice. She sighed. Maybe this change of scenery would be good for him after all.

She leaned forward, arms clasped around her knees, mindful

of the tender sutures in her left hand. The poultice Dr. Foster had made was helping with the pain and swelling.

Going back to St. Joseph wasn't an option, for reasons she'd given Robert earlier. She'd come to Colorado to make a new life for her and Robert, though it would be a far different life than she'd imagined. And more challenging. She had an additional person to provide for now, but at least here they had a place to live, and Mr. Trenton at the livery had already agreed in a letter to hire both her and Robert. She simply had to be strong. To persevere.

She would not allow herself to be broken by this. God would give her the strength she needed—she kept telling herself that.

She was planning on calling on Mr. Trenton the day after tomorrow and would be certain to take the letter he'd written that outlined her and Robert's responsibilities at the livery. She'd written, notifying him of the week of their arrival, but not the exact date. Which, as it turned out, was a good thing.

She spotted Robert walking toward her from the barn. From the set of his shoulders, he looked tired.

He paused at the bottom of the porch stairs. "She okay?"

Understanding who he was referring to, she nodded. "Emma's asleep. Thank you for watching her earlier."

He shrugged, a familiar gesture for him.

McKenna loosened the leather tie from her braid and began unraveling the strands of hair. "She knows her mama is in heaven, but she doesn't understand what's really happened."

Robert didn't say anything. The darkness obscured his expression, so McKenna couldn't read his mood—which seemed to change with little notice these days.

"I guarantee you she doesn't understand," he finally whispered, his tone surprisingly tender. "Not yet." He bowed his head. "But she will, soon enough."

McKenna stared, unaccustomed to the emotion in her younger brother's voice.

After a long silence, he looked up. "But I wouldn't push it with her. She'll have the rest of her life to try to make sense of it all." He took the porch stairs in twos and walked past her into the cabin.

The next morning, a knock sounded on Emma's bedroom door, and McKenna looked up from buttoning the child's dress. "Yes?"

"Miss Ashford," Dr. Foster spoke softly through the closed door. "The pastor has arrived."

"Thank you, Dr. Foster. We're almost ready."

As she straightened the ribbon in Emma's hair, McKenna caught the reflection in the mirror that hung askew on the wall. What she saw tugged at overfrayed emotions. With their best frocks pressed and their hair combed and arranged, she and Emma were dressed for the funeral, but McKenna knew that neither one of them was ready for what lay ahead.

She turned the child to face her, not surprised at the ill-tempered expression she received. Since telling Emma about Janie's passing, the child hadn't looked at her without displeasure. McKenna reached out to smooth a piece of lace on the child's dress—a dress Janie had sewn for Easter—but Emma pulled away.

McKenna formed a smile. "Emma, do you remember what I told you last night before you went to bed?"

Uncertainty penetrated Emma's scowl, and the child shook her head. But McKenna knew she wasn't telling the truth.

What she'd planned on telling Emma about the funeral and what would be happening in the next few hours suddenly seemed unfitting, and she decided to tell her what was in her heart. "I know this is hard for you to understand, Emma. And I know you're not happy with me right now, so I hope you'll listen."

The dainty furrows in Emma's brow deepened.

"I want you to remember, above anything else, that your mama and papa love you, very much. As do I, and Uncle Robert. And that no matter what happens, nothing can take away that love."

A second knock sounded, and through the closed door McKenna heard what she assumed was the pastor's voice, as well as Dr. Foster's. People would be arriving soon. It was nearly time.

Movement from outside the window drew her attention. She spotted a blurred figure cresting the hill behind the cabin. The person made his way down the path toward the homestead. At first she thought it was Robert, who had let her know earlier that morning that he refused to attend the funeral. She'd told him he didn't have a choice and then hadn't seen him since breakfast.

She stepped closer to the window and squinted. It wasn't Robert . . .

It was Marshal Caradon, and he was walking back toward the cabin, cradling something in his arms.

NINE

Wyatt looked down at the tiny bundle he held. The infant hardly weighed anything at all. He couldn't help but wonder what this child was doing now, in the hereafter. He hoped he was running and playing, doing all the things he hadn't a chance to do here on earth. And with his papa and mama beside him, no less.

Dr. Foster had swathed the boy snug in a thin quilt before burial, presumably one Janie had made. Wyatt hadn't removed it, nor had he pulled the edge back to peer into the infant's face. He already had an idea in his mind of what the baby looked like, and he preferred to commit that visage to memory instead of the other.

He'd purchased a baby's blanket from the mercantile yesterday and had wrapped the babe in it, layering the new over the old, and hoping to diminish the effects of the body being in the earth for several days. Seemed to him the child should be buried in clean swaddling with his mother too. Somehow he knew Janie Talbot would have appreciated that, even if Miss Ashford might not.

It hadn't taken him long to exhume the body, but it had taken a while to dig the hole deeper, as he'd told the doc he would do, in preparation for the funeral. The morning air was uncustomarily cool, but he'd still sweated through his shirt. He'd brought a fresh one along and brushed the dirt from his pants as best he could.

Drawing closer to the homestead, he spotted three men standing to the side of the barn. He recognized one of them as Pastor Vickery, the pastor of the church he visited the last time he came through Copper Creek. Wyatt skirted his way around the back of the cabin and through the front door. Dr. Foster requested he be discreet when bringing the body into the house, in case people from town were present. The front room was empty, but he saw the doc, Miss Ashford, and Emma in Janie Talbot's bedroom.

He stayed by the door, not wanting to sit.

He hadn't attended a funeral in seven years and didn't fully know why he was here today. But having been present for Mrs. Talbot's passing and learning about the deaths of her husband and son, it felt like the right thing to do. Even though it stirred images he'd laid to rest long ago. Ones he preferred would remain undisturbed.

Knowing what Miss Ashford was going through had influenced his decision too. Not that it mattered to her if he was present or not. He'd received the distinct impression that she didn't really care to have him around and—though he wasn't overly confident when it came to women—he couldn't quite figure out why. Normally women acted as if they would be open to his company, if he was open to offering it.

"Marshal Caradon!"

He looked up. "Miss Ashford."

Dark half circles beneath her eyes betrayed a lack of sleep. She looked tired—beautiful, but tired—and the droop of her shoulders revealed the invisible weight she bore.

"I saw you coming down the hill just now, Marshal. Please . . ." Her gaze darted to the bundle in his arms and quickly away, as though not wanting to acknowledge it. "I prefer that Emma not see this. She's already upset enough with having to say good-bye all over again to—"

"Mr. Wyatt?"

The small, hollow voice drew his attention, and he spotted Emma standing in the doorway. She'd been crying, as Miss Ashford had alluded, and when she ran full out toward him, Wyatt didn't know what else to do. Abiding by Miss Ashford's wishes—or at least trying to—he deftly placed the infant in her arms and bent to capture Emma in a hug. The girl's tiny arms came around his neck and felt better than anything he could remember in a long time.

He drew back and gently chucked her beneath the chin. "How are you today, Miss Emma?" He regretted the question as soon as it was out.

Her pretty face crumpled, and she snuggled close again.

He smoothed a hand over her back and chanced a look at Miss Ashford—whose arms were stiff with the bundle and whose expression alternated between disbelief and brokenness.

The front door opened. When he saw the coffin the men were carrying in, he moved to a side window and tried to interest Emma in what was peering out from one of his saddlebags—something he'd seen while settling up with the mercantile owner for the blanket. "Can you see it right there? Sticking out at the corner?"

Her posture went straighter. She sniffed and wiped her nose. "Can we go see it, Mr. Wyatt?"

"Emma, please address him as Marshal Caradon," Miss Ashford said from somewhere behind them.

Emma looked back and threw Miss Ashford a frown that communicated plenty.

Thinking that was a mouthful of a name for a child Emma's

age, Wyatt kept the opinion to himself. They'd cross that later, if need be. "Let's ask Miss Ashford if she minds if we go outside for a minute."

He turned to find Dr. Foster holding the infant and quietly giving the pallbearers instruction on how things would proceed. Wyatt approached Miss Ashford. "Would you mind if I take Emma outside, ma'am? We won't go wandering."

Relief eased some of the tension in her face and hinted at forgiveness for what he'd done moments earlier. "I'd be most appreciative, Marshal. Thank you."

Outside, a crowd of people had already gathered, and he saw three more wagons heading down the rutted path. The Talbots must have been well loved. Several of the women turned his way as he carried Emma down the stairs, but none approached.

His horse was tethered by the barn, and he carried Emma to it and held her close enough so she could pluck the surprise from his saddlebag.

"Is it mine?" she asked.

"It is."

She beamed and clutched the rag doll tight against her chest. "Her name's gonna be Clara."

"Sounds like a good name to me." He shook the rag doll's limp arm. "Nice to meet you, Clara." That drew a giggle from Emma.

The crowd across the way quieted, and Wyatt turned to see them filing in small groups up the porch stairs and into the home. Miss Ashford stood inside the doorway, greeting people. He couldn't hear what she was saying, but she held herself with grace and poise, despite the difficult task.

A short while later, everyone gathered out front by the porch again. The pastor led the way down the steps with the pallbearers following behind him with the closed coffin. Miss Ashford fell into step, but when she came close to take Emma's hand, the child wouldn't relinquish her hold on him. Not wanting to draw more attention to the child's reluctance, Wyatt guided Emma to walk beside Miss Ashford, though the little girl still wouldn't take hold of her hand.

Nor did she throughout the funeral, or as they walked back to the cabin after the graveside service.

Most folks had brought a dish of some sort to share, and the kitchen table was laden with meats and vegetables and pies. Emma gravitated mainly toward the desserts while, from what he could see, Miss Ashford managed a meager plateful that one of the women had prepared for her.

An hour later, nearly everyone was gone except for Dr. Foster, a handful of women who were cleaning up the kitchen, and a conspicuously dressed gentleman who'd arrived within the last half hour, well after the funeral. He wore a well-tailored suit and stood off to the side. Judging from the way he kept watching Miss Ashford, Wyatt presumed he was waiting for an opportunity to speak with her.

Curious, and feeling unwarranted protectiveness, Wyatt made his way across the front room to join them when he spotted Robert through a window, and paused. Still a good distance away, the boy was walking down the road toward the homestead, as though returning from town. Only then did Wyatt realize he hadn't seen Robert yet that day. He'd assumed he'd been around. But now that he thought of it, he couldn't remember seeing Robert at the gravesite either. He sighed and turned away, well able to imagine what Miss Ashford's response to this would be.

Dr. Foster was speaking with the ladies in the kitchen, and Emma was devouring yet another cookie, but Miss Ashford was nowhere to be seen.

"Please, Miss Ashford, let me apologize again for the abysmal timing of my visit."

The sound of a man's voice drew Wyatt back to the open window. Peering out, he spotted Miss Ashford and the well-suited gentleman standing off to the side. Conscience wrestling with honor, Wyatt glanced around to make sure no one was watching him. He knew he should move away, but concern—and curiosity—grounded him there.

"I accept your apology, Mr. Billings. However, the continuance of this conversation today is inappropriate. And untoward, I might add."

"I assure you, ma'am, I wouldn't be here right now if it weren't imperative that I speak with you immediately. I've been advised, ma'am, that Mrs. Talbot bequeathed to you her—"

"I give you my word, Mr. Billings"—McKenna's tone brooked no argument—"that I'll stop by your office at my first opportunity to speak with you about this, sir. But for now, I'm going to have to bid you good day."

Wyatt watched the man open his mouth as though considering whether to say something further, then clamp it shut again. Telling from the spark igniting Miss Ashford's glare as she strode back to the cabin, the fellow had made a wise choice.

Wyatt purposefully waited around another hour until the other guests had left, including Dr. Foster. He told himself it was silly, loitering like this, but the next morning would see him gone again, and he couldn't set aside the urge to talk with Miss Ashford one last time. And to help her, if she needed it.

"You did well today, ma'am," he said, standing beside her on the porch. "I think your cousin would've been proud."

Her eyes darted to his then away again. "Thank you, Marshal." Fatigue softened her voice. "I appreciate that, and how you helped with Emma."

"It was my pleasure." He briefly glanced behind them to see Emma playing with the rag doll, Clara, on the rug inside the doorway. The child had yet to warm up to Miss Ashford, and he got the feeling they might have a rough road ahead of them. "I'm glad our paths crossed, ma'am."

Miss Ashford looked at him but said nothing.

A moment passed, and he confined his gaze to the plank

board beneath his left boot. It didn't make sense. How could he face down a criminal without a lick of apprehension, and yet standing here next to this woman conjured up all sorts of unease inside him?

He cleared his throat. "I think you and your brother will take to Copper Creek real well. It's a nice town."

She nodded, bowing her head. "I hope so."

"Where did you say you came from?"

The chirrup of crickets filled the silence.

"A town in Missouri."

He snuck a look at her. *A town* . . . Interesting way to phrase it. "What brought you and Robert all the way out here? I mean, that's quite a ways to travel, even with the railroad in."

That brought her head up, and he sensed her guard rise with it.

"Please forgive me, Marshal, but it's late and I need to get Emma to bed. I thank you, again, for all you've done for us."

Wyatt recognized a dismissal when he heard one. He also recognized a deliberate change in topic. She turned to go.

"If there's anything else I can help with before I head out tomorrow, ma'am, I'd be obliged to. All you'd have to do is say the word."

She stilled and looked back. "So you're leaving town?"

The relief in her voice, in her face, quickly set things in the proper light for him, and told him his waiting around to speak with her had indeed been foolhardy, as had his schoolboy notions, which his gut had confirmed earlier. If only he would've listened.

TEN

Wyatt led his horse from the stall, dreading not only the days ahead, but this one specifically. Another full day in the saddle, with a prisoner in tow. But he wanted to make Denver by late afternoon. The livery was quiet this early. The newly risen sun sneaked through crevices in the plank wood walls and stretched shy, thread-width beams of light across the dimly lit interior.

He took in a breath and let it out slowly. Sometimes the life he'd chosen grew burdensome, like a woolen mantle in the dead of summer. Yet there were moments—like last evening, standing on the front porch of the Talbots' cabin with Miss McKenna Ashford—when he almost believed he could leave everything behind him and start all over again. Almost.

"Mornin', Marshal."

Surprised at the voice behind him, Wyatt turned. "Morning, Trenton. You're up awfully early."

"No choice. Got more work to do than I can keep up with." Yawning, the livery owner slipped on a soiled apron and reached for an iron poker beside the forge. "Let me bring this fire back to life and I'll be right with you." He stretched his thick shoulders and rolled his head from side to side, sighing as he did.

Wyatt silently commiserated. He, too, had more work than he knew what to do with, and thinking about escorting the prisoner today wearied him. But he was already a day late in delivering Ben Slater to stand trial for murder, what with staying to attend the funeral.

He arranged a blanket across the back of his horse and reached for his saddle. He'd tried to get Miss Ashford to open up to him, and he still wanted to know who that Billings fella was, and what he'd said to her that had upset her so. A casual question to the livery owner could answer the first of those questions. Casey Trenton knew everyone in this town. Then again, it wasn't any of Wyatt's business. Miss Ashford had made that perfectly clear last night.

He saddled the mare and cinched the leather straps, careful not to overtighten. Miss Ashford's tight-lipped manner raised his natural curiosity. She wasn't much for talking, unlike the majority of women he'd known in his life.

Which could describe McKenna Ashford on several counts.

It had been ages since he'd noticed—*really* noticed—a woman. Seven years, in fact. But standing by the grave yesterday afternoon, doing his best to listen to what the pastor was saying, his attention had repeatedly been drawn to Miss Ashford. And in the space of a breath, his thoughts had skimmed the years and had landed upon a well-worn page of his life, one dog-eared from handling, tattered around the edges. Sort of like him. It was a page from a chapter he'd been certain would end up defining him forever.

That was, until the past few days—when he'd been given reason to rethink otherwise. The funny thing was . . . the object of his interest didn't seem to have the least interest in him. Or if she did, she was doing an awful good job of hiding it. But that was for the best, he knew. He wasn't in a place to commit himself to a woman. His decision to work for the U.S. Marshals Service had seen to that. Sometimes the loneliness he felt occasionally got the better of him, like it had last night. But he wouldn't let that happen again.

He adjusted the blanket on the horse to compensate for a worn place on his saddle, not wanting to cause the mare any discomfort. This saddle had served him well but would need to be replaced soon. He smoothed a hand over the mare's withers, admiring Casey Trenton's hand with a brush. The mare's coat glistened.

"You're headin' out again, I take it?"

Trenton's question drew Wyatt back. "Yes, sir. And I need that gelding I brought in three nights ago, if he's fit to ride."

"He is. I'll get him for you."

"Much obliged. And figure up what I owe you for them both." Wyatt tied his horse out front, grinning when the mare nudged him in the shoulder. "What're you wanting this morning, Whiskey?" Knowing good and well what the animal wanted, he scrubbed his knuckles gently across the amber patch between her eyes and fed her one of the apple pieces tucked in his shirt pocket. "Ready for the trail again?" She gave an opinionated snort, and he laughed. His feelings exactly.

"Here you go." Trenton handed him the reins to the gelding. "How does fifty cents sound, for three days of boarding?"

"Sounds to me like you're not charging enough." Wyatt reached into his pocket.

"Way I figure it, the Marshals Office probably doesn't pay you fellas near what you're worth. And this is my way of tacking on my thanks."

Holding out a dollar, Wyatt shook his head when Trenton tried to offer him change. "I appreciate your service, Trenton. Let's leave it at that." He turned to go—when something on a workbench caught his attention.

As though reading his thoughts, Trenton motioned toward the saddle. "She's a beauty, ain't she?"

"May I?" At his nod, Wyatt ran his hand over the supple leather, admiring the craftsmanship and detail. "Is this your work, sir?"

Trenton laughed. "Not hardly. I don't have the patience for such things, or the know-how. I stick to bridles and reins, the easy stuff. Fella back East sent this to me as a sample of his work."

"Is it for sale?"

"You're only the fourth person who's asked me that. Wish I could say yes, but I'm afraid it's already spoken for. Sold it the first day I got it."

Wyatt ran a hand along the saddle's leather skirts, which were considerably larger than on the one he owned. That meant more comfort on longer rides, for both horse and rider. The leatherwork was intricate too. The stitches precise and evenly spaced. "What does something like this go for?"

Trenton told him, and Wyatt whistled low.

"Course . . ." Trenton grinned. "That accounts for my percentage and for demand bein' so high. I could probably do a mite better for a man of the law."

"Well, I'd like to buy one, if you can arrange that for me. I'll pay for it in advance." Wyatt reached inside his duster.

"Keep your money for now. Fella who made this was supposed to come see me this week, but hasn't yet. If he shows and if he's willin', I'm hiring him on the spot. No questions asked."

"As well you should." Wyatt admired the saddle one last time. "Or he'll open up shop two doors down and you can kiss that percentage of yours good-bye."

"Don't I know it!" Trenton snorted. "If he turns up, I'll get your order in and you can pick up the saddle when you're through here next. Good to see you again, Marshal."

Wyatt tipped his hat and swung into the saddle.

As he guided Whiskey through town toward the jail, the

gelding in tow, he studied the mountains towering over the waking community of Copper Creek. Bathed in hues of purple gray, the rocky range appeared somehow softer, almost welcoming, in the morning light. But he knew better. These mountains could be brutal. Especially to someone who didn't know them.

An elderly Chinaman passing him on the street met his gaze. A young woman accompanied him, her steps short and stuttered, yet graceful and demure. Wyatt nodded in greeting and tipped his hat.

Her gaze barely brushed his before she bowed her head again.

His attention went to her feet, and he couldn't help but wince. In his travels out West, he'd had opportunity to make acquaintances with people of Chinese ancestry. Their traditions were hardly familiar to him, but there was one custom he had seen. And though he found the people themselves to be hardworking and gracious, this particular custom—foot binding, the one imposed on the young woman who'd just passed—seemed barbaric.

The jail came into view up ahead, and he heaved an audible sigh. He'd enjoyed his job as U.S. Marshal at first, but after years of being on the trail, enforcing justice by pursuing the unjust, this nomadic way of life had left a mark on him. And it wasn't one he necessarily liked. He needed to find a way to reconnect with his roots.

The unexpected thought lingered, then swiftly took hold.

He should make a trip home again. Soon. It would do him good. It'd been three years since he'd last visited San Antonio. Too long. Maybe this fall he'd make his way there to see his parents again, his younger sisters, spend some time sorting out his thoughts, deciding what he wanted to do with the rest of his life. Thirty-two wasn't exactly old, but more and more he realized it wasn't young either.

He didn't dread returning home anymore, not like he had in years past. The memories there that once haunted him had finally been laid to rest—first, seven years ago when he'd buried his sweet Caroline and their precious daughter Bethany in the cemetery behind the family ranch. And in more recent months, when he'd finally managed to lay them both to rest, in his heart.

McKenna climbed into the saddle, arranged her skirt over her legs, and then chanced a last look behind her at the cabin. Robert and Emma stood side-by-side on the porch watching her—glaring at her was more like it—with matching scowls on their faces.

Robert's was prompted by having been asked to watch Emma for the morning—and for everything else in his life that was wrong and that was apparently McKenna's fault. Emma's perpetual frown had found its place yesterday morning before the funeral. And hadn't budged since. No matter what McKenna did or said, the child wanted nothing to do with her. Which hurt more than it probably should have.

With a final wave that neither of them returned, McKenna urged Patch, Janie's handsome palomino, toward town, doing her best to appear confident. But when she rounded the first bend and thought of the tasks awaiting her, her fragile facade of strength slipped and her hope began to pall.

An image rose again in her mind, one she'd tried to keep at arm's length but now filled her thoughts and crowded out her last ounce of confidence—the image of Janie with her newborn son nestled close beside her in the coffin. McKenna knew it was an image that would stay with her forever.

Marshal Caradon had been right. She hadn't said anything to him before he'd left the previous evening, but when she'd seen Janie with her precious baby boy beside her, she'd realized that he'd done the right thing in granting Janie's request. Yet she hadn't been able to bring herself to tell him. Even though he'd been the last to leave.

The way he'd waited around, lingering on the porch, she almost thought he was trying to find a reason to stay. But when the questions turned to where she and her brother had moved from and their previous lives, she knew better. And got rid of him as quickly as she could. She didn't need anyone—especially a U.S. Marshal—prying into their past.

Guests at the funeral had also plied her with questions. "*Where are you and your brother from?*" "*What brought you out West?*" "*Do you intend to stay out here?*" "*Will you be seeking a husband now that you have a daughter?*" While McKenna wanted to believe their curiosity was founded in good intention, she decided it would be best, at least for a while, if she and Robert kept more to themselves. Let the dust settle, as it were.

She wanted to make friends here but was none too eager to have new friends forsake her, and Robert, as former friends had done in St. Joseph. And she certainly didn't need someone like Wyatt Caradon learning about Robert's mistakes. Her brother needed a new start as much as she did, and he'd never get it with someone like Caradon watching his every move.

She didn't need someone like Caradon in her life either. She'd had her fair share of attention from men—especially after her father's death—an endless line of crude excuses for males set on "helping her" with the family business.

But Marshal Caradon *had* captured one little lady's heart completely.

McKenna cut down a side street in town, wanting to avoid the group of wagons lined up at the mercantile, all the while remembering Emma's response to him. With little prompting, the child had taken to the man. And the rag doll he'd gotten her—Clara, as Emma named her—hadn't hurt his standing with the young girl.

McKenna didn't begrudge Caradon's kindness to Janie's daughter. Not much anyway. She only wished she'd thought of getting Emma a doll herself, instead of the wooden cup and ball toy. Maybe Emma would feel differently about her now if she had. The child hadn't cared one whit for the wooden toy, and even made a point of hugging Clara tighter while giving the cup and ball a dark stare whenever McKenna was near. Janie was right—McKenna smiled—Emma was every bit as dramatic as she had been at that age.

Spotting the mercantile ahead, she decided to stop and pick up a few staple items. Janie's cupboards were understandably lean. The food left over from the meal following Janie's funeral would last them for a couple of days, so they didn't need much. After gathering some items, she checked her money purse and discreetly returned the jar of maple syrup to the shelf. That would have to wait until next time.

She settled the bill, then back outside, stuffed the items into her saddlebags and rode through the dirt-packed streets of Copper Creek until she spotted the building ahead. She dismounted and gave Patch a good rub. "Good girl," she whispered. The palomino snorted and shook its head. Janie had raised the horse from a filly, McKenna remembered from her letters, and the animal was every bit as well-tempered as Janie had boasted.

McKenna turned and stared up at the structure. She didn't have an appointment with the livery owner, but the moment she stepped inside, she felt at home. Smells of freshly laid straw and days-old embers bedded in the forge mingled with the scent of animals, and took her back. Back to a childhood she'd loved and a father she'd adored. Even the way Mr. Trenton arranged his tools on the wall reflected her father's trademark neatness.

She only hoped the man possessed an open mind when it came to women working in a livery. Her father hadn't. It had been his love for her—and her own bullheadedness—that had finally persuaded him. She doubted Casey Trenton would share a similar affection for her.

A man entered from a side door shouldering a wooden crate,

a soiled apron accentuating the paunch around his middle. "Can I help you, ma'am?"

McKenna guessed him to be in his early fifties, but years of sun and hard work had left their mark in the lines of his clean-shaven face and made it difficult to be sure. He was tall and broad shouldered, and wore a gruffness about his deep-set eyes that she suspected might disappear when he smiled. Which he didn't.

She stepped forward. "I wish to speak with the proprietor, a Mr. Casey Trenton?"

"You're gettin' your wish, ma'am. I'm him." With a huff, he deposited the crate by a workbench and reached for a crowbar. He commenced to prying open the lid, never pausing.

"It's nice to meet you, sir. I'm Miss McKenna Ashford." She paused, waiting for some sign of recognition at the mention of her name.

He only looked up, a single brow arching.

"I wrote to you, Mr. Trenton, about employment on my brother's behalf and also for mys—"

"You're the ones who sent me the saddle awhile back." Straightening, he gestured to a nearby bench.

She followed his focus. "Oh good, I see you received it. And . . . is the workmanship acceptable to you?" His answer showed in the faint turn of his mouth, though she wouldn't really label it a smile.

"Yes, ma'am, it is. Your brothers are real talented fellas. And I've got plenty of work for them, whenever they can start. The sooner, the better." His gaze drifted beyond her. "I hope they came with you."

It took her a moment to make sense of what he'd said. "I'm sorry, but I think there's been a misunderstanding." She smiled, hoping to soften the correction. "I only have one brother. And yes, he's able to start work as soon as you'd like. As am I," she added gently, hoping her expression mirrored the seriousness of her tone.

His head tilted. A bemused look swept his face. "Beg pardon, ma'am?"

"The letter I wrote to you, Mr. Trenton, the one my cousin delivered. It requested employment for my brother and myself."

"I remember the letter being signed by a woman, but I'm fairly sure the lady who gave it to me told me the jobs were for two men."

McKenna gave a soft laugh. "Janie would never have done that, sir. She knew the jobs were for my brother and me."

"I'm only tellin' you that she listed off two names, and they both belonged to men."

McKenna's smile came more naturally this time. "By chance, did she use the names Robert and *Kenny*?"

"That might've been them. All I know is that neither was a woman's name, I'm certain about that. I would've noticed right off."

"McKenna was my mother's maiden name, sir," she explained. "My parents assigned it as my middle name, but I much preferred it to my given name so began using it instead—"

"And just what's your given name?"

McKenna hesitated. "Agnes," she said quietly.

"Agnes." He nodded. "Now there's a good name for a woman. Right off, you know she's a female."

"Yes, that may be true. Nevertheless, Kenny is my nickname. And I'm the Kenny who applied for one of the jobs."

Squinting, he studied her. "I don't mean no disrespect, ma'am, but the day I hire a woman to work in my livery is the day I start sewing petticoats."

He laughed at his own joke and, though she didn't share the humor, she found her earlier guess proven right—the gruffness around his eyes softened instantly when he smiled.

"There's an order to things, ma'am, that's meant to be followed. And it's unnatural for a woman to do this kind of work." He glanced around him. "And a livery's not a fitting place for a woman to work either."

McKenna kept silent and let him say his piece. She'd heard it all before. Not a hint of meanness undergirded his tone or his reaction. He was simply stating his opinion, which he was fully entitled to—as was she.

"I'm sorry you feel that way, Mr. Trenton. I can't say that your opinion is new to me. I guess I was hoping that views out West might be more open. More willing to see past the way things have always been." When he showed no signs of softening, she crossed to the workbench and lifted the decorative skirt of the saddle. She brushed her fingers over the initials *M. A.* that she'd carved into the leather. Her trademark—something she'd learned to do from her father.

She glanced back at Trenton. "If you're still willing to employ my brother, I'll make sure he's here first thing tomorrow morning." At his nod, she hefted the saddle. "Thank you for your time, and I'll seek employment elsewhere." She started for the door.

"Whoa there, missy . . ." He moved into her path. "I'm afraid that's already sold. And I got an order for another one just like it that came in this morning. Your brother's gonna be one busy fella."

She shifted the saddle in her arms, distributing the weight, and enjoying what she was about to say far more than she should have. "Actually, Mr. Trenton, my brother's giftedness lies more in building and repairing wagons than in leather work." She paused to let that soak in, then added with a smile, "*I'm* the fella who made this saddle."

ELEVEN

Suspicion shadowed the livery owner's face. "You're telling me . . . *you* made that?" His attention dropped to the saddle in McKenna's arms.

"Yes, Mr. Trenton, I did. And regardless of the misdirection of your compliments just now, I sincerely appreciate them." And she did. Telling by the number of orders tacked to the wall behind Casey Trenton, along with the nearly full stalls, his livery was well patronized. And such patronage was hard earned, especially with two other liveries in such a small mountain town. But it spoke highly of him, and she could have benefited from his reputation.

Watching him, she shifted the weight of the saddle in her arms and tried to gauge what manner of man he was. And what his response to her would be. Most men either ignored her once they learned what she did, or suddenly changed their minds about the quality of her work, deciding it wasn't what they'd initially judged it to be. Which her father once said spoke more about them than they likely cared to reveal.

But judging from the way Mr. Trenton stared at her now, his opinion about her work hadn't changed. On the contrary. If she wasn't mistaken, he was counting the money he would forfeit if he *didn't* hire her, which gave her fresh hope. She needed this job. She only hoped Casey Trenton's need for income outweighed his conventional opinions.

"You make fine saddles, ma'am." The lines of his brow gradually smoothed. "Finest I've ever seen. And nobody could say you don't have a talent for it."

She warmed beneath his praise, and what it likely meant. Working in a setting like this, one that reminded her so much of home, and where she could keep a needed eye on Robert would be the answer to her—

"But what I said earlier still stands, ma'am. A woman working in a livery . . . It's just not something I can agree to. Goes against what I hold is right, and I doubt my customers would care for it much either. I'm sorry, Miss Ashford."

She struggled to keep her disappointment hidden. "I see," she whispered, a tangle of emotions unraveling inside her by the second.

"But I want to do right by you, ma'am. You sent me that saddle to show me your handiwork. Not for me to sell. So I might owe you an apology on that count. But from what you penned in that letter you wrote, I kind of figured you might be needing the money."

Sincerity colored his tone. She looked at the saddle in her grip and recalled who she'd had in mind when making it. "You figured correctly, Mr. Trenton. I *could* use the money."

"Name your asking price then. Whatever it is, I'll pay it."

She glanced up at him. *Such trust.* Somehow, despite having only met this man, she wouldn't have expected any less. "I usually sell my saddles for thirty dollars."

He shook his head and laughed beneath his breath. "Well, that's what I get for pricing it without knowing." He pulled a wad of bills from his pants pocket. "I asked forty-five for it and the guy who bought it didn't blink."

McKenna's mouth slipped open.

"He's supposed to come back for it this week. Paid for it up front but was on his way to Denver on the stage, so he asked me to hold it for him until he gets back." Trenton gave her a look that made her feel naive despite her twenty-three years. "Things cost more out here, ma'am. Harder to get supplies up the mountains, and skilled labor such as this isn't that common in these parts."

As he sorted through the dollar bills, she returned the saddle to the bench and ran a hand over the soft, supple leather, thinking of the hours she'd spent laboring over it, wanting to make sure it was her best. She fingered the decorative strands of braided leather on the saddle skirts. No reason why something serviceable couldn't also be pleasing to the eye. This had been the last saddle she'd made in her father's livery, with his tools, and she'd planned on giving it to Janie as a gift.

But seeing how things had worked out . . .

"That's fine that you sold it, Mr. Trenton. You're right, the money will come in handy, sir."

She took the stack of bills he held out.

"I hope your move to Copper Creek turns out to be a good one, ma'am. I've been here since '60 when the place was founded. We got mining towns on all sides, which means lots of business. But once a month, when the miners get paid, things can get a tad rowdy in town for a few nights. Mostly it's a safe enough place, though. Just mind yourself and you'll make it fine."

She acknowledged the warning with a tilt of her head.

"And tell your brother I'll look for him at sunup tomorrow. I've got orders for three new wagons, and two out back waiting to be repaired. So we'll make the most of daylight hours."

"I'll tell him, sir. And he'll be here. Thank you."

Trenton turned to the forge and stoked the fire, while she

walked to the open doorway, discreetly counting the money. *Forty-five dollars.* He hadn't kept a penny for bartering the deal. She retraced her steps. "Mr. Trenton . . ."

He looked back. His attention went to the bills she held out, but he made no move to take them.

"I wouldn't have made this sale without you, sir. I appreciate your reputation in this town . . . and your honesty. Both about what price the saddle brought, and for the manner in which you expressed your opinion a moment ago."

Slowly, the firm line of his mouth turned upward. He accepted the money. "If your brother's half the worker you are, Miss Ashford, it won't be long 'til I have the most profitable livery in town again."

Wishing she could answer in the affirmative about Robert, she simply smiled and prayed again that her brother would make the most of this opportunity. And that he would act with better judgment here than he had back home. Without a doubt, Robert possessed broader talents than she did, but somehow he didn't see it.

She turned to leave, and an idea came.

"Mr. Trenton?" She waited until he looked her way again. "What would you say if we could work out a sort of . . . partnership between us? A silent one," she added quickly. "Where I would work for you making saddles, but not here in the livery." Caution crept into his eyes and she rushed to expel it. "I need a place to sell my wares, and if the majority of people in Copper Creek share your opinion about women working with leather"—his expression said he was tracking with her—"then one way this might work for me—for us both—would be for me to work at home. At the Talbots' home, I mean."

Something changed in his expression. "You mentioned something about your cousin . . . That'd be Mrs. Talbot I take it?"

McKenna nodded.

"Then let me offer my condolences, ma'am. I had occasion to do business with her husband, Vince. He was a fine man, and he was going to make something of that ranch too. He had it in him to do it." His voice softened. "How's Mrs. Talbot gettin' along since he passed?"

Emotions rose, and McKenna spoke past the lump in her throat. "Mrs. Talbot . . . Janie"—she spoke the name softly—"passed away earlier this week, along with her newborn son."

He looked away and didn't speak for a moment. And seemed hesitant to meet her gaze again. "What about their little girl?"

"Before she died, Janie asked me to look after Emma. I promised her I would." Hearing that promise again from her own lips made her responsibility all the more real, and the pressure of all that rested on her shoulders returned. "So, Mr. Trenton . . . would you be willing to consider buying my saddles and selling them through your livery? No one in town need know about it. I won't say anything to anyone, I give you my word."

A man walked in. "Morning, Trenton. Got my wagon ready?"

"You bet. It's out back ready to go. I'll get right with you."

"Ma'am . . ." The customer tipped his hat to her and slowed. "I'm not in a hurry, Trenton. Finish with this lady here." His smile was kind and held invitation. "She was here before me."

Mr. Trenton motioned McKenna over to the side, and she followed. She noticed the other gentleman looking closely at her saddle. But even more, she noticed that Trenton was watching him too.

Mr. Trenton leaned close. "You have all your own tools, ma'am?"

"Most of them," she whispered, matching his muted tone. "And if I need to use any of yours I can come in after hours, at night, when the livery is closed. I promise I won't be an intrusion."

Biting the inside of his lip, he finally sighed. "Where'd you learn to do this? Work with leather like you do?"

She smiled, hearing the decision in his voice. "From my father. And I promise you, Mr. Trenton, you won't be sorry about this. I'll always deliver on time."

He glanced at the man across the room. "How long does it take you to make a saddle, from start to finish?"

"About two weeks if I've got all the materials ready. But I'll need to find a supplier for the leather."

"I'll get you that. And it'll be top grade too. Same as what you've been using. Come early tomorrow morning, before I open, and we'll work out the details."

McKenna left the livery smiling—*really* smiling, for the first time in a long time, her steps lighter than when she'd first stepped inside. She swung into the saddle and Janie's palomino pranced beneath her, spirited and eager. McKenna reached down and rubbed the horse's neck. "Atta girl," she whispered, appreciating her enthusiasm. Casey Trenton had said yes! She had a job! Robert did too! Which meant an income, a livelihood. They were one step closer to having some stability to their lives again.

If only Janie were still here—to share the news . . .

McKenna reached the corner of the crowded thoroughfare and reined in to let a line of loaded freight wagons pass. She stared upward into a sky so rich in blue it almost didn't seem real and hoped Janie knew she was doing her best. *I won't let you down, Janie.*

The reminder of her promised meeting with Mr. Billings interrupted the moment, and McKenna's exuberance swiftly found its footing. She'd promised Mr. Billings a visit to his office, and though she wasn't looking forward to it, the meeting was inevitable. Best get it over with and discover the reason behind his insistence that she come by.

With a sigh, she gave Patch a gentle nudge, then sharply reined in. "Marshal Caradon!"

There he was, directly in her path, astride his mare. She'd nearly run into him. The prisoner from the other night Slater, if she remembered correctly—was on horseback behind him, bound at the wrists, oddly stoic. A fresh bruise marked his right cheek, and she could well imagine who had administered it.

Gripping the reins to both mounts, Caradon lightly touched the rim of his hat, his expression inscrutable. "Morning, Miss Ashford."

If ever someone's gaze felt intimate, his did. She felt as if she could read his thoughts, and a warm blush crept from her chest up into her face. It had been a long time since she'd welcomed a man's attention, much less encouraged it. She couldn't deny her attraction to him. And though she'd done her best to hide it in recent days, she had the feeling he knew. Perhaps if circumstances were different, if she didn't have the responsibilities she had, if he didn't work for the U.S. Marshals Office, she might have been more open to the idea. But as it was, she was relieved he wasn't staying in Copper Creek.

"You're leaving town, Marshal Caradon?"

His eyes took on a gleam. "No need to sound so broken up over it, ma'am."

Slightly embarrassed at her transparency, she attempted to cover it with a laugh. "Not at all. I was simply making an observation."

Wordless, his look said, *Sure you were.*

Tugging at the rope encircling his wrists, Slater kept quiet. Still, McKenna sensed a danger about him and hoped Caradon would be careful. Then again, looking at Marshal Caradon and at the bruise purpling Slater's right cheek, Slater would do well to be on his best behavior.

Her mare sidestepped and whinnied. McKenna tightened her grip on the reins. "Well, I—"

"Well, I—"

She and Caradon had spoken at the same time, and she smiled.

His eyes narrowed the slightest bit and his slow-coming smile made it impossible for her to swallow without deliberate concentration. Marshal Wyatt Caradon was a man women noticed, as evidenced by the number of females staring at him as they passed by on the boardwalk. He had a commanding presence about him that went beyond his build or his badge. And having spent time with him, McKenna suspected he was as good-natured a man as he was handsome. But even that wasn't enough to tempt her.

Even good-natured men made mistakes that others ended up paying for. Sometimes for a lifetime.

"Well, I'd better be going," she said. "I have an appointment this morning. Do take care of yourself, Marshal Caradon."

"You do the same . . . Miss Ashford." He ran a hand along his unshaven jaw, his gaze appraising. "And tell that sweet little Emma I said to be good."

Responding to his tender mention of the child, McKenna nodded and took her leave, eager to complete her business with Mr. Billings and to relieve Robert of Emma. Or Emma of Robert, depending on how they were getting along.

As she rode on down the street, she sensed Caradon's gaze following her.

When she reached the bank building and dismounted, she chanced a backward look in time to see him rounding the corner. His back to her, she watched him go and felt a tug deep inside her, in a place long ago locked away and unaccustomed to intrusion. A place where she used to imagine what it would be like to be loved by a man who would always be there. Who would keep his promises, no matter what. And who would do as he said he would.

After a long moment, she turned toward the bank, torn between her promise to meet with Mr. Billings and her desire to ride like the wind back to the cabin. All she knew was that the banker had some question about Janie bequeathing her the ranch. At least that's what she'd gleaned from their brief encounter following the funeral.

She stared up at the building. She hadn't always been so

uncomfortable around bankers, but her experiences in St. Joseph—with Robert—had taught her to be.

The door to the bank opened.

"Miss Ashford, how kind of you to stop by this morning." Mr. Billings stepped outside, a ready smile in place. "Please, come right in."

She tethered her horse, climbed the steps, and accepted his outstretched hand as she crossed the threshold, but quickly let go once inside. His greeting her at the door couldn't be a good sign. It meant he'd been watching for her.

He gestured. "Let's talk in my office. We'll have more privacy there."

Following him, McKenna wondered if she was only imagining the stares from the other bank employees. Three in all, two sat behind a teller counter and one at a desk outside of Mr. Billings' office, and all of their gazes followed her.

"Good morning," she said to each, smiling as she passed.

Their subdued reactions only deepened her angst, and as Mr. Billings closed the office door, his expression dour, she had the distinct impression they knew something she didn't. But soon would.

TWELVE

Mr. Billings motioned for McKenna to sit in a chair opposite his desk. "May I offer you some refreshment, Miss Ashford? Perhaps a cup of tea? Or coffee? My secretary, Miss Thomas, would be happy to get it for you."

McKenna's throat was parched, but the knot in her stomach prevented her from accepting. "No . . . thank you. I'm fine." Being back in a bank, and in the bank manager's office specifically, prodded memories best left undisturbed.

Billings's office smelled of fine aged leather, expensive cigars, and money. Reminders to her that she was not from that same world. Just as Vince and Janie hadn't been. She smoothed the wrinkles from her skirt, conscious of the dress she'd chosen that morning—a rich blue frock with lace along the bodice and sleeve cuffs. It was her best, though it fit more loosely around the waist than when she'd worn it last.

Mr. Billings seated himself behind his desk and pulled open a large side drawer. He withdrew a file and placed it between them on the desk. With a discreet glance, McKenna tried to read what was scribbled on the edge, and failed.

"May I offer my condolences again, Miss Ashford, on the passing of your cousin and her husband. And my deepest apologies for coming at such an inopportune time yesterday afternoon."

Not yet convinced of his sincerity—or his motives—McKenna kept her responses courteous but brief. "I appreciate that, Mr. Billings. Thank you."

The silence lengthened, and she sensed he was waiting for her to comment further. Unwilling, she attempted a pleasant countenance and hoped it masked her unease.

"I realize you're busy, Miss Ashford, and I appreciate your time. So I won't claim more of it than is needed." He leaned forward in his chair. "I've spoken with Dr. Foster, and he's agreed to act as a witness on your behalf. He confirmed that Mrs. Talbot did indeed bequeath to you the homestead, the ranch, the cattle, everything that belonged to her and her husband. As well as entrusting to you the guardianship of their only child, Emma."

It took a few seconds for what he'd said to sink in.

He wasn't calling her here to contest anything. He was calling her here to validate Janie's last wishes! "That's correct, Mr. Billings." Relief urged her guard lower. "I—I'm so glad you spoke with Dr. Foster. Thank you for doing that."

"My pleasure, Miss Ashford." His smile was short-lived and a paternal look moved in behind it. "In cases such as these, however, where there's no written last will and testament, matters can sometimes get . . . complicated. But since Dr. Foster was present and there are no living relatives of whom we're aware . . ." He paused. "The Talbots had no other relatives that you know of, is that correct?"

"Yes, sir. That's correct. Mrs. Talbot was an only child, as was her husband, as she told me. And both of their sets of parents are deceased."

"Very good," he whispered more to himself, making notes. "I'll file the appropriate paperwork. That makes this part of the transition much easier for everyone involved."

Thinking his manner somewhat callused, it crossed her mind to tell him that the *transition* didn't feel very easy at the moment, but she refrained.

"If you'll permit me, Miss Ashford, I'll come directly to the point."

She felt a check in her spirit.

"I leave tomorrow on the stage to Denver where, on Monday morning, I must give an account to our board of directors about this bank's current holdings—Mr. and Mrs. Vince Talbot's account being among those holdings, of course."

Listening to him, watching him up close, McKenna tried to pinpoint what it was about him that bothered her. And it finally became clear.

Billings was a much younger man than she'd initially judged him to be. Five years her senior, at most. But his formal manner—a trait she was certain he'd worked to cultivate—lent him an older, more mature first impression. And she might have been convinced too, if not for the single bead of sweat trailing down his left temple.

She found the discovery both revealing—and disturbing.

"Our bank has held the Talbots' account since they first moved here, and we've long appreciated their business. They were both fine people, Miss Ashford, and well respected in this community. I think it's important for you to understand that, especially at this juncture."

"Thank you, sir. That's most kind."

"And even though there's another lending institution in town, a smaller one"—his tone held the slightest condescension—"Mr. Talbot entrusted us with his venture, and we were very optimistic about its success."

So *that's* what this meeting was about. Billings was concerned about her keeping Vince and Janie's account—now *her* account—with his bank. Relaxing, she was eager to allay his misperception. "Let me assure you, Mr. Billings, I have no intention of withdrawing any of the Talbots' funds from your bank. My cousin didn't have occasion to brief me on their holdings, but rest easy . . . I'll only be withdrawing funds as they're needed to care for their daughter, Emma, and for operating the ranch. To which I'm committed to continue building, as the Talbots would have wanted."

She read surprise in his features. Surely he didn't think her some kind of gold digger come West only to claim the family fortune and leave. "In fact, after our meeting today, I plan to post an advertisement for a ranch hand to assist with the cattle. And my brother and I have each secured employment as well." Surely that bolstered her level of commitment in his eyes. "Come fall, we'll take the cattle to market, at which time I have every hope of returning with a sizable deposit. Of course," she said, inclining her head, "I'll entrust those funds to your fine institution."

Not sure what she expected his reaction to be, she *did* expect at least some enthusiasm. Yet Mr. Billings appeared unimpressed. He was staring at her, but she got the peculiar feeling he wasn't hearing anything she'd said. "Forgive me, Mr. Billings. But . . . have I spoken out of turn?"

His smile looked forced and ill-fitted. "You're new to Copper Creek, Miss Ashford. I realize that, and . . ." He sighed, his gaze suddenly captive to his desk. "I wish fate had allowed us more time to work out this situation. But, as it is . . ."

He sat straighter in his fine leather chair and clasped his hands before him on the desk. Suddenly he more resembled a boy trying to fill out his father's suit than a grown man in charge of a bank. Regardless, he held her future in his hands, pasty white and thin-fingered as they were.

"Last summer, ma'am, Vince Talbot took out a second mortgage on his ranch to pay for the cattle he purchased. He experienced some setbacks in the fall. Several, in fact, and eventually fell into arrears on his loan payments."

A sinking sense of déjà vu settled inside her. "Fell into arrears?"

"Yes, ma'am. More simply put, that means that he—"

"Fell behind in his payments. Yes, I'm familiar with the terminology." More familiar than he knew. Then it struck her—could Mr. Billings have wired the bank in St. Joseph and attained her financial history? That information was supposed to remain private, but she hadn't left St. Joseph in the best of standing. And Robert's behavior the day their home and family furniture was auctioned off hadn't helped any.

She needed to word her responses carefully. No need to call attention to something that wasn't an issue—yet. "Exactly how far behind were the Talbots in their payments, Mr. Billings?"

He withdrew a sheet of paper from the file atop his desk and laid it before her. McKenna shifted in her chair so she could read it. Her gaze ran down the right column of the ledger sheet and the unpleasant feeling inside her expanded. *December* was the last month recording a payment, and if she read the history correctly, that had only been a partial payment.

Suddenly the miles separating her from all they'd left behind in St. Joseph seemed to vanish. She was right back where she'd started—a bankrupt homestead and business, and more bills than she had money to pay.

"I realize, Miss Ashford, that this has caught you without warning," Mr. Billings said, his voice softening. "And for that, I apologize. Customarily, when we reach this particular impasse, there's culpability on the part of the person sitting in your chair. But in this instance, there isn't any. I realize that. You're an innocent party, and I wish I could allow you the time to try to turn things around. But . . ." He appeared unwilling to meet her eyes. "I regret to inform you that I'm going to have to proceed with the foreclosure of the—"

She heard him—and didn't—at the same time. His voice faded in and out. Clear, then fuzzy as scenes flashed through her mind. She was standing beside her mother's grave. Then her father's. She was in the sheriff's office, posting bail, anything to keep Robert from going to jail.

She broke out in a sweat. She'd already lost one home. One life. She wasn't going to lose another.

"I will not give in." The words were out of her mouth before she'd had time to filter them. And despite their whispered tone, a will of iron rushed in to shore them up.

From the look on Billings's face, he was as surprised as she was.

His mouth hung open for a beat. "I beg your pardon, ma'am?"

She swallowed, willing her voice not to tremble like her hands. *I will not be broken. I will not be broken.* It became like a mantra inside her. "I arrived in Copper Creek four days ago, Mr. Billings." She drew a deep breath. "And *nothing* has been as I expected. I realize that's not your fault, and I'm not blaming you or your bank, for this situation." She studied him, her mind going multiple directions at once, seeking a way through this. "How much needs to be paid on the account in order to keep the bank from foreclosing on the property?"

"I fear we're past that now, Miss Ashford. It's been over six months since the bank has received a full payment. I'll know more this next week after I meet with my fath—" His face reddened. "With the stockholders in Denver," he covered quickly.

But not before McKenna glimpsed the chink in his armor. *My father.* That gave this a whole new perspective. Mr. Billings was only trying to do his job, while also earning his father's approval. Which made her feel even worse about what she was about to attempt. But she had no other choice.

She kept her tone cordial. "Mr. Billings, did Vince Talbot keep you informed of his inability to pay in a timely manner?"

"Oh yes, ma'am. Mr. Talbot was always forthcoming with me about his situation. As I said, he and his wife were fine people, and very well liked. We all feel very badly about how things have worked out, Miss Ashford. For them, and now for you."

She nodded, searching her memory. This could either work for her, or against her. Heaven knows, she'd already had enough of the *against* in her life—maybe heaven would see to it to send some of the other her way. "When did you inform Mr. Talbot about the possibility of having to foreclose on his ranch, sir?"

"Mr. Talbot visited my office"—he flipped to a page in the back of the file—"the last week in April to, again, request more time for repayment of his loan. I explained the situation to him, about the likelihood of a foreclosure, and he said he understood completely."

Her next question poised and ready, McKenna held back, acting as if she needed time to ponder what he'd said. "I see . . . And when was it exactly that you served Mr. Talbot with *written* notice of your intention to foreclose?"

The change in his demeanor was barely perceptible. But it was there. She was certain.

His brow rose, and she knew the rules of the game had changed.

"Written notice?" he repeated.

"Yes, sir. It's my understanding that, by law, a property owner must be given notice in writing of a bank's intention to foreclose . . . before that action can be pursued."

A glimmer of admiration filtered through his surprise, but it was briefly lived. "You're right, Miss Ashford. That is the proper procedure."

Her mind racing, McKenna took heart—until he withdrew another sheet of paper from the file.

"Which is why I drafted written notice of the intent to foreclose on the twenty-seventh of April."

Her hopes fell as swiftly as they'd risen. "I see."

He laid the page before her with a flourish that pressed every emotional bruise she still nurtured. And when she read Vince's name at the top, her heart sank. Why hadn't Janie told her about this? Warned her? Then again, would it have made any difference? She and Robert had nowhere else to—

The bottom of the document drew her eye. McKenna flipped the page over and checked the back. Her pulse quickened. Experience was often a harsh teacher. But once learned, the lessons were not easily forgotten. "Might I see a copy of this declaration that Mr. Talbot signed, please? The one serving as his receipt of notification of your bank's intention to foreclose on his property?"

The look on Mr. Billings's face told her she'd just bought herself more time, and had also sacrificed any hope of forging an unlikely friendship with Copper Creek's most prominent banker.

THIRTEEN

"Aunt Kenny!"

The blade slipped in McKenna's hand, narrowly missing her finger. Teeth gritted, she threw the knife on the workbench and stepped back, her body flushing hot and cold at the near miss. The cut on her left hand had finally healed. Dr. Foster had only recently removed the sutures, and here she'd almost—

"Aunt Kenny!"

As Emma's voice came closer, McKenna ran her hands through her hair, willing a calm that wouldn't come. It was nearly dark outside. Robert had promised to watch Emma and should have put her to bed by now. "I'm in here, sweetie. In the barn." Her cheerful tone rang false, not that Emma would notice.

Head pounding, McKenna gripped the hair at her temples and squeezed tight. The pressure actually helped her headache, but didn't ease the throb in her lower back that spiraled up the length of her spine.

Over two weeks had passed since her meeting with Mr. Billings, but the outcome was never far from her mind. She'd stopped guessing why Janie had never mentioned the seriousness of their situation in a letter. Whatever her reason, it didn't change the circumstances. After meeting with Mr. Billings, she had shared the outcome with Robert over dinner that evening, phrasing it carefully so as not to alarm him. No need for both of them to worry.

McKenna heard a noise behind her and turned.

Emma toddled barefoot into the barn, her nightgown dragging behind her in the dirt. Her blonde hair was mussed, and she looked like a little ragamuffin dragged in off the street. The same could be said for Clara, the rag doll clutched tight in her arms. The doll had been everywhere with her over the past two weeks. It needed a good washing, but every time McKenna tried to take it away, Emma threw a fit. The child had already cried enough tears for a lifetime.

"I'm thirsty, Aunt Kenny."

"Then you should go back inside and ask Uncle Robert for a drink."

"Uncle Robert isn't there."

McKenna looked beyond her to the homestead. "What do you mean he isn't there?"

Emma scrunched her shoulders and let them fall.

Robert, so help me if you . . . A flush of anger swept through her. He'd left a child of five in the house *alone*? "Come on, sweetheart." McKenna took a measured breath and slowly let it out. "I'll get you a drink of water and then it's back to bed."

"But I want milk."

"We don't have any more milk, remember? You drank the last of it at dinner."

"But we got a cow." Emma looked pointedly at the cow in the stall.

"I don't have time to milk her again right now, Emma."

"My mama used to milk Summer before I went to bed."

McKenna searched for a smile. "Yes, I know. But I haven't

had time to do that this evening." Milking was one of Robert's responsibilities. One of the growing list of responsibilities he'd been shirking recently.

She glanced at the pieces of leather on the workbench. She'd been cutting them in thin strips for braids, the finishing touch to this saddle. The knife had veered to the left, cutting several of the pieces too short. More leather wasted. She reminded herself that she still had her finger, but that wouldn't pay for the extra leather. She only hoped the next order from Mr. Trenton's leather supplier had arrived.

This saddle was due to the livery in two days, and it would take every spare minute between now and then to get it finished.

"Are you mad, Aunt Kenny?"

Yes, at Robert. "No, honey, I'm just tired." Letting Emma know how angry she was wouldn't help matters any. Better to maintain a calm exterior for the child's sake. McKenna blew out the oil lamp on the workbench and extended her hand.

Emma looked at it, turned on her diminutive heel, and walked back to the cabin. McKenna trailed behind, mindful of all the little girl had endured in past weeks. Even longer, with Vince's passing.

Dr. Foster's counsel from the last time she'd seen him in town came back to her now: *Give her time. She'll warm up to you. She's no doubt resentful of you right now because—in her eyes—you're trying to take her mother's place.*

Emma still asked for her mother several times a day, sometimes in tears, sometimes in passing, as though she'd forgotten what had happened. "Your mother's in heaven now," McKenna had gently explained a dozen times. "But she still loves you very much."

But that didn't erase the child's tears or her stated wish that her mother was still here instead of McKenna.

McKenna followed Emma through the open front door and, sure enough, saw no sign of Robert. "Robert?" She peered inside the two bedrooms and then turned to Emma. "Did he say where he was going? Or when he'd be back?"

Emma shook her head matter-of-factly. "He's just not here." She climbed into a kitchen chair and situated Clara close beside her. "Clara wants a drink too."

Sighing, McKenna poured the last of the water from the pitcher, her back and shoulder muscles aching from bending over the workbench for the past two hours. She set the tin cup on the table. "You'll need to share this with Clara until I can pump more water later. Be sure to use both hands."

Emma gripped the cup with her right hand and took a sip. She drew her mouth into a bow and smiled.

McKenna chose a firmer tone. "I said to use *both* hands, please."

"I don't need to. See?" Emma brought the cup to her lips again, sipped, and moved to set it down. The cup caught the edge of the table and dropped, drenching the front of her gown. "You filled it too full, Kenny!" Tears erupted. "My *mama* never did it that way!"

Reaching for a rag, McKenna felt her patience thinning, more so with each of Emma's high-pitched screams. The most mundane things set the child off these days. *And where on earth was Robert!*

Emma's tears became more pitiful, and McKenna found herself tempted to join in. The pounding in her head grew to a steady thrum. She'd never felt so tired, so defeated, in all her life. "We'll get it cleaned up, sweetheart. Don't worry. It's only water."

"I—I'm"—Emma hiccupped and took stuttered breaths—"still . . . thirsty, Kenny."

The child had taken to calling her Aunt Kenny, and on occasion shortened to it Kenny. No doubt from Robert's use of the name. It didn't sit well, but seemed a small thing in light of everything else. Especially with the closeness McKenna hoped to cultivate.

She finger-brushed the hair hanging in Emma's eyes, surprised—and heartened—when she didn't pull away like usual. Emma offered the tiniest pout of a smile, but it wasn't enough to change McKenna's mind about giving her more to drink. Not when she'd changed the sheets on Emma's bed three times this week. The soiled laundry sat waiting in a basket on the front porch, probably soured by now.

She leaned down and kissed Emma's cheek. "You've had enough to drink for tonight, sweetie. Remember what happened—"

"*Please*, Aunt Kenny?"

"I said you've alrea—"

"I'll be good," she said in a singsong voice, smiling and tilting her head to one side.

McKenna smiled. "The answer is still no, Emma. You've already wet your—"

"I don't like you!" Emma pulled back, her brow dipped low. "And you're not my *mama*!"

McKenna stilled, feeling as if someone had slapped her across the face. "No, Emma . . . I'm not your mama." She spoke over the child's whimpers. "But your mama asked me to take care of you, and I'm doing that. As best I can. I think we can be very good friends, if you'll only give me a chance."

Emma's glare said the possibility of that was slim.

After an hour of her getting out of bed and McKenna putting her back down again, Emma finally fell asleep. And McKenna collapsed onto the couch, completely spent. She really needed to return to the barn to work on the saddle. Either that or milk the cow, pump more water, or wash the laundry.

Tears edged the corners of her eyes, but she determined not to give in to them. She determined to remain strong. *I will not be broken.* She repeated the phrase, over and over. *I will not be—*

Footfalls outside brought her upright. The door handle turned.

Robert stepped inside, and his eyes widened when he spotted her. "You're still awake."

McKenna stood. “Yes, I’m still awake. And Emma just now went to sleep.”

He made a face. “She was asleep when I left.”

“When you *left*?” She didn’t even try to keep the harshness from her voice. “You agreed to watch her this evening so I could work. You promised, Robert!”

“What . . . ?” He shrugged. “She fell asleep, and there was nothing else to do. Besides, you were in the barn if she needed anything.”

“You can’t leave a child her age alone, Robert. It’s dangerous. And I was *working* in the barn. I’ve got a job to do, same as you. Only I can’t get mine done if I have to take care of Emma too.”

“Well, maybe you should’ve thought of that before you agreed to do this.”

He’d said it beneath his breath, but she heard every word. “I can’t believe you’d say that.” She caught a whiff of something. Or thought she did. She moved closer and took another sniff.

Robert looked away, confirming her suspicions.

“You’ve been drinking?”

He crossed to the kitchen cupboard, a familiar swagger in his step. “I had a beer in town. One beer. I wouldn’t call that drinking.” He rummaged through the shelves. “Do we have anything to eat?”

McKenna could only stare. She’d felt slapped in the face earlier, but this felt like a punch in the gut. Disbelief fed her anger. “Robert, we’ve talked about this before. Alcohol isn’t something that I’m going to toler—”

“For God’s sake, Kenny. It was one drink! Don’t make this into more than it is.”

“I’m not making this into more than it is. I just—”

“You’re not my mother!”

She blinked, caught off guard by the vehemence of his statement. And its similarity to Emma’s earlier. Robert looked away muttering something low and foul. And every syllable delivered a wound.

He was right. She wasn't his mother. She'd been a friend and confidant when he was younger. A sustainer and a lawgiver as the years passed. And though she'd tried to be a mother to him, to fill that gaping hole, she'd obviously failed. After the incident in St. Joseph, their pastor had told her to make a decision: either choose to trust Robert again or continue to harbor suspicion. "It's impossible, McKenna," the pastor had said, "to truly believe that someone can change for the better, if you're constantly dwelling on his past." For a while, she'd walked a tightrope between trusting and suspicion with Robert. But then she'd come to the point when she'd decided to trust him again, to believe in him, and not to withdraw from him as others had done.

And then something like this happened . . .

"Just forget it." Robert slammed the cupboard door and grabbed the blanket from the couch where he usually slept, then headed for the door. "I'll bed down in the barn."

He was halfway out the door when McKenna found her voice. "Robert . . . "

He stopped, his back to her, and finally turned. Contempt riddled his eyes—eyes deep set and stormy gray, like their father's.

She chose her words with care. "You're right. I'm not your mother. But I've done the best I could." She bit her lower lip. "We can't afford for this move not to work, or for you to lose this job. For either of us to lose our jobs. Mr. Billings has already started foreclosure proceedings against the ranch. If I don't deliver that payment to him by September, then—"

"I know what he said. You've told me . . . three times. We'll lose this place."

She heard the helplessness in her sigh. "This is all we have now." Her gaze swept the tiny three-room cabin, one-fourth the size of the house they'd left behind in St. Joseph. "We've already lost one home, we can't afford to—"

"Why do you keep saying *we*? When really . . . you mean *me*?"

He retraced his steps, and as he drew closer it registered with her how tall and broad-shouldered he'd become, how strong. Far more a man than a boy.

"Isn't that what you mean, Kenny? *I'm* the one who lost everything back home. The house. Pa's livery. It was *my* fault. Why don't you just say it out loud for once? You say it every day in the way you look at me."

Oh, she was tempted . . . His words lit a fire inside her. "You're not being fair to me, Robert. I've worked hard to give us this fresh start. To make sure you have a chance at a new—"

"Don't say you're doing this for me, Kenny. To give me a new life. You're doing it for yourself! You were embarrassed by what happened back home. You were embarrassed by me and wanted to get away from everyone who knew us, who knew what happened. So don't you dare stand there and tell me this is all about giving me a chance to start over. I was fine with staying put. I didn't give a . . ."

She cringed at the language he chose but let him speak. At least this was a chance to find out what was going on inside him. However much it hurt.

"And as far as helping with *her*"—he threw a look at Emma's closed bedroom door—"I've got enough to do on my own. Trenton is working me like I'm three men. Sometimes I just need to get away to clear my mind, and if I want to go to town on occasion, I'm going to." Defiance hardened his eyes, daring her to try to do something about it.

McKenna stared up at him, wondering exactly where it was she'd gotten so off track with him. Her chest ached remembering how she'd cradled him as a baby beside their mother's graveside. The memory of their father's burial rose in her mind, and she could still feel the clammy hand of a somber nine-year-old boy clinging tight to hers. Robert had fought back tears that day—tears he hadn't even understood at the time. But she had. Just like she understood the defiance in him now, and saw through it to the hurt inside.

The pain in her chest grew more severe. "Robert, I'm sorry if you think I've—"

His harsh laugh cut her off. "I don't want your pity, Kenny." His smile was almost feral. "And I think you're right . . . Moving here is going to be a good thing." An emotion moved in behind his eyes, one she couldn't define but didn't like. "I think I'm going to end up liking Copper Creek better than I thought."

The slam of the front door reverberated inside her.

And when she awakened the next morning, the sting of their argument was still fresh.

With Emma by her side, morning chores took twice as long. The child seemed intent on making a mess everywhere they went—nearly tipping over the milk pail, pulling laundry from the line . . . The only time she came close to compliance was when McKenna promised to read her an extra book at bedtime that evening. On those occasions, Emma would cuddle close, so that was a promise McKenna didn't mind making.

Noon came and they stopped briefly for a lunch of cornbread and beans. The combination was warm and filling, yet all McKenna could think about was that she hadn't returned to the barn to work on the saddle. Nor had she fed the cattle in the lower field. Robert was supposed to have done that before he left for work, but he'd gotten up late. She hitched the horses to the wagon and loaded the hay, able to manage the bales with effort. Working in the livery full-time for the past five years had strengthened her muscles, but still they burned from the exertion.

She wiped her hands on her skirt, wishing she'd thought to wear an old pair of Robert's trousers. But she managed as best she could. By the time she and Emma returned to the cabin early that evening, they were both covered in hay and were famished. There was no way she could keep this up on her own. But neither did she have money to hire a ranch hand like she planned. Not with what little she had to pay them.

Absent of Robert's company, she and Emma ate a dinner of beans and rice and shared the remaining square of corn bread.

Twice McKenna tried to coax a smile from Emma, and twice the little girl schooled a frown, only to turn right around and reward Clara with a big kiss and a grin. Seeing her react that way to the doll brought thoughts of Wyatt Caradon close. And for some reason, thinking of him deepened McKenna's sense of fatigue and loneliness.

She wondered how he was. Where he was . . . If he'd delivered his prisoner without mishap. Or if the prisoner was even still alive. She pushed aside the silent barrage of questions and rose from the table. "It's time for bed, Emma."

Emma did her best to mask a yawn. "But I'm not tired."

McKenna read one bedtime book, and another as promised. Lacking the strength to endure their normal bedtime routine, she decided to lie down beside Emma for a while. As Emma drifted off to sleep, the child reached out and took hold of a lock of McKenna's hair. With her eyes closed, she held the curl tight.

"Aunt Kenny . . . can we go to church?"

The question was unexpected, and McKenna was unprepared to answer. People at the funeral, from the church where Vince and Janie had attended, had invited them to visit, and she'd considered it, even planned on it—eventually. After she and Robert were more settled, and hopefully after the questions died down. But the more she thought about it, the more McKenna realized she'd missed going to church. And Janie certainly would have wanted it. "Yes, I think that's a very good idea, Emma. We'll do that."

Emma's breathing gradually evened. McKenna pulled her closer and kissed her forehead, then briefly closed her eyes.

Sometime later, she awakened to darkness with Emma cuddled close beside her, the child's breath warm against her cheek. McKenna kissed the crown of her head and inhaled her sweet scent, something Emma wouldn't have permitted if she'd been awake. So she did it a second time, smiling.

"I love you, Emma Talbot," she whispered, meaning every

word, regardless of how Emma felt about her. She prayed Dr. Foster was right and that, in time, Emma would grow to feel something for her too.

A thought occurred, and she nestled Emma closer. She was holding a piece of Janie in her arms. Like a swath cut from a bolt of fine silk, this precious little girl was like Janie in so many ways.

Beyond the open window, the wind rustled the aspen leaves, bringing a familiar sound, and a memory. *You should see them come fall. That's when they're the prettiest,* Caradon had told her. She could still hear the deep timbre of his voice, could see his face so clearly in her mind.

She lay awake, listening to the tinkle of a thousand tiny bells, trying to imagine what the trees might look like three months from now. But would she even be in Copper Creek come fall to see those aspen trees? Not if Mr. Billings had his way . . .

She eased off the mattress, careful not to awaken Emma, and crept into the main room. The couch was empty. Robert could have come home and decided to sleep in the barn again, but a quick check confirmed that he hadn't. *Oh God, show me what to do. Should I trust him? Should I not? Show me how to reach Robert before it's too late.*

Pausing on the darkened porch, a full night of work awaiting, she reached inside her skirt pocket for her mother's handkerchief, and remembered—for the hundredth time—the Chinese woman who had taken it from her to launder.

She would seek out the woman tomorrow—as soon as she finished this saddle and delivered it, along with the bridles she'd made, to Mr. Trenton. Then, for what it was worth, she would finally post an advertisement in the mercantile for an experienced ranch hand. One who would work from dawn to dusk for next to nothing, and who would help with extra chores around the place, without being asked and expecting nothing in return.

The mere thought prompted a bitter laugh. No man in his

right mind would take the job. Not with the lure of gold mining a few miles up the mountain. She stared up into the myriad of stars flung with perfection across the inky night sky, and felt so small and insignificant by comparison.

Ask and you will receive. Seek and you will find. Knock and the door will be opened.

The paraphrase of scripture was familiar. Perhaps too familiar.

She'd asked for God's help so many times, only to be met with His silence. She'd sought to understand why Michael had been taken from her, but still didn't. She'd sought to right the wrongs done in St. Joseph, but had found no way. She'd knocked on the door of heaven's throne room until her knuckles were bloodied and bruised. Yet the door remained locked fast. But surely . . . *surely*—she swallowed the bitterness of her disappointment—there was someone out there who would be willing to help her build this ranch.

And in doing so, would help rebuild her failure of a life.

FOURTEEN

McKenna watched, cringing inside, as Casey Trenton inspected the saddle. She held her breath as he ran a hand along the cantle, then slowly over the side skirts and braids.

For some reason, making this saddle had been excruciating for her. Perhaps it was the pressure she'd put on herself to make it her best—for each stitch to be perfectly spaced, for each braid to be cut to the precise measurement, twisted in like pattern, and tied off at exactly the same angle and length. Or maybe it was everything else going on in her life that had made it so hard to concentrate for any length of time. Whatever the cause, she'd wanted this particular saddle to be better than any before.

And slowly . . . it dawned on her why—

Because in some odd way, this saddle represented the life she hoped to build here in Copper Creek. For *both* her and Robert, no matter what he'd said the other night about this move being only for her. And now this new life also included Emma—who kept yanking on her skirt. McKenna peered down.

"I'm hungry, Aunt Kenny," she said in a loud whisper.

McKenna shot her another warning glance, having told her before they entered the livery to be quiet and not to touch anything. Sore from an earlier mishap in the barn that morning, she reached up to rub her shoulder and caught Casey Trenton studying her stitching. He shook his head, and her anxiety spiked.

"Miss Ashford, this saddle . . ." He sighed, and laughed under his breath. "This is even finer than the first one you sent me by mail."

She exhaled, too relieved to speak.

"I tell you, I'm half tempted to keep this one for myself, ma'am. But I'm sure the fella who ordered it is worthy. And he'll be well pleased with your work." He withdrew some bills from his apron pocket. "I'll pay you for it now. Then I'll collect the money from him when he passes back through."

"But what if he doesn't come back for it?"

"Then I'll do as I'm tempted and keep it for myself." His wink said he would do just that. "But he gave me his word, and I've known this man for a while now. If he says he'll do something, he does it. Now you go ahead and take the money. You've earned it, Miss Ashford."

She only hesitated for a second. "Thank you, Mr. Trenton." She slipped the stack of bills into her reticule, already knowing where most of the money would go—straight to Mr. Billings.

She glanced toward the rear of the livery, where Robert was working on a wagon. He'd scarcely acknowledged her when she arrived and hadn't looked up since. At least his behavior was consistent. He rarely spoke to her at home either. She lowered her voice. "I'm wondering how my brother is doing. Are you pleased with his work?"

Trenton didn't answer right off, and she detected dissatisfaction in his pause.

"He's a talented young man, Miss Ashford." His subdued tone matched hers. "He has the same streak of giftedness in him as you do. Only his is for carpentry, like you said. He can build about anything and has a way of knowing how things are put together." He gestured for her to follow him to the front of the livery, and McKenna drew Emma along with her. "My only complaint," he said once they were outside, "which I've already spoken to him about—is that he's late for work. And sometimes takes off without finishing an order that's due." He opened his mouth as though he might say more, but apparently decided against it.

"Is there something else, Mr. Trenton?"

He ran a hand along the back of his neck. "I'm not sure it's anything, ma'am, but . . . The other day a fella came in. Don't know him personally, don't even know his name. But he didn't strike me as the type of man your brother would be spending time with. Or that you would want him to."

McKenna stole another glance across the shop at Robert, who looked up at that precise moment. Straight at her. She tried to keep the disapproval from her expression but knew she'd failed when his scowl deepened. He turned back to his work, pounding a nail with such force she was certain the wood would split.

"And you said you didn't know this man's name?" she whispered.

Mr. Trenton gave a shake of his head. "No, ma'am. And it's just a hunch on my part. I could be wrong about the man." But his demeanor said he didn't think so.

And McKenna tended to trust that intuition. Trenton struck her as being a fair judge of character, which only deepened her concern. "I'll speak to Robert at home. I'll gently broach the subject and remind him that this behavior won't be tolerated long term."

Mr. Trenton studied her for a beat. "That's all good and fine, Miss Ashford. But I've already . . . *broached* the subject with him." He said the word as though it didn't suit him.

"Though I can't say I was real gentle about it. As his employer, I felt it was within my right. I told him that if he was late again, I'd let him go. With his skill level . . ." He glanced behind him, and it was all McKenna could do not to interrupt. "He should've been done with that wagon two days ago, when it was promised. My patron was understanding this time, but he's also got work that needs to be done on his ranch, and I can't afford not to meet the commitments I make to my customers. I know you understand."

Thinking of how she'd barely finished this saddle in time, McKenna took the admonition to heart. "Of course I do. And I'll be sure to reinforce that at home too. Both Robert and I appreciate the opportunities you're giving us, and we'll work hard not to disappoint."

"I'm not worried about you, ma'am. Your word is your bond, I can tell." He glanced down at Emma, and his sun-wreathed features softened. "And you'd at least have an excuse. How are things going for you . . . with the little one?"

McKenna schooled a smile. "They're going very well, thank you. We're all getting along quite well."

As if on cue, Emma whined, "Aunt Kenny, I'm hungry. You promised!"

Shushing her, McKenna tried to give her an endearing pat on the head, but Emma squirmed from her reach. Looking at Mr. Trenton, McKenna pretended it didn't bother her. "Actually, we've already had breakfast. But she hardly eats enough to keep a bird alive." She didn't want him to think she was starving the child.

"That's cuz your biscuits are *hard*." Emma held up her doll. "Clara didn't like 'em either."

Mr. Trenton laughed softly.

"Kenny knocked over the milk pail too." Emma's bottom lip pudged out. "So we didn't have no milk."

Embarrassed, McKenna grasped Emma's hand, despite the

child's attempt to avoid her. "So we didn't have *any* milk," she gently corrected. "We had a bit of an accident this morning is all, Mr. Trenton. Everything is fine. I've milked cows before. I just need to get to know Summer a bit better."

Emma nodded. "Cuz she kicked you real good, huh, Aunt Kenny?"

"The cow kicked you, Miss Ashford?" Mr. Trenton frowned. "Are you all right?"

"Oh . . ." McKenna waved him off. "I'm fine. I've worked around animals all my life. An ornery cow isn't going to get the best of me." Though it nearly had this morning. She resisted the urge to rub her shoulder. The same one she'd hurt when she first arrived in town. The cow had given no warning and, before she knew it, she was on her back in the hay, staring up at the rafters with the wind knocked out of her. And with shards of pain shooting down her arm and back. A bruise was already forming—again.

Bidding Mr. Trenton good day, she and Emma took their leave and were headed in the direction of the laundry where she'd met the Chinese woman when a delicious aroma drew them off course.

Emma sniffed the air. "I'm hungry."

"Yes, I know. I am too."

Hand in hand, they set off down the boardwalk and paused in front of an open door. *Ming's Bakery*. Whatever was baking smelled of cinnamon and sweetness, and seeing the anticipation on Emma's face, McKenna decided to take advantage of the situation.

She knelt. "Emma, if you promise to be a good girl and to do as I say today, I'll get you something special from the bakery. Do you promise?"

Emma's eyes went wide. Her head bobbed up and down.

"All right then." McKenna extended her hand and Emma took it without hesitation. This was more like it.

They stepped inside and were immediately met by waves of heat coming from an oven somewhere in the back. No one worked the front counter, but fresh-baked goods occupied every inch of shelf space. Loaves of bread all fluffy and tall, not a fallen one in the bunch. Along with crusty-looking rolls whose golden sheen promised soft, airy textures within, unlike the *hard* biscuits McKenna had made that morning. She gave Emma a sideways glance.

The cute little urchin . . .

She'd wanted to wring Emma's tiny neck when she'd said that about her biscuits to Mr. Trenton. If she didn't know better, she would've thought Robert had put her up to it as a joke.

But Robert didn't kid around like that. Not anymore . . .

A pounding drew her attention, and she stepped to one side to peer through an open door into the kitchen. A dark-haired woman stood with her back to them, an apron cinched about her tiny waist. She raised a balled fist and brought it down with surprising force.

She did this repeatedly, and it took McKenna a few seconds to realize what she was doing. She was kneading dough. Pounding it into submission was more like it. And she talked while she worked, except McKenna couldn't see anyone else in the room, and she didn't understand the language.

She took a step forward. "Excuse me?"

The woman kept pummeling the dough, then picked up the complacent lump and slammed it down again. Flour plumed white around her, and the sound of her voice grew more ragged.

McKenna stepped closer. There was no one else in the kitchen, and if not mistaken, she guessed the woman was crying. Not knowing what to do—whether to go or stay—her hunger made the final decision. "Excuse me, ma'am?"

No response.

She tried a third time, louder this time, and the woman jumped and turned, her dark eyes going wide.

McKenna recognized her instantly, and the grief she'd only glimpsed in the woman's face on her first day in Copper Creek now shone undeniably. Tears streaked her cheeks, leaving lines in the flour that dusted her flawless complexion. Remembering the Chinese man she'd been with—her husband?—McKenna couldn't help but wonder if the woman's tears stemmed from something having to do with him. He'd seemed a stern man, and not an easy partner to live with.

She tried offering an apologetic smile, feeling very much an intruder at the moment.

The Chinese woman removed her apron, brushed the flour from her clothes, and made her way toward them with the same short, measured steps McKenna remembered from before. And she bowed repeatedly. "Most sorry, ma'am." With movements smooth and graceful, she tucked errant strands of straight dark hair back into the bun at the nape of her neck and moved behind the counter, where she could barely see over the top. "Serve, please?"

Her voice was soft. What few English words she spoke, she did with clarity and perfect pronunciation.

McKenna motioned behind them, including Emma in the gesture. "We smelled your bread from the street and couldn't resist coming inside." She realized she was speaking louder than normal and purposefully quieted her voice. "Something smells delectable."

The woman squinted ever so slightly. "De-lec-ta-ble?" She glanced at the array of baked goods and shook her head.

McKenna breathed in. "They smell *delicious*." She licked her lips. "*Mmm* . . ."

"Ah." The woman's face lit. "De-li-cious." She patted her stomach. "*Haochi*."

McKenna repeated the words, butchering both the pronunciation and the voice inflection. But with accustomed graciousness, the woman gave an affirming nod, and a smile gradually dispelled the sadness from her features. McKenna felt an instant connection with her, as she had the first time they'd met. But there was something else too . . .

Being in her company made her realize how much she missed Janie. And she wondered if the ache inside her—the wound left at Janie's death—would ever fully heal.

Staring at the Chinese woman before her, McKenna questioned whether the woman remembered who she was, then caught the answer in her gesture.

"All . . . better now?" she said, dark eyes expectant.

McKenna held out her left palm. "Yes, all better now. Dr. Foster stitched it up for me and it healed with barely a scar."

Again, uncertainty fogged the woman's countenance.

McKenna mimicked threading a needle and pretended to sew her hand.

Understanding slowly dawned. "Ah . . . *Xian*." The woman made a similar stitching motion. "*Thread*," she said, pronouncing the "th" with purposed care.

"Yes, very good!" Enjoying the exchange, McKenna felt a tug on her skirt.

"I want that one, Kenny." Emma pointed to a pastry on a lower shelf. Something similar to a cake, except small like a muffin, and round. Symbols of some sort were imprinted on the top, along with what looked like a half moon.

The woman moved from behind the counter and knelt, matching Emma's height. "Moon cake." She held a hand out toward the pastry Emma had indicated. "You . . . like?"

Emma nodded and plucked at Clara's yellow yarn hair, summoning a most pitiful look. "I'm still hungry." She peered up briefly. "Kenny's biscuits aren't very good."

McKenna resisted the urge to roll her eyes. Quite the little stage actress—like Janie used to accuse *her* of being when they were girls. *Emma's just like you, Kenny. When we were young*. The words reached out to her from Janie's deathbed, and only in that moment did McKenna begin to see the similarities between herself and Emma.

The child mirrored Janie's lithe build and fair coloring, but she also possessed an independence that had never described Janie Talbot. And for once in her life, McKenna began to question whether that particular characteristic was as admirable a trait as she'd thought when applied to herself.

The Chinese woman brushed a finger against Emma's cheek, and Emma gave her a smile reminiscent of an angel. *Unbelievable . . .*

"Moon cake," the woman said again, rising and motioning McKenna toward a piece of paper on the counter.

On the page was a description of the pastries written in English. McKenna found "Moon Cake" . . . made of egg yolks and lotus seed paste filling. She glanced back at the Chinese pastry, not at all sure if Emma would like it. She started to inquire as to the cost, then saw it written out to the side. Very reasonable. Especially in light of all that this dear woman had done for her. "Yes, I think she would like a moon cake very much."

The woman wrapped the pastry and presented it to Emma. "*Feichang piaoliang*," she whispered, looking back at McKenna and pointing at Emma. "*Feichang piaoliang.*"

McKenna gently shrugged. "I'm sorry, I—I don't understand."

The woman closed her eyes as though she were searching for the right words. She lightly patted the sides of her face and motioned to Emma, who was stuffing bites into her mouth, and smiled. "*Feichang piaoliang.*"

McKenna studied her for a moment. "Oh! Pretty? Is that what you mean? She's *pretty*?"

"Pret-ty." The woman nodded. "*Feichang piaoliang.*"

"She *is* very pretty. She looks exactly like her mother."

The woman's expression changed, and McKenna sensed she'd understood that last word. And that she might understand more English than she spoke. With Emma's attention on the pastry, she spoke slowly and in a hushed tone. "She's not my daughter. Not . . ." She raised her brows. "In *that* sense. Her mother was my cousin . . . my dearest friend. She passed away not long ago."

Tenderness marked her expression. "Her . . . mother . . . die?"

"Yes," McKenna whispered. "Her mother die."

The woman dipped her head, and when she looked up, tears rimmed her eyes. She did nothing to wipe them away. Nor did she seem discomforted by them. She bowed slightly, pressing a hand to her chest. "My . . . name . . . Chin Mei."

McKenna couldn't explain why, but she mimicked the woman's motions, bowing slightly. "My name is McKenna Ashford."

Chin Mei watched McKenna's mouth as she said her name and then repeated it back slowly.

"Yes, very good! But please, call me Mc-Ken-na."

"Mc-Ken-na," Chin Mei said softly.

"And may I call you Chin?"

Chin Mei laughed, then pressed her lips together as though she shouldn't have done such a thing. "Chin," she said, and motioned behind her.

McKenna looked past her. "There's something behind you?"

Chin Mei kept repeating the gesture.

McKenna shook her head, not understan— "Oh! *Behind?* Chin is your last name. Mei is your first name?"

Chin Mei nodded. "Mei . . . f-irst name."

The woman learned quickly. "Well, it's a pleasure to meet you, Mei." McKenna pointed to the healed palm of her own hand. "And thank you, again, for what you did for me."

Mei's brows disappeared behind the fringe of evenly cut hair on her brow. "Please . . ." She gestured for McKenna to wait, and she disappeared into the kitchen. Returning minutes later, she held something in her hand, and McKenna could hardly believe her eyes.

Her mother's handkerchief. With every last bloodstain washed clean.

FIFTEEN

As soon as the "amen" to the closing prayer was said, McKenna reached for Emma's hand. She'd felt like the center of attention since they'd arrived at church that morning and still sensed stares even now.

People were eager to see Emma, of course, and were interested in knowing how she was getting along—and they still had questions for McKenna. Well-meant, McKenna had no doubt, but with every question she felt herself becoming more distant to the idea of returning anytime soon, which sat ill because she'd benefited from having been here. More than she'd expected to.

The pastor's chosen text that morning had spoken to her in a way those specific scriptures hadn't before. She'd turned in her Bible to follow along—and to make sure he was reading them correctly. He was. And what the verses said described her recent life, her feelings, exactly. It felt as if someone had taken the contents of her heart—the fears and doubts—and poured them onto the page.

Holding Emma's hand, she made a beeline for the back door, but was stopped before she'd gone two pew lengths.

"Miss Ashford, so nice to see you again. And Emma too, but is your brother not with you?"

"How are you getting along? Will you be seeking employment in town?"

"There's an opening at the dry goods store."

"You must miss your cousin. We loved Janie and Vince so much."

McKenna fielded the questions and comments as best she could, all while keeping an eye on Emma, who played with a group of children nearby. Finally, she and Emma made it back to the cabin an hour later than planned and found a note waiting from Robert. He'd gone shooting for the afternoon. So on a whim—ignoring the voice inside her that kept repeating everything else she needed to be doing—McKenna packed a simple picnic. And she and Emma climbed the hill behind the cabin and ate lunch in the valley where Emma had taken her first steps.

It was a peaceful place, and as Emma picked wildflowers and chased butterflies, McKenna retrieved her Bible from the basket and revisited the verses from earlier that morning. The first time, she read the passage to herself, then read certain verses again. *"Blessed be the God and Father of our Lord Jesus Christ, which according to his abundant mercy hath begotten us again unto a lively hope by the resurrection of Jesus Christ from the dead. To an inheritance incorruptible, and undefiled, and that fadeth not away, reserved in heaven for you . . ."*

She ran a hand over the words on the page, dwelling on the one word that stood out above the others. *Inheritance.* She read on . . .

"Wherein ye greatly rejoice, though now for a season, if need be, ye are in heaviness through manifold temptations: That the trial of your faith, being much more precious than of gold that perisheth, though it

be tried with fire, might be found unto praise and honour and glory at the appearing of Jesus Christ."

"Aunt Kenny, do you like butterflies?"

McKenna looked up to see Emma beaming, her cheeks flush from running. "Yes, I do." She tugged the hem of Emma's dress. "What's your favorite thing about them?"

"I like how they're pretty. And how they can fly."

McKenna smiled. This was the happiest she could remember seeing Emma since Janie's passing, and it felt good to see her enjoying herself.

"Do you think we can catch one, Aunt Kenny?"

Hearing the invitation, McKenna laid her Bible aside, then stood and hitched up her skirt. "I don't know." She gave Emma a conspiratorial wink. "But we can sure try!" She set off across the field, keeping a pace Emma could manage.

They spent the afternoon chasing after butterflies and walking the lower pasture. For some reason, McKenna felt closer to Janie here. And even though nothing had really changed about her situation, she felt more at peace about the future than she had in a long time.

Wyatt stared at the advertisement on the mercantile bulletin board, then at the date written on it. Didn't take much to figure why this particular notice was still tacked there after two weeks.

What was the woman thinking, offering so little in pay? Didn't she know they were in gold country? A man could make twice in *one day* what she proposed for a full month's work—even if ranching held less risk than handling dynamite or drilling in a cave. He guessed money might be an issue for her, but if she planned on running a ranch, she'd have to pay more than that for good help.

He gathered the few items he needed from the mercantile and paid his bill. He didn't need much, since he was only in

Copper Creek for the weekend. He glanced at the advertisement one last time as he left the store. If not for the past few weeks spent clearing his mind and refocusing on his job, he might've been tempted to head on out to Miss Ashford's house tonight. Just to see how she and Emma were getting along.

But thankfully the time away had given him the chance to straighten out his priorities, to see his life more clearly. And nowhere did a woman fit in. Much less a woman like McKenna Ashford. Not with the way he lived, always moving from town to town, and not with the places he had to frequent while in those towns.

Lengthening his strides, he passed from the respectable part of Copper Creek into the more suspect. A warm July sun nestled itself deep between the uppermost peaks in the west and cast an orange glow on the weathered clapboard buildings, giving them a deceptively welcoming appearance.

He slipped his badge from his outer vest into an inside pocket and stepped inside the saloon. He scanned the room, finally choosing an open seat at a table of men whose luck appeared to be running dry, based on the shortness of chips before them. He pulled out his money, ordered a drink, and picked up the cards dealt him.

Minutes later, a woman set a glass before him. She leaned low, bodice unlaced, and whispered something in his ear about what was being served upstairs.

"Not now, ma'am," he said, needing to play the part but hoping she'd take the hint. "I need to win some first."

She pressed closer against him from behind and moved her hands down his chest. "Looks to me like you're already pretty well loaded."

Wyatt caught her wrists halfway down, and when she emboldened her intent, he tightened his hold. "I said . . . not now."

She walked away, her soft chuckle full of lingering promise.

Wyatt pulled his focus back, aware of the effect she'd had on him. But her hands on his chest just now hadn't stirred him so much as they'd stirred the memory of what sharing Caroline's bed had been like. And those sweet memories, long buried, rose vivid inside him like a long-denied thirst. As much as he hated to admit it, fleeting moments with a woman in places like this were a temptation on occasion. He'd be a fool to think he was immune.

But when he remembered the intimacy he'd shared with his wife—what their union had meant, what they had made together—women in places like this and the so-called comfort they hocked took on a truer tarnish.

He tipped his glass and swallowed slow this time, eying his cards, waiting for the bet to circle the table to him.

He hadn't been with another woman since Caroline. After she died, he'd asked God to take away his physical desire. And God had answered his prayer, but not in the way Wyatt had expected. The job of marshaling had presented itself soon after and, for years, there was rarely a night he hadn't fallen onto his bedroll exhausted and spent. The Almighty had His own way of reckoning with a man's petitions, and Wyatt rarely understood them.

He studied the hand he'd been dealt—a four, five, six, and seven of hearts. And a two of spades. "I'm in," he said, and anted up, keeping tabs on the man two tables over in the reflection of the bar's mirror.

When the dealer called, Wyatt sacrificed his seven of hearts. It wouldn't do to start winning. Not yet. Men of this ilk preferred a loser.

He threw the first few hands, keeping an eye on the door and on the fellow across the room. The man was only a means to an end, not Grady Polk, the man he was after.

Watching the dealer shuffle the cards, Wyatt's thoughts turned to the telegram back in his room—a commendation on a job well-done. The Marshals Office was more positive than ever about his future with them. His superiors were more than pleased at his recent progress. He'd caught another of Ben Slater's accomplices—two of them, actually, including Ben's younger brother, Jimmy—though only one was alive to stand trial.

For the hundredth time, the scene from a week ago played out before him. He'd reexamined his options, and each time his gut told him the same thing—that his final decision had been the right one. The only one. And it had saved an innocent woman's life . . .

At least that's what he kept telling himself.

But all he could see—both in waking hours and those spent chasing sleep in recent days—was the look on Jimmy's face the instant he realized he was going to die. It was a look Wyatt would never forget, but would spend a lifetime wishing he could.

Fifteen was too young for a boy to be living that way. Much less, dying.

SIXTEEN

Sunlight streamed in through a slit in the curtains, and Wyatt slung an arm over his eyes to block the glare. He rolled over in the bed, every muscle in his body aching. He'd gotten in late last night. The man he'd been waiting for had never shown.

Enjoying the comfort of bed sheets and a freshly ticked mattress, he remembered a time when he'd thought marshaling would give him a break from the rigors of ranching. The pillow muffled a bitter sigh. Right now, he'd gladly trade a few days of ranching for these endless days in the saddle.

He stared at the empty place beside him and ran a hand over the rumpled sheets. A woman's face entered his mind. Only it wasn't Caroline's this time. And the realization was disarming.

Mindful of where his imagination was taking him, Wyatt swung his legs over the side of the bed and stood. Still, images of Miss Ashford crowded the corners of his mind. He stretched, pulled on his trousers, and walked to the window where he edged back the curtain. From his second-story room of the boardinghouse, he had a view of the Chinese Quarter, as this section of Copper Creek was called.

Shoppers crowded the boardwalk below—mostly Asians, a few whites—and wagons lined the street. Typical for a Saturday morning, and all under the watchful eye of the Rockies standing sentinel above. He liked Copper Creek, liked these mountains, and was glad his travels brought him through here on occasion.

Which reminded him—he needed to stop by the livery to see if the saddle he'd ordered was ready. He'd like to have it come Monday when he rode out again.

He turned from the window, then quickly looked back.

It was *her*.

He could tell by the way she carried herself, self-assured and seemingly in command. Two men tipped their hats as she walked by. Either unaware or too intent on her task, Miss Ashford offered no response from what he could tell. But it didn't stop her admirers from turning to appreciate her lovely aftermath.

Seeing their reactions struck a chord of protectiveness inside him. And yet . . .

McKenna Ashford *was* a striking woman. But she'd made it plain she didn't desire his company. Short term, or long. Which somehow still didn't diminish his appreciation of the sway of her hips, the curves of her waistline, and the way she filled out her—

Realizing his own stare had grown too bold, he turned away and let the curtain fall back into place, reminded of something she'd said to him the first night they met, while she rode behind him out to the Talbot's. *"Marshaling must be lonelier work than I thought, Marshal Caradon."*

He sighed, staring at the empty bed. The woman had no idea . . .

He dressed quickly. When he reached the boardwalk ten

minutes later, he turned in the opposite direction Miss Ashford had gone.

A few doors down was the restaurant where he'd taken his meals the last time he'd stayed in Copper Creek. The food—different from his normal fare—was good, served in generous portions, and was fairly priced. Nearly every table in the dining room was occupied.

The majority of patrons looked up when he entered, pausing from their meals. And he knew why. He was the only white man in the room.

Nearly every mining supply town had a Chinese Quarter—a place where the Asian population seemed to migrate. And while some of the white townsfolk looked down on the foreigners, said they weren't hospitable and didn't belong here, he'd found their boardinghouses cleaner, their services more affordable, and their work ethic second-to-none.

"You back, Marshal Caradon." Mr. Ming, the proprietor, bowed low. "You honor my family by eating with us again."

"Good to see you, Mr. Ming. And you honor *me* with your wife's cooking, sir." He enjoyed Ming's smile, glimpsing the spark of a boy in the wizened face of a man. He looked forward to more of Mrs. Ming's steamed dumplings and hoped they were serving them for breakfast like last time. He followed the older man to an empty table by the front window.

As they walked, Ming caught him up on his family's news. Like many Chinamen, Ming had come to America first, made some money, then brought the rest of his family over, along with other relatives.

"You like house breakfast this morning, Marshal? My wife fix it special for you."

"Sounds good to me, sir. Thank you." Wyatt took his seat at a table for two, glad to see the patron before him had left a copy of the *Copper Creek Herald* behind. "But I may need two of them. I'm awful hungry."

"My wife be pleased." Ming thrust his thin chest out. "She

like big man with good appetite!" He laughed before bowing and disappearing into the kitchen.

When Wyatt's meal arrived, he wasn't disappointed. His plate was piled high with food, and even though he didn't recognize every serving, without exception it was all delicious. As he ate, he scanned the latest issue of the *Herald*. His attention snagged on the word *Brinks*, and he brought the paper closer. Two more Brinks stagecoaches had been robbed, one outside of Denver and another on the way to Copper Creek. More lives lost. It wouldn't be long before the Marshals Office got involved.

Staring out the front window, he sipped a cup of hot tea, sifting through the details reported about the robberies, and wondering what brought McKenna Ashford to this side of town. The Chinese Quarter was safe enough during the day. He just didn't know why she'd be over here. And why Emma wasn't with her.

Sensing someone watching him, he turned to find Ming's wife peering around the corner through the kitchen doorway. He smiled and raised a fork in mock salute. She grinned and ducked back around the side. So much for the Chinese not being a hospitable people.

He finished his meal and paid his ticket, then offered a peeking Mrs. Ming one last grin before he left.

He chose the dirt-packed street over the crowded boardwalk, and each step kicked up more dust. A summer sun beat down and, without benefit of cloud cover, the mid-July day promised to be a scorcher. Ming had said they needed rain, and Wyatt believed him.

Passing by the jail, he thought of Slater, who still awaited trial in Denver. He'd delivered Slater to the jail there, glad to be rid of him. But as he'd headed from town, court authorities caught up with him and said the circuit judge had been delayed in another murder trial. They called on him to officiate in the man's stead.

Bringing a felon to justice was one thing. Holding that man's life in your hands, judging what to do with his future, and whether he should live or die, was a responsibility Wyatt never wanted. To his great relief, the circuit judge arrived before the trial was underway.

Wyatt turned down a side street toward the livery, his thoughts turning with him. Sometimes justice was meted out slower than he liked, and other times, it was rendered swiftly. As was the case for Ben Slater's kid brother last week.

He'd cornered the fifteen-year-old boy in a shack on the outskirts of town. And just like his older brother, Jimmy Slater had refused to surrender. "Toss the gun out the window and walk on out, Jimmy," Wyatt yelled. "I don't want things to end bad for you here."

Jimmy answered with gunplay. Wyatt fired back, and the boy dove for cover.

"Sorry, Marshal," the kid shouted, his voice carrying through a paneless window. "But there ain't much chance of that happenin'!"

"I'll make sure you see your brother again. Before he hangs."

Wyatt ducked, anticipating the gunfire that comment would draw—emptying the boy's gun faster. Bullets whizzed past him. One came especially close to his right ear, and he inched farther to the left. Jimmy was a crack shot, just like his older brother, and was headed down the same destructive path.

"You take me in, Marshal, and I'm gonna hang. That don't sit too well with me!"

Wyatt couldn't argue that point. A handful of witnesses in Denver said they'd seen the boy shoot a man down in cold blood, for not liking the way the fellow had looked at him. Jimmy Slater also allegedly took part in the rape of a teenage girl in a neighboring town. She'd been about the same age as Jimmy—fifteen. Wyatt had spoken to her and her family some weeks afterward, gathering information, trying to piece things together, and he still remembered the haunted look in the young woman's eyes.

"You promise to let me go, Marshal, and I'll come out. I know why you're after me . . . it's that girl over in Bixby. But you can't do nothin' to me for that. You got no witnesses. My brother says you don't make deals you don't keep. So tell you what, you just give me a two-minute start on you, then . . ."

Wyatt bided his time, listening to the boy talk nonsense and move around inside the shack.

There were no windows or doors on the back or far side of the shack where Jimmy was holed up. The only exits were within Wyatt's sights. If Jimmy tried to leave, he'd be shot. And the kid knew it.

His orders were to bring the boy in, dead or alive, and the boy was right. He would hang, same as his brother. But Wyatt didn't want to kill this kid. No, it was more than that. He didn't want Jimmy Slater to die this way. It felt wasteful to snuff out a life this young, even with it being squandered.

Jimmy suddenly emerged out the side window, gun raised, and got off two shots—both hitting way too close to Wyatt's head. Wyatt answered once, grazing the boy in the shoulder. Jimmy staggered back but stayed standing. He held his shoulder with one hand, his gun clutched loosely in the other.

Senses alert, Wyatt rose and slowly moved toward him. "Put it down, Jimmy. It's over."

A wildness glazed the boy's eyes, and Wyatt felt he was reliving the scene with Jimmy's older brother all over again. Behind him, down the street from the sound of it, Wyatt heard a door open but didn't dare turn. Jimmy suddenly raised his gun.

But he aimed for something past Wyatt. Or *someone*.

Wyatt fired a hair breadth before the boy got off his shot. A woman's scream competed with the gun's blast as Jimmy fell back, shock twisting his youthful features. A crimson pool formed in the dirt around him. Certain of the boy's fate, Wyatt turned to find the woman shaken but unharmed. He stood there for what seemed like forever, a part of him wishing he'd met Jimmy Slater earlier in life. Maybe he could have made a difference in his life. One thing was certain—he would have tried.

Wyatt blinked and the memory began to fade, but the feelings stayed strong within him. What bred such meanness in a boy so young? Such lack of respect for innocent life? Staring at the dirt his boots kicked up as he walked, he wondered how much longer he could be a U.S. Marshal before this job completely jaded him. He used to have such faith in people. In what a person could accomplish if they only put their time and talents toward something worthwhile, something good. Maybe he needed to give some serious consideration to doing something else with his life.

He spotted Casey Trenton up ahead in the livery. Trenton glanced up, and their eyes connected.

The livery owner paused from his work, staring him down, *hard*. "And here I was hopin' you wouldn't come back this time, Marshal!"

Wyatt stopped short, scouring his memory for how he could've wronged the man. Then he caught a flicker of mischief in Trenton's expression.

"I'm just kidding with you, Caradon. Well, halfway anyhow." Trenton motioned behind him. "I think I know what you're here for."

Wyatt turned to see something draped beneath a blanket on the bench. "It's ready?"

"Yes, sir. Been ready for about two weeks now. And it's a beauty. If you've changed your mind, I'll gladly take it off your hands. And throw in five bucks for your trouble."

With a tug, Wyatt removed the blanket.

Slowly, he ran a hand from pommel to cantle, and along each perfectly braided tassel. He'd never seen a saddle so fine, with such detail. Much less owned one. And he'd seen and owned plenty of them, being raised on a Texas ranch, herding cattle.

"Nice, isn't it?" Trenton said, wiping his hands on a rag.

"*Nice* doesn't begin to describe it. I should pay the man five dollars more for the detail on the saddle horn alone." This saddle would last him for years. Wyatt thought of his father and of how much he would appreciate owning a saddle like this. At fifty-two, twenty years Wyatt's senior, Rayford Caradon still rode and roped with the best of them. "Tell your man he should charge more for his work, Trenton." Wyatt peered over at him, returning the leveled stare from moments earlier. "And not so you can line your pockets with commissions either."

Trenton raised his hands, palm out. "I'm being fair in my dealings, Marshal, don't you worry. I decided on my own to raise the price. Didn't feel like enough was being charged."

"I can see why. I'd like another one just like this come fall, for my father, if your fellow can manage it."

Trenton nodded. "I'll pass the order along, and tell you what comes."

Wyatt heard footsteps behind him.

"I fixed the wagon, Mr. Trenton. Do I have your *permission* to leave?"

The voice was vaguely familiar, thick with belligerence, and Wyatt guessed who it belonged to before he turned.

Robert Ashford's gaze was as hard as Trenton's had been moments earlier. Except Robert didn't look like he was kidding. The chip on the boy's shoulder still begged to be knocked off, and from the looks of Robert's right eye, someone had apparently already tried.

Trenton gestured to the wagon in the back. "You fixed the tongue? And the cracked felly on the left rear wheel?"

"I just said I fixed the wagon . . . *sir*."

Trenton's eyes narrowed for an instant. "You can go on then. Thanks for your work today, Robert. You did a good job, son."

Not answering, Robert gave Wyatt a cursory glance and tossed his work apron on the bench. He strode from the livery, not looking back.

"That boy . . ." Trenton said, rubbing his jaw. "He's just as talented as his sis—" He stopped for a beat. "As his sister said their father was, but he's as muleheaded as they come. And the way he acts toward my customers isn't doing me any favors either. But his work . . ."

"He's good?"

Trenton humphed. "Better than good." He showed him repairs Robert had made as well as a wagon he'd built from the spindles up. "He's got a gift, Marshal. But he doesn't know it. Doesn't seem to care about it either."

Wyatt looked in the direction Robert had gone. "I take it he's had problems getting to work on time?"

Trenton nodded. "And leaving without his work being done. I spoke to his sister awhile back and things got better . . . until this week. Two days ago he came in late with that shiner." He sighed. "I don't mean to speak out of turn, Marshal Caradon. It just bothers me when I see fellas so young with so much ahead of them, if they would only try. Yet they seem intent on throwing it all away."

"I couldn't agree more." How closely those thoughts matched his from earlier. "And you're not telling me anything I didn't already know or suspect. I met his sister, Miss Ashford, the last time I was through here." He softened his voice. "I attended her cousin's funeral, so know a little of their situation."

"She's got her hands full. Miss Ashford, I mean. What with the little girl, and the ranch, and now her brother." He shook his head. "My gut tells me he's gettin' mixed up with the wrong group of fellas. Only reason I didn't fire him yesterday was because of Miss Ashford. I know they need the money, but I tell you, if things keep going like this . . ."

Wyatt could predict what was coming and wished there was

something he could do to intervene. For Miss Ashford's sake, certainly. But even more, for the boy's.

Robert was on a short fuse, begging to be lit. And if he got mixed up with the wrong crowd, they'd ignite the keg building inside that boy and no telling what would happen. Because the only thing more volatile than anger was hurt. And Robert Ashford was chock-full of both.

Wyatt led Whiskey from a back stall and slipped a bridle over her head, eager to try out the new saddle. He spent the afternoon trekking high-country trails to the surrounding mining towns in the mountains above Copper Creek, on the lookout for his target, Grady Polk.

As the sun set, he returned to town, his scouting efforts proving fruitless. He reined in outside a saloon—Harley's—a different place from where he'd gone last night, but one he'd frequented before. Bone-weary and thirsty, he dismounted and stretched. Considering all the riding he'd done, he wasn't nearly as sore in the backside as usual. This new saddle was worth double what he'd paid.

Wyatt stepped inside the saloon and nearly collided with a barmaid. She somehow managed to keep hold of the two trays crammed with brimming glasses she balanced above her head. He moved from her path, offering a whispered apology.

The mingled smells of sweat and stale cigar smoke hit him in the face, making it a challenge to draw a deep enough breath. Across the room, a stalk-thin, wiry sort of man pounded out an off-key tune on a piano—though it was doubtful anyone heard it above the raucous laughter and incoherent drone of liquored-up men.

Wyatt determined to stay for one hour. No more. If Grady Polk didn't show himself in that amount of time, he was going back to his room at the boardinghouse for a hot bath, a warm meal, and a clean bed. In that exact ord—

"You're a cheater! You been cheatin' me ever since I got here!"

The scrape of chairs and angered curses brought Wyatt around.

Two tables over, one man lunged at another, knife drawn. Cards and money scattered, as did the players. Conversation in the room dropped to a simmer. The fellow brandishing the knife brought it to the man's throat, acting like he intended to use it.

Wyatt started toward them, hand on his holster. He hadn't taken three steps when he heard the unmistakable cock of a rifle.

"Put the knife down, son!"

The place fell quiet at the deep-throated command. The man holding the knife turned, and Wyatt went stock-still. Harley, the bartender and owner, stepped out from behind the counter, his rifle trained and steady on Robert Ashford.

SEVENTEEN

Wyatt caught the bartender's subtle glance, and he could see Robert Ashford's hand shaking as the boy pressed the tip of the blade against the man's neck.

"But he's dealin' crooked!" Robert yelled. "I can prove it!"

Rifle aimed, Harley took a step. "Son, you can't prove anything if you're dead. Now . . . you're stickin' that blade into one of my finest dealers—"

Wyatt moved slow and silent.

"—and I'm not takin' too kindly to that right now. So you best pull that knife away, real easy. Then we'll take ourselves a walk outside and have a—"

Wyatt grabbed Robert's wrist from behind and wrenched the knife free, then twisted the boy's arms back in a tight hold. Robert didn't so much groan as he growled. And he fought with surprising strength, his breath heavy with the tang of whiskey.

"Outside, Ashford," Wyatt said low. "Now!"

Robert bucked and cursed, kicking at chairs, kicking at anything he could connect with as Wyatt forced him out the front door. Harley followed, rifle lowered, and soon the piano music resumed to fill the unaccustomed silence.

It took all of Wyatt's strength to subdue Robert until they reached the street. "I'm going to let you go now. But if you so much as move wrong, you'll regret it. Do you understand me?"

Breath coming hard, the boy stilled.

Wyatt released him, hoping he wasn't reading Robert right, yet certain he was. Maybe if he could teach him a lesson tonight, someone down the line who would just as soon shoot him as look at him wouldn't have to.

Robert spun and took a swing at him.

Prepared, Wyatt blocked him with one arm and caught him low in the ribcage with his fist—intentionally holding back. Robert buckled at the knees and went down, sucking air.

Wyatt stood over him, coal-burning street lamps illuminating the night. "You ready to cooperate now?"

After a moment, he nodded, and Wyatt offered his hand.

Robert took hold with his left and, in a flash, was on his feet and caught Wyatt across the chin with a hard right hook. Wyatt stepped back, pain exploding across the side of his face. It felt like he'd been hit with a brick.

He managed to block Robert's next punch and delivered a solid blow to the boy's chin. The kid staggered back a step, eyes glazed, and landed flat on his backside in the dirt.

"Stay where you are this time, son," Harley said, the rifle poised low on his hip.

Robert angled his head from side to side, then swiped at his chin. His hand came away bloody and he cursed Wyatt. "You busted my chin!" He proceeded to curse Harley too, with everyone gawking from the boardwalk.

A crowd had formed. Not only men and women from inside the saloon, but passersby as well.

"That's enough, Robert," Wyatt worked his jaw back and forth, tired of listening to the filth from the boy's mouth.

Robert glared at him. Then surprisingly, he grinned. "You hit all right . . . for an old man."

Wyatt quickly calculated the differences in their ages. Eighteen years separated them, if he remembered right what McKenna had told him. He hated to admit it, even to himself, but if Robert were sober, the kid could probably take him if it came down to it. But he'd give Robert Ashford everything he had if it ever did.

Harley gestured with the rifle. "You takin' him in? Or am I?"

Wyatt retrieved his hat from the dirt where it had landed and brushed it off, only mildly surprised at the question. "Are you saying you want to file a complaint, Harley?"

"I do. Sheriff Dunn can decide what to do with him. Unless you want me to." The man smiled.

Wyatt shook his head.

"It's not the first time this kid's accused one of my dealers of cheatin'." Harley's gaze slid to Robert. "It takes a man to know when someone's cheatin' him, and when he's cheatin' himself."

Wyatt pulled Robert up, watchful. "Come on."

"You're not really takin' me in, Caradon?"

"I am." He shoved Robert forward, not liking the boy's casual tone. "Now move!"

Robert stayed quiet as they walked the darkened streets, but when Wyatt reached to open the door to the sheriff's office, Robert looked back and said something vulgar to his face.

Wyatt stared, not shocked by his language, but finding it hard to reconcile that this boy was McKenna Ashford's brother.

When they walked inside, Sheriff Dunn glanced up from behind his desk. He looked between them. "Trouble, Marshal?"

Wyatt urged Robert forward, seeing the muscles cord tight in the boy's neck. "Had some trouble over at Harley's place. Ashford, here, accused one of his dealers of cheating. Pulled a knife on him."

Dunn laid aside the quill in his hand and stood. He came

around the desk to stand before Robert. "Harley's place draws a mean crowd, but he runs clean tables, Robert. He always has."

Wyatt wasn't surprised at Sheriff Dunn knowing Robert's first name. It wasn't that big a town, and Dunn always made it his business to know who came and went. He was a good lawman. And people like Robert Ashford tended to make themselves known early on.

Using his shirttail, Robert wiped his bloodied chin. "I saw the guy draw from the bottom, sheriff. I know I did."

Sheriff Dunn's stare turned appraising. "How much did you lose?"

Robert looked away, murmuring.

"Say again?" Dunn's voice gained an authoritative edge.

"Forty bucks," Robert said.

Forty bucks! Wyatt could well imagine what McKenna's reaction to learning this would be. Since when did working at a livery pay that kind of wage? It didn't. But a few good hands at a poker table might.

Dunn shook his head and laid a fatherly hand on Robert's shoulder. "What you've done tonight deserves jail time." He sighed. "But I know you're new to Copper Creek, so I'm willing to—"

"Sheriff Dunn, could I speak to you for a moment, sir?" Wyatt indicated with a nod. "Outside?"

The sheriff hesitated, then gestured for Robert to step inside an empty cell and closed the door behind him. "We'll be right back." He followed Wyatt outside.

Aware of the open side window, Wyatt kept his voice low. "Sheriff, this is your town and you're free to run it however you see fit. So don't hear me saying otherwise. But I know something about this situation, and about that boy in there. And I believe that . . ." He had trouble voicing it. Not because he didn't feel it was the right thing to do, but because he knew Miss Ashford would probably never speak to him again if she ever found out he'd encouraged this. "I believe letting the boy spend time in one of those cells would do him good. I see the path he's headed down, sir, because I walked that very—"

Dunn raised a hand. "Marshal, I appreciate what you're saying." He glanced at the closed door. "But I've seen a lot of boys from back East come through this town. They sow a few wild oats and then manage to settle down. A firm warning goes a long way with most of them. And from the looks of things, you've already administered that yourself tonight."

Wyatt looked at the bloodied knuckles on his right hand, doubting that what he'd done to Robert would even faze the boy.

"Robert Ashford's not the felon you're used to dealing with, Marshal. He's young. And he's cocky, to be sure. But I think jail time would only fuel the fire inside him right now, and it would embarrass his sister something fierce. Which I'd like to avoid, if I can. Seems she's already been through enough since they moved here." He leveled his gaze. "My thinking is that some of Robert's problems stem from that. And that they'll work themselves out, given time."

Wyatt thought about what he'd said and considered respectfully disagreeing with him, yet he knew Dunn well enough to know the man's mind was made up. He remembered what his own father had done to him in a similar situation, years ago. Or rather, what his father had allowed him to do to himself. Finally, he nodded. "I appreciate you wanting to help the boy, Sheriff. And I hope you're right."

But deep inside, Wyatt knew he wasn't. Because some lessons just couldn't be taught. They had to be learned. And they always came at a price.

EIGHTEEN

What happened to your chin?" McKenna set the coffeepot on the kitchen table and touched the side of Robert's face.

He flinched and pulled back. "It's nothing. I got hurt yesterday at work, that's all."

"Got hurt? How?" She poured Emma's glass half-full of fresh milk and took her seat.

"Cutting some wood," he answered, avoiding her gaze. "A board popped up and hit me."

Taking a bite of eggs, she eyed him, skeptical. He reached for the loaf of bread between them. It was overly browned and hadn't risen this morning, like always. If anything, it was even more concave than usual. Whether because the yeast was old or she wasn't getting Janie's oven hot enough, she didn't know. But baking bread in these mountains was presenting a new level of challenge for her. Not that she'd ever mastered the basics.

Robert picked up the bread and, after closer inspection, set it down again. He ate a piece of bacon in two bites and started in on his eggs.

McKenna sipped her coffee, trying for a casual tone. "Did you think to check the lever on the vice? Maybe it wasn't tight enough."

He shrugged. "I don't know. It all happened pretty fast."

"Because if it's the equipment, then maybe you should speak with Mr. Trenton about—"

"I'm fine, Kenny! Don't worry about it."

"I'm not worried, Robert. I'm only suggesting that if it's the equipment, then perhaps you should let—"

"I said don't worry about it!" He exhaled through clenched teeth. "And I don't need your advice."

She set her cup down, wondering what she'd done to elicit such a reaction. Watching him—the way he wouldn't meet her eyes, the surly air about him—suspicions rose inside her, one after the other. She swallowed the lukewarm coffee, its taste more bitter than usual.

Two mornings ago, he'd come to breakfast with his right eye swollen and purpling. He'd told her it was the result of hefting crates onto a high shelf. One of the crates had slipped, he'd said. She'd chosen to believe him. Accidents happened—that was part of working in the livery. But something didn't feel right about this.

Robert finished his eggs, grabbed the last two slices of bacon, and rose, shoving back his chair. McKenna hadn't eaten any bacon yet but said nothing. She noticed Emma watching him, eyes wide. Emma scooped up the half piece of bacon left on her own plate and tucked it deep in her lap. Emma was usually more subdued when Robert was around, which was probably for the better.

Anticipating Robert's response to her next question, McKenna readied herself. "Did you get paid yesterday?"

He paused, cup midway to his mouth, and the tension in the room thickened. He stared straight at her, which made what she was certain he was about to say all the worse.

"Trenton said he was short on funds. Said he'd pay me double next week."

McKenna lowered her gaze to her plate, unable to connect with the familiar gray of her brother's eyes and the telling tilt of his head. Her eggs had grown cold, like her faith in him. She kept her voice calm, not wanting to alarm Emma. "I'm going to ask you a question, Robert, and I want a straight answer." Slowly, she raised her head, her anger bled free of compassion. "Where is the money?"

His face was a smooth mask. "I told you. Trenton said he'd—"

"I raised you, Robert . . . Don't forget that. I know when you're lying." Just like he'd lied to her that night in St. Joseph nearly a year ago, when the livery two streets over from theirs—belonging to their longtime competitor—had been torched to the ground.

The muscles in his jaw went taut, and she read his thoughts as easily as if they were written on his forehead. He didn't care if they lost this place. He didn't care if they faced the same disgrace and humiliation in Copper Creek that they'd endured back home.

Anger rose inside her. Not for Robert—that was already there. But for their father—for him having left them this way. For his contribution to the current condition of their lives.

Despite her attempt to stop it, a single tear slipped down her cheek. She bowed her head, feeling old inside. And tired. Tired of being strong, tired of being the one who always held everything together. Who had to be responsible, no matter what. Every day they fell further behind with the farm work. Two weeks had passed, and still no one had answered her advertisement for a ranch hand. And no one would. Not with what she could afford to pay them.

The slam of the door brought her head up. She walked to the window and spotted Robert going into the barn. She waited, dabbing her face with her apron, fully expecting him to ride out on the gray dappled mare and race toward town. Again.

But when he emerged from the barn, he was leading the pair of work horses. She could only stare as he began hitching them to the hay wagon. As well as she thought she knew him, he could still surprise her. Still, he hadn't explained where last week's pay had gone—though she could imagine. And she still didn't know how she was going to provide Mr. Billings with the next installment on the homestead.

"*An inheritance incorruptible, and undefiled, and that fadeth not away, reserved in heaven for you.*"

Like a familiar whisper, the fragment of scripture came softly. She'd read the passage often in recent days, asking God to make it clearer. She thought she understood about the heavenly inheritance, but the part about faith being *tried* with fire—that gave her pause. She could honestly say she didn't doubt God's existence. She'd seen His undeniable hand often enough to recognize His sovereignty. It was the manner in which He chose to display that sovereignty that proved most difficult for her. And the hardest to understand. Yet she was determined to remain strong, however much it seemed that, almost at every turn, she was being beaten down.

The sound of lips smacking brought her around. Emma was on her knees in a chair, pulling out chunks of bread from the underside of the deformed loaf. She dipped them in the honey bowl then slurped off the sweet syrup.

"It's good like this," she said, licking her fingers. "Want some?"

McKenna returned to the table, appreciating the playfulness in Emma's tone. Hand in her pocket, she fingered her mother's handkerchief nestled there and gained strength from it. Every stain was gone. How had Mei done that?

A thought came . . .

She knew the likelihood of its success was slim since it was Sunday. But still, the possibility offered a welcome diversion.

She pulled off a chunk of bread and dipped it as Emma had done, then popped it in her mouth and chewed. Then quickly spit it out again.

Emma giggled, wrinkling her nose. "You're not supposed to eat it. Just suck the honey off."

McKenna laughed softly. "*Now* you tell me." She drank a sip of Emma's milk to wash away the taste and then leaned forward, summoning her most conspiratorial tone. "Would you like to go into town with me this afternoon? After we finish our chores?"

Eyes bright, Emma scrambled down from her chair. "Can we go see Miss Mei? And get a moon pie?"

McKenna tousled the child's soft blonde hair and earned a grin in return. "That's exactly what I had in mind."

Later that afternoon, with Emma's hand tucked sweetly inside hers, McKenna knocked again and tried the latch on the bakery door. It was locked, as she'd suspected.

"Mei's not here?"

She squeezed Emma's tiny hand, appreciating the lack of whine in her voice. "No, she's not. But that doesn't mean we still can't have a nice treat somewhere. The three of us!" She playfully plucked Emma's nose, then the button nose of the rag doll. "Come on, let's go!"

They set off down the boardwalk as though starting an adventure. And for the moment, McKenna pushed aside thoughts of Robert and chose to concentrate on the little girl beside her.

Before coming into town, she and Emma had visited the graves on the hilltop behind the cabin, and Emma had picked wildflowers to put on Vince, Janie, and baby Aaron's graves. It wasn't the first time they'd done that, but McKenna had been struck again by the peacefulness of the spot, nestled on a bluff overlooking the valley.

Over the past two weeks, the emotional tug of war between her and Emma had lessened. They weren't growing closer as much as they were still getting to know each other. McKenna drew strength from something her mother had often said—that a person had to learn to walk before they could run. So she tried to view these small steps as progress, even though Emma wasn't yet affectionate with her like she'd been with Dr. Foster. Or for that matter, with Wyatt Caradon—

Wyatt Caradon . . .

Without trying, she remembered so much about him. The commanding way he carried himself. That funny little half smile he gave when he was amused by something she'd said, whether she'd intended it to be humorous or not. And the way he'd held Vince and Janie's precious baby boy in his arms, as though the infant had still been delicate with life.

He'd been so determined to follow through on that promise to Janie. And yet, before that night, he'd never met her. McKenna felt a twinge of conviction remembering how she'd tried to talk him out of it. Yet he'd remained faithful to his word. Recalling his resolution, she couldn't help but question if something else had influenced him to say yes to that—

"Mei's pretty, huh, Kenny?"

McKenna pulled her thoughts back and peered down. "Yes, honey, she is. She's very pretty."

Emma kicked at a pebble on the boardwalk and missed. McKenna paused as she tried again a second time and sent the rock flying.

"Mei's different from us, huh, Kenny?"

"Yes, she's different. But she's also very much like us too." She could see Emma's mind at work yet decided not to comment further. They were in the part of Copper Creek called the Chinese Quarter—as she'd learned—and were surrounded by Mei's countrymen.

The boardwalk ended, and they negotiated the stairs to the street.

A warm, sunny July afternoon encouraged people outdoors, and groups of townsfolk, mostly men, gathered outside the closed shops, sitting on chairs and stools, conversing in their native language. The inflection in their voices had a singsong quality and was quite beautiful to listen to. Yet they laughed and spoke intermittently and so quickly, it was a wonder they understood each other at all.

McKenna smiled to herself, thinking they probably thought the same thing when hearing people speak English.

The men were dressed in wide-legged pants and long tunics, all with partially shaved heads and long braids similar to that of the man she'd seen in Mei's company. A few looked up when she passed, but they never held her gaze.

Despite her and Emma being in the minority, she felt comfortable here. More so than when they'd passed the saloons earlier and men had whistled and called out to her. She'd learned over time to ignore behavior like that—though it still bothered her. Thankfully, Emma hadn't understood what the men were saying.

Coming to a corner, she was starting to doubt whether they'd find a place open for a "nice treat" when Emma tugged on her hand.

"There she is!" Emma tugged harder. "I see Mei!"

McKenna looked in the direction she pointed and sure enough, there was Mei in a crowd of people crossing the street—along with that man.

"Let's go see her!" Emma yanked on her hand.

"We will. But you mustn't pull on me." McKenna raised a brow.

Emma stared up, and then nodded. "Yes, ma'am, Aunt Kenny."

Witnessing the child's compliance, her spirits lifted. Another small victory, and an encouragement that perhaps she could make this work with Emma after all. "Thank you, Emma," she whispered. "Now let's go see Mei!"

As they drew closer, McKenna noticed that the man with Mei had his arm draped around an elderly gentleman, supporting the man's stooped frame. The two men maneuvered their way up the stairs to the planked walkway and Mei followed, her tiny steps mirroring the older man's. The three paused by an entryway—the laundry where she and Mei first met.

As the younger man opened the door and assisted the elderly man inside, Mei happened to glance in their direction. Her smile was instant and full. And McKenna couldn't help but wave in response. She and Emma quickly closed the distance and climbed the stairs.

"Miss Mei!" Emma called, and reached out to touch the ornate fabric of Mei's tunic. McKenna gently restrained the child but could hardly fault her curiosity. Mei's tunic was exquisite, and she couldn't help but wonder if Mei was wearing it for some special occasion.

The tunic was the blue of a summer sky after a storm and crafted with multicolored embroidered detail on the front and sleeves. Mei wore a coordinating slender-fitting skirt that accentuated her petite frame but seemed to only further inhibit her walking.

Mei took hold of Emma's hand and gave it a gentle squeeze, then moved closer and held the material out for her to feel.

The crowd of people Mei had accompanied stood below the boardwalk a short distance away, talking to one another, and sneaking occasional glances. McKenna spotted a little girl about Emma's age in the group. The little girl watched Emma, a curious smile on her face.

Footsteps drew McKenna back, and she found herself face-to-face with the younger Chinese man. He was scarcely as tall as she, yet he had a muscular build. His arms were folded across his chest and deep lines furrowed his brow. She resisted the urge to take a backward step.

He looked at Mei as if expecting an explanation. Mei whispered something to him and he fired back in rapid Chinese, his tone hushed, but halting. Mei flinched, her smile fading. Blinking, she finally bowed low. He turned and walked inside.

A rush of indignation heated McKenna at the impertinence.

How dare he—whoever the man was—treat Mei that way! To demand such subservience! Already deciding she didn't like him, she worked to mask her disapproval. "Good afternoon, Mei. How are you today?"

"I . . . good. Mc-Ken-na."

"Very good," McKenna said, pleased.

Mei's focus shifted to Emma. "Em-ma . . . moon pie!" she said, her countenance brightening.

Emma stepped forward. "Kenny and I went to your bakery, Miss Mei, but you weren't there. Kenny says we're going to get a treat! You wanna come with us? You can if you want!"

Soft crinkles at the corners of Mei's eyes revealed her confusion. She gently shrugged and shook her head.

For a moment, the three of them stared at each other.

"Better . . . now?" McKenna finally asked, recalling Mei's tears from the day at the bakery, and fairly sure she'd remember the phrase.

Mei smiled, seeming to understand. "Better now. Th-ank . . . you."

McKenna caught Emma waving to the little Chinese girl. Suddenly shy, the girl lowered her eyes, then snuck another look at Emma and put her hand over her mouth, giggling.

"Can I go see her, Aunt Kenny?"

"Yes, you may. But stay right there."

Emma took off down the boardwalk.

"Be sure and tell her your name," McKenna called after her, knowing she probably couldn't hear over the rumble of a passing wagon.

Emma approached and spoke to the girl, who seemed to develop a sudden interest in Clara. Emma held out the doll and the girl fingered the edge of Clara's dress, soiled though it was.

McKenna looked back to find Mei studying her. They smiled at each other.

"Better now?" Mei asked after a long moment.

McKenna nodded, finding the question both sweet and frustrating. She wished they could communicate beyond a handful of words. She checked on Emma only to see her talking nonstop to the little girl about something. The girl's expression hinted at amusement, but was void of comprehension. McKenna knew the feeling.

"Wish . . . I . . . talk better."

McKenna looked back to find Mei's head bowed. "Oh no . . . you talk very well, Mei. Your English is very good."

Mei shook her head. "Wish . . . I . . . talk better."

"And I wish I could bake." McKenna smiled, trying to soften the moment.

Mei's head came up. Something flickered in her eyes. "Bake?" She mimicked patting something out in her hands. "You?"

"No." McKenna laughed. "I said I *wish* I could bake." She pointed to herself and lifted her shoulders. "No bake."

"Ah . . ." Seconds passed, and Mei's dark brows arched. "I . . . bake," she said, making the patting motion again. She gestured to McKenna. "To you."

McKenna didn't know which pleased her more—that she'd understood what Mei was saying, or Mei's offer to teach her how to bake. "Yes! I would like that very much." And since turnabout was fair play . . . "You teach me how to bake. And I teach you how to . . . talk better English."

Slowly, Mei began to nod, and kept nodding. Her eyes glistened. "I bake . . . to you."

"And I talk . . . to you!" McKenna laughed, knowing she was getting the better end of the deal.

Mei reached out and put a tentative hand on her arm. McKenna covered it, surprised at the kinship she felt. What an unexpected friendship she'd found. And right when she needed one.

She turned to check on Emma and the little girl—and didn't see them. Either of them. The crowd of people was gone. The street was empty but for a gathering of men down the way and a couple of wagons passing by. McKenna walked to the edge of the boardwalk and scanned the street in both directions.

"Emma?"

She walked to the corner and looked up and down the thoroughfare, vaguely aware of Mei following. "Emma!" she called again, fighting a rising tide of panic. Her insides twisted tight. A cold seed of fear took root as she screamed Emma's name over and over.

But Emma was gone.

NINETEEN

The shores of Copper Creek were muddy and slick. With the final lingering vestiges of winter succumbing to summer's warmth, the mountain-fed stream ran high with snowmelt from the peaks perched loftily above the town.

As he'd done many times before, Wyatt followed the creek bank as it ribboned around and through the community, drawing unexplained comfort from the melody of water coursing over smooth rock. And with each note played, he imagined snowflakes, fallen months ago, now skimming past him toward the valley below, fulfilling their purpose. Everything came full circle in this life. It was part of nature, God's design. And he sensed that same thing happening inside him. Only, he didn't know what it meant.

Or what God had in store for him.

He only knew that no matter what it was, he was determined to follow the path God wanted for his life. If he could only figure out what that was . . .

He removed his hat and ran a hand through his hair. Was it

staying with the Marshals Office? Or maybe heading back to San Antonio to help with the family ranch? His sisters and their husbands were there, but he knew his siblings would welcome his help. Maybe even expect it, seeing as their parents were getting on in years.

He stooped to pick up a rock and noticed the bruised flesh covering the knuckles of his right hand.

Robert Ashford . . .

He was one young man who had no idea what path he was headed down. That became all too clear last night. But Robert would have to figure that out on his own. Wyatt only hoped the boy would learn it sooner rather than later, and that McKenna wouldn't end up paying too high a price for her brother's mistakes. He rubbed the rock between his thumb and forefinger, fearing his first hope held greater likelihood than his second.

He paused for a moment, certain he'd heard something. He looked downstream, saw no one, and took another step—then heard it again.

A faint cry . . .

He dropped the rock and followed the sound as best he could over the splash of the creek. When he rounded the corner, he saw her.

Even at a distance, he recognized Emma sprawled headlong in the street, and he broke into a run. The road was empty, so was the boardwalk. He knelt beside her and helped her sit up. "Emma . . . honey, are you okay?"

Tears streaked her dusty cheeks. "I-I lost my Aunt Kenny, and"—she hiccupped a sob—"m-my mommy's gone." Her face crumpled.

"Oh, little one . . . come here." He gathered her to him, and she came without hesitation. He stood and wiped her tears, and checked for injuries. No broken bones. Nothing but a skinned knee that a little soapy water—and maybe a sugar stick—would fix right up. "Shh . . . it's okay." He smoothed the hair on the back of her head, and her little arms came around his neck. A lump rose in his throat. "I won't let anything happen to you."

Her sobs came harder. "Clara fell down too, Mr. Wyatt." She drew back and held up the doll. "She's all dirty. And she stinks."

Wyatt tried his best not to smile. Clara was indeed filthy. And wet. Apparently she'd gone for a swim in the same mud puddle Emma had fallen in. Only it wasn't just mud, judging from the smell.

"Here . . ." He gently chucked her beneath the chin. "Let's see if we can find your Aunt Kenny. You want to?"

The little girl nodded with a hint of uncertainty. "But I got my dress all dirty. She's gonna be mad."

Knowing there might be some truth to that, he also knew Miss Ashford would be worried sick. "Do you remember where you were with Aunt Kenny before you got lost?"

Emma shook her head. "I was talkin' to my friend, and I looked up . . ." She sniffed and wiped her nose with the back of her hand. "And Aunt Kenny was gone."

Wyatt knew better than to think it was McKenna Ashford who had wandered away. "We'll find her, don't you worry."

"Clara's dress is dirty like mine, huh?" She held the doll right in front of his face.

Wyatt paused, unable to see it clearly. Easily supporting Emma's weight, he took Clara and did his best to wipe the dirt and mud from the doll's dress and its once-yellow strands of hair. His efforts only made a bigger mess, but Emma's smile said she was grateful.

"She likes you." Emma put a hand to his cheek, then frowned. "Your face is itchy."

Knowing what she meant, he laughed and rubbed his stubbled jaw. He'd bathed and shaved last night in preparation for church this morning, half hoping he might see McKenna and Emma there. But they hadn't attended. "My face is itchy, huh?"

She squeezed his cheek in response, and he made a chomping noise, pretending he was trying to bite her. She pulled her hand back, giggling. Instinctively, he hugged her close and she laid her head on his shoulder. Something deep inside gave way. This is what it would have been like if his precious little Bethany had lived.

He rubbed Emma's back, taking on fresh pain as he glimpsed a fragment of what he'd been denied by the deaths of his wife and infant daughter so many years ago.

"Here, you can carry her." Emma tried to stuff Clara into his outer vest pocket, but the doll wouldn't fit.

Wyatt tucked her inside his vest instead and positioned its scraggly yarn head to poke out over the edge, hoping it would draw a smile. Which it did.

Carrying her, he walked to the end of the street and looked both ways. No sign of McKenna. He'd taken a handful of steps when he heard Emma's name being called frantically from somewhere behind him.

He turned back in the opposite direction and no sooner had he and Emma rounded the corner than he spotted McKenna Ashford at the far end of the street. Her back was to him.

He called her name, and she slowly turned. Then she gathered her skirts and ran.

"Emma Grace Talbot! Where did you go?"

Out of breath from running, McKenna pulled Emma from Wyatt Caradon's arms and crushed the child close, relief coursing through her. Grateful Emma was safe, she also had the overwhelming urge to spank the child's bottom. "I told you to stay right there! That means you're not supposed to wander off!"

She inhaled the familiar scent of Emma's hair—along with something not so fragrant—and felt her pulse begin to slow. She drew back to inspect Emma closer. Other than being slathered in muck and sporting a bruised knee, she appeared to be all right.

Emma's lower lip trembled. "I'm sorry, Aunt Kenny." She blinked and pooled tears spilled over. "I didn't mean to lose you."

McKenna hugged her again, and saw only Janie's face. *I'm sorry. I'm so sorry, Janie . . .*

"I found her a couple of streets over, Miss Ashford. She took a spill, but she seems to be fine now."

"Thank you, Marshal Caradon," she said, forcing her gaze upward. Not that she didn't want to look at him. She did. She just didn't relish seeing herself through his eyes at the moment—the woman who'd lost Janie Talbot's daughter.

A moment ago, when she'd glanced down the street to see Emma, the invisible hand gripping her heart had suddenly loosened its hold. But when she'd recognized the man holding Emma—and when he'd called her by her first name—her heart had done something altogether different. Something pleasant—and wholly unsettling.

"You're back in town . . . I see."

A slow smile tipped one side of his mouth. "Yes, ma'am, I am. But don't let that upset you. I'll be leaving come morning."

She laughed and it came out high-pitched and telling. "Well, thank you, Marshal, again. I'm so grateful you found her." She cradled the back of Emma's head and brought their foreheads together. Emma pressed a kiss to her lips and McKenna laughed again, surprised, in a good way.

Aware of Wyatt peering past her, she turned to see Mei making her way down the street. Her steps seemed hobbled, and worry etched her features.

McKenna met her halfway. Wyatt followed.

"Emma?" Mei said, drawing closer, her hand outstretched.

McKenna squeezed it briefly then nodded toward Emma, still in her arms. "She's all right. Marshal Caradon found her."

She gestured to Wyatt. "Marshal Wyatt Caradon . . . please meet my friend, Chin Mei."

Wyatt tipped his hat. "Pleasure to meet you, Chin Mei."

Mei bowed and when she straightened, McKenna noticed the hair on her forehead was damp with perspiration. Mei briefly closed her eyes. It was warm out, but—

"Mei, are you all right?"

Mei nodded. "I . . ." She swallowed. "Fine." She glanced in the direction of the boardwalk.

"Why don't you sit down over here for a minute, ma'am." Wyatt held out his arm.

Surprisingly, Mei slipped her hand through.

McKenna caught the look Wyatt tossed her and followed them to the steps. Mei sat, wincing as she did. Her skirt rose slightly and before she tugged it down, McKenna noticed her shoes. The same pair she'd been wearing before. Pretty blue slippers made of embroidered silk. Tiny, and so pointed.

McKenna studied them closer. The shoes couldn't have been more than four inches in length! How had she not noticed that before? And how could Mei walk in them? She was a petite woman, but surely her feet were longer than that.

"How far did you and Mei walk just now?" Wyatt asked.

"Three streets over . . . that way." McKenna motioned.

His attention hovered on Mei, whose head was lowered. "If you'll wait here, I'll get my horse from the livery and take you back."

Not understanding his offer, McKenna started to protest. But his pointed nod toward Mei kept her from it. "Oh . . . yes." She looked at Mei. "Get your horse, Marshal. That would be very—"

"I . . . fine." Mei slowly stood, her smile tremulous. Apparently she'd understood enough of their exchange to object, in her own gentle way. "I . . . fine," she insisted, and started down the street, hobbling.

McKenna didn't know what else to do other than to follow. Wyatt fell in step beside Mei. Their progress was slow. They reached the end of the street and when McKenna glanced at Mei, she found her face ashen, her delicate jaw clenched tight.

Mei paused and blinked, then her eyes stayed closed.

"Wyatt—" McKenna said, but he was already there.

He caught Mei as she went limp. He lifted her in his arms and her head dipped forward against his chest. McKenna moved to pull Mei's skirt down for modesty's sake and noticed one of her blue slippers on the ground.

She bent to pick it up and saw Mei's foot. She stilled. And felt sick inside. *Oh . . . what had happen—*

"Can you put her shoe back on?" Wyatt asked.

"Have you seen her foot?"

Wyatt nodded. "They're both like that."

"But . . . wh–what happened?"

"Let's just get her shoe back on. Quick. I'll explain later."

McKenna did as he asked, a dozen questions begging to be asked. But those questions all disappeared when she looked up and saw the young Chinaman storming toward them.

TWENTY

Fury darkened the Chinese man's face, and Wyatt quickly gathered that Chin Mei somehow belonged to this man. Clearly the man was none too pleased with either Mei wandering off, or with seeing another man holding her. Either way, Wyatt's dealings with Chinese men in the past told him this situation would call for delicate negotiation.

"Don't worry, I'll speak with him," McKenna said and took the lead.

Wyatt tried to stop her. "No, McKenna, don't—"

"My name is McKenna Ashford, sir." She moved into the man's path, hands lifted in a halting gesture. "Mei fainted a moment ago, and we're—"

Dark eyes fierce, the man plowed right past her—which was preferable to his plowing *through* her, as Wyatt half expected. The man's attention was fixed on Mei.

Wyatt stopped and secured his hold on Mei, in case the fellow tried to deck him for some reason. He'd seen the damage a man of such a stocky build could inflict, especially when the fellow was properly riled. People who didn't know better gauged a Chinese man's strength on his stature alone—a crucial miscalculation.

The man stopped, jaw tightly clenched, cheeks puffing out with each labored breath as he stared up. He spoke rapidly in Cantonese, his voice low, as Wyatt expected. In all his dealings with the Chinese, never once had a voice been raised to him.

But Wyatt couldn't get a handle on anything he'd said. He'd learned a few words and phrases of Cantonese years ago when the railroad was being built. Just enough to help him investigate some complaints made against the Union Pacific. But there was one word he always made a point to learn when interacting with people who spoke in a different tongue. He dredged that word from memory, hoping his pronunciation and voice inflection weren't too rusty. Those things made such a crucial difference in this dialect.

"*Pengyou,*" he said, and waited.

The man's eyes narrowed but his scowl remained.

"*Pengyou,*" Wyatt tried again, more gently this time, accompanied by a brief bow of his head. He hoped he was saying what he thought he was saying—"*friend*"—and not something offensive to the man or his family.

"What are you say—"

"Not now, McKenna." Wyatt kept his focus on the man, sensing McKenna's frustration beside him. He guessed she didn't like being told what to do, or what not to do. But Chinese men didn't take kindly to assertive women. Nor did he, usually. But he was willing to make an exception in this case.

After sizing him up, the man spoke again, his tone still hard but a shade less antagonistic.

Wyatt caught a couple of the Cantonese words this time, and he stepped forward. The man took Mei from him, holding her in his arms, but not in an overly gentle way. Mei murmured something unintelligible and tried to lift her head, with little success. The man spoke to her, his voice hushed but halting. If Wyatt didn't know better, he'd think the man was angry with her.

But the subtle manner in which he held her told a different story. In his experience, people of this culture rarely showed affection in public, other than women and children. And even those occasions had been infrequent.

"I'm fairly sure this is her husband," he whispered to McKenna. "And please, whatever you do . . ." He said it so only she could hear, practically mouthing the words. "Don't say anything about her feet."

She nodded, but her frown expressed her true feelings about his request. Wyatt sensed something familiar about her reaction, and then it hit him—it was the same obstinate frown he'd seen from Emma on occasion.

Mei stirred and raised her head, blinking. "Li . . ." She slipped her arms around the man's neck and hugged him tight. "*Duyum jeh*," she said, repeating the phrase softly. Then she whispered something Wyatt couldn't understand.

The man tightened his hold on Mei, then focused on Wyatt and spoke again.

Wyatt thought he caught the Chinese word *jia*—home—somewhere in all he'd said, but couldn't be certain. He raised his hand in a parting gesture, and to show he harbored no ill feelings.

But the man didn't leave. He said something else and craned his neck toward the street behind him.

This time Wyatt was certain he'd heard the word "home." Believing he understood, he indicated for the man to start on ahead with Mei, and motioned that he and McKenna and Emma would follow.

With McKenna and Emma walking beside him, they followed a few paces behind, and he kept his voice low. "I think he said he wants us to follow them."

"You speak Chinese?" Disbelief weighed McKenna's tone.

He laughed softly. "No, I don't. That's why I said *I think* he wants us to follow them. For all I know I just agreed for us to plow his field." He smiled. "But no matter what he says, would you please let me answer for us? And if he's inviting us to their home, it's a great honor. Be sure to take off your shoes before you step inside. Both you and Emma. It's part of their culture."

"How do you know all this?"

He couldn't explain it, but he liked having the upper hand on this woman. He had a feeling it wouldn't happen often. "A few years back, I was assigned to investigate several complaints filed by Chinese workers against the Union Pacific." He told her how he'd lived in their camps and had opportunity to learn something of their culture. "I picked up a little of the language while I was there."

At the corner, Mei's husband crossed the street and headed toward the opposite boardwalk.

Wyatt felt a touch on his arm and slowed his pace. The stubbornness in McKenna's expression from moments before was gone.

She paused beside him. "What happened to Mei's feet?" She glanced at the couple ahead of them. "Did *he* do that to her?"

The bitterness in her accusation caught him off guard, and it took him a few seconds to realize who she was referring to. "No, he didn't do that to her. It was done to her a long time ago . . . by her parents, most likely. I'll explain more once we're—"

"What happened to Mei's feet, Marshal Caradon?"

At her repeated question, Wyatt guessed she wasn't going to be easily put off. This wasn't the best time to be discussing this, but if she and Mei were going to be friends, it was best she know. He waited for two elderly gentlemen to pass. "It's a custom among the Chinese people called foot binding. They're also known as Lotus feet. When a little girl reaches the age of about six . . ."

Reminded of Emma standing beside them holding McKenna's hand, he further lowered his voice. "They take bandages and bind the girl's toes under her feet, to prevent her feet from growing." He couldn't keep from wincing, remembering what he'd been told. "Eventually her toes break. And her feet become concave."

The color drained from McKenna's face, and he wondered if he'd done the right thing in telling her now.

"Go on," she finally whispered.

"I don't know much else about it. Other than, even as an adult"—he glanced to see Mei's husband climbing the stairs to the boardwalk—"it's impossible for a woman with Lotus feet to walk any distance without a lot of pain."

Tears of compassion rose in McKenna's eyes but couldn't extinguish the fire of indignation there too. He'd reacted much the same way when learning about the practice, minus the tears.

"Aunt Kenny, you're hurtin' my hand!"

"Oh!" McKenna sucked in a breath. "I'm sorry, sweetie. I didn't mean to." She blinked as though trying to clear images from her mind and turned back to him. "You've seen other Chinese women who've had this done to them?"

He nodded. "Unfortunately, it's common in their culture. Has been for years, is my understanding."

"Can anything be done to heal her?"

"Nothing that I know of, but Doc Foster could speak more to that than I can." He'd anticipated her concern for a woman like Mei, but not this fierce sense of protection for Chin Mei in particular.

She didn't speak for a moment, and Wyatt had no doubt in his mind that Doc Foster would be receiving a visit from her real soon. He only hoped she'd use discretion when speaking of this to Chin Mei.

Across the street, Mei's husband had stopped in front of a shop and was steadying Mei as she stood and gradually regained her balance. The man turned and looked in Wyatt's direction.

Wyatt took the hint and led McKenna and Emma to join them.

Mei was the first to speak. "Thank you . . . sir." She bowed. "You . . . good help."

Her husband nodded as though in agreement.

Wyatt tipped his hat. "It was my pleasure to help, ma'am. Sir."

Mei directed her attention to the man beside her and she touched his arm, her eyes shining with pride. "*Zhangfu* . . . Chin Li."

Husband. Wyatt recalled the word. He extended his hand and bowed briefly. "Good to meet you, Mr. Chin. My name's Wyatt Caradon."

Chin Li's grip was plenty firm. "Mr. Caradon." He pronounced the name swiftly and with confidence, then shifted his gaze to McKenna. And wariness crept in.

Wyatt curbed a smile, seeing the man had good instincts.

"My name is McKenna Ashford, Mr. Chin." McKenna spoke with surprising grace, given her earlier accusation against the man.

Chin Li didn't say anything but gave a curt nod, and Wyatt stared between the two of them. He'd figured they had just met. But they obviously shared a history, and he was curious to know what it was.

"Caradon," Chin Li said, and motioned above him.

Wyatt peered up to see a wooden shingle hanging over the doorway. *Laundry*.

Chin Li pointed to the sign again. "Wash," he said. "For you."

Wyatt gradually gathered his meaning. There was no call for the man to offer to launder his clothes, but refusing would be rude. He bowed again. "Your generosity honors me, Mr. Chin. *Xiexie*," he added—*thank you*—hoping again that his memory held.

A smile teased the corners of Chin Li's mouth. "*Xiexie.*" He nodded, then looked at McKenna. His smile vanished, his lips went firm. Mei whispered something to him, and Chin Li shot back a response. Mei lowered her eyes.

"Aunt Kenny?" Emma pulled on McKenna's shirtsleeve. "What about our treat? You promised."

McKenna shushed her, which only encouraged a pout.

Awkwardness stretched the moment taut.

Without a word, Mei raised her chin and peered up at her husband. A subtle glance passed between them before she quickly bowed her head again. But Wyatt watched as a fraction of Chin Li's stubbornness evaporated. A thin layer, and not without effort, telling by Chin's furrowed brow. But the challenge in his eyes lessened. Seeing the exchange tugged on Wyatt's emotions, and turned time back on itself. With a similar touch, Caroline used to communicate so much to him. Without ever saying a word. He missed being known so intimately by someone.

No, not just known by someone . . . but by a woman.

Chin cleared his throat and lifted his head by degrees. "Wash . . . for you," he said to McKenna, with far less enthusiasm.

McKenna's expression remained guarded, and Wyatt prayed she wouldn't refuse the offer. As her silence lengthened, so did his unease.

"That's very generous of you, Mr. Chin," she finally said, with the same scarcity of feeling with which the gift was offered.

After several awkward bows and backward waves, Wyatt and McKenna rounded the corner—Emma filling the space between them—and Wyatt peered down beside him. "So I take it that you and Chin Li have met before?"

"Yes, we have. On the same day you nearly ran me over."

A faint smile touched her mouth, and he listened as she told him about what Mei had done for her that day. "But that man . . ." She shook her head. "The way he speaks to her—I don't like it."

Wyatt chose his next words carefully. "So you understand what he's saying to her then?"

That earned him a raised brow. "I understand his tone."

He nodded, letting the silence answer for him.

"Don't tell me that's part of their culture too. For husbands to speak harshly to their wives."

"I didn't say that."

She huffed. "You heard him speak to her today."

"I saw a husband concerned about his wife. And, I'm not saying it's best, but sometimes concern like that can come out a little harsh . . . based on how much a man loves a woman."

McKenna held his gaze for several beats then stared straight ahead, and he got the feeling his answer hadn't been well received. They walked in silence until they reached the corner, and she paused.

"Thank you, Marshal Caradon, for your help with Chin Mei. And for bringing Emma back to me safely. I appreciate what you did, and I . . ." She looked at him briefly, then away. "I wish I could think of some way to thank you, but, since you're leaving in the morning . . ."

Her expression was the picture of remorse, but unmistakable relief tinged the edges of her voice.

Wyatt eyed her, not wanting her to go. And not willing to let her off so easy. "It was my pleasure to help, Miss Ashford. On both counts." With her sudden shyness, it felt as if they'd taken a step back in the familiarity department. Wyatt stared at his boots, juggling the nervous pangs of a schoolboy while struggling with the desires of a man. "If you and Emma don't have plans for dinner, ma'am . . . I'd consider it an honor to treat you both."

Emma perked up. "Dinner! I'm hungry!"

"You're always hungry." Her smile a mite too perfect, McKenna tapped the child's nose. "We both appreciate the offer, but I need to get Emma home and cleaned up."

Wyatt glanced at the child's clothes, having forgotten about that. "Tell you what, I'll go get us some dinner and we can eat under the trees across the way there." He pointed to a grassy spot alongside Copper Creek. "Wouldn't take but a few minutes, then I could see you home. Since it'll be dark soon."

Blue eyes wide, Emma nodded. "Yes, Kenny. *Please*, can we?"

"That's most kind of you, Marshal. But I've still got a lot of work to do this evening."

"But I'm hungry, Kenny!"

McKenna shook her head. "I'll fix us something once we're home."

"Can Mr. Wyatt come with us? Please?"

Wyatt's affinity for the child deepened, as did the humor in the moment, and he decided to let things play out. He noticed McKenna didn't correct the child and tell her to call him Marshal Caradon, which suited him fine. Emma looked up at him, expectant, and he shot her a quick wink. McKenna seemed intent on looking anywhere but at him, which only increased his patience. And his hopes.

Finally, McKenna scraped together what looked like the remnants of a smile and met his gaze. And he knew her answer.

"I'm certain Marshal Caradon's responsibilities keep him very busy, Emma." She addressed the child, yet aimed the words at him. "He's got an important job to do, and he has to get up very early in the morning to leave again. We don't want to interfere with his plans."

In all his years of marshaling, he'd never been shot down so fast.

Watching her, hearing what she *wasn't* saying, Wyatt clearly heard what she meant. She said she didn't want to interfere with his plans, but what she really meant was that she didn't want any part of his life. And he couldn't blame her. Hadn't he just come to grips with that himself? His responsibilities as a U.S. Marshal left little room for anything else. Or anyone . . .

They said good-bye. And when he reached the corner, he

snuck a backward look behind him, wondering if McKenna might do the same—she didn't.

He walked to Ming's alone and ate a too-quiet dinner at a table for four and returned to his room at the boardinghouse, dreading the deafening quiet yet unable to stomach another evening at a saloon. Not tonight. He opened the door and spotted something on the floor.

An envelope had been slipped beneath.

He picked it up. A telegram. From the U.S. Marshals Office. Groaning, he tossed it on the bed along with his hat.

He stood at the window for the longest time and stared up at the mountains. Painted in shades of molten steel, the lofty peaks gave him comfort. He didn't know why, they just did. Maybe it was because they'd been here for so long. They'd withstood so much and still rose proudly, a testament to things that lasted. He sighed. The languid summer sun was barely touching the highest peaks in the west. Thirty minutes to sunset at least, maybe forty-five, this being the middle of July. Plenty of time for them to get back to the ranch before dark.

He'd wanted so badly for her to say yes. He hadn't realized how much until she'd said no. He didn't blame her. He blamed himself. For making choices in his life that had led him to this. He ran a hand through his hair, then turned back to the telegram.

He snatched it and tore open the envelope.

The Marshals Office was forever changing his orders, sending him here and there on a whim of a rumor that someone had seen so-and-so here or there, and he was sick and tired of—

He stopped. He read the brief message again. They'd given him a lead on Grady Polk, the man he'd been looking for, which was good enough. But it was the rest of the telegram that turned his mood for the better. Finally, after all these years, the Marshals Office had gotten something right. And he might just get another crack at that dinner with McKenna Ashford, and that sweet little Emma, after all.

TWENTY-ONE

No, Emma! Don't touch th—" McKenna dropped the saddle and lunged for the pitchfork, barely catching it before its heavy handle smacked Emma in the forehead. She exhaled. Was the child intentionally trying to hurt herself? "I told you not to play over here! It's not safe! Now get back over there to your blanket and—"

Turning to put the pitchfork back on the hook, McKenna caught the bottle of leather oil with her elbow and sent it clattering across the workbench. Half the contents spilled before she could reach it. Midday temperatures soared to sweltering in the barn, along with her temper, and she bit back a word she'd heard men use repeatedly in the livery as she was growing up.

She'd been so irritable for the past two days—and she knew why. But knowing didn't help, and neither did this heat. It had taken her every last ounce of creativity to come up with a reason to turn down Wyatt Caradon's offer for dinner.

Oh, but she'd wanted to go . . .

Yet no matter how she looked at it, spending time with

him wasn't a good idea. Emma was far too fond of the man as it was and, though it felt selfish, she needed Emma to start cultivating those feelings for her. Not someone who wasn't going to be here.

Then there was Robert. Having Marshal Caradon around her brother wouldn't help that situation either. Robert was surly enough these days. Best not spit directly into the wind, as she'd heard Casey Trenton say recently.

But the reason she was most hesitant to say yes to having dinner with him was that . . . she liked him. Very much. Too much, considering the man was a U.S. Marshal who came and went as freely as Wyatt Caradon did. And she couldn't help but see a similar thread between Marshal Caradon and Michael Seaton. Michael had just been sworn in by the St. Joseph's sheriff's office. He'd told her he'd be right back. And he'd been killed that same hour. Standing by his graveside, knowing he'd saved one person's life had offered some consolation, but it hadn't restored the gaping hole in her own life. Made by a man of honor . . .

No matter how much she might grow to care for Wyatt Caradon—or perhaps already did—she wasn't going down that particular road again. Trusting a man, especially a man in Caradon's line of work, and letting yourself rely on him only led to disappointment and hurt. She'd been making it fine by herself, and would continue to.

She shoved damp strands of hair from her face, aware of Emma's glare. She pointed to the blanket. "Go on back over there like I told you to do."

"But you said we'd go for a walk when you finished." Emma peered up, sweat plastering her hair to her head, not looking the least penitent.

"We will. But I'm not finished yet."

"But you said it wouldn't take long."

"It wouldn't—if you'd stop getting into things. I just need for you to sit still for a few minutes." She motioned toward the blanket she'd spread out by the front barn door. "Read the books I brought out here for you."

"I don't know the words."

McKenna leveled her gaze, knowing that was something else she needed to tackle. Emma knew her alphabet and a few numbers, but that was it. Robert had been reading words by Emma's age. "I meant you could look at the pictures."

"I already looked at 'em."

"Well, look at them again!" Hot, tired, and hungry, McKenna pointed to the blanket until Emma trudged back over—frowning the entire way—and plopped down.

McKenna slid a couple more buttons free on her bodice and dabbed at the sweat dampening her chest. Even with the front and rear barn doors propped open, there was little cross breeze. Colorado nights supplied a needed reprieve, but the days weren't nearly as forgiving—as she feared Mr. Trenton wouldn't be either if she didn't deliver this saddle to him by this afternoon. She was already two days late.

So much for her promise to always be on time.

She leaned the pitchfork against the workbench and began cleaning up the oily mess. Reminding herself that Emma was only five, she decided to try a more optimistic approach. "Maybe Clara would like for you to draw her a picture of a bird."

"Maybe Clara wants to go for a walk like you promised!"

Something triggered inside her at the challenge in Emma's tone. "Well, you can just tell Miss Clara that she's not going *anywhere* if I don't get this saddle finished! And neither are you!"

Emma picked up her favorite book and threw it down on the blanket.

McKenna pressed the palms of her hands against her eyes, summoning patience she didn't have. She hadn't intended to raise her voice, but she'd never dealt with such an obstinate child before. Robert had been a quiet boy at this age, so easily appeased.

Deciding to ignore Emma, she retrieved the saddle and brushed off clinging pieces of hay, wondering if parenting might have been different for her if she'd sought it out, instead of it seeking her. She poured more oil onto the cloth and worked it into the rich leather of the saddle skirts. At least a dime's worth of oil had spilled. Just add it to her ever-increasing tab.

Standing back, she inspected the saddle, the muscles in her arms and shoulders fatigued from work. This was her second saddle to sell through Trenton's livery—not counting the one she'd sent to him by train before they arrived in Copper Creek. She needed to work faster, to make more money. But the thought was ludicrous. She was doing as much as she could and still needed more hours in each day.

Something she looked forward to doing was setting a time with Mei for their first lesson. Or lessons. She enjoyed being with Chin Mei—as long as her husband wasn't around. *But the woman's feet* . . . How could parents do something like that to their little girl? She looked at Emma again and couldn't fathom purposefully hurting the child in such a way. Maiming her like that . . .

Seeing Emma hold Clara close and whisper something to her softened McKenna's earlier frustration. "Ten more minutes, Emma. That's all I need."

"You said that before," she replied, head bowed, apathy flattening her tone.

McKenna opened her mouth to respond, then caught herself. Emma was right. She had said that—at least thirty minutes ago. She crossed the barn and knelt beside her on the blanket, aware of Emma edging from her reach.

"Tell you what. I'll finish rubbing down the saddle, then we'll take it into town to Mr. Trenton."

Emma looked up, her expression skeptical. "Can we get a treat?"

McKenna blew out a breath. They barely had enough money

for necessities, much less treats. Yet if she delivered this saddle to Mr. Trenton, she'd get paid. And maybe they could afford a tiny little something, especially if it helped her regain ground with Emma.

"All right, we'll get a treat. But it won't be something large. We'll need to make it something small that—"

"Don't cost much." Emma nodded. "Right?"

Said sweetly enough, Emma's reply pricked her pride like a barb. "Yes," she whispered. "Something that doesn't cost much." Hearing the crunch of hay, she turned and sucked in a breath. A man stood only a few feet away.

"Good day, miss." He tipped his hat to her.

McKenna glanced past him to the door on the opposite wall. He'd come in the back way? She could smell him from where she stood. His clothes were filthy, and he wore a jacket. In this heat . . .

His gaze slid past her to Emma on the blanket. He smiled and McKenna felt a chill. She moved into his line of vision, not taking her eyes off him, and prayed that Emma would stay quiet.

He blinked and nodded once, then pursed his lips as if acknowledging her dislike of how he'd looked at Emma. "She yours? She don't look like you."

"Please state your business, sir."

He looked around and took his time in answering. "I read a note in the mercantile, says you're needin' work done. Cattle to herd, fences to mend. That cabin could stand some repairs, same as this barn."

His gaze snagged on the blanket Robert had left on the pile of hay where he usually slept—whatever hour the boy decided to come home.

"So, tell me, ma'am, you got anything around here that could use my attention?"

When he looked past her again, McKenna's thoughts went to

the rifle in the kitchen, kept loaded atop the cupboard. "There's nothing I can think of. And we're not hiring right now, so you best be on your way."

He squinted. "That so?" He nodded slowly. "I don't know . . . I ain't seein' much evidence of a man's mark on this place. Leastwise not one who's doin' right by you." His eyes took on a gleam. "You got a man who's doin' right by you, ma'am?"

Heat poured into McKenna's face. He wasn't carrying a gun—that she could see anyway. But she guessed the sheath peeking from beneath his jacket held a knife. No way could she reach her knife on the opposite end of the workbench. Nor beat him in a fight. He was of thin build and had a sallow look about him, like he hadn't eaten well in a long time. But desperation clung to him, telling her there was little he wouldn't do.

Her eye went to the empty hook on the post beside him. The pitchfork . . .

She'd leaned it up against the workbench. It was just behind her, to her right. She didn't allow herself to think of what might happen if she didn't get to it first.

He was quick on his feet, but surprise gave her the advantage.

She caught him in the chest with the sharp prongs. Emma screamed behind her. The man's eyes went wide. He cursed and took a step back. The pitchfork left holes in his jacket but if she'd drawn blood, she saw no sign of it.

Fatigue weighted the muscles in her arms, but McKenna wielded the pitchfork with confidence, knowing her and Emma's well-being depending on it. "You leave here right now, and don't you ever come back."

The man moved toward her and she jabbed at him again. But lower this time, where he wasn't expecting it.

Covering himself with one hand, he raised the other in truce. "All right! All right now! Just calm down there . . ." He drew back. "I'm leavin' the same way I came in."

"No! You're leaving out the front. Where I can see you walk

down that road to town." The road went for a good quarter mile before curving behind some boulders. McKenna angled herself where she could see both him and Emma. "Child," she said, not wanting to use her name. "Get behind me."

Eyes like saucers, Emma did as she asked.

McKenna sickened inside at the way he watched Emma, and she motioned again with the pitchfork, her arms starting to shake. "Next time I'll have a rifle, and I'll just as soon use it as look at you."

He turned and grinned as he walked from the barn, and again as he started down the road.

McKenna kept her focus on him while ushering Emma inside the cabin. Following the man's progress through the front window, she grabbed the rifle and positioned herself on the front porch. She watched him through the rifle sights until he rounded the corner, and she stood, keeping vigil, as long as she could.

Until her legs betrayed her. Then she sank to the floor, bile rising in the back of her throat.

TWENTY-TWO

Wyatt was determined not to shoot the man. He was going to take Grady Polk alive and, if he could help it, without injury. Wyatt peered around the edge of an old mining shack in time to see Polk raise his gun, then he ducked in case Polk's aim had gotten any better.

A bullet zinged past him, a good two feet over his head.

Nope, Polk's aim hadn't changed. The man's grandmother could probably shoot better than he did.

Wyatt's thoughts went to the telegram in his vest pocket. He'd been carrying it with him for the past week, and though it was only a piece of paper, what it represented gave him fresh hope like he'd not known in a long time.

GAMBLING RING LINKED TO ROBBERIES *STOP* BIXBY

SEVERANCE COPPER CREEK *STOP* DETAILS COMING BY MAIL *STOP*

STAY IN COPPER CREEK *STOP*

It was reading that last part that had given him hope. He'd be working from Copper Creek for a while. That'd probably mean he'd be there for a couple of months, maybe more, if past experience held. So delivering Grady Polk to the Denver jail was all that stood between him starting his new assignment with the Brinks robberies—and being near to her . . .

McKenna Ashford had certainly given him no encouragement to hope for anything more, and his being in Copper Creek wouldn't guarantee anything. But there was something there. He'd sensed it when he was with her. Or else his imagination was deceiving him. 'Course, she'd turned him down for dinner, so that didn't bode well.

He wasn't going to push things with her, but if their paths happened to cross again somewhere down the road—something inside him softened at the thought, and he felt a smile—he might just be open to that. He wasn't against "helping" their paths cross either. Sometimes things needed a little nudge.

Another bullet whizzed past him. Up around the roofline.

"Polk, we've been at this for two hours," he yelled, inching out from behind the building. He fired and Polk's hat went flying. He heard Polk cussing.

"You did that to my last hat, Marshal! This one's brand new! I just broke it in!"

"You're trapped, Polk. Walk on out of there, and I'll tell the Denver judge you were civil about things. They might go a little easier on you this time."

"I don't know, Marshal. I'm thinkin' I can make it out. I made it clear of Denver, didn't I?"

"There's a rock wall behind you, Polk. You're not going anywhere!" Growing weary of the back-and-forth, Wyatt fired two more shots to keep Polk pinned down, and then skirted the mound of scrub brush. He'd tracked Grady Polk from Copper Creek all the way to Boulder, and as Polk left the brothel this afternoon, he'd been waiting for him.

What Wyatt hadn't counted on was the owner of the livery yelling a big hello across the street to someone at that same minute. Polk had spotted him, and the game was afoot.

A good distance from the mining shack where he'd been, Wyatt fired another shot at the rock where Polk was holed up. But lower this time. An experienced gunman would have known Wyatt was on the move, but not Grady Polk.

Polk's specialty was knife fighting. Wyatt had seen two corpses of men unfortunate enough to have drawn knives with Polk. So while he knew the man couldn't shoot a fish in a barrel, he held a high amount of respect for Polk's "talent," and the man's earnest desire not to return to jail any time soon.

"Why don't you just come on out from behind that fancy badge of yours, Marshal, and we'll talk things through. Man to man. I'll even let you choose—guns or knives." Polk had a high-pitched laugh that carried for miles. Made tracking the man a little easier.

Wyatt spotted him, fifteen feet away. Polk's back was to him. Polk kept peering above the rock, watching the mining shack. It wouldn't take him much longer to realize Wyatt wasn't there anymore.

Wyatt readied his gun. "Polk!"

The man turned and Wyatt fired. Polk's pistol went flying.

The man cussed a blue streak and rolled on the ground, holding his hand. "I told you before, I *hate* it when you do that! Takes me a week to shake off the sting!"

"Be glad you still have your hand." Wyatt gestured. "The knives . . ."

Feigned innocence swept Polk's expression.

Wyatt cocked his gun.

Polk pulled a knife from his left sleeve and dropped it, then his right. One from his belt and another from inside his boot. Wyatt waved the gun again, and Polk scowled and pulled a ten-inch curved blade from his back waistband.

Wyatt approached, cautious. "That all of them?"

"Why don't you come on over here and find out, Marshal Caradon."

"I'm not of the mind to play games with you, Polk. I'll shoot you, if you choose to go that route. But I don't want to."

"Didn't stop you from shootin' Slater's kid brother, now did it?" He spit a dark stream. "That's what I hear anyway."

Mention of the boy soured Wyatt's mood even further. He gestured. "Down on the ground."

Polk was a wiry little man, but he was fast and made up in speed what he lacked in muscle. "Mind if I get my pack right over here? It's got some special things from my mama in it."

"I'll get your pack. Down on the ground. Now!" Wyatt knew that pack no more contained items from Polk's mother as it did a stash of gold.

Polk lay facedown on the ground, legs spread wide and arms behind his back. Wyatt bound his wrists and helped him up. Keeping an eye on the man, he gathered the pack and the knives. Two of the blades probably cost more than Wyatt made in six months.

"If you wouldn't spend so much on knives, Polk, you wouldn't have to rob so many stores."

"A man's gotta have somethin' he loves, Marshal. And I love knives."

Wyatt whistled for Whiskey, who came trotting from over behind the shack. Gun trained on Polk, Wyatt swung into the saddle. Polk stayed a few feet in front of him—he knew the routine by now.

They made the Boulder jail in about a half an hour. A deputy met them at the door.

Wyatt glanced inside. "Sheriff Tanner in?"

"No sir, Marshal, he's not. He's over at Lou's having some lunch. He'll be back in a while."

Wyatt hesitated, not knowing this particular deputy but thinking the boy was nearly of age to start shaving. These guys seemed to be getting younger all the time. Or he was getting older.

"I can take him for you, Marshal. I've got a cell open right here." The deputy drew his gun.

Wyatt stared at the jail cell a few feet beyond, then at the young deputy, sizing him up. He seemed eager but capable. Wyatt finally nodded. "Much obliged. I'll stop back by before I leave town to see Tanner. And be careful. The man's fond of sharp objects, knives especially."

Wyatt was back on his horse when he heard the crash. He made it through the door in time to see Polk wielding what looked to be a letter opener. The deputy had a fresh cut across his left cheek. But to his credit, he was up and fighting.

Polk stabbed at the deputy again, lightning fast, and got him across the back of the hand. He turned toward Wyatt. "I'm not of the mind to mark you up, Marshal. I'll do it though, if you choose to go that route. But I ain't wantin' to," Polk said, repeating Wyatt's earlier threat, laughing high-pitched and squeaky at his own joke.

"You want me to shoot him, Marshal? I can! I'm ready!" The deputy cocked his gun, then turned and looked at Wyatt.

Wyatt saw it in Polk's eyes. And knew the deputy didn't.

Wyatt drew his gun as Polk grabbed the deputy's hand that held the pistol. Polk aimed it at Wyatt, and fired.

Wyatt dove behind a desk and the back of his head met a sharp edge. He felt a flash of pain and a warm gush as a second shot landed somewhere in the wall a foot from him. His head screamed and Wyatt knew he'd busted his skull open.

He heard scuffling, then heard the deputy cry out. Taking a breath, he prayed, and rose up on one knee.

With vicious delight in his face, Polk raised the letter opener and brought it down, aiming straight for the deputy's gut. Wyatt fired. Polk fell back, eyes round with shock. He clutched his right hand, or what was left of it.

"You shot me, you—"

Wyatt dragged Polk by his good arm, threw him in the

cell, and locked it up, with Polk kicking and screaming the entire time.

Polk had sliced the deputy on the jaw and on his hand. But thank God, nowhere else. Wyatt knelt beside him and leveled his gaze. "Never . . . never . . . *never* take your eyes off the prisoner, son."

Tears rose in the deputy's eyes. "Yes sir, Marshal. I'm real sorry."

Wyatt clasped his shoulder and helped him up. The young man swiped at his tears, obviously embarrassed.

"And don't you be ashamed of those either. We see the worst that goes on in this world, and those'll help keep you from getting hardened to it."

He nodded. "Yes sir, Marshal."

"Now you go fetch the doc." Wyatt fingered the back of his head and came away with blood. "Tell him he's got three patients who need his attention."

The deputy closed the door behind him, and as Polk still raged and cursed and cried, Wyatt thought of the telegram in his pocket—and of her—and held on to that hope.

TWENTY-THREE

Late the next afternoon, an hour out of Copper Creek, Wyatt urged Whiskey onto a side trail that wound upward some seven hundred feet to the town of Severance—site to one of the biggest gold strikes in Colorado history.

Caves surrounding Severance had shown more gold to men plumbing the mountain's depths than any others. But that was years ago, and since that time, the mountain—if she had anything left to give—had been holding back. Rumor in recent months was that she was reawakening, hinting at color even richer than before. And the almost-forgotten town of Severance was being birthed again. That wasn't necessarily a good thing.

Severance was rough, even by Colorado standards, and drew the kind of men Wyatt usually kept in his sights, which was why he was headed that direction. The Marshals Office listed Severance as a town involved in a gambling ring, along with Bixby and Copper Creek, and his meeting with one of the higher-ups in Boulder that morning had shed new light on the assignment.

Gambling was a lucrative business, and the Marshals Office had no intention of trying to shut it down. That'd be like holding back an ocean. Their focus was narrower in scope. They were after the key conspirators in the ring, the handful of men who had orchestrated the robberies.

Wyatt guided Whiskey around a larger boulder in the path.

A man by the name of Brinks owned a fleet of stages used for transporting money and valuable goods across the mountains, and to towns on the plains. After numerous robberies, Mr. Brinks approached the Marshals Office about investigating the incidents, which they'd been obliged to do—seeing as the two men killed in the last incident were two of their own. Wyatt had known the marshals. They were good men. Or had been.

His visit to Severance today was more for scouting, seeing what and who was here. He'd been to Severance twice before, and had been warned by his superiors to keep a low profile, as he typically did at this stage of an investigation. No one knew his occupation in Severance, that he knew of, and the Marshals Office had made it clear it was to stay that way. If he lost that advantage, the chance of finding the men responsible for the crimes was slim to none. And like his superiors, he was eager to see justice meted out, before anyone else was killed.

He'd been given no names yet, no arrests were to be made. Right now, he only wanted to get something to eat and down a cool drink to ease the ache in his head, then he'd start scouting the place.

The winding trail opened into the main—and, only—thoroughfare in Severance. Clapboard buildings and shacks lined the road, most either built adjacent to the other, or sharing common walls that looked weary of shouldering the load. With few exceptions, the structures housed saloons, brothels, or the larger and more lucrative gaming halls—which typically offered both gambling and "comfort," as it was called. The places were open for business all hours. And were always busy.

As he rode, Wyatt gently probed the back of his scalp, feeling the prick of stitches. A good bit of the swelling had gone down, but the gash was still tender. And would be—the doc had said yesterday—for quite a while. The young deputy in Boulder would bear the scars from his run-in with Grady Polk for the rest of his life, but at least he still had his life.

With that in mind, Wyatt tethered Whiskey in front of Clell's Eatery. He spotted the same red-and-white checkered curtains framing the splintered glass window from the time before. "*Providin' the boys with a touch of home*," is what Clell Watson, the proprietor, had said when Wyatt commented on the curtains his last time through.

Clell's daily special was the same as before. It consisted of a plateful of beans, a generous portion of venison, and buttered cornbread, and was as filling as it was tasty. Wyatt ate it, grateful, and left Clell Watson a tip that showed his appreciation.

Back outside, he stared up into the night sky and took in a lungful of cool mountain air. How could a place he didn't hail from feel so much like home?

He started down the street, taking the town in, when a shout coming from a gaming hall next door drew his attention. It wasn't so much the familiar voice as it was what the fellow had said. Wyatt paused—listened again—and bowed his head. It couldn't be. Not all the way up here.

He walked the short distance to the gaming hall and peered inside.

"Not bad card playin' . . . for an old man," Robert Ashford yelled again, his voice slurred.

Wyatt could only stare. What was the boy doing in Severance?

Seated across from Robert, a bear of a man slowly rose from the card table. Robert laughed, too drunk to realize he was about to get payback—in spades. The man's fist was about as big around as Robert's head, and when the two connected, Robert fell back like a two-ton stone, chair and all.

Every seat at every table was occupied, and the rabble of miners, both young and old, applauded and whooped, urging the big man on. Men on their way upstairs paused to watch, and scantily clad women leaned over the railing to get a better view, while also giving one. Wyatt purposefully looked elsewhere. Everybody in the place had apparently had their fill of Robert Ashford. And from the looks of Robert, he'd had his fill too.

Wyatt walked on in, but left Robert where he lay. Bloodied face and all.

If he interfered now, he'd draw attention to himself—not what the Marshals Office had in mind—and he might make things worse for Robert. He hoped when the kid came to, that the last fistful might've knocked some sense into him, and they could head on down the mountain together.

But he had his doubts.

He took a seat at the bar, near the end where he could keep an eye on things. He ordered a drink and watched Robert taking up floor space across the room. Hard to reconcile that boy being related to McKenna Ashford.

From what little he'd seen of Miss Ashford with her brother, Wyatt figured if she were here, she'd be asking him to carry Robert out right now, or would've dragged him out herself. She'd be tending her brother's wounds and trying to sober him up with black coffee. Loving on him like she thought a big sister should. When really, she'd only be digging a little deeper the hole Robert had already dug for himself.

The bartender set a whiskey before him, and Wyatt sipped slowly, willing the drink to ease the dull thud inside his brain.

Sometimes you had to let a person stumble, let 'em fall flat out—no matter how much it hurt to see—before they could come to grips with how bad off they were. Because until a person realized that, there wasn't much helping them. He knew that well enough, but doubted McKenna would agree when it came to her kid brother.

He scanned the faces in the room, most grizzled and rough from years of hard work, some young enough they hadn't had their spark snuffed out yet.

Robert stirred on the floor, and to Wyatt's surprise, the boy got up, righted his chair, and seated himself at the table again. The kid's skull must be made of oak! Robert swayed for a few seconds, his eyes going wide then squinting again as though he were having trouble focusing.

Wyatt noticed the bartender motion to one of the women, who sauntered over and situated herself on Robert's lap, facing him. Wyatt held back, waiting. If Robert headed for the staircase with her, he'd find a way to intervene. Money was one thing to squander and lose, his innocence was another. If it wasn't already too late for that.

Focusing on the woman's low-cut bodice, Robert dug into his pockets and came up with a few coins. Palm up, he held them out to her. She looked at him and huffed, and called him a coarse name that drew laughs from those nearby—especially the brick wall of a man sitting across from him.

Robert shoved back his chair and threw the coins on the table. One of them bounced up and hit the man in the face, and the fellow reacted. His punch sent Robert sailing again. He went down, but didn't stay down this time.

Robert gave his head a quick shake, let out a low growl, and charged.

Wyatt shook his head. The kid was outmuscled and outmatched. He'd be sore and bruised tomorrow, and his head would hurt something awful, but so far it was just fists. He'd live to tell the tale—if he weren't too far gone to remember.

When two more men teamed up against him, Wyatt's concern notched up. He'd been ordered not to do anything to draw attention to himself. The assignment demanded it. Lives depended on it. But he wouldn't stand by and watch Robert get beaten to a pulp either—despite the kid asking for it. Yet he and Robert couldn't take on the entire room, which is what it could come down to if he jumped in now.

Robert got in a couple of respectable licks on the two men closer to his size. Even drunk, the boy held his own fairly well. Until the large man penned him from behind.

Wyatt stood up and pushed his way through the crowd.

Being cheered on, the men delivered repeated blows to Robert's face. And with each one, Robert's taunts grew more unintelligible. Was the kid trying to get himself killed?

Wyatt was a few feet from Robert when the cheering fell silent. All heads turned toward the staircase.

He followed their line of vision to see a man descending the stairs, a woman by his side. The man was well dressed—too well dressed for Severance—and surveyed the room below him with an air of bored distraction.

Wyatt felt like he should know him, but couldn't place why. Maybe he'd seen a drawing of the man's face on some poster, though he couldn't recollect it. He did, however, get the strong impression that if there was some kind of criminal activity being headed up in Severance, this man would not only know about it, he'd be calling the shots.

At the man's faintest nod, the men holding Robert let go.

And Robert fell to the floor, motionless.

"—And then Aunt Kenny *poked* him with a big fork, and he went away!" Emma said, acting out the scene as Mei's eyes grew wide.

The seriousness of what could have happened days earlier was never far from McKenna's mind, yet Emma's dramatic retelling of the events prompted a smile. As did watching Mei who sat beside her, nodding and smiling politely as though the child were recounting the antics of a Sunday afternoon picnic.

"I think Mei understands me, Kenny."

Certain that Mei didn't, McKenna wasn't about to dash Emma's hopes. "I think Mei likes you very much and enjoys listening to you."

Looking around Chin Li and Mei's second-story apartment, McKenna was glad she and Emma had stopped by the bakery that afternoon. She'd wanted to share a book with Mei in preparation for their first lesson. As it turned out, Mei was just leaving and—through a series of amusing charades—invited her and Emma to follow her home. Sensing the invitation was a great honor, McKenna prepared Emma on the way, thankful Wyatt had told her about the custom of removing shoes.

But she was even more thankful that Chin Li apparently wasn't home. She didn't look forward to their next encounter.

Emma reached for one of the pastries Mei had offered upon their arrival. Before her fingers touched the moon cake, Emma turned in McKenna's direction and batted her big blue eyes, her question clear.

McKenna nodded, pleased she'd sought permission.

With her sparkling eyes and honey blonde hair, Emma was a beautiful little girl, despite her stubborn disposition. A shiver worked its way up McKenna's spine as she remembered how that man had looked at Emma. Things could have turned out much differently that afternoon, which was why she'd already made changes to their routine at the homestead—to lessen the chance of being caught unaware again.

"You . . . like?"

McKenna turned to see Mei cupping her hands to her mouth as though she were drinking something. Understanding, McKenna nodded. "Yes, thank you. That would be nice."

As Mei left the room, McKenna's focus trailed downward. She'd visited with Dr. Foster about Mei, and he'd told her there was little that could be done for her feet. He'd seen Lotus feet before, but not often. The Chinese were a very private people, he'd explained, especially the women. And they usually depended on physicians in their own community or counsel from elders for their remedies.

Chin Li and Mei's home was located above the laundry. The apartment was small and the furnishings sparse, but it was very well kept. Everything had its place. And McKenna admired the neatness, quite a difference from the cabin where boxes and crates occupied nearly every corner, still waiting to be unpacked.

McKenna looked around the room, noting the vivid colors Mei had chosen in decorating, namely a vibrant shade of red. It was in everything—the cushions on the furniture, the wall hangings, tiny statues on tables, and pottery on the mantle. Even the ornate rugs covering the plank wood floor were fringed in scarlet hues. Calligraphy adorned one wall, painted with a wide brushstroke, and below it there appeared to be an altar of some sort, with a plate of food set before it.

Footsteps sounded and McKenna looked up, expecting to see Mei returning. Instead, the front door opened. From where she sat, she couldn't see who it was. But fairly certain it was Chin Li, she fought the urge to grab Emma and make a run for the next room.

Chin Li stepped inside, but with his back to her. Seconds passed, and she discovered why . . .

He was assisting the same elderly gentleman from before, helping him maneuver the corner, and both men were laughing with each other, obviously unaware of her presence. Chin Li's voice sounded higher-pitched than usual. He turned and it struck her that he actually looked friendly when he smiled. Even handsome, in a fearsome warrior-ish sort of way.

But when he saw her, his smile died. Back came his customary frown. He spoke to the older gentleman, who peered at her beneath deeply hooded eyes.

She glanced in the direction Mei had gone and silently begged her friend to return. Not certain what was customary in this instance, she began to rise, then paused and sat back down again. Men were supposed to stand up when women walked into a room, not the other way around. But what if the Chinese custom was different? What if the women usually rose or bowed low when men entered the room?

Catching Chin Li's disapproving look, McKenna decided that if she was supposed to do something other than sit there and muster as sweet a smile as she could, Chin Li would just have to be disappointed.

He bowed. "Miss Ashford."

Surprised at how well he pronounced her name, McKenna matched his civility. "Hello, Mr. Chin." Doubting whether either man would take kindly to one of Emma's outbursts, she was grateful the child remained seated quietly beside her for the moment, albeit Emma's eyes brimmed with curiosity.

With a bow, Chin Li presented the elderly man beside him. "My honorable father . . ."

He said the name so quickly, she didn't understand it—but she wasn't about to ask him to repeat it. It hadn't sounded like Chin, but it had to be.

Deciding to err on the side of caution, McKenna bowed her head low to the older gentleman, and lingered there longer. "Very nice to make your acquaintance, sir." Where *was* Mei!

The two men exchanged a flurry of words, then stared at her again, their expressions identical, easily classified as suspicious. And the silence stretched beyond uncomfortable to excruciating.

"Ah." Mei entered the room carrying a tray, and McKenna wanted to hug her.

Mei set the tray on a low-legged table in front of McKenna then turned and bowed to her husband and his father. Her voice was soft and inquisitive, and both men responded with a nod to whatever she'd said, then walked into the next room. But Chin Li's backward glance revealed his displeasure.

The pot from which Mei poured the hot tea—at least it looked and smelled like tea—was one of the most beautiful McKenna had ever seen. The china cups shared the same exquisite design of blue and red flowers along the sides and stem, and she wondered if they might be a family heirloom.

"This is a very pretty tea set." McKenna gestured to the pot and cups.

"Th-thank you." Mei smiled and briefly closed her eyes in what looked like an abbreviated bow. They drank in silence, but every few seconds, Mei glanced at the door leading to the next room.

McKenna sipped, disappointed that their first lesson had been interrupted before it had even begun. She pointed to the clock on the table beside her. "Is now still a good time?"

Mei squinted and smiled, a sure sign she hadn't understood.

McKenna reached for the book she'd brought with her. It was one she'd purchased for Emma, but as she and Emma had read through it last night, she realized it would serve well for her first few lessons with Mei.

Deciding to simplify things, McKenna held up the book. "Learn to . . . talk better?"

Mei nodded and touched the cover. "Yes! Talk better . . . to me." She smiled.

Enthused once again, McKenna set aside her cup and opened the book. Mei leaned close. And as McKenna had done with Emma, she turned to the page with all the letters and sounded out each one, then flipped to the hand-drawn pictures, and started with the apple. Soon she moved to the boat, the cat, and the dog—corresponding words printed below each of the pictures—and marveled at how quickly Mei learned.

Mei retrieved a pad of paper and a quill, and she took notes as they went along. Mei copied each letter—jotting a series of symbols beside each one—and then repeated each one aloud, getting it near perfect the very first time. Mei was a bright pupil and much farther along in her basic knowledge of the English language than McKenna had thought.

"She's learning to read just like me, huh, Kenny?"

"Yes, just like you."

"Can I have a turn too?" Emma asked, cuddling close.

"Yes, but I'm going to give Mei more turns while we're in her home, because you and I get to do this when we get home later, all right?"

Nodding, Emma threw a grin at Mei and scrunched closer to McKenna.

When McKenna looked at the clock again, an hour had passed and she thought of all the work waiting for her at home. She reached the end of the page and closed the book. "That's all for today." She laughed softly when Mei and Emma both sighed with disappointment. "You did very well, Mei." Far better than she had expected. "You too, Emma. I'm proud of you both."

"Thank you," Mei said, mastering the "th" sound that had been difficult for her at first. "You . . . good." She pointed to the book.

McKenna smiled. "Thank you. And next time, you teach me to bake"—she made a motion like kneading bread dough—"okay?"

"O-kay," Mei said, her dark eyes dancing.

To McKenna's relief, Chin Li never reappeared. They said their good-byes, and by the time she and Emma returned home, precious few moments of daylight remained.

As McKenna guided the wagon up to the barn, she spotted a piece of paper tacked to the door of the cabin. It looked like an envelope, but it was hard to be sure from this distance. It was probably a note from Mr. Billings. Another *gentle* reminder about the payment due on the ranch. Or perhaps a *not-so-gentle* reminder that he was proceeding with the foreclosure in an effort to throw them off of this land. She sighed, deciding that kind of news could wait.

By the time she unbridled the horses and finished the outside chores, the sun was nearly set. Robert was working late at the livery and had told her he might not be home until after midnight. She appreciated the extra hours he'd been working recently. He seemed to be taking more of a share in the responsibility facing them, and she wanted to believe that would last.

McKenna closed the barn doors and scanned the road, the corrals off to the east, the outhouse and the woods encircling the property. She briefly touched the bulk in her apron pocket, far more aware of her surroundings these days than before.

Emma reached up and took hold of her hand. "I like it when you don't work in the barn, Kenny."

"Me too, sweetie," McKenna answered, gently squeezing her tiny fingers. Another change she'd made was to push Vince and Janie's bed to one side of the bedroom and move her supplies for finishing saddles into one of the corners. It was a tight fit, but it allowed her to keep the cabin locked when they were there alone, and prohibited Emma from constantly getting into things she shouldn't. The change also meant she could work later into the night, with Emma sleeping in her bedroom only feet away. Making saddles faster, she could earn more money, if she could keep up with everything.

She opened the cabin door to let Emma run on inside, and tugged the envelope free from the nail. The feel of the paper—heavy and expensive—confirmed the note was from Billings. Who else in Copper Creek used such fancy stationery? Or would come all the way out here to deliver it?

She stepped inside and bolted the door behind her, and paused, resting her hand on the latch. How many times had Janie touched this lock? How many times had she latched out the world at night, feeling safe with her husband and her daughter, never knowing that the world would still manage to creep in through the crevices . . . creep in and steal everything away . . .

When Emma wasn't watching, she removed the Derringer from her apron pocket and slipped it into a cupboard drawer. Since *that* day, she'd carried it with her, and she wouldn't hesitate to use it if that man—or anyone else meaning them harm—ever showed up here again.

"I'm hungry, Aunt Kenny."

"Okay, sweetie. Run and change into your nightgown, and I'll make us some dinner."

"Then will you read me a story?"

McKenna smiled. "After we've eaten."

Emma scampered off, and McKenna moved to the front window and opened the envelope. It was from Billings. She read the note in the waning light, her brow furrowing. He wanted to meet with her—*posthaste*, was the wording he'd chosen.

He offered no particulars in the note about the purpose of their meeting, only that it was "imperative for their schedules to coincide at the earliest possible moment."

That man . . . Were all bankers so eager to disrupt lives and remind a person of their failings? A bitter taste rose in her mouth. She slid the letter back into the envelope and laid it aside. She was doing the best she could with what she had. Mr. Billings's pressuring her wasn't going to change that.

TWENTY-FOUR

Robert didn't move. But Wyatt could see him breathing. He needed to get the kid out of here.

The man on the stairs motioned, then looked pointedly toward the bartender. "Take him out back." He scanned the crowd, a slow smile turning the corners of his mouth. "Drinks and girls half off for the next fifteen minutes!"

A riot of cheers erupted, and Wyatt watched as the two men dragged Robert out, facedown and body limp, through a side door. In a blink, Robert was forgotten.

Wyatt slipped out the front and skirted down the side of the building. He stuck to the shadows—easy to do with the sun now set—and spotted the men as they dumped Robert by a rubbish pile. Talking in low tones, one of them gave the boy a swift kick to the gut before they went back inside.

As soon as the door closed, Wyatt moved.

Robert was out cold, his pulse shallow but steady. No broken bones that Wyatt could tell, but he felt a lump in the right forearm. Severance didn't have a physician. He knew because Doc Foster had mentioned making rounds up here on occasion.

Voices floated toward him on the cool night air. "I'll finish him all right. Talkin' to me that way, the puny little . . ."

Gritting his teeth, Wyatt heaved Robert up onto one shoulder. The kid was solid muscle! The wound on the back of his head pounded hot, and his head swam. He blinked to clear his vision and moved as quickly as he could down a side street toward Clell's, where he'd tethered Whiskey.

With little time to act, he situated Robert across Whiskey's broad back and swung up behind him, in time to see three men saunter from the alley. He recognized one of them as being the huge brute of a fellow from the gaming hall.

They looked in his direction.

Mounts were tethered in front of the hall, but Wyatt had no idea which one belonged to Robert. He thought he'd seen the tan palomino once before at Trenton's livery, and maybe the sock-footed black mare on the end, but horses were easily mistaken and he couldn't be sure. It was dark, and there was no time. And since stealing horses was a hanging offense and somewhat frowned upon for a U.S. Marshal, he decided to let it go. Robert needed to learn to clean up his own messes.

Holding on to the boy, Wyatt negotiated the steep trail downward, riding as fast as he dared. Moonlight silvered the shadows on the trail, and Whiskey hit a patch of shale and slipped, but regained her footing. Wyatt reined in, slowing their pace. Halfway down, he stopped to listen for pursuit.

All he heard was the faint keening of wind sweeping across the snowcapped peaks above, and the soft wheeze of Robert's breath. He rode on, not stopping again until they made the outskirts of Copper Creek.

He stopped by Doc Foster's clinic and pounded on the door. No answer. The office was dark and unlocked. He didn't know what medicinal supplies would be needed, but McKenna would. If she needed anything to tend her brother, he could make a run back into town.

The boy began to stir, and by the time they reached the

Talbots' cabin—*McKenna's* cabin—Robert was coming around. The front windows overlooking the porch were dark. It was well past midnight. McKenna and Emma were no doubt in bed by now.

"My head hurts . . . bad." Robert moaned. "My gut . . . does too."

Wyatt reined in by the porch, trying to scrape up some sympathy—and failing. Especially when imagining what McKenna's reaction would be at seeing her brother like this. "You should've thought of that before, son."

"I'm not your son," Robert whispered low and cursed him.

Wyatt could only stare, most of him wanting to knock the kid's head the rest of the way off. But a part of him wanted to take the boy and hold him tight, like his own father had done to him before allowing his only son to go to jail.

"How did you get up to Severance tonight, Robert?"

Robert moaned, clutching his stomach. "I hitched a ride . . . with a guy on a freight wagon."

Wyatt shook his head. Well, that took care of having to go back for a horse. "It should probably pain me more to say this, but you're going to feel a whole lot worse before you start to feel better."

Robert leaned forward, groaning."I think I'm going to be sick."

"Okay, hang on and I'll get you—"

Robert vomited, dousing them both.

Another bout of sickness followed before the kid's legs gave way. Wyatt managed to catch him. Supporting his weight, he started for the stairs.

The front door opened and Wyatt looked up, expecting to see McKenna.

And saw a Winchester aimed straight at him instead.

TWENTY-FIVE

Stop right there! Come any closer and I'll shoot!" Heart pounding, McKenna opened the door a few inches more, rifle in hand. She squinted, seeing only shadows moving in the dark.

"It's Wyatt Caradon, ma'am! With your brother!"

"Marshal Caradon?" She squinted. What was he doing back here? His voice sounded both familiar, and yet different, at the same time.

"Yes, ma'am. It's me. And I've . . ." His breath came heavy. "I've got your brother. He's been hurt."

Hurt? Guilt pinched a nerve. *The lever on the vice at the livery* . . . Robert had told her the contraption wasn't working right, but she hadn't believed him. She propped the rifle by the door and hurried out to meet them, not understanding why Marshal Caradon was bringing Robert home.

From what little she could see, Caradon was carrying her brother up the porch steps, Robert's body limp against him, his head lolled to one side.

"What happened?" She slipped an arm around Robert's waist

and grimaced at the overwhelming stench of liquor and vomit. Truth hit her full in the face, and something broke away deep inside her. As she helped Caradon carry her brother inside, she felt herself inwardly reaching, grasping for something solid to hold on to. Yet the familiar tide of betrayal swept her out farther with each wave.

"He got into a fight. He's pretty beat up, but . . ." Caradon paused inside the doorway. "I think he's going to be all right."

She threw a blanket over the couch and motioned for him to lay Robert down. Caradon did so gently, not like she would've been tempted to have done. Cinching her robe tighter about her, she retrieved the lamp from the kitchen table and brought it close to Robert's face. *Oh dear God . . .*

Tears welled in her throat.

Robert had come home roughed up before, but he'd never come home this bad off. Bathed in an umber glow, his face was almost unrecognizable—his left eye a narrow slit, the skin surrounding it puffy and mottled with blood pooling beneath the skin. His right eye wasn't much better. Both sides of his face were swollen and, if she wasn't mistaken, his nose was broken. An ache clenched her chest.

"I stopped by Doc Foster's on the way over, ma'am, but he wasn't in. I can ride back out for him if you think we need him."

Something about the way Caradon used "we" stirred unexpected emotions. In their final weeks in St. Joseph, she'd handled these situations alone—when Robert would return in the wee hours of the morning, full up on whiskey and spite. Though she'd never had to carry her brother inside before. Not that she could have, even when he was younger.

"Thank you, Marshal Caradon. I appreciate you bringing him home." She set the lamp on the side table.

Robert moaned and lifted his hand to his face.

Anger warring with concern, she gently urged his hand back down. "I'm here, Robert," she whispered. "I'll take care of you." *Like I always do.* He stilled. "I'll get you something for your pain." She rose, wishing there were something she could take for hers.

From the pantry, she gathered clean cloths and what poultices and herbs she had on hand. A pitcher of water, a spoon, a tub of salve, and the bottle of laudanum she'd found following Janie's death. She slipped a spoonful of the medicine through Robert's swollen lips and glanced up at Marshal Caradon, who still stood quietly beside her.

She nodded toward the chair. "Please, have a seat."

"I'm fine, ma'am. Thank you."

She unbuttoned Robert's shirt and ran her hands over his abdomen and down along the sides, checking for telltale signs of internal bleeding. His chest bore marks from the altercation, as did his back, but no swelling or deep bruising that she could see. Still, she'd want Dr. Foster to examine him to be sure. "Do you have any idea what happened? Who did this to him?"

"Yes, ma'am. I came across your brother in a gaming hall in Severance earlier tonight."

She looked up. "Severance?"

He nodded. "It's a mining town up the mountain about an hour north of here. Rough place. Makes Copper Creek look almost civilized. Robert said he hitched a ride on a freight wagon heading up there."

She dabbed the blood from Robert's face, her ministrations becoming less gentle. "Robert told me he'd be working late this evening at the livery, finishing a wagon."

"All I can tell you, ma'am, is that he was in Severance. And he wasn't there building any wagon. He was gambling. Drunk and mouthing off to men he had no business looking cross-eyed at, much less speaking to that way."

Caradon's statement sparked defensiveness inside her, but she tempered her reaction, knowing it was unwarranted. He was only telling her what happened.

His sigh drew her attention. She noticed his shirt and pants, and understood now why he hadn't taken a seat. His clothes were covered in Robert's vomit. She breathed in the stench again, and though her robe was clean, she felt just as soiled as these men.

"Marshal Caradon, I'm sorry. I-I didn't realize . . . I think Vince Talbot was about your size. I'll check the chiffarobe when I'm finished and get you a change of clothes."

"I'm fine for now, ma'am. I can take it, if you can."

Touched by the kindness in his voice and in his smile, she pulled her focus back to Robert. Who was this man standing beside her, and why did he keep walking back into her life? Whatever the reason, she was thankful. Especially tonight. If he hadn't been there to stop the fight and bring Robert home . . . She couldn't let herself think too long about it.

She blinked to clear her vision. "Did you see what transpired?"

He didn't answer right off, and she looked back, getting the feeling she wasn't going to like whatever he was about to say.

"When I walked in, your brother was playing cards. Or losing at them was more like it. He spouted off to a guy twice his size, and the fellow punched him in the face. Robert went down. He was out for at least a couple of minutes."

She folded the cloth back to reveal a clean edge, dipped it in water and held it against Robert's swollen lower lip. He winced, and she wondered if he was more awake than he was letting on.

"I'm grateful you were there to intervene on his behalf, Marshal. It seems I owe you yet another debt of gratitude."

The rhythmic tick-tock of the mantle clock—a wedding present to Vince and Janie crafted by McKenna's father—marked off the seconds. Caradon shifted beside her. She'd expected him to have some smart response to her comment. Had hoped for it, actually. Maybe make mention of that offer for dinner she'd turned down last time. Whether wise or not, she hoped he would ask her again. Her answer would be very different this time.

"I don't want to mislead you, ma'am, about what happened tonight. When Robert went down, I . . . I didn't exactly come to his rescue."

She glanced at him and read shyness—or was it apprehension—in his expression. "No need for false modesty, Marshal. Robert's here now, isn't he? And all because of your kindness."

Caradon got an uncomfortable look on his face, and she knew why. He was still wearing those filthy clothes. She finished rubbing salve into Robert's cuts and set the jar aside.

"I'll get you a clean shirt and pair of pants." She went to the chiffarobe in the bedroom and sorted through Vince's clothes, quickly coming up with a change of clothes she thought would do. "Here you are," she said, keeping her voice quiet.

The last thing she needed now was for Emma to waken and see Robert this way, or for her to see Wyatt Caradon again. Emma would be thrilled to see Caradon, but knowing what type of man he was, McKenna knew he wouldn't be staying in one place for long. And that would only translate to more disappointment for the little girl.

Caradon took the clothes. "Thank you, ma'am. I'll be back shortly." He excused himself and closed the front door softly behind him.

McKenna removed Robert's pants and covered him with a blanket. His soft snores—effects of the laudanum—only served to irritate her. Dwelling on the selfishness of her brother's actions, she bundled his soiled clothes and set them outside on the porch to be washed. She spotted Caradon's horse but saw no sign of him. Back inside, she exchanged her dirtied robe for Janie's clean one and was back in the kitchen when she heard a soft rap.

She opened the front door and, for a moment, could only

stare. Seeing Wyatt Caradon dressed in worn dungarees and a soft chambray shirt took her aback.

"Thank you for the clean clothes." His voice was soft. "This is much better."

She completely agreed about the "much better." The black duster he customarily wore was impressive, but there was something about seeing him dressed this way that showed another side of him. A side she liked. Very much. She ushered him back in—catching the scent of fresh river water and soap—and matched his soft tone. "I'm glad they fit. And the smell's a definite improvement."

He smiled, his hair still damp and curling at his neckline. He glanced in Robert's direction. "Would you like for me to ride for Doc Foster?"

"Yes, I would appreciate that. Thank you."

He didn't move. "There's something I—I want you to be clear on. About what happened tonight, when your brother was fighting." He hesitated. "After he was knocked out, Robert got up a few minutes later . . . of his own accord. He started back in on that same man, egging him on. The fellow was huge. He punched Robert a second time, hard. Your brother went down again. But he got right back up fighting."

She shook her head. "That sounds like Robert." Then something occurred to her. Something Caradon had said. "Wait . . . you're telling me that *one* man did all this to him?"

"At first . . ." His expression went solemn. "And then two more joined in."

Something about his manner, his recounting of events, sat ill with her maternal instincts. "And then two more joined in," she repeated, trying to make the images in her mind fit with what he was describing.

"Yes, ma'am. But your brother picked the fight, Miss Ashford. You need to realize that."

In light of all he'd done for Robert tonight, and for her, she tried to find a smile, not wanting to appear ungrateful. "Surely you're not suggesting that Robert deserved this?" She gestured toward Robert. "That whatever he did or said gave grown men the right to do this to a boy?"

Caradon stared, unblinking. "What I'm saying is that Robert holds some of the responsibility for what happened to him this evening. A lot of responsibility."

She searched his eyes. He thought *she* shared some of that responsibility too—she felt it from him. "I see." She brushed past him and gathered the bowl of bloodied water and cloths from the table beside the sofa, trying to sort out why she was trembling. She set the bowl down on the kitchen table harder than intended, and some of the water sloshed over the edge and onto the front of Janie's robe. If she understood this right, he'd stood by and watched her brother get beaten by three burly men.

Furious, disappointed, confused, she exhaled. "I realize, Marshal Caradon," she kept her voice low, knowing Robert could hear if he were awake, "that my brother can be hot-tempered and obstinate at times. I'm not excusing that, believe me, but you don't realize all we've been—" The words caught, and she stopped to swallow. "All that's *he's* been through in his life. Our mother died when he was born, and our father . . ." She looked to see if Robert's eyes were still closed. They were. Still, she spoke even softer. "Our father died seven years ago, leaving us in a . . . very difficult situation. But in many ways, we'd already lost him years earlier, the same day we lost our mother."

She hadn't planned on telling him all this, and wondered now if she should continue. But perhaps he would be more understanding if he knew a little about Robert's past. She certainly didn't need her brother getting on his wrong side. "After our mother died, our father buried himself in work, until finally . . . work buried him. Every day, he grieved her passing, and no matter what I did or what I said, he pushed Robert away. He never gave his son what he needed."

"I've given you and Robert all I have, McKenna. You and your brother will have a roof over your heads," her father had said days before he passed. If only William Ashford had known that the inheritance he'd worked so hard to leave his son wasn't the one Robert needed most.

McKenna prayed she could make Caradon understand. "He blamed Robert—a *child*—for what had happened, and never was a father to him. I can count on one hand the times my father—*our* father—held him, as a baby or as a little boy. I'd ask him to, but . . . he'd just stare at Robert and . . ." Her voice broke. "And then walk away."

Caradon moved closer. At this angle, she couldn't see his face, but she could feel the warmth from his body. He wasn't even touching her, but something inside her changed—responded—with him so near. It was silly, but her heart raced and her breathing became more of a conscious act.

"Miss Ashford . . . McKenna," he said, his voice tender. "I understand, and I'm so sorry. For you both."

If she thought she'd had trouble breathing before, now it felt as though her lungs had completely lost their memory. "I've tried to do right by him, Marshal, to give him what he's needed. Maybe knowing this about my brother will . . . help make things clearer for you."

"They're *much* clearer now, thank you. And please don't think I hold you responsible for what happened tonight."

She smiled up at him and nodded, relieved.

"You're only doing what you think is best for your brother," he said softly. "And I appreciate that. But in my line of work, I see men all the time who've never been made to learn to take responsibility for their actions, and they end up—"

"Been made?" She blinked. It felt like the conversation had changed midsentence. *His line of work?* He was comparing

Robert to hardened criminals? So he *did* hold her responsible for what had happened tonight, at least partly. She heard it in the smooth velvet of his voice, wedged between his carefully chosen words. "Surely you're not comparing my brother with the men you track down and take into custody . . . just so they can be hanged?" She'd said the last part off-the-cuff, but hoped to get a reaction. And she did.

He stiffened. Then slowly shook his head. "Now's not the time for us to be discussing this. I'll ride for the doc."

He turned and walked to the door, but she strode after him, a question burning the tip of her tongue. Knowing she should let it go, she couldn't. "What responsibility do *you* hold for what happened tonight, Marshal Caradon?"

Hand on the door, his eyes narrowed. "Beg pardon, ma'am?"

"You said my brother got into a fight with one man. And then two more joined in. What were *you* doing during this time?" She wanted to add, "*When my brother was being beaten senseless*," but refrained.

"Don't be lured down a false road, McKenna. You weren't there. You don't know how things played out. Robert kept coming at them. He wouldn't back down, even when he knew he couldn't win."

She didn't know why, but the calm in his manner, the confidence with which he spoke, and—unlike before—his use of her Christian name, infuriated her. She spoke slowly, each syllable deliberate. "What were you doing while those men were beating my brother . . . Marshal Caradon?"

He held her gaze for the longest time. "No matter what I say right now, you're not going to take it well. So why don't we agree to speak on it more tomorrow . . . if you're still wanting to? I'm going to fetch the doc."

She took a breath. Opened her mouth to speak. Then emptied her lungs and let him go. Because she knew—in that secret, hidden place inside her, that slender space between the reality of what men were and the dream of what a man could be—that come tomorrow, or the next day, or the next . . . Wyatt Caradon would be gone.

TWENTY-SIX

After escorting Doc Foster back to the cabin, Wyatt bedded down in the barn, exhausted and frustrated. He rose with the sun the next morning. The same thought rankling him when he closed his eyes was still rankling him when he opened them. He'd known the timing last night hadn't been right to talk to her about Robert, so why on earth had he even tried?

He wanted to be completely honest with McKenna about why he hadn't acted on Robert's behalf sooner, and it bothered him that he couldn't. Trusting her wasn't the issue. Trusting Robert was. And if for some reason, she let it slip to the boy about his assignment from the Marshals Office . . . His gut told him Robert would turn on him in a heartbeat.

As it always did up here in the mountains, early dawn held a chill. He opened the double barn doors and sunlight poured in, warming him where he stood. He looked toward the cabin and spotted movement through a front window. A curl of smoke rose from the chimney. Someone was up.

He brushed bits of straw from his clothes. Turned out

McKenna—or rather, *Miss Ashford*, remembering her tone last night—was right. Vince Talbot had been about his size. The work-worn dungarees fit comfortably, as did the shirt, and took him back to younger days spent working the family ranch.

Wyatt surveyed his surroundings. It'd been dark last night and he hadn't been able to see much of the barn's interior. He'd agreed to meet Samuel Ramsey, his boss, this morning in Bixby to discuss the robberies. But he had a good hour before he needed to leave, and his natural curiosity got the best of him.

He inspected the two stalls, both in bad need of mucking out, then noticed the tools left in disarray on the workbench. A dark stain marred the surface. Something had been spilled—his guess would be saddle oil—and cleaned up none too well. He knew better than to attribute that to Vince Talbot. Robert was the first one who came to mind.

He walked out back where a pile of fresh-cut pine lay scattered, needing to be chopped and stacked. Three cords, at least. It being summer, the horses were loose in the corral adjacent to the barn. Doc Foster's gray mare was among them, which meant the doctor had stayed the night. Wyatt hoped Robert was faring better this morning and that the boy had learned something from last night's brawl.

His focus went to a portion of fencing along the corral that needed mending, as well as the sagging gate. Last night he'd noticed the handle on the front door was loose too, and a couple of boards on the porch stairs had given in spots. Work was never at a shortage on a homestead like this, and he didn't know how Miss Ashford and her brother were going to make a go of the place. Not by themselves, anyway.

He grabbed a bale of hay in each hand and loaded the feed bins, then emptied the brackish water from the troughs and filled them with fresh water from the stream. Vince Talbot had chosen his land well, and the location of his barn and cabin too. Right where Wyatt would have built them.

The lonesome coo of a mourning dove drifted to him on the cool breeze, and he stood still, bucket in hand, and let the moment wash over him. This was his favorite time of day, when the world was just beginning to stir, when the air was cool and crisp, and the hours lay ahead pristine and yet to be written upon.

What he found surprising was the enjoyment he felt in doing this kind of work again. The satisfaction in living by your own hand and in seeing the product of your labors lent him a sense of purpose he hadn't felt in a long time. He walked back inside the barn and lifted the pitchfork from its hook, then dragged a work cart to the edge of the first stall and soon found his rhythm. He'd been mucking stalls since he was about Emma's age, his father had seen to that.

A short while later, when the wound on the back of his head started pounding, Wyatt slowed a mite. But he knew the ache in his head wasn't half as bad as the one Robert would be nursing this morning, that was for sure. Finished cleaning the first stall, Wyatt scattered fresh straw over the floor and moved to the second.

Something McKenna said to him last night still weighed heavy on his mind. About the men he took into custody . . . *just so they can be hanged.*

He sank the pitchfork into a pile of soiled straw, tossed it into the cart, and repeated the motion. He'd always considered his role as a U.S. Marshal to be one that helped society—what little of society there was out West. And he figured being a marshal did contribute to that, certainly made things more civil for the law-abiding folks. But when it came right down to it, her implication was right. He wasn't making much of a difference in the lives of those men he took into custody. Unless you counted helping them to their deaths as doing something worthwhile, which he—

The steel tines of the pitchfork hit something solid beneath the straw in the corner.

He poked at the object and leaned down to see what it was. He pulled out a bottle of whiskey. Half empty.

He knelt and turned the bottle over in his hand, thinking again of what McKenna had told him about their mother and father. She'd asked if her telling him all that had made things clearer for him. And it had. Only not in the way she'd probably meant for it to.

McKenna Ashford was a good-hearted woman, trying to make up for the love and guidance her younger brother had never received. Trying to make sure he had the opportunities any young man deserved. But in doing that, she was making excuses for him, shielding him from bearing the consequences of his actions. And in the end, her actions were going to have the exact opposite outcome of what she desired. They already were . . .

Knowing about their parents shed some light for him on Robert's poor choices, but it didn't excuse them. When a man was born, he got dealt a certain hand right off, and he had to play that hand, whether good or bad. He'd sampled enough of people's lives—and hands of poker—to see those born into a royal flush throw it all away. While those given a meager two pair ended up with a life most people would've traded their eyeteeth for. It wasn't the hand a person was dealt that determined the outcome—it was the person holding the cards who made the difference. And he'd laid his cards down long ago. At the foot of the cross.

Wyatt stared at the bottle in his hands, at the amber-colored liquid . . . *God, would You do something to turn that boy around before it's too late? Love him, Lord—*hard*—like You did me at that age.*

The crunch of boots on straw brought his head up, and he peered through slats in the stall to see McKenna. He hid the bottle back in the straw—she didn't need to deal with that this morning—and slowly stood, as much for the sake of the gash on his head as to not scare her.

"Morning, Miss Ashford."

She stopped short. "Marshal Caradon!" She let out a breath. "You startled me. I thought you'd be gone by now."

Why was this woman always trying to get rid of him? "No ma'am." Smiling, he raised an apologetic brow. "I'm still here."

He walked from the stall, aware of the way she was looking at him—good and long, full up and down—and he couldn't help but hope she liked what she was seeing, at least a little. He certainly liked what he was looking at.

Her long brown hair fell about her shoulders, curly and loose, like it had last night. Her skirt and shirtwaist were simple homespun, yet somehow took on a fancier appearance with her giving them shape. She had a strength about her that was compelling and impossible to miss. Yet if you looked closely enough—if she let you that close—the woman had a vulnerable side too. One she worked to keep hidden behind that wall she kept up. She'd never believe it if he told her, but it was that vulnerability that he found most attractive.

He ran a hand over his shirt. "Thank you again for the clothes. I'll be sure to launder them and get them back."

"No need." She made a waving gesture, her tone nonchalant. "If you can use them, keep them. After all, you were very . . ." Her lips firmed. She looked away.

Whatever she was thinking of saying next apparently wasn't coming easily for her. Either that or she didn't want to say it, which made him hope even more that she would.

"You were very kind to my cousin, Marshal. And I think Janie would want you to have the clothes as"—her voice softened a degree—"a token of her thanks for the kindness you showed her. And her son," she whispered, peering at the dirt floor.

It was her first mention of the promise he'd kept to Janie since the day of Janie's funeral. That she now considered it a *kind* act was surprising to him. "I appreciate that, ma'am, very much." Movement caught his eye through the open barn doors behind her, and he saw Doc Foster step from the cabin and onto the porch. The man yawned and stretched, not looking their way. "What does the doc say about Robert?"

"That he's got a slight concussion and some bruised ribs, in addition to a handful of cuts that needed stitching. Dr. Foster prescribed several days of bed rest." Her gaze grew somber. "But Robert will heal, given time. I'm paying Casey Trenton a visit this morning to speak with him about Robert keeping his job. With the beating my brother took"—her tone turned accusing—"he'll be laid up for a while. Mr. Trenton has work waiting to be done, which—I'm fairly sure—means Robert will lose his job."

And if that happened, she would clearly lay the blame at his feet. Wyatt heard that loud and clear. "I'm sorry to hear that, ma'am." For two reasons. First, that she was going to make the petition on behalf of her brother. And second, that Robert would most likely lose his job. He imagined Robert's income—what little he didn't gamble away—helped keep the ranch afloat. He doubted she realized how close Trenton had already come to firing the boy. "I wish I could do something more to help your brother, ma'am." The hard glint in her eyes told him he'd misspoken.

"Why thank you, Marshal Caradon." False gentility edged her voice. "That's such a comfort. Now if you'll excuse me, I've got work to do." She crossed to the far wall and hefted a bale of hay with more ease than a woman should. Or should have to.

"I've already fed and watered the horses, ma'am. I'm about done mucking out the stalls too, and thought I'd see to the milk cow before I go, if that's all right with you."

Her back to him, she dropped the bale. Dust and dirt plumed. "Actually, I think you've already done enough." She bowed her head, her hands clenching and unclenching at her sides. "I would prefer that you just go."

If she'd yelled the words, it would've lessened their sting. As it was, Wyatt felt the knife enter his gut and twist.

Maybe he should confide in her about his assignment from the Marshals Office. Surely she would understand then. If she gave her word not to say anything to anyone, he could tell her why he'd been in Severance last night and why, on top of wanting Robert to learn a lesson, he hadn't intervened sooner.

Then thoughts of Charlie Boyd and Frank Williams crowded close—the two marshals killed in the recent Brinks robberies—and he knew better. The Marshals Office had assigned him to this case largely due to the fact that he kept a low profile, because of his anonymity. If he lost that advantage, even more innocent lives could be lost.

"Yes, ma'am, I'll go," he whispered, knowing what he needed to do, but still wrestling with what he wished he could do.

McKenna turned, anger awash in unshed tears. "He's only a boy . . ." She took a stuttered breath. "How could you just stand there and let them do that to him?"

No way could he win this fight, yet he couldn't tuck tail and run either. She needed to know the thin line Robert was walking, and how she was contributing to that, even with the best of intentions. "With all due respect, ma'am, Robert may be young, but he's hardly a boy anymore."

"He's only fourteen!" Her voice rose.

"He's old enough to know when to keep his mouth shut. And he's big enough for someone else to shut it for him, if he won't."

She stepped closer. "I *love* my brother, Marshal Caradon, very much. And because I love him, I could never stand by—without feeling, without conscience—and watch him be battered like that! And God help me . . ." Her lips trembled. "I don't understand how you could."

He winced at the callousness she attributed to him. He wanted to touch her, to somehow soften what he was about to say, but she looked of the mind to slap him if he tried, so he curbed that desire. "I think, ma'am, the reason you don't understand is because we have different definitions of what it means to love."

Her mouth fell open. If someone walked in on them now, they would assume he'd just struck her, and they would be half right. Seeing her pain, Wyatt wished he could take back the words, however much he thought they were true.

"Well . . ." She stared. "If your definition of love is to cast someone aside and give up all hope on them, then I wish to have nothing to do with it. And I don't want you near Robert either. He needs someone who's going to be for him, not against him."

"He needs someone, ma'am, who's going to let him stand or fall on his own merit. It'll be good for him." He hesitated, then realizing he'd gone this far, plunged in with both feet. "And about you going to talk to Trenton about his job this morning . . ." He shook his head. "You can't be coming to the boy's rescue every time he gets into trouble."

"Coming to his rescue? That's what you think I'm doing?" Her face flushed crimson. "If that's what you're thinking, then apparently you've never loved someone. You've never cared for someone so deeply that you would give your very life if you could—" She swiped at the tears on her cheeks as if angry they'd fallen. "If you could just keep them from going through any more pain. If you could give them what they should've been given from the very start. I was nine years old when Robert was born. I gained a baby brother and lost a mother in the very same day. My father left everything about raising Robert to me. Do you have any idea how frightening that was? He not only didn't hold Robert, after she died . . ." She took a halting breath. "He never held me again either. Never touched me. I used to stand close and pass him tools in the livery, just so our fingers would brush. I just wanted to touch him."

She licked her lips, and Wyatt could almost taste the salt of her tears on his own tongue. His throat ached with emotion. He stepped closer, but she retreated.

"Miss Ashford, believe me when I say that I'm sorry for all you and your brother have been through. It wasn't my intention to add to your hurt in any way. I'm only trying to—"

She held up a hand, not looking at him. "I think you should leave, Marshal Caradon." She nodded again, more confidently. "I *want* you to leave."

He fought the insane urge to wipe away her tears. Either that or shake her until she could see that his actions toward Robert *were* rooted in love. Just love of a different kind. "I'll go, Miss Ashford. But as far as never having cared for somebody so deeply, I do know what it's like to—"

"Mr. Wyatt!"

He turned and looked through the open barn doors. Emma was headed straight for him, her tiny legs pumping hard. Needing one of her hugs about now, he met her halfway and knelt and caught her in his arms. "Hey, little one! How are you?" Standing, he scooped her up with him and held her close, catching a whiff of maple syrup.

She pulled back and took his face in her hands, her fingers sticky. "You came to see me!"

He smiled and chucked her beneath her tiny chin. "I sure did."

"Marshal Caradon was just leaving, Emma." McKenna's voice was strained. "He has a very important job to do. Please say good-bye to him now, so he can be on his way."

Wyatt peered up. Anger and finality darkened McKenna's eyes.

Emma's smile fell. "But you just got here! I don't want you to go."

"I'm sorry, little one." Wyatt brushed the pinkish hue of her cheek, realizing how badly he didn't want to leave. But this wasn't his family. This wasn't his homestead. And no matter his feelings, he had no claim to anything—he looked up at McKenna—or anyone, here.

He kissed the top of Emma's head, and she grabbed hold around his neck and wouldn't let go.

"I wanna go to dinner with you," she said, crying. "Clara does too."

"Well . . . maybe—" He found it impossible to swallow. "Sometime when I'm back through here, you and me and Clara can go."

She cried harder and held on tighter.

He pried Emma's arms from his neck and handed her to McKenna, who took her—still crying and reaching out for him—back into the house. McKenna closed the door behind them, but Emma's wails breached the walls of the cabin.

He walked back into the barn and saddled up Whiskey, then started down the road without a backward glance. At the far end, just before the curve, he paused, and took one final look. Then raised a hand in farewell, hoping McKenna was watching. But knowing she wasn't.

Wyatt got to Bixby a half hour late, distracted and at odds with himself. Samuel Ramsey, his boss, was already waiting at the restaurant. They ordered breakfast and launched into a discussion of the Brinks' robberies. Ramsey relayed what new details they had while soliciting Wyatt's ideas on how to proceed.

Wyatt kept having to pull his thoughts back to the conversation at hand, his mind repeatedly wandering to the one he'd just left.

"Marshal Caradon?" Ramsey asked at one point.

Wyatt blinked. "Yes, sir." Had Ramsey asked him another question? He sighed. "I'm sorry, sir. Would you repeat that, please?"

"Listen, Caradon, this is a sensitive case. Brinks is a powerful man and has close connections with President Hayes. We can't afford for this investigation to be compromised in any way. If you don't think you can handle it, then—"

"I can do it, sir. I give you my word. My mind wandered there for a minute. It won't happen again."

Wyatt listened, committing to memory every detail Ramsey told him. The burden to find the men responsible for these crimes deepened, as did his awareness of how much the Marshals Office was depending on him. Thirteen people had been killed in the stagecoach robberies so far—two of his fellow marshals, nine men who'd been driving or riding shotgun on the stages, and two female passersby who'd been caught in the crossfire.

Everything Ramsey said to him confirmed that he'd been right not to tell McKenna about this assignment.

Ramsey took another sip of coffee. "We got a lead from the sheriff over in Timber Ridge this week that really helped us out."

"James McPherson?" Wyatt asked.

Ramsey nodded. "You know him?"

"Sure do. He's a good man. Met him when I was back through a year or so ago. He'd make a good marshal."

"I already tried. He said no." Ramsey stood and slipped some bills from his pocket. "He actually reminds me a lot of you." He laid the money atop the receipt their waitress had left. "You're one of our best, Caradon. We chose you for this case because you follow orders. Because you're thorough, levelheaded, and you've never come back without your man."

Wyatt nodded once. "Thank you, sir."

"This case could take weeks or months. We'll meet again in a few days, see what you've found."

Wyatt rose and shook his hand. "I appreciate your confidence, sir. And that of the Marshals Office."

"When you identify the men behind all this, Caradon, we'll send others to bring them in. We'd rather keep your affiliation with the Marshal's Office as quiet as we can." Ramsey smiled.

"We prize your subversive persistence—working in our favor, of course."

Wyatt sat there long after Ramsey left, but his mind was no longer on the assignment facing him. It was on a woman—a stubborn, independent, headstrong, opinionated, beautiful, loving, caring, capable, well-meaning woman. A woman worth fighting for.

Even if it meant fighting against her first.

TWENTY-SEVEN

What if I offer to fill in for Robert? Just until he's well again?" McKenna read skepticism in Casey Trenton's expression and knew he wasn't favorable to the idea. Nor had she expected him to be. This wasn't the best time to talk to him either. Noon hour at the livery was busy. Customers kept coming in and out, and Trenton was flooded with work. But she needed to get this settled.

Mr. Billings's letter was foremost in her mind and told her that the bank was readying the foreclosure. Her ability to keep the ranch depended on the income Robert made from working at the livery, and he needed to have something constructive to do with his time once he got well enough to work again. Instead of gambling his time and money away in saloons. Dr. Foster had agreed to stay with him until she returned. She owed that dear man a fortune in physician fees, and yet he'd charged her nothing. "I'll come in at night, Mr. Trenton, after hours. No one will even see me, I promise."

"Aunt Kenny?"

She rubbed Emma's back. "Just a minute, sweetheart."

"But Aunt Kenny, I really need to—"

"Just a moment, Emma," she said, using a more authoritative tone.

Emma quietly nodded and looked down.

Using a pair of long-handled tongs, Trenton retrieved a horseshoe from the white-hot coals of the forge and positioned the shoe on the anvil. McKenna took a step back, shielding Emma behind her. He brought the mallet down—once, twice—and sparks flew. With every couple of blows, he stopped and studied the horseshoe, then begin pounding again. Finally, apparently satisfied with the results, he plunged the horseshoe into a bucket of water. Steam rose with a hiss.

He tugged a handkerchief from his back pocket and wiped the sweat from his brow. "So you're telling me you can build wagons now too, ma'am? At night? All by yourself?"

"Well . . ." McKenna forced a soft laugh. "No, of course not. But I can follow someone's measurements and I can cut and size boards to fit, so when Robert returns—in only a week, two at the most, Dr. Foster said—he'll have everything ready to build a new wagon." Mr. Trenton started shaking his head and she rushed to continue. "I can shoe a horse. I can clean and organize your tools. I can service the forge." She pointed to the stone furnace to accentuate her point. "And we both know it needs cleaning."

Flames from the forge bolstered the noonday heat, and McKenna felt herself start to perspire. "Mr. Trenton, I can muck out stables, sir. And I'll—"

He turned to her, his bushy brows nearly meeting in the middle. "And just when do you think you're gonna do all this, ma'am? Before or after"—he glanced around the shop—"you make good on all those saddles we've got orders for?" His gaze dropped to Emma. "Not to mention take care of your little one there."

Little one . . .

Emotion burned McKenna's eyes. That's what Caradon called

Emma. She firmed her jaw until the temptation to cry had passed. She'd done enough of that on the way here this morning.

She'd been so angry with Wyatt Caradon she could've spit nails. But as deep as her anger burned, her hurt and disappointment cut a far deeper gash. She'd wanted to trust him. She'd already made the mistake of trusting him . . . And then he'd accused her of not loving Robert! How could he even think something like that? And this after she'd confided in him about all she and Robert had been through as children, all Robert had endured, all she'd sacrificed—and still, he would say something so awful to her.

She studied her hands knotted at her waist. She was glad he was gone. She only wished she could silence that tiny part inside of her that, for some reason, kept wishing he were still here. Seeing how he'd held Emma and how tender he could be, she'd wanted to find a reason to trust him. So he could stay. So he could be the man she'd begun to believe he was. But if last night was any indication of how Wyatt Caradon would "help" Robert if he were around, then they truly were better off without him. Emma included.

With effort, McKenna pulled her focus back to the purpose of this visit. Rehashing the past never did any good, and it wouldn't help her save Robert's job.

"Aunt Kenny?" Emma's voice sounded much smaller this time.

McKenna held up a forefinger. "One more minute, Emma, and then we'll go." Waiting for the last customer to leave, she dared broach the subject with Mr. Trenton one last time. "My brother needs this job, sir. I know you're aware of some of the . . . challenges Robert's personality can present. But he's a good boy, and a fine wagonsmith, and I promise you he won't be late again. From now on, I'll see to it that he gets up on time and gets in here as he should. And stays until his work is completed."

Trenton's brow furrowed. "That's a mighty tall order, ma'am."

"I beg your pardon?"

He rolled his shoulders while massaging one side of his neck. "I mean that's a tall order . . . guaranteeing another person's word. I have a hard enough time keeping my own, much less somebody else's."

His voice held kindness, and yet McKenna felt a hidden barb. She couldn't help but think of what Wyatt Caradon had said to her that morning—about rescuing Robert—which made Trenton's statement sting all the more. But she knew from experience that some people simply couldn't understand, because they'd never loved someone the way she loved Robert, and had quickly come to love Emma.

"If you'll only give me a chance to make this work, sir, I promise you I'll work hard. And Robert will be well before we know it."

"You're about as persistent a woman as they come, ma'am. And a right talented one, too. But you know how I feel about women working in a livery. It's not right in my book. I think Robert's a fine young man with a lot ahead of him—if he can get himself straightened out. But he hasn't worked out well here. I'm sorry, ma'am. I've had customers complain, sayin' he was rude to them. Or that he acted like it was interruptin' his work to stop and help them." He shook his head. "Without customers, ma'am, I ain't got nothin'. You understand that, I know."

He picked up the charred tongs and reached for another horseshoe buried deep in the fire of the forge, yet it was McKenna who felt burned. Not at Trenton's hand, but by Robert's. No matter what opportunity she tried to set in place for her brother, he always seemed to come behind her and set it aflame. And she was growing tired of sweeping up the ashes.

She took Emma's hand and guided the child around the forge.

"Miss Ashford?"

She turned back.

Trenton wiped a hand on his apron, leaving a char-colored stain. "I realize I might've just talked myself out of working with the finest saddle maker in all of Colorado." His smile held uncertainty. "But I sure hope I haven't."

"Our agreement hasn't changed, Mr. Trenton. I gave you my word. And I'll make good on it." Even if she couldn't make good on Robert's.

Holding tight to Emma's hand, McKenna maneuvered a path down the crowded boardwalk. She'd known the probability of Mr. Trenton accepting her proposition had been slim. But still, she'd hoped. And now she didn't even want to imagine what might happen next.

Emma started to lag behind.

McKenna tugged on her hand. "Come on, honey. Keep up, please!" They cut across the street to avoid passing by the bank. She did *not* want to see Mr. Billings today. *Posthaste*, or otherwise. She glanced at Emma—whose head was bowed—thinking she heard the child say something. But she couldn't be sure with the rumble of wagons and blur of conversation around them. Emma probably wanted a treat. Again. And they didn't have money for that today, nor would they anytime in the near future.

Emma's steps grew increasingly lethargic.

"Please, Emma, try and keep up, sweetie! I'm in a hurr—" Looking down again, McKenna saw huge tears slipping down Emma's cheeks. She slowed, squeezing her hand. "Emma, what's wrong, honey?"

Emma shook her head and wouldn't look up.

McKenna negotiated a path to the edge of the boardwalk and knelt. "Tell me what's wrong, sweetie, and I'll try to fix it."

The little girl's shoulders began to shake. "I'm—s-sorry, Aunt Kenny. I-I didn't mean to." She hiccupped a stuttered breath.

McKenna brushed the hair from her face. "You didn't mean to do what?"

Emma cried harder—shuddering, pitiful sobs.

McKenna gathered her in her arms and stood. "If you'll only tell me what's wrong, then maybe I can—" She felt the dampness on her arm, soaking through Emma's dress, and slowly realized what had happened. "Oh, Emma, how could you—?"

Emma buried her face in the curve of McKenna's neck and wept. "I didn't mean to do it, Kenny."

Her voice came out muffled and warm against McKenna's skin, and it dawned on McKenna that the child had tried to tell her. Repeatedly.

Holding Emma tight, she stepped into the alley behind the mercantile, her own tears coming, and knelt. "You tried to tell me, didn't you, sweetie?"

Emma's head bobbed up and down, and McKenna closed her eyes, loathing the image of herself at that moment. *Oh God, how could I be so selfish?*

"Shh . . . shh . . . it's all right, honey. We'll get you cleaned up. This isn't your fault. It's mine. It's my fault." How could she have been so inattentive? So oblivious? "You were trying to tell me and I didn't listen. It's me who needs to apologize to you. And I'm so sorry, Emma."

She tried to coax the girl's head up, but Emma refused. McKenna hugged her tighter, the blatant truth of her own self-centeredness leaving her stark and naked, without excuse. If those who'd gone on before could somehow glimpse their loved ones they'd left behind, McKenna prayed that God would shield her selfishness from the purity and goodness of Janie's heart.

"Will you please look at me, Emma?"

Emma shook her head again.

Using the wall behind her for support, McKenna stood slowly, guilt weighing her down far more than the precious child in her arms. "We'll go on home and get you washed up, all right?"

Emma nodded, sniffing. And as they walked back to the wagon, McKenna felt Emma's ragged breath grow gradually calmer. They were nearly out of town when she heard her name being called. Thinking she recognized the man's voice, she attempted to act as if she hadn't heard him. But he proved persistent.

"Aunt Kenny . . ." Emma pivoted on the wagon seat and peered behind them. "I think that man wants you."

"Miss Ashford! Please, ma'am. I must speak with you!"

Realizing it was futile, McKenna brought the wagon to a stop as Mr. Billings caught up with them.

"Miss Ashford!" The bank manager approached her side of the wagon, hat in hand and short of breath. "I was . . . afraid you didn't hear me, ma'am. Did you receive the letter I couriered to your residence yesterday?"

Couriered to my residence? "Yes, Mr. Billings, I did. And I had hoped to meet with you today, but—" She gestured toward Emma. "As it happens, Emma isn't feeling well and we're headed home. I'm so sorry. But I'll be back in—"

"Miss Ashford, it is imperative that we speak today." He stepped closer. "News of the greatest import arrived in my office late yesterday afternoon."

McKenna had been through this process with a banker before. "News of the greatest import" likely meant that the foreclosure papers had arrived from Denver and Billings was ready to officially serve notice. "Mr. Billings, if this is about"—she lowered her voice—"the foreclosure, then please, may we meet about it in your office in the morning? I'll be there first thing, I promise. *Posthaste*," she added, lifting the reins.

"I must insist, Miss Ashford!"

Emma scooted closer, and McKenna covered her hand. "There's no call to raise your voice, sir."

He firmed his jaw. "This is about the foreclosure, yes . . ." His tone held an urgency it hadn't before. "But not in the way you're thinking."

McKenna huffed, weary of his formality and of the power men like him wielded over others. "Then why don't you tell me what it *is* about?"

"All right, ma'am. I will." He reached up and straightened his tie. "When we first met, I inquired about Vince and Janie Talbot having other living relatives, and you answered that they had none. Do you recall that?"

McKenna nodded once. "Of course, I do."

"So tell me, ma'am. Why was there a man claiming to be Vince Talbot's brother sitting in my office yesterday? With a letter stating that he is to inherit *your* ranch?"

TWENTY-EIGHT

You must be mistaken, Mr. Billings. Vince Talbot didn't have a brother. My cousin would've told me if he had!" Seated in the banker's office, McKenna stared at Billings across his desk. It felt as if someone had shaken her world hard and plunked it back down off kilter.

At Mr. Billings's insistence, she'd agreed to meet with him at his office. But first, she'd taken a chance on Mei being at home. When Mei had answered her door, McKenna relayed as best she could—pantomiming throughout—what had happened with Emma, and also that she needed for Mei to watch her for a short time. Mei's repeated nods and flutter of singsong Cantonese indicated she understood. After McKenna cleaned up Emma in Mei's water closet, Mei motioned her on, saying something about a moon cake to Emma—who was all smiles and waves as the door had closed.

McKenna struggled to temper her accusing tone. "Vince Talbot's parents died a year before he and Janie got married. I don't know who this man is who came to see you, but I can guarantee you he's not Vince's brother. Vince had no siblings. I'm certain of that."

Mr. Billings sat across from her, quiet and reserved, hands folded atop his desk. "I know this has come as a shock to you, Miss Ashford. As it was to me, I assure you. I also realize that . . . due to your past experiences in Missouri, you are most likely predisposed to distrust me." The look in his eyes grew more intent. "And I cannot say that I blame you."

Far too late, McKenna tried to mask her surprise. "I—I'm not sure I know what you're referring to."

"On the contrary, Miss Ashford. I believe you do."

Her world slipped completely from its axis.

If Billings knew about what had happened back home, there was no possibility he'd give her a second chance at keeping this ranch. Whether the stranger claiming to be Vince's brother was authentic or not—and she knew he wasn't. He couldn't be—Billings was going to foreclose on her with lightning speed. He would have her and Emma and Robert off the ranch within two week's time, and gone would be her promise to Janie to take care of Emma as Janie had requested. So here, yet again, she stood to lose everything.

She forced herself to look at him again. "May I inquire as to how you learned this information?"

"The telegraph is revolutionizing the banking industry, Miss Ashford. The world is much smaller than it once was. The foreclosure of your grandparents' house in Missouri, the auction of your family's livery—those events and how they came about, will, of course, have bearing on your situation here. For me to give you any other impression would be misleading. However, I give you my word I'll be fair in my assessment."

McKenna lowered her eyes, feeling little comfort. *God, why are you putting me through this all over again?* She cleared her throat and reached for the glass of water Billings had poured for her when she first arrived. But her hand shook so badly, she tucked it back in her lap and let the water sit. "Most of the cattle are ready to take to market." It was a half-truth at best. She had no idea how many were ready. "I'll be able to make a sizeable payment then. Perhaps even a month or two in advance."

He inclined his head and smiled at her as though she were Emma's age. "We, meaning not only this bank but also the larger bank in Denver that owns us, consider our lenders carefully. In recent years, droves of people moved West thinking they'd find better lives. Most have, I think. Those willing to work hard." He laughed softly. "And those who don't mind numb toes from October to March."

McKenna didn't respond to his attempt at levity. Did he think he could humor her out of the dire straits in which she found herself?

"But our bank also loaned a great deal of money to people whose dreams didn't work out, due either to their lack of initiative or to circumstances beyond their control. Too many loans remain unpaid."

Melancholy layered the seconds.

McKenna sighed. "Which brings us full circle, doesn't it?"

"Yes, ma'am. I'm afraid it does."

The whinny of horses and the muffled clomp of hooves drifted through the open window from the street outside.

"The foreclosure papers arrived yesterday on the stage from Denver. I was going to hand deliver those to you yesterday, until the gentleman showed up in my office claiming to be Mr. Talbot's brother."

"What is the *gentleman's* name?"

"Mr. Harrison Talbot. He seems a nice enough fellow, younger than Vince Talbot by a few years, I'd guess. After I explained the situation to him, he requested to meet you."

McKenna shook her head. "What makes you think any of what he's saying is true? And even if it is, don't Mrs. Talbot's last wishes count for anything? You've spoken to Dr. Foster. He acted as witness on my behalf. You said so yourself."

He nodded. "Yes, yes, this is all very true. Unfortunately, in cases like this—as I mentioned to you during our initial meeting"—his brow rose as if punctuating the reminder—"when multiple living relatives are involved and no written will exists, awarding the inheritance can become tedious. However, it doesn't fall to me to make that final decision in this instance."

She waited. "To whom then does it fall?" she asked, matching his formality and loathing it.

"I wired the bank in Denver this morning and, as we speak, the request for a circuit judge who will travel to Copper Creek is being forwarded to the courthouse. It will fall to that judge to make the final decision. He'll speak with you at length while here, of course. As well as research the facts with utmost care."

McKenna felt as though she might be ill. When Billings stood, she followed suit.

"Would it be convenient for me to bring Mr. Talbot out to the homestead sometime tomorrow morning, ma'am? To meet you? And to see the ranch?"

No, it wouldn't. I don't want that man anywhere near there. She nodded. "Yes, that would be fine." She could hardly refuse under the circumstances.

Billings escorted her through the lobby to the front double doors. "Will the child be there as well? Mr. Talbot indicated an interest in seeing his niece."

McKenna's heart skipped a painful beat. "He wants to see Emma?"

"Yes, ma'am. He made a special inquiry to that end."

The questions bombarding McKenna's mind were almost too much to take in. What if Vince really did have a brother? What if he wanted Emma?

She offered a hasty good-bye and left the bank as swiftly as possible. On shaky legs, she climbed into the wagon and, minutes later, found herself at Mei's, not remembering how she'd gotten there. *What if this man wants Emma?*

Numb, she knocked on Mei's door. Mei answered with Emma holding her hand—both of them smiling—and McKenna hugged the child extra long. She politely declined Mei's invitation to stay for dinner, and they set up a time for another of their lessons that week. Emma chattered the entire way home, and though McKenna pretended to be listening, she barely heard a word Emma said.

Thanking Dr. Foster for staying with Robert, she also promised to reward him for his kindness, and knew just how she would do that.

After Dr. Foster left, she finished the chores, made dinner, and saw to Robert's and Emma's needs before finally crawling beneath the cold bed sheets well after dark. She thought she'd known what desperation felt like. To feel so fragile inside that the slightest bump would break her into thousands of tiny shards. But this pain went far deeper. She reached for the pillow beside her and hugged it tight against her chest, letting it muffle her cries.

Some time later, she awakened to pale fingers of sunlight stretching through the curtains billowing in the breeze. Turning onto her side, she caught the scent of the lavendar Vince had planted for Janie beneath the window and was reminded of the morning Janie had died. It felt like a lifetime ago.

A rooster crowed and McKenna pushed herself from bed, knowing there was more work to do today than she could do in a week. Slipping into her robe, she hesitated, her gaze involuntarily going to the end of the bed.

The night before Janie died, Janie had seen something—or Someone—in that same space. Believing it was God's presence her cousin had seen, McKenna wished she could see Him now. And she envied Janie being in His presence.

Something compelled her to crawl from bed and sink to her knees beside the bed. Unsettled by the uncustomary prompting, she bowed her head.

It wasn't that she didn't pray. She prayed often enough. But she couldn't remember the last time she'd been on her knees before Him. Her heart was overflowing with requests and petitions and pleas, and they all came out in a jumble, one atop the other, and with such desperation that she wasn't sure where one started and the next began.

After a while, with her knees aching on the cold wooden floor, she lifted her head, hoping . . .

She sighed, halfway smiling. The space at the end of the bed was empty. Had she really expected Jesus to appear? To grant her prayers so fully? So quickly?

She found Robert asleep on the couch where she'd left him, his soft snores hinting at a peacefulness she knew was absent from his life. She opened Emma's door and crept to her bedside, careful not to make the loose plank squeak. She covered the girl back up and kissed her hair. So precious . . .

The water in the coffee kettle was nearly boiling when she heard something outside. She peered through the curtain and saw nothing. Surely it was too early for Mr. Billings and that man to—

A knock sounded on the door.

It couldn't be! She glanced at Robert to see if he'd awakened, but the laudanum she'd administered to him before bed was working overtime. She pulled the coffeepot to the side of the stove so it wouldn't boil over. She ought to have known Billings would show up at the crack of dawn. He'd already proven his timing to be atrocious.

She hurried to the door, cinching her robe, smoothing her hair, and asking God to guide her conversation with the man claiming to be Vince's brother—whoever he was. She opened the door.

"Good morn—" She frowned, unable to explain the tiny spark of irritation, but even greater sparks of joy, she felt. "What are you doing here?"

"Good morning, Miss Ashford. It's nice to see you again too, ma'am." With a wry smile, Wyatt Caradon tipped his hat and held up the ragged-looking advertisement she'd posted at the mercantile weeks ago. "I'm here in answer to your notice, ma'am. I'm hoping you can still use a ranch hand."

TWENTY-NINE

Smelling the aroma of freshly brewed coffee, Wyatt was relieved to know he hadn't gotten McKenna straight out of bed. But he didn't think she'd been up long. She still had that just-awakened look about her, a softness that made him wish he'd earned the privilege of touching her face, of tracing a feather-soft path from the curl at her temple down the smooth plane of her cheek. His gaze went to the modest opening at her neckline . . . Remembering the tender passion found only in a woman's arms didn't help his train of thought.

With deliberate intent, he looked away and focused on the piece of paper in his hands. "I hope the position's still open, ma'am."

She stared as though uncertain whether or not he was serious. Or perhaps she was still angry with him. Highly likely with the way things had been left between them.

He shifted beneath her attention, the same schoolboy awkwardness overtaking him as when he'd invited her and Emma to dinner. "I've had experience with this kind of work." He tried throwing in another smile. "And I can provide references, if needed."

Her frown lessened a fraction. "References?" She gave a half-smile and leaned against the doorframe, sizing him up. "Don't tell me you've turned in your badge and decided to settle for a dullard's life on the farm?"

Her sarcasm was gentle—more probing than pointed—and he relaxed a mite, taking no offense in it. "No ma'am, I'm still with the Marshals Office." He edged back his vest to reveal the badge beneath, pinned to his shirt. "They've got me working out of Copper Creek for a while, so I'll be around." He indicated the barn with a nod. "I had such fun mucking out your stalls . . ." He shrugged. "Thought I might try doing it on a regular basis."

She eyed him, the subtle shake of her head saying she wasn't buying it. But that's all he was giving her. For now, at least.

Meeting with Ramsey to discuss the details of this case had confirmed something Wyatt had hoped—that he'd have a few hours each morning to help out here. It'd push him, for sure, what with spending late night hours scouting one gambling house to the next. But considering the woman in front of him, she was worth it. He wanted to make a difference in her life and prove to her that not every man would up and leave when things got rough.

"So tell me, Marshal . . . do you have those references of yours handy?"

She had the upper hand, and she knew it. And he didn't mind in the least.

Feigning a pained expression, Wyatt slipped off his hat and ran a hand through his hair, feeling a film of road dust. "That all depends on your definition of *handy*, ma'am."

She laughed and a sparkle lit her eyes, then just as quickly extinguished. "You know the pay I advertised, Marshal Caradon. I can't afford much. Actually . . ." She shook her head and looked away. "Until I get the cattle sold at market, I can't pay you a single penny. So if it's extra money you're looking to earn, then—"

"No, ma'am, I'm not doing this for the money." He didn't plan on taking one red cent from this woman, but he knew her well enough to know that if he said that now, she'd send him packing.

She had a streak of pride in her, but it wasn't one of vanity. It was the kind of pride that made it difficult for her to accept help, that made her always want to be in control. Or at least give that appearance. It was a pride he understood and had wrestled with most of his life. But time had a way of flattening out a man's pride. Not that a man ever lost it entirely. No fellow he knew, anyway. It just seemed that, with time, a man became more aware of that pride—of what it had cost him—and he learned to view life despite it, instead of through it.

He let the silence draw out, enjoying the suspicion creeping into her face, followed by open curiosity.

"Just why are you applying for this job, Marshal? It's not for the money. And it's certainly not for the excitement."

How honest should he be? Seeing her eyes narrow ever so slightly, he decided to chance a slice of truth. "Ever since you moved to Copper Creek, ma'am, and even before that," he added more softly, "you've been dealt a difficult hand. I'd just like to help out, if I can. Ease a little of the burden. For however long I'm around." Which he hoped was for a long while.

She opened her mouth like she was going to say something. Then hesitated, as if she might regret it if she did. "I can certainly use the help. But the only accommodations I can offer are in the barn."

"I've sampled those already, and they're more than satisfactory. This'll be a nice change from the boardinghouse."

"You're welcome to take meals with us, but I can't promise they'll be as tasty as the ones you get in town."

"I'm fine with that."

"And my bread never rises."

He curbed a grin, seeing she was serious. "I'm fine with that too, ma'am. I make fairly good biscuits when called on to do it."

She nodded, as though considering that. "All right then." She gave an airy laugh that sounded more like a young girl than a grown woman. "Would you care to come inside for a cup of coffee?"

If not mistaken, he'd just been hired by Miss McKenna Ashford! The first woman boss he'd ever reported to.

"Thank you, ma'am. I would."

But despite her invitation, she didn't move. A puzzled look came over her face. Wyatt trailed her focus to Whiskey standing saddled by the porch.

"Is there a problem, ma'am?"

"No." She squinted. "No problem. I'm just wondering . . . where did you get that saddle?"

Now he understood. "You're not the first one who's asked. I bought it from Trenton at the livery. It's a real beauty, isn't it?"

She smiled. But slowly, as if hesitant to. "Yes, it is. And . . . it suits you."

"Thank you, ma'am. It's by far the finest saddle I've ever owned."

"Is that so?" she said, her smile deepening.

She opened the door wider and he stepped inside. Robert was asleep on the couch, and Emma's door was still closed. He hated to disturb the hush that lay over the house. When McKenna handed him his mug, he motioned toward the front porch. "Why don't we take our coffee outside?" he whispered.

"Good idea."

He held the door open for her. "I have those, on occasion."

"I hadn't noticed," she said, brushing by him, a fresh-poured cup of the steaming brew in hand.

Her smirk inspired his, and he followed her outside. He sat beside her on the porch steps and for several moments, they drank their coffee in silence. He didn't feel the need to nudge conversation, and apparently neither did she. His gaze scaled the mountains bordering the fields on either side, and as final vestiges of pinkish dawn surrendered to new day, gray mist that clung to the highest peaks evaporated before his eyes. Never would he tire of these mountains.

McKenna wrapped her hands around the mug. "I imagine it wasn't easy for you to come back here. Took a lot of courage."

Wyatt peered into his empty cup. "Maybe. Or maybe I just like being put in my place."

Her sigh came out part laugh, part huff. "I was so angry with you."

"Yes, ma'am . . . I know."

"And a part of me . . . still is."

He slowly nodded, respectful of that anger. But even more respectful of her—for admitting that to him. He looked over at her hands clasped loosely around her cup and wondered what it would feel like to have one of them fit snug into his. Her hands were small. Not delicate, but slim. Her fingers had strength to them, just like she did.

He felt her staring. "I don't want to start anything back up, believe me, ma'am, but . . . I do want to tell you that my saying all that yesterday wasn't done with any intention to hurt you."

She worried an edge of loose hem on her robe. "I know that . . . mostly." Her smile was weak. "But still . . . it did."

Words failed him. Close enough to see the flecks of gold in the soft umber of her eyes, he reached for her hand. She jumped like a skittish filly. But she didn't pull away. He held her hand in his, memorizing the feel of her soft skin, and of how her fingers gripped his, shyly at first. "I'm sorry," he whispered. "For hurting you." And he was.

He wasn't sorry for what he'd said, because he still believed he'd spoken the truth. He only wished they'd gotten along better from the very start—that day in Foster's clinic. Seems like no matter what he did, she was always letting him know his attention wasn't welcome. But watching her now, feeling her fingers threaded with his, he sensed that might be changing. And he intended on taking full advantage of every opportunity to win her trust.

If there was one thing he knew a little about, it was pursuing a person. And though he wasn't about to give the woman beside him fair warning, Miss Ashford had better be on her guard. Because he planned on doing everything in his power to win not only her trust, but her heart as well.

McKenna was tying the sash on Emma's dress when a knock sounded on the door.

"Is it the mean banker man?" Emma whispered, blue eyes wide.

If she weren't so nervous, McKenna might've smiled. And she would have corrected Emma if what the child had said weren't true. But Billings was not a kind man. "I'm sure it is." She adjusted the bowed sash. "Now remember what I told you."

Emma nodded. "Stay with Uncle Robert. And don't go outside."

McKenna brushed a kiss to her forehead. "That's exactly right." She caught a passing glimpse of herself in the mirror and smoothed the front of her dress. She could still feel the strength of Wyatt's hand as it had held hers. She hadn't meant to jump like she did, but it'd been so long since she'd been touched by a man. Tenderly, like that. And the way he'd looked at her . . . Heat spiraled from her chest down into her belly just thinking about it again.

She searched for him through the window. He'd said he was going to the lower field to check on the cattle, to see how many were ready for market. She still couldn't believe he'd come back. And his timing was . . . She sighed. Nothing short of answered prayer. And that he had her saddle! Her finest work yet. She'd wanted to tell him how much it meant that he owned that particular saddle, but her agreement with Casey Trenton to keep her employment secretive prohibited it. "*It's the finest saddle I've ever owned*," Caradon had said, pride shining in his eyes. And she would carry that light inside her for a long time to come.

A second knock sounded, and she hurried into the main room where Robert was lying on the couch.

"Somebody's at the door, Kenny!" he barked.

"*Robert* . . . I'm right here," she whispered, pointing. "And the windows are open." She headed for the door.

"I don't care who hears me!"

Her face flushed warm. Her brother was in rare form this morning. Part of her wanted to tell him the same thing she'd told Emma—to stay quiet and keep out of sight. But if she did, he'd be up off that couch in the space of a breath, despite Dr. Foster's orders for bed rest.

Hand on the latch, she inhaled, hoping she at least appeared relaxed.

She opened the door, and saw only Billings. "Mr. Billings . . ." She stepped outside and pulled the door closed behind her. "I thought you were—" Then she saw him. The man on the far end of the porch. His back was to her. Feet firmly planted, arms crossed over his chest, he looked out over the fields as though he were a king surveying a conquered kingdom. She bristled inside at his possessive posture.

"I hope you're well this morning, Miss Ashford." Mr. Billings wore a smile that seemed out of place.

I'm not, thanks to you. "I'm fine, Mr. Billings. Thank you." She stopped short of wishing him the same, waiting for the other man to look in her direction. Without question, he heard her. He had to. Yet he didn't turn.

Billings gestured with a flourish. "Mr. Talbot, shall I make the introductions?"

Only then did the man turn, and McKenna felt like she'd been gut-punched. She barely heard Billings' voice as he went through the formalities. She hadn't seen Vince Talbot since he and Janie married seven years earlier, but—she worked to regain her composure—the resemblance this man bore to her memory of Vince that day was uncanny.

"Miss Ashford," he said, tilting his head in greeting. "So nice to make your acquaintance, ma'am. And may I offer my condolences on the loss of your cousin—my sister-in-law, Janie," he added softly. "I also apologize for this rather abrupt, and what I'm sure is a disconcerting, visit."

He'd given her no reason for it, but already McKenna disliked him. Something in his demeanor set her on edge. While outwardly pleasant, shades of insincerity bordered his tone. "Pleasure to meet you, Mr. Talbot. Thank you for your condolences and may I return them . . . on behalf of . . . your brother." It nearly choked her to say it.

He briefly bowed his head. "Thank you, ma'am. I appreciate that."

A soft thud sounded from inside the cabin, and McKenna prayed it wasn't Robert about to join them. At the moment, she didn't care so much about him falling as him making his presence known. All she needed was for Billings to see her brother beaten and bruised, learn about what he'd done, and then portray her as an unfit guardian for Emma.

She hurried to fill the silence. "How long had it been since you'd last seen Vince, Mr. Talbot?" The question felt rude this early in conversation—and Billings's frown confirmed it was—but she didn't care.

Talbot sighed and ran a hand along the porch railing—*her* porch railing—as though it already belonged to him. She studied him, wanting to find fault, hoping for some frayed thread that would unravel this man who bore such a likeness to Vince.

"I hadn't seen Vince in . . . at least a year," he said. "Maybe a little longer. I remember because I was on my way to California last time I was through Copper Creek."

"California? What took you all the way out there?"

He smiled, and a single dimple framed the left curve of his mouth. Vince had been handsome, she remembered, but not like this man. Harrison Talbot was positively striking with his dark hair and dark eyes. *Swarthy* was a word that came to mind. As did arrogant.

"I've been traveling for years, ma'am, seeing the country, watching it grow."

McKenna nodded. In other words, he was a drifter. "And just what is your occupation, Mr. Talbot?"

He moved closer. "I've been many things in my life, Miss Ashford. Right now . . ." His smooth demeanor shed a layer of warmth. "I'm looking forward to doing some ranching."

She stiffened. "May I come directly to the point, Mr. Talbot?"

"You strike me as the kind of woman who would." There went that dimple again.

Heat shot through her veins. "I was with Janie Talbot when she died, and she named me as her inheritor. Witnesses were present. And I've been here ever since, working this ranch, and keeping the promises I made to her that night."

He stepped closer to the rail and pressed down on one of the boards with the tip of his boot. The slat gave easily beneath his weight. "I appreciate that, Miss Ashford. You've been doing a fine job." He took in a breath and let it out slowly. "I feel for the situation you're in. And I know this is difficult for you, having just moved from Missouri all the way out here to Copper Creek. And likely not welcoming the prospect of the long trip back."

Instinctively, McKenna clenched her fists. "There is no money you'd stand to inherit, Mr. Talbot. My cousin and her husband left this farm steeped in debt. As I'm sure Mr. Billings has told you . . ." She glanced at Billings, who stood a couple of feet away, silent, his expression attentive. "The mortgage on this property is currently entering foreclosure. My brother and I have both been working dutifully to make payments to the bank, and—"

Talbot raised his hand. "Mr. Billings briefed me on the situation, ma'am. However, I possess the means to pay off the mortgage, free and clear, so that won't be a problem for me."

McKenna slid her gaze back to Billings, who was suddenly preoccupied with his hands. A dozen questions shot through her mind. Had Billings gone out and found a buyer who would pay his price? And in cash, no less? She wouldn't put it past him. But how did he just happen to find someone who was a dead ringer for Vince Talbot? Even wanting to believe it, she had to admit the coincidence seemed a stretch.

Talbot surveyed the fields again, sighing. "This land meant a lot to my older brother, and I know he wanted to keep it in the family. Family meant a lot to Vince."

"Which makes it even odder that in all the years I knew Vince, he never once mentioned your name. He never even mentioned having a brother."

He glanced down at his boots. "Up until last year, it'd been years since we'd spoken. We had a bit of a falling out, you might say."

"Over what?"

A spark of challenge lit his eyes. "Oddly enough, it was when we were younger, before he met Janie. He wanted me to move out West with him and start a ranch." The hint of challenge faded. "And now I'd do just about anything if I could turn back those years and take him up on that offer."

McKenna was surprised her coffee stayed down. She snuck a glimpse at Billings, wondering if he was buying all this. The banker looked spellbound. And if she wasn't mistaken, his eyes were glistening. She'd had enough. Even if this man *was* Vince's brother—which, despite his uncanny resemblance, she doubted—Janie had bequeathed the ranch to her. Not him. And that should be what counted according to the law. She hoped. "Mr. Billings, have you heard from the circuit judge in Denver yet?"

"No, ma'am. But I only wired the courthouse yesterday. These things take time . . . as you well know."

Ignoring his last digging remark, she took a step toward the door. "Please let me know as soon as the date is set. Now if you two gentlemen will please excuse me, I've got work to do."

"One last thing," Mr. Billings said. "Would you mind if I show Mr. Talbot around? Just the outside buildings. I think it would be appropriate under the circumstances."

Not knowing what else to do, she nodded. "That would be fine."

Mr. Billings set off toward the barn. Talbot started to follow, then turned back.

"One more thing, Miss Ashford." His dark eyes flashed. "I'd like to say hello to my niece, if you don't mind. I'm sure Emma's grown a foot since I last saw her."

Hoping to have avoided this introduction, McKenna had a sudden thought. It was worth a try. "Of course, she's just inside. You know . . ." She smiled. "She bears a real likeness to you, Mr. Talbot."

He stared for a moment. "Really? How's that, ma'am?"

"Your coloring is so similar to hers. Just like her father's." Vince's hair had been dark, like his eyes. Like this man's standing before her. The exact *opposite* of Emma's. But Harrison Talbot wouldn't know that if he hadn't been here before. If he was only someone *pretending* to be related to Vince.

"I appreciate that, ma'am. Emma's a pretty little girl. But if memory serves right, and I believe it does—" His gaze took on a penetrating quality. "She shares her mother's coloring. Not my brother's. Or mine."

McKenna wasn't intimidated by him, but neither was she

completely unaffected. This man could well end up waltzing in and taking everything she'd worked so hard to keep for Emma's sake. And for her own. She returned his glare. "Wait here. I'll get her."

McKenna closed the door behind her and walked to Emma's room. Emma sat on the edge of her bed, holding Clara. "I need for you to say hello to someone, sweetie."

"That mean man who yelled at us?"

"No, it's not Mr. Billings, sweetie. It's another man. All you have to do is say hello."

Emma nodded and slipped down from the bed. "Can Clara go?"

"Of course, she can. And one more thing . . ." McKenna briefly glanced over her shoulder. "I want to play a little game. Just between you and me, okay?"

Emma giggled, nodding.

"When we go outside, I want you to hold my hand. Then I want you to look at the man you're going to meet and if you remember seeing him before, I want you to squeeze my hand really tight. Okay?"

Emma smiled, nodding again.

"Remember, only squeeze my hand if you remember seeing him before. All right?"

"All right, Aunt Kenny."

Harrison Talbot stood right where she'd left him.

McKenna hesitated a few seconds to see if Emma would show any sign of recognition or if she would greet him as *Uncle Harrison*. When Emma didn't, McKenna felt a sense of victory and gestured toward him, not about to introduce him with the endearment of uncle. In fact, best that she not influence Emma's decision with a name at all. In doing so, McKenna knew she was setting etiquette aside, but the situation warranted it. "Emma, this is a friend of Mr. Billings. And this"—she looked pointedly at Talbot—"is Emma."

He knelt to be closer to her height. "Hi there, Emma. How are you?"

Emma pulled back slightly, staring. Just as McKenna had thought she would.

"Emma," she coaxed gently. "Can you say hello, please?"

"Hello," Emma whispered, smiling and briefly ducking her head.

"Hello, Emma. It's nice to see you again."

McKenna waited, but Emma relayed no sign of having seen him before. Which likely meant that this man claiming to be Vince's brother had actually never visited here, as he'd stated. And that her earlier supposition was—

Emma squeezed her hand. *Hard.* Harder than McKenna thought a five-year-old capable of doing. And as Harrison Talbot took his leave and walked toward the barn where Billings stood waiting, McKenna pried Emma's hand from hers.

"Did I do good, Aunt Kenny?" Emma whispered.

"Yes, sweetie, you did very well," McKenna said, her heart clenching tight. "And do you remember where you saw him?"

Emma nodded, her smile blossoming. "Right here. At my house."

THIRTY

"Are you certain you've seen him here before, Emma?" McKenna asked after Billings and Talbot left.

Emma nodded and held on to McKenna's hand as they walked up the rock-strewn hill behind the cabin. McKenna often came up here when she needed to be alone or think things through, though the cool of evening was preferable to the late July sun beating down overhead.

"He and Papa walked outside. I 'member 'cuz I wanted to go. But Mama said no. That I had to help her with the biscuits. My mama made good biscuits, Kenny."

"Yes, honey, she sure did." McKenna gathered her skirt as she stepped over a rock. "But do you remember what that man was here for? Maybe something he said to your papa or mama?"

Emma's brow scrunched. "He liked my mama's biscuits. I 'member that."

He'd eaten a meal with them? Every instinct within her said the man was an imposter. But how could she prove that? When Billings left earlier that morning, he'd told her he would send word when the circuit judge contacted him. That was the next step. As she understood from his explanation, if the judge believed that Harrison Talbot was Vince's brother and therefore the legal heir, then Harrison Talbot would be awarded the ranch, and would have to pay the outstanding balance on the loan. Which, unfortunately, he could do. But if the judge disagreed, and upheld Janie's last wish, then McKenna would be awarded the ranch. At which time she'd be right back in the position of facing a foreclosure because she didn't have the money to pay.

She heaved a sigh as they crested the hill, not liking any of those possibilities. But one thing she was increasingly thankful for—she tightened her grip on Emma's hand—neither man had mentioned anything about getting custody of Emma, and she hadn't dared bring it up.

She breathed deep, her body still not fully adjusted to the high altitude. Emma, on the other hand, didn't seem bothered by it in the least.

"Can I pick some flowers for Mama?"

McKenna glanced at the graves not far away and nodded. "That'd be real sweet. She'd like that."

As Emma set about her task, McKenna cleared off the various offerings they'd left at the foot of the graves through past weeks—wilted Columbine, a dead beetle Emma had been sure her little brother would like, and a chunk of pyrite, fool's gold, as it was called, that Emma had found and wanted to give to her papa. But McKenna left the picture Emma had placed there beneath a rock. The etching was faded and the paper curled at the edges, but she could still make out the childish renderings of Vince, Janie, and baby Aaron "in heaven," as Emma had said. And they were all smiling.

Emma returned with an armful of wildflowers, most of them weeds, some with dirt still clinging to the roots, and she distributed them between the two graves. McKenna thought again of Janie cradling her precious baby boy and felt a rightness about it inside her.

They stayed for only a while—a world of work waited below—and as they walked downhill, McKenna saw Wyatt astride his horse beside the cabin. He cut a fine figure sitting there, broad shouldered, with his dark duster draping the horse's flanks. She couldn't be sure, with the tilt of his hat, but she thought he might be looking in their direction. She offered the tiniest wave and his arm immediately rose in response, which brought a smile.

But her smile faded when she saw him turn his mount and ride down the road toward town. He'd told her he'd be gone most afternoons and late into the night working for the Marshals Office. She didn't know what he did exactly, but seeing him ride away was a sobering reminder that his being here was only temporary. She flexed the fingers on her right hand, remembering his touch, and knowing she'd best not forget that.

That afternoon, she worked on her saddles and the hours passed quickly. Trenton had orders for seven now, and she decided to try something new by making parts for multiple saddles at once, instead of all the parts for one saddle. Today she braided edges to the skirts and carved her initials into the upper corners, as she did on all her saddles.

After dinner and evening chores were done—with Robert helping as little as possible, claiming he still needed bed rest, four days after the incident—McKenna couldn't help questioning Emma about Harrison Talbot one last time. "Maybe," she said, pulling up the covers and walking her fingers from Emma's tummy, to her chest, then to her chin where she tickled her, "you remember that man because he looks like your papa."

Emma didn't answer for a moment. "He looks like my papa?"

Confusion strained her small voice, making it sound even more so in the flickering flame of the oil lamp. Question riddled the child's eyes and McKenna regretted having brought the subject up again. "You know what? Never mind what I said."

She gently kissed Emma's tiny nose and tucked her in. "He isn't anything like your papa was."

Emma smiled and hugged Clara close.

As McKenna closed Emma's bedroom door behind her, Robert walked back inside the cabin. Seeing her, he suddenly stopped and reached for a nearby table. He limped back to the couch and heaved a sigh—a bit too much of one—and eased himself back down.

"Where have you been, Robert?"

"I just went out for some fresh air. Dr. Foster said to be sure and get up and move around a little, as long as I didn't overdo it." He shrugged. "I'm just following orders."

McKenna couldn't remember the last time her brother had followed anybody's orders. Suspicious, she moved closer, alert for the scent of liquor, but caught only that of mint.

He held out a leaf, his eyes brighter than they'd been all day. "I found it growing outside by the barn. Want some?"

"No. Thank you," she said, wondering where he'd hidden the bottle this time, but too weary to go out there and search for it. And too tired of fighting to confront him about it now. "I checked on the horses after dinner and didn't see Patch . . . Janie's horse, in the corral. Do you know where she is?"

Robert nodded. "I think I saw her in the lower field yesterday. Remember she got out that one time and I had to bring her back."

"Tomorrow, *if* you feel up to it . . . would you please go get her and bring her back up?"

"If I feel up to it, I sure will."

Not bothering to say good night, McKenna closed her bedroom door, shed her clothes, and slipped into her gown. She crawled into bed, barely conscious of her head touching the pillow.

Sometime later, she awakened, overly warm.

She kicked off the sheet and lay still, unmoving, in the darkness.

Oblique moonlight painted the bedroom with an otherworldly feel, and she felt the faint throb of her heartbeat pulse gently in the hollow of her throat. *Who was that man?* She'd been so sure Emma wouldn't recognize him. But after questioning the child, all doubt of that had been removed. Harrison Talbot, if that was his name, which she doubted, had been here to the homestead before. But for what purpose?

Unable to sleep, she got up and padded softly out to the main room. Robert was asleep on the couch. The clock on the mantle said it was half past two. She checked on Emma, then opened the front door just enough to slip outside but not enough to awaken the rusty hinges, and settled on the top porch step. She hugged her knees close to her chest. The barn was dark. She didn't know if Wyatt had returned or not.

The breeze off the mountains felt like silk against her skin. She gazed up at the stars flung wide across the canopy of night, and likened it to an upturned bowl of shimmering candles held balanced between the highest peaks. The Colorado Territory in all its colors was more beautiful than any picture she'd seen of it back home. But would it prove to be the saving grace she'd once thought?

The distant thud of horse hooves carried on the night air, and McKenna stood and moved farther back into the shadows of the porch. She kept an eye on the darkened road leading to the homestead. If it were daylight, she could have seen the rider. As it was, the horse's pace slowed a short distance down the road, and the rider's approach grew quieter.

The rifle was just inside, but Wyatt had told her he would be coming in late. She hadn't figured this late, but reasoning told her it was him. And when the rider dismounted by the barn, she recognized Wyatt's stance and the way he moved.

She hadn't made a sound when he stilled. He turned and looked directly at the cabin.

"Miss Ashford?"

She let out a held breath, embarrassed at having been caught spying. "Yes, I'm here."

The chirrup of crickets sounded oddly like laughter to her ears.

"Is everything all right, ma'am?"

"Yes, I was only—" She rolled her eyes in the dark. "Yes, Marshal Caradon, everything's fine. I just couldn't sleep."

He took a step toward her, then stopped. "Is there anything I can do?"

She wanted to say "Come sit with me on the porch step and hold my hand again," but she'd never be so bold. Yet she wasn't ready for him to go just yet. "Would you like a . . . a cup of cider?" She thought she heard him laugh.

"A cup of cider? In the middle of the night?"

She smiled, knowing he couldn't see her, but it felt good after a day spent worrying. "It's silly. I'm sorry. Never mind."

"No! I'd like a cup of a cider. Or a cup of . . . anything . . . with you, ma'am."

The warmth she'd felt when he'd held her hand earlier returned in a rush.

"Just let me get Whiskey unsaddled and seen to. Then I'll meet you on the steps."

Minutes later, in her robe and with two cups of cider waiting, McKenna watched Wyatt walk toward her in the dark. He sat down next to her, not as close as she would have liked, and took the offered cider.

He raised the cup and drank it dry. Moonlight gave his skin a paler appearance than was true and his shadowed jawline stood out darker against it.

"A little thirsty there, Marshal?"

Smiling, he wiped his mouth and laid the cup aside. "Just a little."

Then she caught a whiff of something. At first she thought her sense of smell was playing tricks on her, but she knew it wasn't. She smelled cigar smoke, whiskey . . . and cheap perfume.

"How did your day go here?" he asked, sounding tired. "I don't mean to pry, but I saw Billings and another man as they rode out this morning. But only from a distance. Billings brought good news, I hope?"

The only reason a man came home smelling like a saloon was if he'd been in a saloon. Or a brothel. But she never would have imagined Wyatt Caradon frequenting those places. Having heard his question, McKenna realized then that she'd *wanted* to talk about all that had happened today. About Billings, about Harrison Talbot, about Emma having recognized the man. But now . . . one question crowded all that out. She placed her full cup of cider behind her. "What exactly do you do for the Marshals Office?"

He shrugged. "Different things. Mainly . . ." He laughed softly. "I do whatever they tell me." He leaned forward, clasping his hands between his knees.

"What kind of different things?"

He held off answering. "Is something wrong, ma'am?"

His sincere tone didn't ease her suspicions. She felt him staring but didn't look at him. "No. I'm only wondering what you did . . . What you do for a living."

He cleared his throat and ran a hand over his jaw. "I track down convicts, but you already know that. I transfer prisoners from one place to the next. All in all, I guess you could say I'm a pursuer."

That drew her attention. "A pursuer?"

"Yes, ma'am. That probably sums it up best."

He moved closer to her, and McKenna buried her hands in her lap.

"Just what is it that you pursue, Marshal Caradon?"

"You know . . . I wish we could get to the place where you'd stop calling me Marshal Caradon." He reached over and trailed his fingers along the curve of her wrist and over the back of her hand.

McKenna tried hard to resist the shiver working through

her, and couldn't. So she stood. She'd wanted Wyatt Caradon to be different from the other men she'd known. But maybe she wanted that so badly that she was blind to what he was. "I think a certain formality between a man and woman is healthy . . . Marshal Caradon."

He stood with her. "I'd agree with you on that. Unless the man and woman have earned the right to move on to . . . something more. For instance . . ."

He braced one arm on the post behind her head and leaned in, and the top step suddenly became even narrower.

"Say they've done some things like . . . sew up a man together in a doc's clinic, or shared what it feels like to lose someone precious and then find her again. Or maybe they've gone to a nice dinner togeth—Oh wait!" He snapped his fingers. "We haven't done that yet."

She was tempted to smile, and yet couldn't. He must've sensed her initial reaction because he moved closer. She'd instigated this little *meeting* and yet now she wished she hadn't.

"Miss Ashford . . ." His voice was almost a whisper. "May I please call you McKenna?"

Despite not wanting to, her body reacted to his closeness. And she decided the straightforward approach was best. "Yes, Marshal Caradon, you may." She put a hand against his chest. "If you'll tell me why you smell like stale cigars, whiskey, and cheap women."

THIRTY-ONE

Wyatt stared, his mouth hanging slightly open. He took a step back, feeling like she'd slapped him, but he also felt relief. At least now he understood why she was being so snippy with him. Under the circumstances, and understanding some of what she'd been through, he couldn't say he blamed her. "I appreciate your candor, ma'am." He spoke in hushed tones, knowing Robert and Emma were inside the cabin asleep. "For a minute there, I thought we really had us a problem."

Her hands went to her hips. "And you think we don't?"

"No ma'am, not the kind you're imagining."

She opened her mouth and, with his gentlest touch, he closed it for her. Then drew his hand away before he lost it.

"Like I said, I appreciate your candor, and I can see how you came to your conclusion. I don't blame you for it either," he added, seeing her brow rise. He pointed to her cider. "You going to drink that?"

She shook her head.

He picked up the mug and downed the contents, wishing it were something a little stronger.

He'd sensed she wanted to talk about something, but they'd gotten derailed, as they often did. If this woman wanted to talk, he'd stay up the rest of the night to oblige her, despite being dog-tired. She didn't let her walls down often, and he wanted to be there when she did.

"You remember Slater, the man you sewed up at the doc's clinic?"

She slowly nodded, her skepticism obvious.

"Men like him don't hang around mercantiles or dry goods stores. You find men like him in saloons and gaming halls. So for the most part, that's where I spend my time these days. And yes, there are women there. But . . ." He wanted so badly to touch her face, but the way she'd jumped when he'd taken hold of her hand told him he needed to move slowly with her. More slowly than he wanted to. "I have never . . . *never* been with a woman in one of those places."

McKenna looked at him, really looked at him, and he didn't flinch. He hoped she would stare, study, search, do whatever she needed to do, for as long as she needed to do it—until she recognized the honesty in him.

Gradually relief smoothed the lines from her forehead.

She was the first to look away. "I'm sorry for accusing you falsely."

"Apology accepted, ma'am." If there was one thing he knew she didn't need, it was more guilt. "But you didn't really accuse me. You asked me one straight-out, fully loaded question that half scared me to death. But you didn't really accuse me. Not directly anyway." Laughter played at the corners of her mouth, and he let his smile show through. "I appreciate your honesty, and I wouldn't want things any other way between us . . . ma'am." He'd wanted to use her name just then, but decided to let her take the lead in that.

He could see in the tilt of her head that her mind was working overtime.

"So, if I understand what you've said, Marshal, every afternoon when you leave here, you'll be going to saloons in Copper Creek? Looking for men like Slater. Is that what you do for a living?"

She made it sound so simple and absent of honor. "A lot of the time. But not just in Copper Creek. I also travel to some of the surrounding towns too." How much did he dare tell her about his job? About this assignment? Not much, for her sake, as well as his. "If it makes any difference to you, I don't take any pleasure in it." He rubbed his lower back and sat down on the top step again. "But I agreed to take this case, and I intend to see it through."

He leaned back on the floor of the porch, glad when she finally took a place beside him. He was careful to keep his distance this time.

"So why don't you do something else?"

He smiled. "I've been asking myself that same question recently."

"You might consider working on a ranch. I hear there are some openings around here."

Hearing the playfulness return to her voice, he relaxed. "Yes, ma'am, I've heard about them too. My only hesitation is that I've heard the ranch owners leave something to be desired." He snuck a glance, wanting to see her reaction.

She looked like she tried to quell a smile, and couldn't. "Yes, distrusting bunch that they are."

Much preferring this sense of ease between them to the tense moments before, Wyatt decided not to touch that last comment. Trust didn't come easily for her, he knew that. But with what she'd told him about her father—and having seen her struggles with Robert firsthand—he could understand why.

Her gaze slid to his and their eyes held for a moment.

He saw the invisible burden she carried in the stoop of her

shoulders, and in the way her lips moved as though she wanted to say something but somehow couldn't. He prayed she would trust him enough to tell him, whatever it was. And that he'd be able to help, however possible.

"Wyatt?" she whispered.

He swallowed hard at the softness in her eyes, and at what it made him want to do. "Yes, McKenna?"

She chewed the corner of her mouth. "Would you . . ."

He dipped his head to capture her gaze again. "Yes?"

"Would you mind just . . . sitting here for a while and . . . holding my hand?"

Her simple request, and the ache in her voice, stirred emotions in him he hadn't experienced in a long time. He scooted closer and closer, until their bodies touched. Then he took her hand in his and wove their fingers together.

After several moments, he felt her shoulders begin to shake. He kissed the crown of her head, breathing in the flowery scent of her hair, and—though he knew it was impossible—he wanted to block out everything in her life that had ever hurt her, or ever would.

She leaned into him, her head touching his shoulder, and he closed his eyes.

"McKenna?"

She sniffed. "Yes?"

"I think I can do better than this, if you'll let me."

Nothing for a moment, and he wondered if he'd overstepped his bounds. Then she nodded.

Holding her hand tighter, he slipped his other arm around her and drew her against him. She came without reservation and fit perfectly against him.

She hadn't told him what was bothering her like he'd hoped she would. He wanted to know who the enemy was, so he could go to battle for her. That's what he did. He pursued and he fought. But somehow, in the quiet of this moment, in the hush of her tears, he realized that this had cost her more than if she'd shared her burden with him tonight.

Satisfied with that knowledge, at least for now, he settled against the porch railing, closed his eyes, and asked God to fight mightily for the woman in his arms. Until he could too.

THIRTY-TWO

What do you mean you lost Patch in a card game?" Rage shot through McKenna's body and her hands began to shake.

Inclined on the sofa, Robert cocked his head and gave her a look she wanted to slap right off his face.

During the past week, his cuts and bruises had healed considerably and, according to Dr. Foster, Robert could return to work. *If* he had a job. Which he didn't, and he'd shown no initiative in trying to get another one either. He was in a perpetual foul mood and had done little—even inside the cabin—to help out in recent days.

"I think it's clear what I meant, Kenny. I lost . . . the horse . . . in a game . . . of poker." He spoke the sentence slowly as though she were dull-witted.

McKenna closed her eyes, imagining what it would be like for her fist to connect with that disrespectful mouth of his. The depth of her anger frightened her, and thoughts of retaliation shamed her. Especially after everything he'd been through. But his attitude shamed her too.

A quick glance at Emma, who sat at the kitchen table, a hunk of cheese in hand, confirmed the child was listening to every word. McKenna would never voice it aloud, but she sometimes wished Robert would just leave. That had to be better than his hanging around here all day—sullen, argumentative, and underfoot—acting this way in front of Emma.

Her gaze went to the letter on the table, and she felt her blood pressure rising again. It had arrived moments ago via courier from Billings. The circuit judge would be in Copper Creek on August tenth. One week from today! Billings offered no other instructions on how to prepare for the meeting other than for her to be on time.

Time . . . that was something she needed more of.

Yesterday she'd met with Mei for an English lesson, their second that week. While each visit was no less than two hours—hours she could spend working—she considered time with Mei something she did for herself. Being around Mei was calming, and the woman's ability to learn was remarkable. Following Mei's, she and Emma visited the livery where Trenton gave her orders for four more saddles, which was good. Her business was growing. But she simply couldn't make the saddles fast enough. It was the first week of August, and she had enough work right now to last her through Christmas. Yet Trenton needed the saddles delivered by Thanksgiving.

Fortunately, having Wyatt on the ranch to help with chores and the cattle felt like having three of her. He simply saw something that needed to be done, and he did it. Without question or badgering. She'd seen him in recent days, but only from afar or when he was leaving in the afternoons. He seemed busier than when he'd first arrived and seemed to leave earlier every day. A part of her wondered if he might intentionally be avoiding her. Did he regret having been so tender with her last week? She kept telling herself that wasn't the reason, that having two jobs was the real culprit. Something she could certainly understand.

The smug look on Robert's face drew her back to the conversation at hand. Wanting to run away, she'd let Robert get away with too much for too long. He had to be dealt with.

"Robert," she said softly, feeling like a simmering pot with its lid stuck tight. "Three days after you got back from Severance, you *told* me you'd put Patch in the lower pasture, by the creek. Do you remember that?"

He stared, unblinking and unapologetic. "Stop talking to me like I'm a child. I knew you'd be mad and you wouldn't understand, so I—"

"You're right I don't understand! And yes, I'm angry! It wasn't your horse to bet. And it wasn't your money to bet either!"

He came to his feet. "It *was* my money! I earned every penny! I worked from dawn to dusk for Trenton, and I was tired of it. I'm glad he fired me."

Her body trembled at his admission.

Remembering Trenton's confirmation that Robert repeatedly came in late and left early without finishing his work, another emotion bled through her fury. Disappointment welled up inside her until a physical ache formed in her chest. She thought she'd modeled what it meant to work hard, to take pride in your accomplishments.

It was sobering to stand face-to-face with someone she'd poured her life into, someone she loved with a love she sometimes couldn't even understand, only to have them throw everything right back at her.

Tears slid down her cheeks. She didn't wipe them away this time. She didn't care if Robert saw. She was tired of being the strong one.

His expression hardened. "I didn't mean to lose the horse, Kenny. It just happened! I was winning. The other guy must've been cheating, because that's the only way he—"

"I'm going outside for a while," McKenna said, voice hushed. She turned to Emma and held out a hand.

Emma slipped from her chair, grabbed Clara, and followed.

Robert spat out a curse. "It's just a stupid horse, Kenny!"

Hand on the latch, McKenna turned back, then looked pointedly at Emma. "Don't use that language in front of her. Ever again!" She thought of the night Wyatt had brought him home from Severance, and of the days since. "That was Janie's horse, Robert. She raised Patch from a filly. But what hurts the most is that you knew that . . . because I told you." She shook her head. "Why did you take her that night?"

Robert stared at her for a long moment, varied emotions playing across his face. And in his eyes, for an instant, McKenna caught a glimpse of the infant she'd rocked at night after warming the bottle, then the little boy she'd cuddled close when storms came.

Too quickly, the images faded, and the eyes staring back at her now . . . she didn't recognize.

His stare was dark and fathomless—and frightening. "I took her . . . because I knew you wouldn't want me to."

Wyatt glanced up in time to see the pretty twosome rounding the side of the cabin in the direction of the hill out back. As he watched them, McKenna's determined stride told him something wasn't right. That—and she was going up the hill to the bluff overlooking the valley. He'd quickly learned that's where she went when needing to sort out her thoughts.

Whatever had been bothering her in recent days had only become worse. Her increased anxiety showed in her reticence and in a frown she never seemed to put away. He'd wanted to ask her about it, but working two jobs was making time scarcer than he'd thought. Which wasn't all bad. After the night they'd shared last week in which they'd talked, and he'd held her until the sun had risen, Wyatt found it harder and harder not to want more from McKenna when he was with her.

He finished nailing the new rails to the fence posts, then

gathered his tools and headed to the barn. He'd catch up with her and Emma and see if he could find out what was wrong.

He was quickly coming to covet his mornings spent working the ranch—where there was enough work for two full-time men, at least—while dreading his afternoons and nights spent moving from one gambling hall to the next. Bixby, Severance, and Copper Creek, the towns the Marshals Office had assigned him to scout, were all within a two-hour ride of each other. That made coming and going easier, but the vagabond life had long ago lost its allure. Even time spent riding the mountain trails wasn't as enjoyable as it used to be.

Already, he'd supplied the Marshals Office with one conspirator's name and had a lead for another that he intended to follow up on tonight. To his favor, liquored-up men were loose in the tongue and easily baited. Intentionally throwing a few hands of poker did wonders for lowering their guard. He prodded their egos until their pride pushed back and they started boasting about what they'd seen and done.

He stowed Vince Talbot's tool crate in the barn, knowing he'd have to hurry if he was going to catch McKenna and Emma before it was time to leave for Severance. He was on his way out of the barn when he collided headlong with Robert.

Wyatt reached out and steadied the boy. "Sorry, Robert. I didn't see you."

Robert jerked away, mumbling something Wyatt didn't catch but figured wasn't worth asking him to repeat. He'd seen little of Robert throughout the week. The boy had probably been hiding out somewhere, avoiding work. Or avoiding him. He could tell Robert didn't like having him around.

Wyatt had hoped for a chance to talk to him and, as much as he wanted to see McKenna before he left, maybe this was his opportunity.

Robert pushed past him.

Taking into account the boy's scowl and McKenna walking to the bluff, Wyatt figured they'd had another argument. He could set his pocket watch by their squabbles. The boy knew exactly what to say and do to trigger her temper. McKenna's anger would flare, she'd apologize, and then try reasoning with the boy. What the boy needed right now wasn't reasoning. He needed a good swift kick in the behind.

But Wyatt knew what kind of response McKenna would have if he tried to offer counsel. She'd made it clear she didn't desire his help in that area of her life.

"You're looking better, Robert. How're you feeling?"

"Just dandy, Marshal Caradon."

The kid's sarcasm was thick—and familiar. Wyatt was reminded of himself at that age, and wondered how his father had ever kept from knocking his impudent head clean off his shoulders.

"That's good to hear! Then you can start lending a hand around here again. There's a lot to do, and I'm sure your sister would appreciate your help."

Robert huffed. "I'll bet she would."

"A woman shouldn't be made to do a man's work, Robert. Not when there are men around to do it. They *are* the gentler sex, after all."

"The gentler sex . . ." Robert raised a brow. "Is that right?"

The boy's tone held humor Wyatt didn't catch.

Robert walked back to the stalls and started casually toeing through the straw with his boot. But the boy wouldn't find what he was looking for. That bottle was long gone. As were two others Wyatt had found—one in the grain bin, the other in the loft.

Wyatt came up behind him. "Heads up!"

Robert turned and Wyatt tossed the pitchfork at him, tines downward.

Reflexes sharp, Robert caught it, his eyes wide. "What are you tryin' to do?"

Wyatt shrugged. "Thought you might want to use that instead of your boot. It'll make the job go a whole lot faster."

The kid laughed. "I didn't come in here to muck out stalls."

"I know what you came in here for, Robert. But the bottles are gone."

The boy's eyes darted from one hiding place to the next, then hardened. "You had no right to do that!" Robert turned the pitchfork in his hands.

Seeing the curved tines facing him, Wyatt slowly smiled. He read the boy's thoughts and almost wished he would try something.

Robert eyed him. "I know why you're here. U.S. Marshal just happens to show up in Copper Creek same time I do?" He leveled his gaze. "I'm not stupid."

Wyatt hadn't seen this coming. Did Robert think he'd tracked him all the way out here? If so, then the kid had a much bigger ego than Wyatt had attributed to him. Or maybe, a more serious past.

It also told him Robert had experience with the Marshals Office, the kind a young man Robert's age shouldn't have. Wyatt trailed that thought, and it led him to a possible explanation as to why McKenna had seemed so eager to get rid of him when they'd first met. And why that still might be her goal, if not for her desperate need for help with the ranch.

He decided to help the conversation along, see what he could learn. "I never said you were stupid, Robert. But it certainly wasn't the smartest thing you've ever done either."

The boy got red in the face. "What did they tell you?"

Wyatt only stared. Guilt riddled the boy's expression, telling its own story.

Robert shook his head. "No one was supposed to be inside. We were only going to mess things up a little and then go. It wasn't my idea to start the fire. I didn't even know Keller had matches with him until he—" He clamped his mouth shut, and winced. "It wasn't my idea! Did the judge tell you that?"

Having no clue what the boy was talking about, Wyatt could still guess what was coming, having had plenty of experience filling in the blanks in these situations. "In the end, a person's intent only goes so far. Then what a judge looks at is what happened to the victim due to the direct result of your actions. Or your lack of action. Meaning . . . how you might've helped this Keller do what he did simply by not trying to stop him. Responsibility remains, Robert, even when you choose to do nothing."

Robert raked a hand through his hair. "You can't arrest me for that again!" He raised the pitchfork and stabbed it deep into a pile of straw. "The judge in Missouri said I wasn't guilty. He said the charge wouldn't follow me out here!"

Standing in the doorway of the stall, Wyatt sensed a desperation in Robert Ashford that hadn't been there before, and suddenly the young man's behavior became a whole lot clearer to him. The Missouri judge had apparently acquitted him of his part in whatever crime had been committed. Arson, most likely. That was enough to satisfy Wyatt's curiosity on that point. But the judge, however well-intentioned, had misled the boy.

"The judge did you a disservice, Robert, by saying the charge wouldn't follow you. Nothing could be less true. Until you're ready to face what you've done and make amends, guilt always follows a man. No matter where you go. I'd think you would've learned that by now."

The muscles in Robert's neck corded tight. He licked his lips. "You can't arrest me for that again," he repeated.

"No," Wyatt whispered, feeling as if he was watching a caged animal. "We can't."

The boy's eyes narrowed. "Nothing I did in Severance that night was against the law either. So you can't do anything to me for that."

Wyatt blinked, and saw Jimmy Slater standing in front of him again, blood soaking through the kid's shirt, his eyes going dull. He blinked again to clear the image. "Can I ask you a question, Robert?" Whether it was the calmness in his voice or the question itself, something seemed to throw the kid off balance.

Robert gave a slow nod.

"With all the talent you have, with everything you could do with your life, why are you choosing a path like this?"

Robert stared for a moment, then sneered. "Now you're sounding like Kenny. It's *my* life, Marshal. I can decide what I want to do with it, and what I don't."

Wyatt nodded. "Fair enough. But you still haven't answered my question. I've seen your work. The wagons you build." He gestured over his shoulder. "The saddles you make."

"The saddles I make?" Robert asked, his eyes narrowing.

Wyatt motioned behind him to an out-of-the-way corner where he stowed his gear. "Turns out, I even bought one. I didn't know you'd made it or I would've thanked you personally while I was at the livery. It's the finest saddle I've ever owned, Robert. Talent like yours is rare. It's a gift. And you ought not squander it."

Robert started laughing. "Talent like mine, huh?"

A spark of indignation twisted Wyatt's chest. How could someone with such a gift not be grateful for the ability God had given him? "Casey Trenton told me your father owned a livery." He treaded with care in what he said next. "I know your father wasn't all you needed him to be—and what he should have been in your life. But you still inherited a great gift from him."

Even from where he stood, Wyatt sensed an anger building in Robert.

"That man . . . didn't give me anything," Robert whispered, his voice tight. "Much less an inheritance." He walked to within inches of Wyatt's face. "And if you speak to me about him again, I'll knock you flat . . . *Marshal* Caradon."

Robert shouldered past him, and Wyatt let him go.

"By the way, Marshal . . ."

Wyatt turned to see him standing in the doorway of the barn.

"You think I made that saddle? You might want to check beneath the skirt." He chuckled. "Then get back with me on a woman doing a man's work."

Robert turned on his heel and strode from the barn.

Confused, Wyatt walked to the saddle and lifted the leather skirt as Robert instructed. He found nothing on the right side so moved to the left. There, in an upper corner, he read the initials M.A. carved in the fine-grained leather.

He stared, disbelieving.

It couldn't be . . . *McKenna* had made this saddle? If so, surely Casey Trenton knew. Yet the man had said nothing. Neither had McKenna, and certainly she'd noticed it by now. Then he remembered—the morning she'd hired him, she'd commented on the saddle then. So she did know, yet had said nothing. But why . . .

He fingered the decorative leather braids, his respect for her deepening. McKenna Ashford had more mystery to her than one woman should be allowed. Along the same lines, discovering this about her shed new light on her brother.

Robert Ashford, the son, should have been the child to have learned and carried on his father's trade—saddlery. Yet it was his older sister who had claimed that birthright. Through no fault of hers, she obviously had a gift for it. But in the end, Robert Ashford had been robbed. Not by failing to be shown how to make saddles, but by failing to be shown a father's love and acceptance.

Knowing this didn't lessen Wyatt's frustration with the boy, but his heart somehow opened a little wider where Robert was concerned.

Past time for him to leave for Severance, he saddled Whiskey and was on his way from the barn when he spotted McKenna and Emma walking back. He rode in their direction.

"Morning, ladies. How are you?" He tipped his hat, tempted

to let McKenna know what Robert had revealed to him, while also wanting to thank her for her workmanship—although that last word didn't seem to fit too well in this case.

"Good morning, Marshal. We were just taking a stroll. Are you leaving already?"

Disappointment tinged her voice, and he hoped it was for him. "Yes, ma'am. I got the fence mended on the north pasture. Tomorrow morning, I'll move the cattle over there to graze. Another month of field grass and they'll be ready to take to market." Though he didn't know how he was going to have the time to get them there. That would take weeks. Weeks he didn't have, and neither did she. Not wanting to add to her worry, he kept that to himself.

Emma reached up. "Can I ride with you, Mr. Wyatt?"

"Sure, little one. Come on up."

McKenna lifted the child up, and Wyatt situated Emma in front of him, holding her secure. Whiskey plodded along, and Wyatt relished the way Emma smiled up at him every few seconds.

"Hang on tight, sweetie." McKenna walked beside them as they rode. "I'll be sure and tell Mr. Billings at the bank about the cattle. Just to keep him informed."

Something in her voice—and her short-lived smile—raised questions in Wyatt's mind. "Have you heard from Billings recently?"

"Yes, I just got a letter from him today, in fact."

He waited. "And?"

She looked away.

He reined in. "McKenna, if there's something wrong—and I know there is—I want you to tell me. I know it's not easy to ask for help, but . . ." He waited until she looked at him before continuing. "I hope it's clear that my intent is to do just that—help you . . . in any way I can."

Her smile was fragile. "I appreciate that. And you're already helping me, Wyatt." She fingered a braid on her saddle. "More than you know."

"It's not fair to look at a man that way when he can't do anything about it, ma'am."

He liked the blush that rose to her cheeks. He also liked that she didn't go shy on him and look away, but locked her eyes with his.

"I'll be sure and remember that . . . sir."

He kissed the top of Emma's head and handed the little girl back down. Emma wrapped her arms around McKenna's waist. She pulled her close, brushing the hair from her face. If he didn't know better, he'd think Emma Talbot had been natural born to McKenna Ashford.

"Wyatt . . ." Seriousness replaced McKenna's former flirtation. "I'd like to invite you to dinner this Sunday. I could use your advice . . . on what to do."

Finally, she was confiding in him. "I'll be there." He needed to be on his way, but he hated to leave her with that pained look in her eyes. "But only if you promise to bake some of that bread you've told me so much about."

Winking, and knowing he'd carry her smile with him all the way to Severance and back, he tipped his hat and rode on at a gallop.

He didn't slow until he spotted Robert on the outskirts of Copper Creek, walking into a saloon with two other men. He recognized one of them. The fellow was worse than no good. Torn, Wyatt kept riding. He had a job to do for the Marshals Office, and lives depended on him doing it.

But other lives depended on him now too.

It was a sobering thought. And one that, oddly, warmed him, while also sending a shiver straight through him. He'd told himself he had no right to invite a woman—much less a woman with a child, and with a rebel of a brother, to boot—into his life. Yet that was exactly what he'd done.

And God help him, he'd do it all over again. He was tired of being lonely, and tired of living life for only himself. He'd asked God to guide his steps. Now he had to trust that the Almighty knew what He was doing.

THIRTY-THREE

McKenna peered over Mei's shoulder, half afraid to look. "Did it rise?"

"I wanna see too, Aunt Kenny!"

McKenna lifted Emma up as Mei bent to open the oven. She enjoyed time spent with Mei, but today all she could feel was the jarring tick of a clock inside her. In only five days, she would meet with the circuit judge—a stranger who would determine her future.

She'd awakened in a panic during the night, unable to breathe, feeling the tiny bedroom closing in around her. On her way to the porch, she'd passed an empty sofa. Again. Robert hadn't come home Friday night, *or* Saturday. And he hadn't been there when she'd awakened this morning either.

"I took her . . . because I knew you wouldn't want me to."

What he'd said to her about losing Patch in a card game had hurt more than she could have imagined. She still loved her brother. That would never change. But she realized that whatever she was to him—or had been, or wanted to be—wasn't enough. And that realization brought a hopeless, adrift feeling, like she'd emptied her pockets, pulled them inside out, and still hadn't even begun to pay the debt. *Oh God, would you reach him? Because I can't. Not anymore. I'm so sorry . . .*

The happy sound of Emma's squeals drew her back.

Mei pulled the most scrumptious looking, perfectly rounded loaf of golden brown bread from the oven. The yeasty just-baked aroma wafted through Mei's kitchen, and McKenna felt a flush of pride. Her eyes watered, aided, no doubt, by the heat of the oven. "Finally!" She exhaled, smiling. "I've gotten it right!"

This bread would be the crowning glory to tonight's dinner with Wyatt, especially after she'd told him she couldn't bake. She hadn't seen him since Friday afternoon, though she'd seen evidence of him being there yesterday morning—the cattle and horses were fed, fresh water filled the troughs. But this morning, she'd had to do his chores. He hadn't said anything about being gone, but certainly his job with the Marshals Office held surprises.

She'd been nervous when asking him to dinner. Though, in the end, it hadn't taken her as much courage as it had humility. Asking for help had never been easy for her. Especially from someone like Wyatt Caradon, who seemed so self-sufficient. Asking for help felt like a sign of weakness. Not when others did it. Just when she did. And she so wanted him to see her as strong and capable—the way she viewed him.

When he held her hand the other night and said he thought he could do better if she'd let him, she thought he'd meant something more along the lines of a kiss. And she'd been thinking about it ever since, wondering what it would be like to kiss Wyatt Caradon thoroughly.

Warmer now than before, McKenna focused on the bread again, inhaling the aroma. She couldn't wait to sink her teeth into the crusty feast! Her first loaf of bread that had actually—

Mei withdrew a second pan. She gave McKenna a forlorn

look, and McKenna's pride, and hopes, fell flat—just like her bread had done.

Mei slid the second pan onto the table, her expression brightening. "You will do better . . . next time!"

McKenna offered a deflated smile, proud of her friend's improvement in speaking English, but wishing the same could be said of her own baking skills. She frowned at the traitorous loaf cowering beneath its puffed-up cousin. "For some reason, Mei, I don't think so." So much for serving bread with dinner tonight.

Emma gently patted her on the back. "You make good saddles, Aunt Kenny."

A prick of tears rose at the comforting way Emma said it. "Thanks, sweetie. Maybe I'll just serve Mr. Wyatt one of those for dinner instead." She tickled Emma's tummy, which drew a giggle.

Smiling, Emma framed McKenna's face in her little hands and planted a big, wet kiss right smack on her lips. "I love you, Aunt Kenny."

Taken aback by the show of affection, McKenna searched Emma's eyes so blue and innocent. "I love you too, Emma." She had been nine years old when she first held Robert in her arms. She'd been a child herself. Maybe it was because she was twenty-three now—certainly that had something to do with it—but the love she felt for this child was different from the love she felt for Robert. It felt as if part of her own heart were nestled within the tiny chest of this child. This precious part of Janie that was left to her.

What would happen if she lost Emma? If, for some reason, the judge awarded not only the ranch to Harrison Talbot, but Emma as well? The floor beneath her suddenly felt like a thin sheet of ice which, with the slightest movement, would splinter into a spiderweb of cracks and send her plunging.

She was weary on the inside and out. She'd spent so many

years working to keep the family home in St. Joseph, and the livery business her grandfather had built and her father had continued. Only to lose it all—in a blink. Her whole life, she'd grappled and clawed her way, struggling to provide security for Robert and herself.

But as it turned out, security was a fickle mistress. And was, at best, an illusion.

Emma hugged her neck and McKenna held on tight, realizing that the ranch meant nothing compared to what she held in her arms. But if she lost the ranch, where would they go? How would she provide for Emma, and keep her promise to Janie? Everything rested on the meeting with the judge. She had no idea how to prepare for the appointment, but hoped Wyatt would. She planned on asking him during dinner. Surely a U.S. Marshal had experience with such things.

While Mei's bread cooled on the counter and McKenna's waited in a slop bucket to be fodder for pigs, Mei served them warm rolls with a kind of fruit jam. Realizing what trouble Mei had gone to, McKenna summoned a cheerfulness she didn't feel, and they sat at the kitchen table eating, laughing, and practicing Mei's English.

Until Chin Li walked in.

Their laughter dissolved. Chin Li's stern gaze brushed the three of them before coming to rest on the open book and strewn papers atop the table, then fell hard on McKenna. Mei immediately rose and bowed before her husband. He spoke to her in his regular clipped tone.

While McKenna didn't know what he'd said, she didn't like how Mei jumped every time this man walked into the room. And she didn't like his tone. She looked up to see an elderly gentleman tottering along behind Chin Li with the aid of a cane. Chin Li turned as though following her line of vision. He immediately reached out and took hold of the man, steadying him. He spoke to Mei over his shoulder before disappearing around the corner.

The front door opened and closed, and Mei took her seat once again and started eating, as if nothing out of the ordinary had happened.

McKenna leaned forward. "Should Emma and I go?" She motioned toward the door.

Mei frowned. "Why . . . would you go? We still have lesson. And bread." She held up a roll.

McKenna busied Emma with pencil and paper, and chose her words carefully, not wanting to offend Mei. "I wasn't sure if your husband appreciates our being here." Seeing Mei's expression cloud, she tried again. "Perhaps Chin Li does not like me coming to see you."

Mei smiled briefly. "Chin Li is . . ." She lowered her eyes. "Careful for me."

"Careful for you?"

"He no wish me . . . to be sad."

"To be sad," McKenna repeated, not understanding.

Mei nodded.

"But why would being friends with me make you sad?"

Mei kept her gaze confined to her lap. "Not all people in Copper Creek be . . . kind . . ." She peered up beneath dark brows. "Like you, McKenna Ashford," she said softly.

Liking the way Mei said her full name, McKenna let what she'd said sink in. "Have people treated you badly here?"

Mei didn't respond, but McKenna sensed she wanted to. In watching the way Mei knotted her hands in her lap, the way she pressed her lips together, McKenna wondered if the woman's genteel manner prohibited her from saying anything further—or perhaps it was Chin Li who prohibited his wife from saying anything. Perhaps Chin Li only told Mei that because he didn't want her having friends for another reason . . .

A flurry of possibilities entered McKenna's mind—all casting further doubt on Chin Li—and a wave of protectiveness swept through her. She touched Mei's arm. "Is your husband unkind to you?"

Mei's head came up. "Unkind to me?"

McKenna nodded. "Is he ever harsh with you?" Already knowing the answer to that question, she grew more hesitant, not wanting to overstep her bounds. But her concern for her friend urged her on. "I hear the way he speaks to you, Mei. It makes me sad inside to think he might be hurting you in some way. I want you to know that if you ever need to—"

Mei giggled. Her shoulders started to shake. "You think . . . Chin Li speak harsh to me?"

"Well, yes. I just heard him say something to you a moment— Are you laughing at me?"

Mei covered her mouth. "I sorry. I no laugh at you, McKenna. I laugh at you think Chin Li is harsh man." Her laughter quieted, and her features softened. "In my country, parents choose who children marry. First man who wanted me as wife was poor. He was a . . ." She wriggled her hand back and forth in front of her like a trout running upstream.

"Fisherman?" McKenna supplied.

"Yes, fisherman. His family was fisherman too."

McKenna quelled a smile.

"But my father say no to this man. In harsh way." Mei shook her head. "The man no good for his daughter. My father want better man. Rich man. My father say this to him and hurt him. Disgrace him, very bad. So the man go away." She bowed her head. Seconds later when she looked up, her eyes held tears. "But he not stay away. He say he want my father's daughter, and he will go to America to make business so he be good husband to her. He send money back to father to pay for her."

McKenna saw the love in Mei's expression, and sensed what Mei was telling her. "That man was Chin Li," she whispered.

"That man was Chin Li," Mei repeated softly. "He send money for her to come, and for her father." She leaned forward, her gaze earnest. "At first when I meet Chin Li, I think him unkind, as you say. But it not true. He only want to guard me. So you see, he is good man." A coy smile tipped her mouth. "Like your Marshal Caradon."

Surprised, McKenna felt heat rise to her cheeks. "He is not *my* Marshal Caradon."

Mei's brows shot up.

"He and I are friends. Like you and I are friends."

A knowing look filled Mei's dark eyes. "Chin Li and I were friends when we marry. Then we grow into . . . much more." Mei spoke something in Cantonese, offering a smile. "That is what my grandmother once say. It mean, 'The most fertile soil for love lies in heart of friend.'"

McKenna couldn't imagine entering into marriage as Mei had. Not loving the man. Not even knowing him! But she wasn't about to say that aloud. When she married—*if* she ever married—it would be for love. A love she'd not yet experienced, and wasn't even sure existed.

"You think our way is foolish."

McKenna's face heated at Mei having read her thoughts so easily. "No! No, I never said that."

"You no have to say. I see in your eyes."

McKenna sighed. "I'm sorry, Mei. I just can't imagine marrying a man I didn't know, much less a man I didn't love. Marriage seems hard enough as it is, much less with those challenges."

"In my country, at young age, we teach that being right person is . . ." She frowned.

"As important?" McKenna said, guessing where she was going.

Mei nodded. "Is as . . . important as marrying right person."

Understanding what she was saying, McKenna nodded, still grateful that she would be able to choose her husband. Then something dawned on her. "You said Chin Li sent money back to your father in China to pay to marry you, and so you could come to America. And that he also sent money for your father."

"That is right."

"So, is your father still living?"

Confusion clouded Mei's face. "You know my father. He just here, with Chin Li."

McKenna looked toward the next room where Chin Li—and who she'd thought was *Chin Li's* father—had stood moments before. "That elderly man is *your* father?"

Mei's smile was her answer, and McKenna could only stare. "But Chin Li is so gentle with him, so caring and attentive. Especially after how you described your father treating him."

Unabashed pride shown in Mei's expression. She reached over and, in an unaccustomed display, touched McKenna's hand. "Now you see how kind a man my Chin Li is."

McKenna covered Mei's hand and briefly squeezed it tight. "Yes . . . I do."

When she spoke again, Mei's voice was soft. "When we first come here, people call us names. Unkind names. Many night, as young wife, I cry. My husband hold me and, at first, I . . ." She bowed her head, hands buried in her lap. "I no want to be wife to him." She touched her chest, her lips trembling. "I hurt inside my heart. Deep. Even when he hold me, I feel all by myself."

McKenna nodded, knowing that alone feeling, and knowing what it felt like to want more with a man. Whatever that *more* was.

A tear slipped down Mei's cheek and she wiped it away. "But I learn, over many day and night, that Chin Li choose good life for us. Better life than my father's daughter deserve. And he patient with me . . . in many way." A blush crept into Mei's cheeks.

McKenna nodded, understanding and, yet, at the same time, not.

"As long as Chin Li and Mei . . ." Mei seemed to struggle for the next word, then put her two index fingers side by side. "What is the word?"

"Together," McKenna whispered, feeling more than a twinge of jealousy. "As long as you and Chin Li are together . . ."

Mei nodded. "Then we will be . . . okay."

McKenna forced a smile on Mei's behalf, wondering whether she would ever be *okay* herself again. The panic that so often awakened her during the middle of the night returned and crowded out what little confidence remained. God seemed to be stripping everything away from her—layer by layer, person by person, possession by possession—despite her best efforts to hold her world together.

And if she didn't know better, she'd think He was doing it intentionally.

THIRTY-FOUR

Mr. Wyatt will come. I know he'll come." On tiptoe, Emma peered out the front window. "He said he would."

McKenna dished a piece of cold roast beef onto the child's plate, followed by a dollop of stiff mashed potatoes. "It's bedtime, Emma. You need to go ahead and eat."

"But I'm waiting for Mr. Wyatt."

"He's not coming." Finally, McKenna voiced what she'd known for the past two hours. "I'm sure something came up that he had to take care of." She wanted to believe that herself.

"But I drew him a picture. And he promised he would—"

"People don't always keep their promises, Emma!" Her voice came out harsher than she'd intended, and seeing the hurt on the little girl's face, McKenna wished she could take back the words. She breathed in, held it, then slowly exhaled. "I'm so sorry, sweetie. About yelling and . . . about Mr. Wyatt not coming." She felt her hands start to tremble. The lack of sleep was catching up to her, as was the realization that she had no "together" with anyone. Not like Chin Li and Mei had. She was alone. Again. "Why don't we go ahead and eat something? We'll feel better."

An hour later, with Emma fed and finally asleep, she double-checked the bolt on the front door then snuffed out the flame on the oil lamp. Remembering that closed-in feeling she'd experienced in the bedroom last night, she opted for the front room instead and sat on the sofa in the darkness.

Even drifting off to sleep, Emma had never lost hope, saying that Mr. Wyatt *would* come. McKenna leaned back and closed her eyes, wishing she still possessed that kind of childlike faith, wishing life hadn't snuffed that out for her. She draped a blanket over her legs, not faulting Wyatt so much as she faulted herself.

No matter how much a woman might prefer to lean on a man, to be protected or supported, she needed to make her own way through life. It was safer that way.

Wyatt left Bixby well before sunup. He wanted to get back to the ranch, and to McKenna and Emma, before having to leave again for Severance later that day, which meant he needed to get an early start.

He'd tried his best to get back to Copper Creek last night, knowing they'd been expecting him. But a lead he'd been chasing for weeks had finally paid off, and he couldn't just walk away. Not when he remembered the people who'd been murdered in the Brinks robberies, and the many more who might meet the same fate if the case wasn't solved soon.

His efforts in Bixby had proven fruitful—he'd added two more names to the growing list of conspirators. Yet he knew that not showing up at McKenna's last night had cost him. He'd worked so hard to earn her trust and didn't want to have to do any backtracking there. He patted his coat pocket, making sure the package was still inside. It had originally been a thank-you gift for McKenna, in recognition of making him such a fine saddle. Now it would be a peace offering for missing dinner.

He was beginning to think he might actually make it to her cabin in time to have breakfast with—

Gunfire sounded in the distance.

Wyatt reined in. "Whoa there, girl." Whiskey sidestepped nervously beneath him as he searched both sides of the ridge above. No one. The trail ahead led to Slocum's Pass, the only way to Copper Creek and then on to Denver.

Another shot sounded, followed by an explosion.

Wyatt spurred Whiskey down the trail, a whisper of smoke curling above the peak to his right. He'd ridden this road a hundred times. If his estimation was accurate, that smoke was rising from a spot not two hundred yards ahead where the road took a sharp turn. As he came closer, he heard voices, shouting over each other. He slowed his horse and drew his rifle.

But he wasn't prepared for the scene that appeared around the bend.

Splintered wood and debris littered the trail. Up ahead, a stagecoach—or what was left of it—lay on its side, smashed against boulders edging the path. Wyatt dismounted and tethered Whiskey to a stubby pine. The tang of gunpowder was thick in the air. Passengers were strewn among the wreckage, moaning, bleeding. Some lay still, crying for help, while others attempted to stand and seemed unable.

A man kneeling in the trail some distance ahead drew Wyatt's attention. He didn't fit somehow. His movements were sharp and purposeful. He didn't seem disoriented. On the contrary, he appeared frustrated.

The trail opened up, and Wyatt knew that if the man happened to look his way, he'd have nowhere to—

The man turned. Pistol in hand, he fired at the same time Wyatt pulled the trigger. The man staggered. Wyatt's leg went out from under him and he fell back, a bullet tearing through his right thigh. Wyatt rolled and took aim again, but the man was gone. He heard the pounding of a horse's hooves, heading back toward Copper Creek.

Wyatt eased up on one elbow and saw a man lying in the brush off the side of the road. He recognized the badge on the man's vest, and the absence of spirit from the body. And fury roiled inside him. Using his rifle for support, he gained his footing and made his way down the trail, wary.

Two men lay bloodied, facedown in the dirt, near where the man he'd shot, bullet wound in his head, had stood. As Wyatt came closer, he caught the salty scent of blood, and quickly realized what they'd been after. And what it had cost them.

A strongbox lay opened, one side completely blown away—much like the less fortunate of the two men. The other man lay motionless. Wyatt readied his rifle and nudged him over.

He staggered back when the eyes of Robert Ashford stared up at him, dull and fixed.

THIRTY-FIVE

A distant pounding awakened McKenna and she sat upright, blinking, trying to gain her bearings. Morning light spilled in through the side window.

"Miss Ashford!"

Not recognizing the voice, she threw off the blanket and rose, stiff from sleeping on the sofa, and retrieved the rifle from the top of the cupboard. She switched the safety lever as she moved to the door.

More pounding. "Miss Ashford!"

"Who's there?" she called, checking the bolt on the door again.

"It . . . Chin Li!" he said in a no-nonsense tone. "You come!"

Chin Li . . . That last part certainly had sounded like him. Still suspicious, she slid the bolt from the latch and inched the door open, rifle in hand. Seeing him, she lowered the gun. "Mr. Chin . . . What's wrong? Is Mei all right?"

"Miss Ashford." He motioned sharply. "You come!"

She looked past him. She didn't see anyone else, only a wagon. If Mei hadn't shared what she did yesterday about this man, McKenna might not have been inclined to go with him at all. As it was, she nodded. "I'll come with you, Mr. Chin. But give me a moment to get ready. I need to get Emma up and—"

"Marshal Caradon!" He said the name with authority. "You come!"

McKenna turned back. "Marshal Caradon? He sent you?"

Chin Li didn't answer, he only looked back at the wagon and motioned, every gesture efficient. "You come! Now!"

McKenna did as he ordered and, minutes later, held on tight to a barely awakened Emma as the wagon bounced over rutted roads on the way into town.

They reached Copper Creek, and Chin Li reined in sharply in front of Dr. Foster's clinic, sending dust billowing beneath the wheels. She'd tried asking him questions before they left the cabin. Whether he didn't understand or didn't want to divulge any answers, she couldn't be sure. But he remained silent, his dark eyes somber.

A group of people McKenna didn't recognize were gathered out front of the doctor's clinic. The bystanders turned to watch them. Dust covered their clothes and weariness dulled their expressions. Some had cuts on their faces, and they all shared a common disheveled appearance.

McKenna handed Emma down to Chin Li. Then he assisted her and returned the child to her arms. As they neared the boardwalk, McKenna saw two bundles draped in sheets on the planked walkway.

Only as she drew closer did she realize they weren't bundles at all. They were bodies.

More people arrived by the minute.

McKenna turned to ask Chin Li a question and found him speaking with a group of Chinese men. Their voices rose in a singsong blur. One of the gentlemen kept pointing down the street. McKenna searched the crowd for a familiar face and spotted Casey Trenton.

"Mr. Trenton!" She pushed her way toward him, Emma heavy in her arms. "Mr. Trenton!"

He turned in the direction of her voice. "Miss Ashford!"

She put Emma down and gave her a reassuring look, holding tight to her hand. "Do you have any idea what's happened, Mr. Trenton?"

"They're saying the morning stage was robbed. A ways from town. Three fellas ambushed it. Started shootin'. A U.S. Marshal was riding shotgun. I hear he returned fire as the driver tried to outrun them, but . . ." He shook his head and gave her a cautious glance. "The stage overturned. They're saying the marshal was killed and so was one of the—"

"A U.S. Marshal was killed?"

"Yes, ma'am. I don't know what this world's—"

"Do you—" McKenna could hardly breathe. "Do you know the marshal's name?"

"No, ma'am. Nobody's said yet." Trenton nodded toward the boardwalk where she saw Sheriff Dunn speaking to two other men. "How's that brother of yours doing? I feel bad about how things—"

"I'm sorry, Mr. Trenton. Please excuse me!" She lifted Emma into her arms. Wide-eyed, the child tucked her head into the curve of her neck. McKenna shoved her way through the crowd toward Sheriff Dunn. Then climbed the stairs to the boardwalk only to find her way blocked by a deputy.

"I'm sorry, ma'am, but you can't come up here."

"Can you tell me the name of the U.S. Marshal who died?"

He nodded. "Sheriff Dunn will be answering questions in a while, ma'am. We appreciate your patience."

She felt as if she could plow right through the man. "Sheriff Dunn!"

The deputy put a hand out to stop her, but McKenna pushed past him.

"Ma'am, you can't be up here!"

"Sheriff Dunn!" McKenna glanced at the bodies beneath the sheets as she passed, trying to shield Emma from seeing. Nothing showed other than the men's boots, and it struck her then that she'd never paid much attention to Wyatt's boots. "Sheriff!"

Dunn turned, and his expression went from in charge and commanding, to hesitant with regret. McKenna felt her legs go weak and was grateful when someone momentarily grabbed her from behind.

"I'm sorry, Sheriff, I told her she couldn't come up here!"

"It's all right, Wilson."

"But sir, you told us—"

"I'll handle this." Dunn waved the deputy off. Once the younger man left, Dunn sighed. "I'm sorry, Miss Ashford. I just sent a deputy out to your cabin."

McKenna hugged Emma closer, refusing the reality forming in her mind. She found it impossible to speak.

"I'm so sorry, Miss Ashford. I wished things had worked out differently. Marshal Caradon tried to tell me something like this might happen, but . . . even after all these years, I still tend to give people the benefit of the doubt. Especially young men like your brother."

Feeling like she was blindly groping her way through a fog, McKenna frowned. "Like my brother?"

Dunn stared as though he'd just made a misstep, and an awful fist tightened at the base of her throat. Reason tempted her to look back at the bodies, but she refused. "Sheriff, has something happened to Robert too?"

This time it was Dunn who seemed lost in the conversation. "Why don't we step inside the clinic, Miss Ashford? Dr. Foster can help explain things."

THIRTY-SIX

Wincing as he rose, Wyatt was careful not to put more weight on his right leg than necessary. The wound pulsed hot, and he tightened the tourniquet around his upper thigh.

Through Doc Foster's front window, he saw McKenna walking toward the clinic with Sheriff Dunn following behind. She held Emma in her arms, extra close, which told him something of her frame of mind. She looked like he felt—bone weary and near emptied of hope.

He wondered where Chin Li was, grateful the man had gone to get her. He also wondered what Dunn had told her. Whatever the case, he needed to speak with her before she got inside.

"Don't go too far on that leg, Marshal Caradon." Doc Foster peered up from his examining table. "You're next in line."

Wyatt nodded. "He still holding his own?"

Doc Foster sighed. "From what you described, this boy should be lying out there with those other two. Or should've at least had an arm blown off. As it is . . ." He wiped his brow.

"Yes, he's holding his own, and then some. I'd say somebody was praying for this boy, Marshal."

"I'd have to agree, sir." Wyatt glanced out the front window again. "And she's headed up the boardwalk right now." A group of men had stopped Dunn, no doubt pressing him for information. McKenna continued on without him.

"Do you want to tell her, Marshal . . . Or shall I? I think it'd be better if she's prepared."

"I'll do it." Wyatt reached for the latch. "When will he wake up?"

"Not for a while yet. Why don't you keep her outside? Until I'm done and . . . have it bandaged. I'll come get you."

"Thank you, sir."

"Marshal Caradon?"

Wyatt turned back.

"Did he have any part in the killing?"

Wyatt lowered his gaze to Robert who lay unmoving on the table. "I don't know the answer to that yet, sir." He shifted his weight to his left leg. "But I'm praying for his sake, and his sister's, that he didn't."

He opened the door and his eyes found McKenna's.

She stopped short. Her face went ashen. "Y-you're a-alive." It came out a whispered question. "They told me a marshal had been—" She choked on a sob.

Wyatt slowly realized what she'd mistakenly thought, and the feeling in her eyes softened him in a way he couldn't rightly explain. He took her in his arms, Emma too, and held them close. "I'm fine, McKenna. And very much alive."

She clung to him, fisting his shirt in her hand. Even Emma put her little arm around him and held on tight. He kissed the crowns of both their heads.

After a moment, McKenna stepped away. Her gaze lowered.

Wyatt looked down. Bloodstains, long dried, soiled the front and sleeves of his shirt, along with his right pants leg. Some of the blood was his. But most of it was Robert's, and he dreaded having to tell her about it.

"Marshal Caradon!" Chin Li approached, his expression grave.

But Wyatt knew kindness lay beneath his stern countenance. "Mr. Chin." In lieu of a handshake, Wyatt bowed, feeling his head swim. "My thanks to you, sir, for bringing Miss Ashford and her daughter."

"You have need again . . ." Chin bowed. "I help!"

"I appreciate that. Thank you, Mr. Chin."

Chin took his leave, and Wyatt gestured for McKenna to follow him down the boardwalk, away from the crowd.

But she shook her head. "You're hurt, Wyatt. You need to see Dr. Foster. And Sheriff Dunn said something about Robert. Do you know if he's all right?"

Wyatt took hold of her hand. "McKenna, I need you to trust me. Just for a minute. Dr. Foster has another patient who needs his attention first, then he'll see me."

The struggle was evident on her face. She finally relinquished, and nodded.

He guided her to an empty bench a few paces away, mindful of the pain in his right leg and the churning in his head. Grateful to be seated, he casually leaned forward and braced his arms on his legs, aware of the audience beside him.

McKenna situated Emma on her lap and gently touched his arm. "You're in pain," she whispered.

He closed his eyes at the cool touch of her hand on his skin. "A little . . . it's not that bad." Unable to look at her, he studied a knot in the wooden plank beneath his boots and prayed for her, as he'd been doing ever since he spotted Robert on the other end of that gun this morning.

"I'm not sure what all you know, McKenna . . ."

"That the stage was robbed. That a marshal died. And that it wasn't you."

Head down, his eyes watered. "The six o'clock stage left Copper Creek at daybreak and was ambushed by three men on horseback about a half hour out of town. In Slocum's Pass, on the way to Denver. The driver tried to outrun them, but the stage flipped. A U.S. Marshal was on board and gunfire was exchanged." He looked over at her. "They were carrying a full load of passengers . . . and a strongbox."

She searched his eyes, and he could see her trying to tie the loose ends together. And failing.

Emma raised her head from McKenna's shoulder. "We waited for you last night, Mr. Wyatt. But you never came."

"I know, honey, and I'm so sorry. I wanted to be there." He hoped his smile conveyed sincerity. "More than any other place I could think of . . ." He looked at McKenna. "I wanted to be there."

The disappointment in her eyes drove home how deeply he cared for her, how much he desired for her to trust him.

She smoothed a hand over Emma's hair. "We missed you but, of course, we understand. Don't we, Emma?"

Emma nodded, but due more from McKenna's prompting, he thought, than from truly understanding.

McKenna pulled a little slate and piece of chalk from her reticule and situated Emma beside her on the bench. "I'd like for you to practice your letters. Write as many as you can remember." After a moment, she turned back. "Not long ago, I read about a Brinks robbery in the newspaper." She spoke in hushed tones. "Is that related to this?"

"I'm not sure yet. But my gut tells me no. You asked a while back what I do for the Marshals Office. I wasn't at liberty to tell you then, and I'm not sure I should tell you now, but I don't see how I can avoid it . . . under the circumstances." He glanced around, making sure no one else was within earshot. "The Marshals Office has been investigating the Brinks robberies for months. Not long ago they asked me to investigate a possible connection between those robberies . . . and *murders,*" he said, glancing at Emma and mouthing the word, "with owners of gambling halls in the area."

"So that's what you've been doing when you leave the ranch every day."

He nodded. "I was on my way back here from Bixby when I heard gunfire, then the explosion."

"Explosion?"

"The three men who robbed the stage—or tried to—used dynamite." Anticipating what was coming, a weight settled in the center of his chest. "The strongbox was too heavy to move, so they held the driver and the passengers at gunpoint while they set the charge. But they weren't experienced with explosives. The charge went off before they were ready. Two of the men were injured in the explosion. One of them . . . didn't make it." He stared at the bloodstains on his hands, then forced his gaze back to her. His heart wrenched inside him. He phrased his words carefully, needing to be sure she understood. "McKenna . . . the other man who helped set the charge . . ." He swallowed hard. "It was Robert. That's who Doc Foster is working on right now."

For a moment, her features went slack. She blinked, frowning. "But it can't b—" She searched the street in the direction of Dr. Foster's clinic, shaking her head. "It's not . . . possible." She turned back. "You're certain?"

He nodded. "I'm sorry. I was there. It was Robert."

Tears rose in her eyes. "Is he all right?" She stood. "I need to go to him."

Wyatt rose slowly, taking a deep breath. "You can. As soon as Dr. Foster's done."

Her lips moved but nothing came out. "He was injured." It wasn't a question.

"Robert was beside the strongbox when the charge went off. He . . . lost . . . The doc is trying to save what's left of his hand—his left hand."

She closed her eyes and tears fell.

"Dr. Foster says it's a miracle Robert didn't lose his arm, McKenna. Or his life."

"But he's a wagonsmith, Wyatt. Without his hands—both of them—how is he supp—"

"I know." He wanted to touch her, hold her. "But he's fortunate to have his life, McKenna. He can start over. The man who was beside him doesn't have that option."

She wiped her cheeks. "I want to see him."

"I'll go with you." He took a step forward and had to reach out to steady himself on the back of the bench. Even from sitting for that brief a time, his leg had stiffened up.

McKenna slipped her arm around his waist. "Emma, follow us, please," she said behind her, putting a hand on his chest. "You don't look well, Wyatt."

"Maybe not." He dug deep for a smile. "But I'm feeling better by the minute." He tried not to put too much of his weight on her as they walked.

They were nearly to the clinic when her grip tightened. "Did—Was it Robert who shot you?"

Wyatt leaned against the building for support, feeling his body break out in a sweat. "No. There was a third man. I shot him, but he got away."

Relief cleared the question from her eyes.

Her hand on the door latch, she paused, as though trying to prepare herself for what waited inside. She looked at the two bodies draped in sheets on the boardwalk, and Wyatt found himself praying again that it hadn't been Robert who pulled the trigger on the marshal. He could see in McKenna's face that she was praying the very same thing.

THIRTY-SEVEN

McKenna put her hand on the door latch of the jail and felt a shiver sweep through her. The boardwalk was empty. She'd chosen her visiting time with care. Mei had graciously agreed to keep Emma, even offering to feed her dinner, complete with a freshly baked moon cake. Emma had hardly taken time to blow a kiss and wave good-bye before hurrying back to the kitchen.

McKenna smoothed a moist palm over the front of her dress as memories of Robert lying on Dr. Foster's examining table shoved their way to the forefront.

His left hand—or what was left of it—but also his face, his neck and chest. All bore marks from the explosion.

She took a steadying breath, praying he would be more open to seeing her now than he had been two days ago in Dr. Foster's clinic. "*Give him time*," Wyatt had told her. "*Maybe he needs to be alone right now. He's got a lot going on inside him.*" Yes, well Robert wasn't the only one who had a lot going on inside him. She was scheduled to meet with the circuit judge in the morning at nine o'clock and could scarcely hold a thought in her head, much less be prepared to defend her right to keep Vince and Janie's ranch, and be mother to their daughter. And all this while her brother was in jail for robbery—and possible murder!

Guilt nipped her conscience at her lack of compassion. He'd made such poor choices. And his timing . . . His obvious lack of desire to speak to her—even look at her—didn't help to soften her attitude toward him. And yet she loved him. No matter what he did, no matter whether he deserved it or not, she loved him. That seemed to be the curse of a parent's love. A parent was bound to their child no matter what. Forever. The child could abandon the parent. But never the parent, the child.

Wyatt had encouraged her not to come here. Not to see Robert. That perhaps Robert having time apart from her would be good. But people who loved each other stood by each other . . . didn't they? No matter what . . .

She lifted the latch.

Copper Creek's sheriff stood when she entered. "Miss Ashford."

"Good evening, Sheriff Dunn." No need for her to state why she was here. He knew. "How are you?"

"Doin' well, ma'am." He glanced at the hallway behind him. The door was ajar. "Robert's just had dinner. I'm finishing mine now too. My wife made some of her beef stew with corn bread. She slathers the bread thick with butter and honey." He briefly looked down, fingering the corner of his desk. "He's eatin' real good, ma'am. And . . . I think he's gettin' to a better place inside himself. Better than when you last saw him, at least."

Touched by his statement, McKenna smiled. "Thank you, Sheriff." She removed the basket on her arm and set it on his desk. "I brought him something to eat, maybe for later."

With all the care of a father with a newborn, Dunn peeled back the dishcloth and inspected the contents of the basket, then covered them back up. "This all looks fine, ma'am. Did you get them at Ming's Bakery?"

McKenna nodded, guilt having its second nibble at her for not having baked the items herself. "Robert never has liked my biscuits." She retrieved the basket, trying for a carefree tone. "Honestly, I can't say I blame him. I'm not much good at baking." Or anything else with Robert, it would seem.

Silence answered back, and she bowed her head, wondering if she was wrong to have come here.

"That may be true on the baking part, ma'am. But . . . from what I hear . . ."

Something in his voice drew her gaze.

"You make right fine saddles."

Her eyes widened. How did Dunn know she made saddles? She'd given Casey Trenton her word she wouldn't tell anyone she worked for him. If she lost this job at the livery . . . "I–I'm sorry, Sheriff Dunn. But I'm not quite sure I understand your meaning."

His sheepish smile held mischief, and looked out of place on such a seasoned man of the law. "Let's just say I heard it from someone who's right proud of you, ma'am." He glanced again toward the hallway. "Even though I'm not sure he realizes how true that is just yet."

"Thank you, Sheriff Dunn."

He grabbed a set of keys from his desk. "Come on, and I'll take you back."

The short corridor was better lit than she imagined and had a dank smell. Three cells lined up on the right. The first two were empty. A straight back chair sat lonely and isolated at the end of the hallway. Wyatt had told her that since Robert was under Dr. Foster's care, he'd stay here in Copper Creek, at least until Dr. Foster declared him fit to travel. She suspected Wyatt had pulled some strings for that to happen and was appreciative for it.

He was due home tonight and had said he'd do his best to get back before her meeting with the circuit judge. She hoped he did because she needed him. First to bear witness, along with Dr. Foster, to Janie's last spoken wish and testament. And second, to stand beside her. She couldn't imagine going through tomorrow without him.

Robert lay flat on his back on a bunk, eyes closed. He didn't look up when Dunn announced her, nor when the sheriff unlocked the door and let her inside.

"I'll be at my desk, Miss Ashford." Dunn placed the chair inside the cell. "Call me when you're through."

"Thank you," she whispered, and heard the lock in the door tumble solidly into place behind her. It was a cold, final sound and made her wish already that she was on the other side of those thick steel bars. She looked at her brother. At least she could leave here with one word to the sheriff. Robert, on the other hand . . .

"Hello, Robert. I hope it's all right that I—"

"I don't want you here, Kenny."

His voice echoed in the small space, bouncing off the mortared rock walls and meeting itself again. He rested his hands on his stomach, his right hand covering his bandaged left.

She hadn't expected this to be easy. Nothing was easy with him anymore. But she was determined to bridge the gap between them. "I brought you some things from Ming's Bakery." She considered placing the basket on the edge of the bed, two steps away, then decided against it, thinking he might well kick it off. She set it on the floor between them instead. "Chin Mei baked them herself."

"I *don't* want you here."

He didn't open his eyes. He didn't move, other than to speak. There was a flatness to his voice. Gone was the rebellious undercurrent that had so punctuated his tone in recent months.

The chair beside her looked as if it had served its purpose in this life, and the next, so McKenna sat carefully, in stages. "How is your hand feeling?" she asked, once certain the chair would support her weight. "Dr. Foster told me you should heal well, and that you'll still have use of the fingers—"

His eyes came open.

She didn't finish the sentence.

He stared straight up at the ceiling, unblinking.

She looked down at her own hands, trying to imagine what he must be feeling and thinking right now. And she couldn't. As well as she'd once known him—or thought she had—Robert was like a stranger to her now. But she thought she could reach him, if she just didn't give up.

"Emma's doing well," she tried again. "She asks about you." That was actually helping the truth along some. What Emma had asked was if Robert was ever coming home again. McKenna knew the child liked it better there without him. And she couldn't blame her. "I meet with the circuit judge in the morning. He'll determine whether—"

Robert was up off the cot in the space of a breath. "Sheriff!" He picked up the basket and dropped it in her lap.

Dunn appeared in the hallway. "There a problem?" He looked to McKenna for a response.

She didn't know what to say.

Robert peered through the bars. "Don't I have the right to refuse visitors, Sheriff?"

Dunn hesitated. "Yes, son. You do."

"Then I'm refusing this one."

McKenna rose, numb and unsure. She avoided Dunn's gaze as he unlocked the door. What had she done to Robert to make him hate her so?

The door clanged loudly as it shut behind her. Dunn clicked the lock in place and she followed him down the hall.

"Don't come back here, Kenny . . . *please*." Robert's voice was tight with emotion.

She turned and saw a single tear roll down his cheek. She hurried back to his cell and tried to cover his right hand gripping one of the bars. But he pulled away before she could. His face twisted. He was trying so hard to stuff down the emotions, just as he'd done as a little boy.

"Robert . . ."

He stepped back. "Promise me, Kenny, that you won't come back here."

Throat aching, eyes burning, she shook her head. "I'm sorry," she whispered. "But I can't make a promise like that. I'll be here for you, Robert. I love you too much to ever leave you alone."

But as she left the jail all she could think about was that one, solitary tear rolling down her brother's cheek, and what Wyatt had said about time apart from her being good for Robert right now. And about it being best if she not come here.

After seeing him, she couldn't help but wonder if Wyatt hadn't been right.

THIRTY-EIGHT

Wyatt arrived at the Copper Creek jail at dawn the next morning, certain that what he was doing was for the best. Even Sheriff Dunn agreed . . . now.

The wound in his leg still tender, Wyatt followed Dunn down the short corridor to the third cell. Each step, a prayer. A prayer he'd been praying for Robert for weeks now. And one he'd prayed for himself for years. *Break him, Lord, until he's wholly yours.*

He found Robert seated on his bunk.

"Morning, Robert. You ready to go?"

Dr. Foster had examined the boy late last night and declared him fit to travel. And that's all Wyatt needed. Robert was being transferred this morning to Denver, under escort of a U.S. Marshal. Wyatt had felt in his heart that the plan he'd already put in place this week was the right one. But after McKenna told him about her visit to the jail yesterday, he was absolutely certain.

He'd considered telling her about it last night, but decided to wait until the meeting with the circuit judge was over today. No need in adding to her list of worries.

Robert stood, cradling his bandaged left arm close to his body.

Dunn unlocked the door. "Let's go, son."

Robert walked out, then paused, looking at the handcuffs Wyatt held.

"Are you taking me?"

Wyatt shook his head and was almost certain he saw Robert's shoulders fall. *Break him, Lord, until he's wholly yours.* "I'm staying with your sister to attend the circuit judge meeting today. But I'll be in Denver next week."

Robert nodded. "Does she know?"

"No. I'll tell her later, once the meeting is over."

Robert held out his arms. "I didn't shoot him, Marshal Caradon."

Wyatt snugged a handcuff around his right wrist, then fitted the next more carefully around his left. *Break him, Lord, until he's wholly yours.*

Dunn led the way out of the jail.

Robert fell back a step, and then looked over at Wyatt. "When will the trial be?"

"A month from now. Maybe two. You did good in telling us the name of your accomplice."

When they got outside, Wyatt helped Robert up onto the horse. "Robert, this is Marshal Dalton. He'll see you all the way to Denver."

Mindful of his leg, Wyatt climbed into the saddle and rode with them until they reached the turnoff where he headed back to the cabin. Nothing was said. Dalton and Robert just kept on riding. And Wyatt kept on praying. *Break him, Lord, until he's wholly yours.*

As soon as Wyatt saw Circuit Judge Stewart Hawkins, he knew things would not go well for McKenna. The man went strictly by the letter of the law, to the extent that he often trampled the spirit of the law. The judge possessed no margin for compassion and had even less use for women who insisted on pursuing a "nontraditional role," as Hawkins had stated on more than one occasion. He was the last man Wyatt would have chosen to preside over this ruling.

"I have a bad feeling about this," McKenna whispered beside him, mirroring his own thoughts.

Mindful of Dr. Foster and Judge Hawkins standing nearby, he led her from the church sanctuary where the meeting was being held, out into a small foyer that afforded some privacy. With no courthouse in Copper Creek, the church building served a dual purpose as town hall.

He was grateful to Chin Li and Mei for agreeing to keep Emma this morning. McKenna couldn't afford to be distracted today. Although he didn't want to frighten her, he *did* want her to understand the seriousness of what she faced. "Just remember what we discussed. Answer the questions as briefly as you can. Don't wander in your response, and try not to give answers that prompt more questions. Be sure and—"

"I remember everything you said, Wyatt." She offered a tiny smile. "You were very thorough."

He nodded, wishing it were him being questioned by this man, instead of her.

A degree of optimism faded from her expression. She glanced back inside the church. "Do you know something about Hawkins? You said you've worked with some of the circuit judges before . . ."

Wyatt debated whether to say anything. If he warned her, she would be even more nervous than she already was. But if he didn't, and she inadvertently said something that ended up costing her the ranch—or worse, Emma—she'd never forgive him. And he'd never forgive himself. She deserved the truth. "Judge Hawkins wouldn't have been my first choice to preside over this ruling. I don't know him personally. I only know his reputation. But his rulings—the ones I'm familiar with—have been harsh. As is often his manner. And he doesn't think highly of women who seek to live more . . . independent lives."

She eyed him. "What does that mean?"

"You know exactly what it means, McKenna. Women who take on the world and never back down. Women whose hearts have so much love, they give even when that love isn't returned." He was reminded of what he had in his vest pocket for her—the thank-you gift for his saddle. The gift had since turned into the peace offering for missing dinner that night, and now represented so much more . . . Now that he knew how much she cared for him. Even though she might not be able to voice it, or even want to admit it to herself. But he would forever remember the moment she looked up outside the doc's office, thinking he was dead, and found him alive.

The timing hadn't felt right to give it to her then, but it did now. He reached into his pocket. "I'm talking about a woman who faces life with a courage and a persistence that astounds me. Who has endured so much difficulty in her life and yet keeps pushing on with stubborn grace, step-after-step, day-after-day." He softened his voice. "A woman who, at first, didn't trust me." He touched the side of her face. "But a woman who might just be beginning to trust."

Tears glistened in her eyes.

"And who makes this man want to spend the rest of his life proving to her that she can." He held out the box. "Not to mention a woman who makes the best saddles in all the western territory."

Her eyes widened. "You know?"

Oh how he wanted to kiss her. And if he was reading her right, she was more than open to the idea. "What did I tell you about looking at a man that way when he couldn't do anything about it?"

She grinned, and he pulled her to him and kissed her. He'd meant for their first kiss to be more tender, slow and gentle, but the way her arms came around him, pulling him closer, the way she responded, deepening the kiss, drove the desire inside him. Their bodies touching, he memorized the curves of her waist, the small of her back, how she felt pressed up against him. The warmth of her hand as she cradled the back of his neck encouraged him further—

Remembering where they were, Wyatt drew back. "McKenna!" he whispered.

Her eyes were still closed, her lips parted. She was wearing a purple dress today, one he hadn't seen before. But he liked it, very much. Especially on her. It buttoned up the front, and the lacey curve of the bodice revealed her neckline. The dress wasn't at all improper, but the thoughts he was having about her right now bordered on being just that.

She blinked. "Y-yes?"

He smiled and ran a finger over her mouth, and put more distance between them. "You need to open your gift."

She gave him an intimate look. "I thought I already had."

Oh this woman . . . It was a good thing they were in church.

She opened the box in her hand, and giggled.

He didn't mind in the least. He'd had about the same reaction when he'd first seen it. The woman in the store in Denver had called it a charm bracelet. But it was the tiny saddle hanging off it—among other miniature trinkets—that had gained his attention.

She held up the bracelet and fingered each tiny charm. "I love it! Thank you, Wyatt." For a long moment, she stared. "I wish you were presiding over this today."

He cupped her face in his hands. "We'll get through this. God's waiting for you in there, right now, just as surely as

He's already waiting for you . . . in the moment this ruling is decided."

They heard footsteps, and Wyatt put more distance between them.

Billings and another man, one Wyatt assumed was Harrison Talbot, walked into the church and nodded in their direction. Wyatt did likewise but couldn't shake the feeling he'd seen the second man before. Yet he knew he'd never met him. He'd only seen him from a distance on the ranch.

McKenna worked to open the clasp on the bracelet. Wyatt helped her put it on her wrist, feeling clumsy with the delicate chain.

Dr. Foster peered around the corner. "Judge Hawkins says he's ready, Miss Ashford."

She nodded. "Thank you, Doctor. I'm coming."

"Ma'am, may I say again how sorry I am about all this with your brother. I stopped by the jail and checked on him last night before he was transferred. He's doing fine and—"

"Robert was transferred?" McKenna looked from the doctor to Wyatt.

Wyatt watched a blush creep into her cheeks. But this time, it wasn't from his kiss. "I was going to tell you, McKenna. When the timing was right."

Dr. Foster's expression turned sheepish. "I'm sorry, I assumed you knew, ma'am. I–I'll see you both inside." He disappeared around the corner.

McKenna took a step toward Wyatt. "When was Robert transferred? And where is he going?"

"He left this morning, and he's on his way to Denver."

She searched his eyes. "And you knew?"

He nodded. "I arranged it, this past week. He's in good hands. With another marshal I've served with for years. Robert will stay in the Denver jail until he stands trial in a month or two."

"A month or *two*?"

"It could be longer, depending on when we track down the third man. But we'll get him. Then he and Robert will stand trial together for what they've done."

"Robert didn't kill the U.S. Marshal. I'm sure of it."

Wyatt wanted to be certain too, but wasn't.

McKenna turned and walked to the door of the church. She took several deep breaths. "You could have told me."

He came up close behind her, but didn't touch her. "If I had, what would you have done?"

She gave an abrupt laugh. "I would have tried to stop you. I would have tried to change your mind."

He spoke as tenderly as he could. "Neither of which would have happened, McKenna."

"I know," she whispered, and bowed her head. "Will you be going there? To Denver?"

"On occasion."

"Will you see him?"

Wyatt knew where she was headed. "Yes, I'll make sure I see him."

"Perhaps I can go with you, on occasion."

When he didn't answer, she slowly turned back.

Her eyes said she already knew, but Wyatt stated it so she would understand what he'd done. "I've asked the judge to limit Robert's visitors. Not to punish him, but in the hope that, given time, alone, with the right people helping him, he'll realize what path he's on and decide to make better choices."

"And my name won't be on that list, will it?"

"No, it won't." Wyatt took hold of her hand, and was grateful when she didn't pull away. "That's not because you don't love him, McKenna. I know you do. I've seen it. But what Robert needs right now is a different kind of love."

She looked down at their hands.

It had taken him years to learn this, and he'd learned it in the crucible. From God. He didn't know how else to say it, other than this. "Break me, Lord, until I'm wholly yours."

Her head came up.

"That's been my prayer for years . . . for myself. And it's been my prayer for Robert, since the day I met him."

She squeezed his hand tight. "How are you so sure that this is what he needs?"

Wyatt saw the fledging trust in her eyes. She was struggling, wanting to understand. And like blowing softly on kindling until it caught flame, he wanted to nurture that trust. "Because it's what I needed when I was about Robert's age—and nearly killed a man."

Seconds passed in silence. She slowly shook her head. "No . . . that's not possible."

"I'm not the same man now that I was then, McKenna. My father loved me enough to let God deal with me in the consequences of what I'd done. And God did. He'll do the same for Robert, too, if we'll only let Him."

THIRTY-NINE

Mr. Talbot, I appreciate your testimony today. Miss Ashford, yours has been . . . enlightening." Seated at a desk on the platform stage, Judge Hawkins glanced at his notes, seeming to enjoy the elevated position. "Vince and Janie Talbot's daughter is a most disarming child, and meeting with her this afternoon greatly aided my ability to make this decision so swiftly. So my thanks to you, Miss Ashford, for your assistance in that."

McKenna heard a trace of sarcasm in his voice, and she forced herself to maintain Judge Hawkins's appraising stare. Something in his manner, in the way he looked down at her over his glasses made her stomach churn.

Seated beside her, Wyatt gave her hand a discreet squeeze on the pew between them. He moved to pull away, but she held on. It still didn't seem possible—she tried to picture Wyatt at Robert's age, nearly beating a man to death for cheating at a hand of poker. While she wasn't fully convinced that Wyatt's approach with Robert would work, she knew with growing certainty that whatever she had been doing hadn't.

The proceedings had been surprisingly informal, given they were being held in a church. Wyatt had told her Judge Hawkins could be harsh. But Judge Hawkins had given new meaning to that word. How he'd learned about what had happened in St. Joseph, she didn't know. But as Billings had alluded to that day in his office, the world wasn't nearly as large a place as it used to be. Seeing herself through Judge Hawkins's eyes had been a most unpleasant experience. Especially with Wyatt present. She'd never before had her shortcomings and failures painted in such a stark light.

They'd taken a brief recess for lunch, and she and Wyatt had gone to Chin Li and Mei's to see Emma. Mei had served a delicious-looking meal, but McKenna hadn't eaten much. Neither had Wyatt. All she'd wanted to do was to hold Emma.

She'd been so sure Harrison Talbot was a fraud, yet it seemed as if he could actually be Vince Talbot's brother. He'd produced private documents substantiating his claim, and he also knew personal information about Vince and Janie that an outsider could never have known. Still, McKenna's instinct told her something was amiss, and he wasn't the man he professed to be.

But Judge Hawkins clearly didn't share her opinion.

"First, my ruling on the property belonging to Vince and Janie Talbot." Judge Hawkins looked down at his notes. "Based on the absence of a written will from Mr. Vince Talbot, in whose name the land deed was registered, I must rule in compliance with the laws of land ownership in the State of Colorado. Mrs. Janie Talbot's name was not recorded on the deed. She did not have legal ownership of the property, and thus did not possess the right to bequeath the property to her cousin.

"However, the property was in foreclosure at the time of Mr. Vince Talbot's death. Therefore, the statutes of foreclosure supersede those of inheritance law. And I am hereby recommending to the State of Colorado that the property be sold at auction on the fifteenth of October, at the courthouse in Denver." He peered down at her. "Miss Ashford, you have until that date, and no longer, to vacate the premises. You may take with you from the home only what you brought. Everything belonging to Vince and Janie Talbot must remain."

Feeling her hope being ripped from her, McKenna managed a nod. In itself, losing the homestead wasn't nearly as important as it once had been. Her heart was fixed solely on the one thing she wanted to leave here with today—her true inheritance from Janie—Emma Grace Talbot. But if she didn't have the ranch, she didn't have a place to raise Emma, to provide a stable home for her. Perhaps Judge Hawkins would overlook that in light of the obvious care she'd given the child, but that hope was a thinning ball of twine quickly unwinding.

"Miss Ashford . . ."

She looked up at Judge Hawkins.

"As I stated earlier, your testimony has enlightened these proceedings. Though I dare say, not in the light you might have desired. That being said, I assure you that the care you attempted to give this child was taken into consideration."

McKenna's breath caught. *Attempted to give?*

Wyatt gripped her hand.

"In ruling on the custody of Mr. and Mrs. Vince Talbot's daughter"—Judge Hawkins glanced again at his notes—"I am recommending to the State of Colorado that Emma Grace Talbot be removed from Miss Ashford's care and that a home more comparable to what Vince and Janie Talbot provided for their daughter be sought on the child's behalf."

Numb and disbelieving, McKenna remained seated on the pew, but she felt as if she were not in her body anymore. She saw the judge's lips moving but didn't hear him. She blinked hard, knowing she needed to be paying attention. Wyatt had said God was with her in the moments before they'd walked in here, as surely as He was waiting for her when Judge Hawkins made his ruling. But she couldn't see God anywhere in this.

"Emma Talbot is very young," Judge Hawkins continued, "and I believe that with the proper nurture and emotional stability that a home with both a father and mother will provide, the child will flourish and will little remember the difficult time she's endured in recent months." The judge leveled his gaze. "You are a most enterprising woman, Miss Ashford." He said it in a way that didn't sound complimentary. "While that is of concern to me, for many reasons, it did not influence my final decision. The motivation behind my decision today is your inability to provide for the child's basic physical needs, as well as your inability to provide a traditional, nurturing environment for Emma Talbot, such as, I have no doubt, her parents would have desired for her."

Feeling herself unravel, McKenna bowed her head, unable to maintain his gaze.

"I will add, Miss Ashford—at the risk of causing further injury, but in the hope of providing understanding—that I did consider the recent path your brother has taken. His . . . altercations shed light on himself, most certainly, but also on you. After all, you were and are the main parental influence in his life. I felt I would be remiss in my duties had I not taken that into consideration when making my decision."

Looking sternly in her direction, he straightened his notes and slipped them back into the folder, then made parting comments McKenna only half heard.

She closed her eyes and tears spilled over. How could God possibly be in this decision? Was she that horrible a parent? The answer came back swiftly as she pictured Robert arriving in Denver and being led to his jail cell. *Oh Janie . . . I'm so sorry.*

McKenna stood, clutching the pew in front of her, grateful she hadn't eaten anything for lunch. She looked beside her, expecting to see Wyatt, but he wasn't there. Somehow she'd missed him leaving.

Both Mr. Billings and Harrison Talbot briefly met her gaze

before walking from the church. Dr. Foster made his way toward her, his eyes filled with remorse. “Miss Ashford, I’m stunned, and so very sorry. I want you to know that I spoke to the judge privately on your behalf, and will do so again before he leaves town this afternoon. Emma Talbot should be with you. That’s what Janie wanted. That was her last wish.”

She tried to choke out a thank-you, but could only nod.

His hug was unexpected, and it was all McKenna could do not to crumble into a heap on the floor.

When Dr. Foster took his leave, she noticed Wyatt near the pulpit speaking to Judge Hawkins. If there was anyone she would want to plead her case, it would be Wyatt. But not even the word of a U.S. Marshal would change Judge Hawkins’s mind. Much less, his verdict.

FORTY

Wanting to see Emma, needing desperately to hold her, McKenna slipped from the church, leaving Wyatt to speak with Judge Hawkins in hushed tones. Shaking, she half-walked, half-ran to the Chinese Quarter.

She knocked on Mei's door, short of breath, and was tempted to take Emma right then and flee Copper Creek and never come back. They could go somewhere far away from here, where no one knew them. They could start over and—

Even as the thought took shape, she realized how foolish it was. She couldn't abandon Robert that way, even though for a time, he'd been "taken" from her by Wyatt's decisions. Yet how could she live apart from Emma, this child she loved like her own? And how would she ever come to terms with not keeping her promise to Janie?

Mei opened the door, her beautiful almond eyes full of hope. McKenna didn't have to utter a word, to see Mei's hope drain away.

"It not be true," Mei whispered, then took McKenna's hands in hers. "You good mother. She your child!"

McKenna lifted her shoulders and let them fall. "The judge doesn't think so." She tried to stem the tears for Emma's sake, but still they came. "He says Emma must go and live with someone else."

"Aunt Kenny?"

Emma came barreling around the corner. McKenna quickly wiped her tears, then bent down and scooped her up. Normally, she would have scolded the child for running in the house, but this afternoon she only held Emma close and breathed in the precious girl's scent—lavender, sunshine, and . . . moon cake. McKenna kissed her cheeks and felt crumbs at the corners of Emma's mouth.

"Miss Mei made us cookies to take home, Aunt Kenny."

"And did you eat one?"

"No." Emma shook her head. "I ate two!" She giggled and hugged McKenna's neck, and it was all McKenna could do not to start crying again.

She set Emma down. "Go gather your things. We need to get on home and do our chores."

"Yes, ma'am."

Emma ran back down the hallway, and part of McKenna's heart went with her. She heard steps behind her and turned.

Wyatt filled the doorway, his breath coming heavy. "I hoped . . . to catch you here." He stepped inside. "Chin Mei." He bowed.

Mei reciprocated. "Marshal Caradon," she said softly.

McKenna read hope in his eyes, which seemed incongruent to the day.

He stepped closer to her and reached for her hand. "McKenna . . . I have some news . . . from the judge." He glanced at their clasped hands, and moved closer still. "If I had my way, I'd give you more time to make this decision, and I'd do it all right and proper."

A wry smile tipped his mouth, and she stared, confused.

"Then again . . ." He laughed softly. "I'm not sure I'm that patient of a man, especially when it comes to you."

He brought her hand to his lips and kissed it—once, twice—and despite the turmoil inside her, McKenna thought of their shared moment back in the church foyer, and a shiver stole through her.

"I've spoken with Judge Hawkins, McKenna, and he's agreed to rescind his ruling about Emma . . ."

Her breath caught, wanting to believe this but unable to. "You were able to change his—"

He held up a hand. "But only if you marry."

"Marry?" she whispered, not understanding.

"Before he leaves town . . . in one hour."

FORTY-ONE

Having anticipated the drop of her obstinate, enticing little chin, Wyatt didn't dare let go of McKenna's hand. "If you choose not to marry now but want to wait, which Judge Hawkins says is an option, he'll go ahead and submit his ruling. Then you'll need to travel to Denver and file an appeal, appear before a judge there, and have another hearing in coming weeks."

McKenna stared, wide-eyed and wordless, while Mei stood off to the side, her head bowed, with a demure smile bunching her cheeks. Wyatt wished McKenna would smile, would cry, would do something to let him know what was going on inside of her.

He reached for her other hand and held them both between his. "And in case it's not clear to you . . ." He smiled, wanting to take her in his arms and kiss her again, maybe try and help her decision along. "I'm the one you'll be marrying. Unless you have someone else in mind." *Lord, please let her say yes . . .*

With a nervous laugh, she lowered her eyes, her grip on his

hand turning viselike. She glanced down the hallway, then back at him. “Would I be able to keep Emma with me? If I waited?”

Wyatt tried not to take the implication of her question too personally, yet felt a slight sting. He knew she was scared to death. And she’d been through fire today. First with finding out that he’d transferred Robert, then with Judge Hawkins. And now this . . .

Several times he’d wanted to take Judge Hawkins out behind the church and show the man a different kind of justice. But he also knew that if God had wanted McKenna in another situation, He could have arranged it. As hard as Wyatt had found it to sit there and listen to her answer Hawkins’s questions, to witness her ability and even her character be called into question, he’d sensed God restraining him. And he’d found himself praying the same prayer for her that he’d prayed for Robert, and that he prayed for himself.

He shook his head. “If you chose to wait, Emma will be temporarily placed with a family in Denver. One experienced with assisting in situations like these. Hawkins said you could visit her though, on occasion.”

With each passing moment, he grew more certain about his love for her. And as the frown deepened on her face—less certain about her affection for him.

“Mr. Wyatt!” Emma came at him at breakneck speed down the hallway.

He caught her up and hugged her tight. She kissed his cheek, and Wyatt glanced at the clock on a nearby table. Thirty-five minutes and counting until Hawkins boarded the Denver stage.

“Mr. Wyatt, can we have dinner tonight? You promised, ’member?”

“I do remember, little one. And I’d like that . . . very much.” He looked at McKenna and saw her watching the two of them. “But that all depends on what your Aunt Kenny says.”

Emma's expression turned pleading. "Can we, Aunt Kenny? *Please?*"

Wyatt had never seen so many varied emotions flit across a young woman's face.

McKenna slowly drew herself up. She smoothed the front of her dress and offered a brave smile that might have appeared convincing—if not for the tremor in her hands.

"All right," she said finally, her tone none too confident. "We'll have dinner with Mr. Wyatt—"

Squealing with delight, Emma hugged his neck.

"—after he and I visit with Judge Hawkins."

"Marriage is a holy institution." Judge Hawkins pierced McKenna with a look. "Not to be entered into lightly."

She lowered her gaze to the open Bible in his hands and tried to recall some of the scriptures she'd recently committed to memory. Wyatt shifted beside her, and suddenly her mind went blank. She sensed he was watching her, but she didn't turn. Doubt bombarded her from all sides. This was happening too quickly. If only she had more time to consider her options.

But there were no other options.

"The union between a man and woman is to be entered into with all reverence and consideration . . ."

She kept her eyes on the floor, focusing on a portion of a wooden plank that had soaked in more of the stain. It was darker and stood out from the rest.

They'd found Judge Hawkins waiting for the five o'clock stage to Denver, just where he'd told Wyatt he would be. Yet he'd appeared none too pleased when he saw them coming. When they first arrived back here at the church, Hawkins attempted to speak with her alone, but Wyatt had circumvented the man's efforts. "If you have something to say, I'd appreciate it if you'd address us both, Judge Hawkins. Since we are to be husband and wife."

Husband and wife . . .

Fear looped another knot in her stomach. But at least Wyatt had saved her from another conversation with Judge Hawkins. She looked down at her dress. *Purple*. She cringed. What a color to be married in. If she'd known she would be getting married that day, she would have chosen something else that morning.

"This union was instituted by God to provide a place wherein a woman is to be a helpmeet to her husband, and wherein a man is to love his wife as Christ loved the church. God designed this relationship to be shared between a man and woman for their mutual edification and for the purpose of procreation . . ."

McKenna's face heated at the word, then at how her imagination began filling in the blanks in her mind. But her imagination ran out long before all the blanks were penciled in, and she swallowed hard, clenching her eyes tight at what remained unknown.

"Marriage is intended to last a lifetime . . ."

She stared at her hands resting in Wyatt's. His were warm, large, and rough, browned by the sun. A rancher's hands, familiar with work. A puckered scar ran the length of the top of his left thumb. She'd never noticed that before. The skin looked long healed. Perhaps it was something from boyhood . . .

His thumb began to make slow, patient circles over the tops of her fingers, and the effects of his tenderness spread throughout her entire body. Her thoughts took a backward skip to Judge Hawkins's comment about procreation, and she blushed as her thoughts penciled in another blank.

"Wyatt—" Judge Hawkins stopped. His brow knit. "What is your full name, Marshal Caradon?"

"Wyatt Thomas Caradon, sir."

"Wyatt Thomas Caradon," Judge Hawkins continued, "do you take this woman to be your lawfully wedded wife? To have and to hold, from this day forward . . . ?"

McKenna glanced beside her. His middle name was Thomas?

She hadn't known that. There was so much about this man she didn't know. Oh God, what was she doing? Her heart started pounding. A ringing filled her ears. She was famished, yet she couldn't have eaten a bite at that moment if she'd tried. She cared deeply for Wyatt. But caring for a man and loving him the way a wife should love her husband were two very different things. Maybe she was making a mistake. Maybe she should—

A quick glance over her shoulder at Emma seated on the front pew beside Mei, Chin Li, and Dr. Foster bolstered her decision. Again. Emma waved, and McKenna smiled back, knowing she couldn't live without this child. And she wouldn't risk having Emma live with someone else for weeks on end, with the possibility that Judge Hawkins might change his mind at any time. And she could never live with herself knowing she'd let Janie down.

She faced forward again. *Janie, I'm keeping my promise . . .*

"I do," Wyatt said, and gave her hand a gentle squeeze.

He didn't sound as nervous as she was. In fact, he didn't sound nervous at all. McKenna slid her eyes to the right and stole a furtive glance, trying to see his face. But she couldn't, not without being obvious.

"Miss Ashford?"

"I do," she forced out, trying not to wince as she said it. Then she met Judge Hawkins's stern gaze and realized she wasn't supposed to have said that yet.

"State your full name, please, Miss Ashford."

"Oh, yes. I'm sorry. It's—" She hesitated, cringing. "*Agnes* McKenna Ashford."

Wyatt sighed beside her. Or had it been a laugh? She couldn't be sure.

"*Agnes* McKenna Ashford," Judge Hawkins repeated with the same emphasis, his gaze weighed with displeasure. "Do you take this man to be your lawfully wedded husband? To have and to hold from this day forward? For better or worse, for richer or poorer, in sickness and in health? Do you pledge yourself unto him, and him only? Do you promise to love, honor, and obey him as your rightful head in the sight of Christ?"

My rightful head? Honor and obey? A cool wind of reality swept through her. She thought of Chin Li and Mei, and didn't think she could ever be that subservient to a man. Would Wyatt Caradon expect her to be? He certainly wouldn't expect her to bow to him, but what might he expect of her in other ways? And what if—

Wyatt's grip suddenly tightened and she looked up.

He was smiling. Only it wasn't a full smile. It was one of those ghosted little grins that masked a secret. And it gave her a glimpse of what he must have looked like as a little boy. *Adorable . . .*

Her gaze inched upward to his eyes and all traces of boyhood vanished.

A wave of desire, powerful and unexpected, swept through her. Her memory traced a path back to the way he held her in his arms earlier that day, and of his kiss. He hadn't been the least bit shy then, and at the slightest bit of encouragement, had grown undeniably bolder.

"McKenna." Wyatt's voice was soft.

She blinked, and recognized the earnestness in his eyes.

"Will you take me as your husband?" he whispered, indicating the judge with a tilt of his head. "He has a stage to catch."

She thought of Emma, and of Janie. And of all she'd done wrong with Robert in her life. Then she thought of what little she knew about this man before her. He already loved Emma, and Emma loved him. He was a man of honor, kind and— "Yes," she whispered, forcing the words over the *tick-tock* of the imaginary clock. "I do."

Judge Hawkins closed his Bible, his sternness only slightly less diminished. "By the power vested in me by the State of Colorado, I now pronounce you man and wife. What God has joined together, let no man put asunder. Mr. Caradon, you may kiss your bride."

McKenna froze. What if he kissed her here like he'd done

when they were alone in the church foyer? His hand covering hers urged her toward him. Readying herself, she turned.

His smile was gone and in its place was a look she couldn't define. If she hadn't known better, she might've thought they were alone. He leaned down. His lips brushed hers, and lingered. His mouth was soft against hers, and so sweetly tender that her worries began to lose their footing. A man who could ride and shoot like Wyatt Caradon ought not be able to kiss like this.

He drew back before she was ready for him to, and when she opened her eyes, that smile of his was back in place. Only with a wicked little gleam this time. She forced her gaze elsewhere, knowing she'd have to be careful not to encourage him in this area. Until she was ready anyway . . .

Kissing was one thing. But what lay beyond that was another. And knowing the mind of a man as she did, she knew Wyatt would want the "what lay beyond" to come sooner rather than later.

She remembered that night on the porch steps when she'd accused him of having been with cheap women. He'd told her then that he'd never been with a woman like that, and she'd believed him. She still did.

What was even more reassuring was knowing—when the time came for them to truly become husband and wife—they would share that experience for the first time . . . together. Just as God intended.

FORTY-TWO

Draped in dusk, the homestead came into view as Wyatt guided the wagon down the road. McKenna saw it all so differently—the cabin, the barn, the corrals—and sorrow settled inside her. She thought she'd prepared herself for what this moment would feel like—when she knew with certainty that the ranch was no longer hers. Between Mr. Billings's foreclosure notices and his visit with Harrison Talbot, reality should have sunk in by now.

But it hadn't.

With Emma asleep in her arms, it hit her full force that this precious child would not grow up in the home Vince and Janie built for her. Nor would she inherit the land her parents worked so hard to keep. But she *would* grow up knowing she was loved. McKenna could guarantee that, so would Wyatt, she knew. And Emma would know how much Vince and Janie had loved her too.

Wyatt pulled the wagon to a stop in front of the cabin, climbed down, and came around to her side. Wordless, McKenna handed the child down, and warmed at the way he cradled Emma in his arms.

"I'll carry her inside," he whispered.

Nodding, McKenna started to climb down too, but he turned back.

"Wait here, please," he said softly, that semblance of a smile returning. "Agnes."

Seeing the mischievous gleam in his eyes, she bit her lower lip to keep from smiling. She kept her voice low. "I've always hated that name."

"And I've always loved it. It's my mother's name."

"It's not!" she mouthed.

But he nodded and winked.

Watching him walk into the cabin, she felt a nervous tickle reawakening inside her. They'd eaten dinner at a place in the Chinese Quarter called Ming's. The food was delicious, though not the type of fare she'd dreamed of having at her wedding reception. Nothing about this day had been as she'd dreamed. Having Chin Li, Mei, and Dr. Foster's company kept conversation between her and Wyatt to a minimum, as had Emma falling asleep on the way home.

Just then, her thoughts were interrupted as Wyatt took the porch steps by twos. She suddenly felt conspicuous sitting there, waiting for him. So she quickly folded her hands in her lap then changed her mind and put a hand on the bench seat and one on her reticule. Her fourth finger on her left hand was bare. No time to buy a ring, if Wyatt planned on making that purchase. Not every wife wore one, nor could every husband afford it.

Seeing the way he stared up at her, a wedding ring was suddenly the least of her concerns.

"May I have the honor . . . Mrs. Caradon?"

Mrs. Caradon. Mrs. Wyatt Caradon. She leaned down and he lifted her into his arms. She kept her eyes averted as he carried her up the stairs and across the threshold of the cabin, yet she was aware of every place their bodies touched, and of where his hands were on her—chaste and proper—which only accentuated what he was probably thinking about. And what she was trying her best not to.

Emma's bedroom door was closed. Vince and Janie's wasn't.

Wyatt lowered her to the floor, then paused, his hands on her waist. "McKenna?"

His breath was soft on her face. "Yes?"

"You can look at me, you know. I'm not going to bite."

Something about the way he said it made her smile, and she lifted her gaze. The room was cast in shadows, and she could make out only the faintest outline of his stubbled jaw. She fought the sudden urge to touch his face.

"Thank you," he whispered. "For making me your husband." His hand moved, ever so slowly, around her back. "And for giving me the chance . . ." He nodded toward Emma's bedroom. "To be a father to that sweet little one in there."

The anxious tickle expanding inside her, McKenna matched the softness of his voice. "And thank you for making me your wife, Wyatt. For allowing me to keep her, and to keep my promise to Janie. It was very . . . honorable of you." She was achingly aware of the progress of his hand on her lower back as it moved upward.

As though acting on its own volition, her hand rose to cradle his face. *This man* was her husband. This man was *her husband*! He pulled her closer. The rise and fall of her chest met his, and the cabin suddenly seemed overly quiet. And dark.

He leaned down and she sucked in a breath.

He kissed her forehead and the curve of her cheek. "I love you, McKenna. I have for some time now. And when Hawkins mentioned the option of you marrying today . . ."

He brushed the hair from her temple and kissed her there. Twice. A weakness settled in her knees.

His laughter came soft. "It wasn't hard for me to know what I wanted to do. So just to be clear . . . honor had little to do with my actions today. They were mostly selfish at heart."

McKenna let out a held breath. Her hand trembled against his face. He kissed the corners of her mouth, and lingered. His breath was warm and his question clear. She answered by turning toward him, and he drew her into his arms and kissed her full on the mouth.

After a moment, she grew heady with being so close to him, and with the possibilities that lay beyond this moment. How could she want two such opposite things at the very same time? She wanted to be close to him, exactly like this, with his arms around her. Maybe even closer. Yet she wasn't ready for . . . *more*. Not now. Not yet.

His hands grew bolder, his intent clearer, and she was on the verge of rethinking that last thought, when he drew back.

She couldn't see his face, but she felt him staring. His breath was audible. He kissed her again, but this time on the crown of her head, like he might have Emma, and then he held her. Just held her. And she clung to him, burying her head in his chest.

They stood that way for the longest time—in the dark, in the quiet, the clock on the mantle ticking off the lengthening seconds.

Until he lifted her chin. "We're husband and wife now, McKenna. But . . . I realize that doesn't mean things are going to change between us all at once. It'll take time." He ran his hands down her arms and rested them again on her waist. "We'll be patient with each other. We'll take things slow."

She loved the way his hands rested on her waist—strong, possessive. "Thank you," she whispered, then felt as though she needed to state the obvious. "It's just that I've . . . never—"

He kissed her forehead. "I know."

She smiled, waiting. For what, she wasn't really sure, until the thought struck her—she'd expected him to say, "Me neither," or to somehow echo what she'd professed. But he hadn't. She reached into her memory for his response when she'd accused him of keeping company with cheap women. *"I have never . . . never been with a woman in one of those places."*

She stepped back, wishing she could see his face, wondering now if she'd assumed too much from his statement. Maybe he *had* been with a woman before, just not a woman from one of those places. "So . . . have you ever . . . ?" She gave a tentative shrug, unable to voice the question outright.

He didn't move. It was such a simple question, yet seemed to take him forever to answer. The longer he took, the more unsure she became. And when he finally looked away, she knew.

After what felt like an eternity, he turned back and met her gaze. "Yes . . . I have, McKenna. But it's not what you're thinking. It was with . . . my wife."

FORTY-THREE

Your *wife*?" McKenna whispered, disbelief weighing her tone.

Wyatt moved to light the lamp on the kitchen table. He needed to see her face, and for her to see his. He'd planned on telling her about Caroline and Bethany, he simply hadn't anticipated telling her tonight. The oil lamp cast a dingy orange glow on the space around them. McKenna's expression held surprise, and a trace of disappointment.

He encouraged her to sit beside him on the sofa. She did, but kept her distance.

"Caroline died seven years ago. After giving birth to our daughter, Bethany." Images flashed through his mind—of Caroline and Bethany, of his years on the trail, of pursuits and shoot-outs. Of nights spent lying on a bedroll staring up into a night sky so dark and fathomless he'd often wondered how God ever remembered his name. Why all of that converged in this moment, he didn't know. He only knew that McKenna Ashford—no, McKenna *Caradon*—held his heart, which was fine with him. As long as God held their future, which he knew He did.

Wyatt told her about his wife and daughter, about how he hadn't been able to bring himself to stay and live within the walls that held memories of Caroline's laughter and Bethany's sweet coos. "Bethany went first, two days after she was born. Caroline followed a week later. Before Caroline died, she asked me to bury her with Bethany, but . . ." He shook his head, recalling the scene. "Afterward, her family insisted that Bethany stay buried where she was. I gave in, and—"

"You've regretted it," McKenna said softly. "Ever since."

Wyatt saw tears in her eyes. He nodded. "Yes, I have."

Her gaze went briefly to Vince and Janie Talbot's bedroom. "So when Janie asked you to bury her with her son . . ."

Wyatt didn't need for her to complete the sentence. "I was keeping not only my promise to Janie, but my promise to Caroline too, in a way, after all these years."

An errant tear wove a path down McKenna's cheek. "I sensed there was something more to what you did for Janie that day."

To his surprise, she scooted closer.

"Do you think we could just . . . sit here for a while? Together? I'm tired, but . . ." She stifled a yawn. "I'm not ready to go to bed yet."

He wasn't either. Especially knowing he wouldn't be going with her, at least for now. He leaned back on the sofa and drew her close. She laid her head on his chest and sighed, then suddenly raised up.

"I'm not hurting your leg, am I?" She looked down.

He smiled and urged her back against him. "Believe me, I'm feeling no pain right now."

A pleased look on her face, she tucked her head beneath his chin and was asleep within minutes.

After a while, he eased her down beside him and lay behind her on the couch, holding her close, and thanking God for this second chance at a family he thought he'd never have.

McKenna awakened early the next morning, fully clothed and in bed. Alone. She brushed a hand across the empty space beside her, and realized she'd never thought of it as being empty before. But she did now.

Wyatt had been married. Discovering that last night had come as a surprise. All this time, he understood far more about pain and loss than she'd given him credit for, and as she viewed the past few weeks through that filter, her affections for him only deepened.

She turned over, the straw ticking crunching in the mattress beneath her, and she stared out the window onto a world bathed in the pale half light of dawn. Surely Robert was settled in the Denver jail by now. Was he alone in his cell? Was someone else with him? Did he miss her, or home, yet? Doubtful . . . But even more—was he guilty of shooting that U.S. Marshal?

Everything within her said he wasn't. But there was just enough of the unknown—that part of Robert she didn't understand anymore—to keep that niggling possibility alive, and to keep her repeating, with increasing earnestness, Wyatt's prayer for her brother. *Break him, Lord, until he's wholly yours.*

She rose to find Emma still tucked deep in slumber. The blanket on the back of the couch was neatly folded. She assumed Wyatt had slept there last night, but he could have bunked in the barn. The possibility of that sat ill with her. It didn't seem right for a groom to have spent his wedding night alone in a barn.

Looking out the front window, she spotted him riding across the field on Whiskey, headed for the lower pasture. He'd risen early, as she'd learned was his custom, and she doubted that he'd eaten anything yet.

Having breakfast waiting when he returned would be a nice gesture.

An hour later found the table set with fresh wildflowers, the coffee brewing, and eggs and bacon sizzling on the stove. Biscuits were in the oven, but she had full confidence they would turn out as hard and tasteless as usual. Scoops for honey, at the very best.

Footsteps sounded on the porch, and she felt a twitter of excitement as Wyatt walked in, hat in hand.

He stopped and stared. First at the table, then at her. "Well . . . this is sure a nice welcome."

She grew warm beneath his attention, and warmer still as he crossed the room toward her.

He lifted a curl from her bodice and rubbed it between his thumb and forefinger. "It smells good in here."

He smelled good too. She caught a whiff of fresh soap and sunshine, and his hair was still damp. "You bathed in the creek," she said softly.

"Yes, ma'am, I did."

"Well . . ." She gave a breathless laugh. "Breakfast is ready. I hope you're hungry."

"Yes, ma'am." His gaze captured hers and held. "I am."

If not for his self-declared patience, she might have been unnerved by the transparency of desire in his eyes. But Wyatt Caradon was her husband. She could stand on tiptoe right now and kiss him full on the mouth if she wanted to. That was her right. And the thing was—she slowly realized—she wanted to.

Even more, *he* wanted her to.

Yet he didn't move. However, he did smile, ever so slightly, and it gave her the encouragement she needed.

She rose on tiptoe, and could all but reach him. "You might want to meet me halfway, Mr. Caradon."

Wordless, he did, but stopped just short of completing the journey.

Their breaths mingling, she sensed his growing lack of patience, which, oddly enough, only increased hers. She ran a finger along his stubbled jawline and saw his eyes narrow ever so slightly. She'd never been one to toy with a man, but then she'd never been married to one with whom she could toy.

She kissed him on one corner of his mouth, then the other. On his cheek, and then gently on the lips, like he'd done with her yesterday at the ceremony. His arms didn't come around her like she half expected, but not for a moment did she question his response. He was letting her take the lead . . . and she liked it.

For as nervous as she'd been with him last night, she felt quite the opposite this morning.

Hearing the creak of Emma's bedroom door, McKenna ended the kiss and turned, but not before she caught Wyatt's subtle wink. Resisting the urge to fan herself, she met Emma halfway, still smiling. "Good morning, sweetie."

Emma reached for her, yawning.

"Are you ready for some breakfast?" McKenna scooped her up and nuzzled her neck.

Emma nodded, and looked in Wyatt's direction. "I like it when you're here."

Wyatt moved to kiss her forehead. "I like it too, and I plan on being here every day. Is that all right with you?"

Her grin was affirmation enough.

Wyatt motioned for them to sit, then retrieved the skillet from the stove and doled out eggs and bacon to each place setting. He followed with her over-browned biscuits and two cups of coffee. After he offered thanks, conversation came easily.

He bit into a biscuit, and McKenna grinned at his hesitation. He looked up, realizing he'd been caught.

"They're not bad," he said quickly.

She laughed. "They're not good either."

His expression remained noncommittal. "Let's just say I don't mind handling the biscuits next time. It's the least I can do."

The first to finish, Wyatt carried his dirty plate to the wash bucket. "Did Vince or Janie ever mention anything to you about running irrigation on their land?"

McKenna swallowed the sip of coffee in her mouth. "Not that I recall. Why?"

"It's probably nothing. I saw pipes down by the creek this morning and wondered. Makes sense that's what they'd be for, but I'm not sure." He came around and knelt beside Emma. "Would you consider giving me a hug good-bye, little one?"

Emma complied without reservation.

McKenna sought his eyes. "You're leaving so early?"

He stood, taking Emma with him. She laid her head on his shoulder and he rubbed her back. "I've got a meeting in Bixby this morning. And if I want to get home earlier in the evenings . . ." He paused. "And I do . . . I need to leave earlier in the day." He set Emma back in her chair and came around to McKenna's side. He leaned down and kissed her cheek, and lingered.

Sensing what he wanted, McKenna turned her head and met his lips. How quickly she was becoming accustomed to this.

"Thank you for breakfast," he whispered.

"You're welcome." She brushed his cheek with her hand. "Come home soon."

"I wish I never had to leave."

FORTY-FOUR

The wind blew hard from the north, swirling the snowcapped peaks above the cabin and ushering fall in with a chill. Wrapping her shawl tighter about her, McKenna stood on the porch and kept a watchful eye on the thunderhead building in the distance. It was mid-afternoon, too soon to expect Wyatt.

In the past month, he hadn't returned home before eight o'clock at the earliest. But still, she hoped he'd be home soon, both considering the coming storm but especially knowing he'd been in Denver, visiting Robert. She could hardly wait to hear how Robert was doing and if Wyatt noticed any change in him. And whether he had news on the upcoming trial.

The horses were safe in the barn and Emma was inside napping, though, with this wind, surely she wouldn't be able to sleep much longer.

Wyatt was right. Aspens in fall were more beautiful than McKenna could have imagined. But right now the wind was stripping the bright golden leaves from their branches, sending them scurrying down the road in a swirl of dust and dirt.

The first raindrop landed with a resounding *plop* on the bottom porch step, followed by another and another. McKenna walked back inside and closed the door. She slipped the bolt firmly into place, accepting with sinking certainty that Wyatt wouldn't make it back home tonight. Nor would she want him to try, considering the weather, despite what plans she'd had.

Back in the bedroom, she lit a lamp for extra light, and picked up a clean cloth, doused it with saddle oil and continued her slow circular motions, working the oil into the leather. Every few minutes, listening to the wind howl outside, she found her focus drawn back to the bed.

She'd underestimated Wyatt's patience and overestimated her own confidence. The fact that he knew what to expect from the intimacies between a husband and wife should have lent her comfort. But it didn't. All she could think about was his disappointment if she didn't meet his expectations. And that one single fear had been enough to curb her enthusiasm. But tonight she had planned on putting aside that fear once and for all, and would simply follow his lead. That, she knew she could trust.

A loud thud sounded outside the bedroom window. She rose and peered out in time to see an empty whiskey barrel careening down the road. A crack of thunder rolled across the sky and the dark gray thunderhead opened wide. Within minutes, the sun-drenched earth formed pools of mud that congregated to flow downhill toward the road.

Thunder rolled again and a cry came from Emma's bedroom. McKenna laid her cloth aside, grabbed the oil lamp, and hurried to check on her.

"Hey, sweetie . . ." She sat down on the edge of the bed. "It's all right, I'm here."

Hair mussed and tangled, eyes squinty with sleep, Emma crawled from beneath the covers and into her lap. She wrapped her arms around McKenna's neck and, seconds later, McKenna heard her soft cries.

"Oh honey . . . what's wrong? Are you sick?" She felt Emma's forehead and found her burning up.

Eyes red-rimmed and swollen, Emma managed to suck in breaths between sobs.

"Oh sweetie . . ." McKenna cradled her close.

Emma cried harder. "I'm scared. I—I want m–my m–mama."

McKenna's heart broke. She took Emma into the kitchen and sat her in a kitchen chair. Emma's sobs became more broken and the child shivered uncontrollably as McKenna poured water into a bowl and wet a clean dishcloth. She dabbed Emma's forehead and cheeks, then her neck and chest.

She held a cup of water to Emma's lips, but Emma refused it.

"Emma, you need to drink something to get your fever down."

Emma shook her head harder. "It hurts . . . my throat."

McKenna couldn't help but remember that illness that had taken Vince and Janie. But she knew better than to panic. She remembered Robert having sore throats when he was younger. The doctor always prescribed willow bark tea and plenty of rest. She made Emma comfortable on the sofa and gathered ingredients for the tea.

Soon the kettle whistled on the stove.

She let Emma see her stirring honey into the cup. She tasted the concoction first, checking the temperature. "Mmm . . . it'll feel good to your throat."

She lifted Emma's head. Emma drank, wincing. But at least she drank. The tea had a sedating effect and, shortly after, Emma slipped back to sleep.

With the storm still raging outside, paling daylight took an early leave. She rinsed the compress on Emma's forehead every few minutes, while bathing her skin with a cool cloth. Soon, her own eyes wouldn't stay open either and she dozed in small snatches.

She awakened after midnight to Emma's cries and found her still hot to the touch. McKenna repeated the tea with honey, the compresses, the cool water baths, and moved Emma back to her own bed, thinking she'd be more comfortable there.

But when she tried to lay her down, Emma clung to her and wouldn't let go.

"Mama? Mama?" she cried, over and over.

Tempted to cry with her, McKenna shook her head. "*I'm* here, Emma. Aunt Kenny's here."

Clinging to her, Emma's sobs grew more hoarse. "I want M-mama . . ."

Knowing she had to calm Emma down somehow, McKenna cradled her close. "Shh . . ." Closing her eyes, she hoped Janie would forgive her. "Mama's here, Emma. It's okay, Mama's here."

Emma's breath caught, and in the dim light from the lamp in the other room, McKenna saw the child looking up at her. Any minute, Emma would see she wasn't Janie and would—

Emma nestled closer and snuggled her head into the crook of McKenna's neck. This time it was McKenna who sobbed. She rocked Emma back and forth, back and forth, and thought of the many times Janie had surely sat right here in this very same spot and done the very same thing.

Finally, worn out from crying, Emma went limp in her arms. McKenna laid her down on the bed and covered her with a light sheet. She checked her forehead again. Then felt of her cheeks.

She was cooler! Her fever wasn't gone, but it was definitely subsiding.

Grateful and exhausted, McKenna was about to lie down beside her when she heard a knock on the front door. She pushed up from the bed, found her way into the front room, and was reaching for the rifle atop the cupboard when she recognized Wyatt calling out to her.

She unbolted the door and he hurried inside, bringing torrents of rain and wind with him. He pushed the door closed and turned, and McKenna threw her arms around him. The wetness of his coat seeped through her dress.

He hugged her tight. "Are you okay? Where's Emma?"

McKenna nodded, so happy to see him, and so relieved all at the same time. She drew back. "She's running a fever, but it's breaking. I think she's going to be okay."

Wyatt shrugged off his duster, hung it on a peg, and headed for the bedroom. A puddle of water marked the spot where he'd stood.

McKenna met him by the bedside.

"What have you given her?" His voice sounded tight.

She told him everything she'd done, and how much tea she'd managed to get Emma to drink.

He felt of Emma's forehead. "She's still a mite warm." He turned. "I'll ride for Doc Foster."

At that moment, a peal of thunder cracked overhead. Emma jerked but didn't waken. McKenna hastily soothed her back to sleep and caught Wyatt at the front door. Already in his duster again, she grabbed his arm. "She doesn't need Dr. Foster, Wyatt. Her fever's breaking."

He reached for the door, not seeming to hear her.

She reached up and took his face in her hands. He stilled.

"Emma's going to be okay. Her fever's breaking." His face was a mixture of pain and fear, and suddenly his actions made more sense to her. "Did your Bethany die of fever?" she whispered, already seeing the answer in his eyes.

"I can't—" His voice caught. "I can't lose another child that way."

She hugged him to her as tight as she could, wanting him to feel every part of her loving him. "You won't. You won't lose Emma."

He lifted her face to his, and McKenna met his kiss and returned it.

"You're sure she's all right?" he said.

McKenna nodded. "Yes, but . . ." She looked down and away. "I did something I shouldn't have done."

"What? What did you do?"

Shame poured through her. "Emma kept crying for Janie, asking for her mama." She shrugged. "I couldn't console her, her fever was high." She closed her eyes. "I told her that . . . *I* was her mama. I know it was wrong. I don't want her to forget Janie, it's just that—"

"You remember that night, McKenna," he said, his voice soft, "when Janie asked you to take care of her?"

She nodded. "I'll never forget it."

"Janie asked you to take her . . . and *make her your own*. Those were her exact words."

Not following him, McKenna waited from him to say something else.

He took her in his arms, his eyes at once both steel and velvet. "Am I your husband, McKenna?"

She stared. "I don't understand what you're—"

He kissed her long and hard. Pressed against him, McKenna began to feel something deep inside her slowly unfurl.

Breathless when he finally drew back, she blinked to refocus.

She searched his eyes and, for a moment, thought he was going to kiss her again.

He trailed a finger across her lips. "Let me ask this another way. Even though we haven't known each other as husband and wife, *yet* . . ." Intimacy deepened his expression. "Is there any doubt in your mind that I'm your husband? Now, in this moment?"

It took her a few seconds to form the right syllable. "No," she finally whispered, swallowing. "There's no doubt."

"As sure as you are of that, even without the closeness we'll share one day as husband and wife, that's the kind of certainty Emma needs in her life right now. She needs a mother,

McKenna. I'm not saying for you to step in and replace Janie. No one can ever do that, and I know you'd never try. You loved Janie too much. But you can be to Janie's daughter what Janie can't be anymore. God put you into Emma's life to be"—he wiped the tears from her cheeks—"her mama."

As though standing by Janie's bedside again, McKenna heard the distant echo of her cousin's fragile voice. *"Take her as your own."* And for a second time, she silently pledged to do just that.

They checked on Emma together and found her sleeping soundly, her fever all but gone.

When Wyatt started for the sofa, McKenna took hold of his hand and led him into their bedroom, and closed the door. Remembering something from their wedding one month ago, she reached for his hand and found the scar on his thumb. She kissed it—once, twice—and noticed the subtle shake of his head.

"You're testing your husband's patience, Mrs. Caradon," he whispered, his voice husky.

She drew him down beside her on the bed and kissed him, long and slow, as she'd thought about doing for days now. Loving his response, she also loved the way she felt when he took over. His clothes were soaked, but she soon found his skin beneath to be warm. And by the time the sun rose, McKenna knew with certainty that Mei was right—the most fertile soil for love truly did lie in the heart of a friend. And in the heart of her husband.

A heart that had been broken by God and made whole again, just like hers.

FORTY-FIVE

In a room reserved for family members of defendants, McKenna surveyed the courtroom through a narrow slit in the window covering. Seeing jailers lead Robert in through a side door off to the right, her heart ached. His wrists and ankles were shackled. She couldn't see his face from where she stood, but he looked as though he'd lost weight through his shoulders.

Over three months had passed since she'd last seen him in the jail in Copper Creek. But it felt like much longer. She glanced back to see Wyatt seated on the couch beside Emma, who was practicing letters on her slate. His head was bowed.

Fingering the handkerchief in her pocket, she thanked God again for bringing him into her life, for so many reasons. For the fullness he added to her, for the change she trusted was taking place in Robert's heart, and for the ability to keep the ranch and raise Emma in the home Vince and Janie had built for their family.

What had seemed nothing at the time, Wyatt's discovery of the irrigation pipes near the creek bed had led them to uncovering the truth, and had proven her instincts right about Harrison Talbot. When Vince hired a prospecting company to survey a large patch of "heavy sand" by the creek, Harrison *Taylor* was the employee they'd sent. He'd accepted Vince and Janie's offer to stay for dinner and had gotten to know them over several days of surveying their land. That explained how Emma remembered him so well. But the company went bankrupt before the report to Vince was completed, and then Vince died. So he and Janie never received the final report of what had been found.

But Harrison Taylor knew.

And after reading a newspaper account of residents who had succumbed to cholera, he decided to pose as Vince's brother—the strong resemblance between them only aiding his cause. But in the end, the far-reaching connections of the U.S. Marshals Office and a string of fraudulent bank drafts caught up with him. And when it came time for the auction of the property in Denver, Wyatt and Chin Li's combined efforts in butchering the cattle themselves, then selling and delivering the meat to contacts Wyatt had made in mining towns, provided nearly enough money to purchase the homestead outright. It took slaughtering all the cattle Vince and Janie had bought, and every penny of income from the saddles, but at least they still had the land and the possibility of something more for the future.

Yet one piece was still missing—that final surveyor's report. It was due back any day now. Finally after weeks of waiting.

"Are you ready for this, McKenna?"

Wyatt's question coaxed her back. And hearing the trepidation in his voice, McKenna drew herself up.

"No . . . and yes." She moved to stand before him. He looked handsome in the formal judicial robes. "Are *you* ready?"

His gaze was somber. "I didn't ask for this case. You know that."

She eyed the still-healing gash on his right cheek. "I know you didn't."

For weeks, the third man involved in the robbery with Robert had eluded the Marshals Office. Finally, they tracked him to the town of Severance. Wyatt had been called to help bring him in, but the man hadn't come without a fight. The wound would leave a scar, but that was a small price compared to what could have happened.

"I know you didn't ask for Robert's case, Wyatt. But ever since he was arrested, I've been praying about who would decide his fate. And I've asked God, many times, to provide a judge who would decide for my brother what God desires be done."

Two feet of snow had fallen in the past two days since they'd arrived in Denver. The accumulation impeded travel and, combined with the Thanksgiving holiday just around the corner, judges were scarce. This particular case had been reviewed by the Marshals Office and Wyatt's ruling confirmed by a judge, so he was delivering the verdict today—something she'd learned the Marshals Office was called to do on rare occasions.

McKenna knelt in front of her husband, loving the way he looked at her. "So it was no surprise to me this morning when they asked you. I believe it was an answer to my prayers, Wyatt."

He shook his head, a faint smile seeping through his seriousness. "I've got to stop you from praying that prayer for me, woman." He traced the curve of her cheek, then wove a path down her neck. She loved the way he touched her in intimate moments like this, when they were alone. But even more, she loved the way she felt inside when he did.

A knock sounded on the door, and they both stood. Wyatt's superior, Samuel Ramsey, walked in and closed the door behind him. He carried a file.

"Mrs. Caradon." He nodded her way before turning to Wyatt. "They're ready for you, Caradon. They're waiting to bring in the other prisoner until you're ready for him. He's still a little . . . unruly, you might say. And he for sure won't be happy about seeing you again."

Wyatt huffed, fingering his cheek. "I'm sure he won't."

"We've got a double guard on him, so there shouldn't be any problem. But if there is, are you—"

"Yes, sir," Wyatt answered, not looking in her direction. "I'm sure things will be fine."

McKenna looked between the two men, sensing there was more to this exchange than their conversation revealed.

"Good then, I guess we're set." Ramsey nodded. "The Marshals Office appreciates you filling in like this, especially on such short notice." He extended his hand, and Wyatt gripped it. "I know it's not the first thing at the top of your list."

"No, sir, it's not. I turned in the names of the final conspirators for the Brinks case last week. By chance, do you know if—"

"They've picked up all of them but one. And he won't get far. They turned on each other so fast, we have all the evidence we need to convict the whole slew of them. You did well, Caradon," Ramsey said. His voice quieting he continued, "The families of Charlie Boyd and Frank Williams are here today. They were in town for one of the convictions and heard you were holding court. Their wives want to thank you personally for tracking down the men who killed their husbands." He looked at McKenna. "Mrs. Caradon, they'd like to meet you too, if you've got time. They're waiting downstairs. You and your daughter can go down anytime you like."

Wyatt briefly bowed his head, and McKenna could only imagine what the wives of the two U.S. Marshals slain in the Brinks robberies were going through. Wyatt had told her he'd be open to doing something other than marshaling after the Brinks case was closed. She hoped they were quickly approaching that juncture.

"One more thing." Ramsey held out the file. "Curtis asked

me to give you this. Something about a surveyor's report. Said it was personal."

Wyatt took the file, and McKenna caught his sideways glance in her direction. She knew by the way he wouldn't look directly at her that he was hiding something.

Ramsey touched the rim of his imaginary hat. "Mrs. Caradon, a pleasure as always."

She nodded. "Mr. Ramsey." He left the room and she followed Wyatt to the door. Curious about the file, she was even more concerned about this second prisoner. "Be careful," she whispered. "This other prisoner. He sounds dangerous."

Wyatt ran his hands slowly down her arms and rested them about her waist. "He's nothing to worry about. I'll see you and Emma back here afterward."

She hugged him, and froze when she felt the pistol on his hip beneath the robe. She looked up at him.

"It's just precautionary, McKenna. Ramsey insisted on it. Everything's going to be fine."

He kissed her, not lingering like he normally did, and then knelt down and hugged Emma close before leaving the room.

McKenna watched through the curtained window minutes later, pride and concern swelling inside her as he took the judge's seat in the courtroom. Yet in the same breath, apprehension for Robert and what his future held, crouched hidden in a far corner of her heart.

Without fail, Wyatt had visited Robert every week since Robert arrived at the Denver jail. He'd also studied the evidence against Robert but hadn't been at liberty to share it with her. She understood, yet she still didn't like the not knowing.

The same prayer she prayed for her brother, she now also prayed for herself, and for Wyatt, and—which often proved hardest—for Emma. Would there ever come a time when her faith would be so refined that she would whisper that hushed petition—*Break me, Lord, until I'm wholly yours*—without cringing the slightest little bit. She trusted the Lord. It wasn't that. She simply didn't trust Him enough. Not yet.

She'd once thought God would never intentionally hurt her. But looking back over her life, she'd had cause to rethink that. She was certain nothing touched her life that didn't first filter through the loving hands of her heavenly Father. But she was also convinced that God sometimes wounded, in order to bind up. And that He shattered, so that His hands could heal. This was part of His inheritance she'd overlooked before, but never would again.

The formal court proceedings took longer than she'd anticipated. Fifteen minutes later, a bailiff was still reading the summary account of Robert's trial and the evidence in the case. The walls of the waiting room started to feel as if they were closing in, and McKenna remembered the wives of the slain officers who were waiting downstairs.

She bent down and brushed a kiss to Emma's forehead. "Please gather your things, sweetie. We're going to take a walk."

Emma complied. "Isn't Mr. Wyatt coming?"

McKenna smiled. "He's got some work to do. But we'll meet him back here shortly."

Their footsteps echoed down the long marble corridor as they walked hand in hand.

Passing the doors to the courtroom, McKenna was tempted to stop and peer through the window in the door, but she didn't want Wyatt—or Robert—to glance up and see her there. Robert hadn't wanted her present in the courtroom, and Wyatt had encouraged her to respect his wishes.

Only, now she couldn't help but wonder if the real reason Wyatt hadn't wanted her in there was rooted more in why Ramsey had insisted he wear a gun, rather than in Robert's desire for her absence.

At the far end of the corridor, three men rounded the

corner, and McKenna instinctively tightened her hold on Emma's hand.

Flanked on either side by guards, a prisoner shuffled along, his shackled steps heavy, each one coerced. The chains encircling his ankles made a dull clanking noise when he walked—metal rubbing metal—and the sound echoed down the empty corridor.

The closer the men came, the more difficult McKenna found it not to stare. The prisoner looked so familiar. Had she seen him before? No, that was impossible.

His right shoulder appeared bulky, as though bandaged beneath his shirt. His face was cut and bruised. This had to be the prisoner Wyatt and Ramsey had spoken of earlier. The one Robert had been involved with in the robbery. The man Wyatt had apprehended in Severance.

Still a few feet away, the guard on the prisoner's right, a U.S. Marshal she'd met that morning, acknowledged her. "Mrs. Caradon," he said, face somber.

The prisoner locked eyes with her—and recognition washed over McKenna in a thick, sickening wave. The prisoner shifted his attention to Emma, and the same repulsive chill McKenna had felt that afternoon, months ago, in the barn when he'd first looked at the child, returned.

Question lit his face. "Caradon?" he whispered and looked from Emma back to her.

McKenna saw it in his eyes, the same as when he had accosted them in the barn—the intent to do harm.

A knife slid from his sleeve into his palm, and the man grinned. In a flash, he sank the blade into the leg of the guard who had greeted her. The guard went down.

Bending to pick up Emma, McKenna saw the second guard draw his gun. But he wasn't fast enough. The prisoner delivered a swift elbow to the guard's windpipe and the gun went off. A window exploded beside them and glass showered the hallway. Emma screamed and tightened her hold around McKenna's neck.

The guard dropped the gun and fell to his knees, gasping, choking for air.

McKenna's gaze went to the gun on the floor—the same time as the prisoner's did. He lunged for it, and McKenna turned and ran, Emma in her arms.

The hallway was empty. And suddenly seemed endless. Every step was an inch compared to the distance to the closed courtroom doors. Even holding Emma, McKenna knew she could outrun the prisoner. But there was no way she could outrun the bullet. The fleeting thought of what a bullet would feel like piercing flesh came and went. And left her body cold and clammy.

She crushed Emma to her chest. How many bullets were left in the chamber? And would her own body be enough to stop them from penetrating through to Emma?

Heart pumping, she chanced a look over her shoulder, careful to keep Emma protected.

The prisoner took aim.

Oh God . . . She tried to pray but only one word passed her lips. "*Jesus.*"

She turned back, hearing a gunshot behind her, and fell forward—into someone's arms.

She looked up, shaking, breath coming hard, and made out the blurred image of Robert's face. He steadied her and Emma as another deafening blast filled the hallway.

Shielding Emma's face in the curve of her neck, McKenna saw Wyatt standing beside them, readying to fire a second time. Chains rattled behind her. A shuffling sound. And Wyatt fired again, in quick succession this time, the tang of gunpowder thickening the air.

EPILOGUE

May 27, 1878

As McKenna peeled potatoes for the roast, she found her gaze returning to the road, as if her heart was tethered to whoever might appear around the bend. Because it was.

Feeling a tug on her skirt, she glanced down. "Yes, sweetie?"

"Can—I—" Emma tried to speak around a mouthful of warm bread.

"Finish your bite first." Smiling, McKenna tweaked her chipmunk cheeks.

Rocking back and forth on the heels of her feet, Emma nodded, her eyes squinting at the corners, so much like Janie's.

McKenna glanced behind her at Mei, who was kneading more dough on the kitchen table. Mei pounded the lump again and again, rotating it a quarter turn each time, and forming a rhythm as she went along—*Thwack!*, *turn—Thwack!*, *turn—Thwack!*, *turn*—which is probably why her bread came out so fluffy and perfect every time. Something McKenna had come to accept would never be said of hers. Although it *had* improved.

Emma made a show of swallowing. "Mama, can I go with

Mr. Chin? He found a nest in the trees and it's got baby birdies in it."

McKenna glanced through the window and saw Chin Li waiting by the porch steps. "Yes, you may. But remember not to touch the birds."

"Yes, ma'am!" Emma was out the door in a flash.

Smiling, still loving the sound of *Mama* on Emma's lips, McKenna added the potatoes to the roast and returned the pan to the oven. She peered through the window and followed Emma and Chin Li's progress as they walked toward the stand of aspen growing along the edge of the field. Emma's endless stream of chatter drifted through the open window, and McKenna wondered if Chin Li ever grew weary of it. He didn't seem to.

Just then, Emma reached up and grabbed his hand. Chin Li's arm went stiff, and he pulled away. McKenna cringed. She'd spoken with Emma about this before. Chin Li was such a private man. Not even he and Mei held hands in public.

Chin Li peered down, and slowly—very slowly—wrapped his fingers around her hand.

Beaming up at him, Emma started chattering away again as they continued on. McKenna's appreciation for the man deepened tenfold. Then something drew her gaze back to the road and her pulse kicked up a notch.

But no one was there. It must have been the wind in the trees.

Wyatt had been in Denver for the past three days, arranging for Robert's release. Memories of what happened in the courthouse weren't as clear as they once had been, but there were moments, like now, when they crept closer than she would have liked. The prisoner—scheduled to have been hanged for his crimes—had been served justice swiftly that day, more swiftly than his wrongs demanded.

That day had also served as the final turning point for Wyatt's career. He'd resigned as a U.S. Marshal one week later.

Robert was found innocent of shooting the U.S. Marshal, but

guilty in the charge of attempted robbery. Understandably so. The maximum sentence for his part in the crime was seven months, and Robert had served every day of his seven-month sentence. McKenna hadn't spoken to him once during that time. She'd written letters, but had stopped hoping for a response months ago.

Wyatt told her Robert was quiet these days and that he wasn't exactly sure what was going on inside her brother, which only encouraged McKenna to pray more fervently.

A wave of dizziness came over her, and she gripped the edge of the washbasin, suddenly overwarm.

"You want tea?" Mei asked behind her.

McKenna turned to see Mei holding up the pitcher. "Yes, I'd love some, thank you."

Mei was as at home in this kitchen as she was in her own, and her green tea rivaled her moon cakes. She poured a glass and McKenna took a long satisfying drink.

"Mmm, that's delicious. Thank you."

Mei smiled, her eyes lowering to McKenna's rounded abdomen even as she covered her own. "Our babies be good friends. Like you and me."

McKenna laughed softly. "We'll make certain of that." Her gaze dropped to Mei's feet. Wordless, she crossed the room and dragged a stool over to the table. "You have to be hurting, Mei. Please sit down."

Though she and Mei had grown close in recent months, McKenna had said nothing to Mei about her Lotus feet. What was there to say? Nothing corrective could be done at this late stage, as Dr. Foster had confirmed. And she wasn't even sure that Mei would want anything to be attempted in the first place.

Mei looked at the stool, then at McKenna. "Thank you," she said, easing her still slight weight onto the seat. She sighed. "Much better now." She smiled that special way a person did when recalling a shared joke, then just as quickly, her smile faded. She looked down at her feet. "If we have daughter, Chin Li already say . . ." Her voice broke. Her face crumpled. "We no do this to her."

Hurting for her friend, McKenna hesitated, unsure about the emotion behind Mei's reaction. Was she happy at Chin Li's decision? Or sad? Hugging her from the side, she smoothed a hand over Mei's back.

Mei sniffed and sat up straighter. "You saw . . . my feet. That day Emma was lost." Her eyes said she already knew the truth.

"I saw," McKenna whispered. "But only briefly."

Mei nodded and lifted the hem of her full pants to display an exquisite slipper beneath. Her smile trembled. "Can you reach for me?"

Understanding her request, McKenna bent, grasping the edge of the table for balance, and carefully removed Mei's slipper. Mei's foot was bound with cloth.

"It is custom among my people that started long time ago. Nine hundred years." Mei tried to lean down, as if wanting to remove the binding from around her foot, but she couldn't quite reach.

McKenna situated herself on the floor and began unwinding it for her. "Does it hurt all the time?" She chanced a look up.

Mei's expression was bathed in gratitude. "Not all the time."

It took a couple of moments, but McKenna removed the strip of cloth. She tried not to wince, but what she'd only glimpsed one afternoon months ago, she saw now in excruciating detail.

The shape of Mei's foot could best be described as bent, concave. There was a cleft, on the underside of each sole, between the ball of Mei's foot and the heel, that was at least two inches deep. Her entire foot, measuring from heel to toe, couldn't have been more than four inches in length. And from what McKenna could tell, every toe but the large one was missing on both feet. This was a barbaric custom. How could anyone do this to their child?

"You wonder why parents do this to daughters they love?"

Tears in her eyes, McKenna nodded. Mei read her too well.

"This custom is sign of wealth in China. I was four"—she held up that number of fingers—"when my mother and grandmother bind my feet for first time. My mother, her mother, and her mother before . . . all women in family have Lotus feet. All husbands want wives to have such feet. Girls who do not . . ." She shook her head. "They no grow up to marry. And if woman no marry, she disgrace to family, and parents are shamed."

McKenna accepted what Mei was saying as truth in the Chinese culture, but she still couldn't get that truth—and what she was seeing—to make any sense in her head. Not with such deformity before her. She rose slowly and retrieved a fresh towel and a bowl of water.

When she returned, Mei was shaking her head.

"You no need do this. Chin Li help me at—"

"I want to do this, Mei. Please," McKenna whispered.

After a long moment, Mei gave a bow from her seated position, emotion glistening in her eyes.

McKenna returned the bow and then knelt. She removed the cloths from Mei's other foot and washed both of Mei's feet in the lukewarm water. "You did something similar for me the very first day I arrived in town. Do you remember?"

"I no forget. Ever." Mei smiled. "You no want me to take kerchief."

McKenna laughed softly. "But once you returned it, I was so grateful you had taken it."

When she finished, she dried Mei's feet and rewrapped them in the bandages. Then she slipped the tiny, exquisite slippers onto Mei's feet and vowed never again to take for granted how easily she laced up her boots. Nor would she complain when her feet grew sore from too much walking.

With care, she broached Mei's original statement. "If you have a daughter, Mei . . . will you be happy, or sad, about Chin Li's decision?"

"Both, I think. Happy that daughter will run and play like Emma, and no have pain. But part of heart will also be sad. She will be . . . different from her mother and all women in her family before." Mei rose from the stool and smoothed her tunic. "But mostly, I am happy. And grateful to Chin Li."

She reached out to hug McKenna but their bellies met first, which caused them to giggle.

Even warmer now than before, McKenna gestured toward the door. "I won't be long."

"You take time. Dinner almost ready." Grinning, Mei made a shooing gesture. "I bake bread now and no need you to stay and help."

Not hurt in the least, McKenna walked on outside and eased herself down on the top porch step. She breathed the cool, dry air of spring and mentally counted the days until July when Dr. Foster said the baby was due. She hoped for a boy, but Wyatt kept saying it didn't matter to him. He hadn't said it aloud, but she knew he only wanted her and the baby to be well.

She glanced at the saddle on the far end of the porch. Dr. Foster was joining them later today, and she looked forward to giving it to him. A long-overdue token of her appreciation, the saddle was custom-made with bags to match that would hold Dr. Foster's bottles and supplies. She'd even etched the medical insignia into the leather, along with his name.

Her gaze traveled the homestead. It was still hard to believe that all of this was theirs. The surveyor's report that came back the day of Robert's sentencing revealed silver lead deposits dotting Vince and Janie's property down by the creek. It certainly wasn't a gold strike, but it was enough to buy a few head of cattle and to breathe renewed life into the dream that Vince and Janie had for this ranch and for the life they'd wanted to give their daughter. The barn boasted a fresh coat of red paint and the porch swing Wyatt had made for their evenings out here together creaked softly behind her, pushed to and fro by the breeze. But where she sat now offered a better view of the road.

Chin Li and Emma were slowly making their way back to the cabin. Emma waved her little arms wide, and McKenna waved in return—then stilled. Her gaze slowly trailed to where the road switched back on itself, and her throat closed tight.

Two riders, one taking the lead, one following behind, made their way toward her.

Gripping the porch rail, she stood, the tether on her heart tugging hard.

A short distance away, Robert reined in. For a moment, she wasn't sure whether he was going to turn and ride away, or keep moving forward. But she stayed exactly where she was. Wyatt had told her it was important to let Robert take his own first steps in the coming days. And she agreed. But oh, it was hard to keep her feet planted where she stood when her mother's heart wanted to ease his journey home.

Robert continued on and dismounted beside Wyatt near the barn. Even yards away, his discomfort was palpable. Wyatt laid a hand to his shoulder and whispered something to him. Robert nodded, and stood staring at his boots for the longest time. Then slowly, he lifted his eyes, smiled in McKenna's direction, and took his first step toward home.

He stopped a short distance away from her, head bowed. He removed his hat and stood twisting it in his hands, until finally he peered up. "Hello, Kenny."

He looked different. Even his voice sounded different—deeper, more . . . centered. She'd promised herself she wouldn't cry. "Hello, Robert. It's good to see you again."

"It's good to see you again too." He smiled an all but forgotten smile. "I've missed you, Kenny. More than you know." He stared at the hat in his hands for the longest time before looking at her again. "I'm sorry . . . for what I did. I was wrong, in lots of ways. And I want to do better now. I want to make things right." His jaw firmed, but in a noble way. "You have my pledge that I'll work to make things right."

Catching Wyatt's subtle nod behind Robert, McKenna

closed the distance to her brother and put her arms around his neck. She couldn't remember the last time she'd done this—held her younger brother close—and she relished it, not wanting to take this for granted either.

Once they drew apart, she patted his chest. "Supper's about ready, and I've got all your favorites."

Robert slipped his hat back on. "Sounds good," he said. "I think I'll go wash up then." He started to walk away, then stopped and surveyed the surroundings. "The place looks real fine, Kenny. Real fine. Wyatt says things have really turned around."

"Yes," she whispered, so much meaning in one word. "They certainly have."

She watched him cut through the barn to the well, and she felt Wyatt's arms come around her from behind.

"You were perfect, McKenna."

She leaned into him, mindful of Emma running straight for them. Chin Li nodded their way then averted his gaze. But McKenna saw the smile on his mouth.

"Papa!"

Wyatt caught Emma up and gave her a big hug. "How are you, little one?"

Emma's eyes sparkled. "Did you bring me anything?"

"Now what makes you think I'd bring you anything?"

She stuck her hand into his outer vest pocket, which earned a raised brow from Wyatt. So she immediately went for his inner pocket, and her grin widened.

"Another doll!" she squealed.

Wyatt tugged the red-yarned head of the rag doll. "I figured Clara needed a sister, since you'll be getting either a new brother or sister yourself real soon."

Emma hugged his neck tight. "Thank you, Papa."

"Now," he said, kissing her forehead and setting her down. "We're going to have Uncle Robert's welcome home dinner in just a minute, but first, I'd like for you to run on inside and show Chin Li and Mei your new doll while I kiss your mama good and proper. Think you can do that for me?"

Grinning, Emma nodded and set off.

McKenna was grinning too, until Wyatt pulled her close. Seeing the desire in his eyes sparked her own, and she slipped a hand beneath his vest to finger a button on his shirt. "I've missed you, Mr. Caradon." No longer *Marshal*, and she was so thankful.

His hand moved lower down her back, pressing her closer against him. He smiled. "I think I've warned you before, ma'am"—his gaze went from her eyes to her mouth—"about looking at a man that way when he can't do anything about it."

Remembering the first day he'd said that to her, McKenna cradled the back of his neck and drew his face down to hers. "Then I suggest, sir, that you do something about it. Right quick."

And he did.

AUTHOR'S NOTE

Nearly fifteen years ago, on a wintry Colorado day, I dropped our only son off for another morning of kindergarten. I don't remember the exact day, but it had to have been late October because I *do* remember that I planned to head home after work and finish sewing Halloween costumes. I say "late" October because sewing (especially Halloween costumes, or anything other than a garment that requires straight hems) has always been something I've put off for as long as possible. My skills are sorely lacking in the sewing department.

While our son usually enjoyed kindergarten, on that particular day, for some reason, he was hesitant for me to leave. But we finally made the separation and I headed on to my job as a secretary at our nearby church (my hat goes off to every church secretary out there! While rewarding, it can be an endless and often times thankless job). I was almost to work when I remembered something I needed to get from home.

Since we didn't live far, I turned around and headed back home as it began to snow. After retrieving what I needed, I retraced my path to work. On the way, I saw a child—all bundled up against the cold, chin tucked against the wind—walking up the sidewalk adjacent to a high traffic four-lane road that ran in front of the school. A semi-truck rumbled up the road, gaining speed.

What kind of mother would let a child that young walk this busy road all by himself? And why wasn't the poor child in school? Slowing my car, I huffed to myself, "Parents need to make sure their children are safely inside the school building instead of just dropping them off and then driving awa—"

The little boy looked up, and my heart stopped. The child was mine! And *I* was that mother.

My son saw me and started toward the curb. I stopped my car in the middle lane, watching the approaching semi barreling down the road. I got out of the car and yelled at my son to stay where he was. Not to move. I could tell he'd been crying. He took another step toward the road, almost to the curb now. Couldn't he hear the oncoming truck?

I screamed again for him to stay right he was. The truck's horn blasted, and my son froze. For a few terrifying seconds, the semi passed between us and I couldn't see him. I waited—heart in my throat—for that truck to pass. And I prayed he would still be standing on the curb on the other side.

He was.

I ran over and grabbed him, hugged and kissed him, shook him, hugged and kissed him and shook him some more, crying along with him now. Turns out, he'd left his "show and tell" item at home and had gone back to get it (without telling the teacher, of course). Never mind that he didn't have a key to the house or that it was freezing outside.

As I carried him back to the car, I heard an inaudible confirmation inside me. It wasn't even a voice really. No words that I remember. I simply recall that I knew a prayer I'd been praying had been answered. I was thankful beyond words that I'd "just happened" to forget something that morning, and that the Lord had nudged me to turn my car back toward home. I shudder to think what might have happened had I not come upon my little boy as he trudged along that busy highway.

And the answer to my prayer? I'd been asking God to make me more grateful for what I had in my life and to break me until I was wholly (and holy) His. I'm not saying God led my son out there that day into the cold to teach me a lesson. But I am saying that God used that incident to answer my prayer, in a big way.

The theme of this book is brokenness and it's a theme God has been working on in my life, and in my heart, for a very long time. A broken and contrite heart, the Lord will not despise, the psalmist says in Psalm 51. I so wish I were already "there" in this respect, but I still have so far to go. So much to surrender and so much yet to entrust to Him. But He's shaping me, bit by bit, step by step, day by day.

So my continued prayer—perhaps along with you now—is *break me, Lord, until I'm wholly yours.*

Until next time,
Tamera Alexander

Reading Group Guide

Note to readers: As would be expected in a discussion guide, crucial plot points and events are revealed in the following questions. So if you haven't finished reading *The Inheritance* and don't wish to have these "surprises" spoiled, you might want to skip reading the group guide until you have.

1. When you first glimpsed the title *The Inheritance*, what's the very first thing you thought of? An earthly inheritance? Or a spiritual one?
2. McKenna Ashford is a woman who's been handed a lot of responsibility early in life. She didn't ask for it, and she hasn't handled it all well. Can you identify with some of her struggles in the story—her anger, her confusion—and the question of "why" God has allowed these to happen in her life?
3. In Chapter Five, McKenna is faced with a situation she hadn't anticipated and one that pushes her to the brink. Have you ever experienced a "domino effect" of stressful

events in your life? How did you get through it? How does John 16:33 speak to this?

4. The last three paragraphs of Chapter Five describe a deep friendship that has stood the test of time, and that—even though interrupted for a time—will last throughout eternity. Have you ever experienced a friendship like this? If yes, what made that friendship so special and how did it change your life?

5. In Chapter Eight, McKenna must explain "death" to Emma (five years old). Do you agree with how she chose to explain what happened to Emma's mother? How might you have explained things differently?

6. In Chapter Nine, Wyatt Caradon fulfills a promise he made to Janie Talbot. This event in the book was taken from an actual historical account. If Janie had made this request of you, would you have done it?

7. McKenna's relationship with her brother, Robert, is a dysfunctional one, for many reasons. In Chapter Thirteen we get a glimpse (in their argument) of just how dysfunctional it is. What happens in this chapter with Emma? And what would you say is the biggest underlying issue for Robert and McKenna?

8. McKenna finds an unexpected and unlikely friend in Chin Mei, a Chinese woman she meets (in Chapter Fourteen) for the second time. Have you ever had a "fated" friendship? One that seemed prearranged by God from the very beginning? Someone with whom you felt an instant kinship? Describe what that felt like and how you met that person.

9. Wyatt's life crosses that of Robert Ashford, and Wyatt sees himself in the young man. In Chapter Twenty-Three and Twenty-Four, he intentionally chooses not to intervene in a situation with Robert. Do you agree with Wyatt's decision?

And have you ever known someone like Robert Ashford who seems to have an unquenchable need to prove him/herself, almost to their destruction? Where do you believe these feelings, these needs stem from? And how would you attempt to help someone like this?

10. Like many of us, McKenna faces significant financial struggles amidst her emotional challenges. Have you ever faced financial struggles similar to this degree where the future seemed so bleak, you didn't know what to do or where to turn next? What was your greatest source of comfort through this time?

11. As McKenna faces challenges, she's determined to not "be broken" by them. When she first stated that desire (to remain strong and not be broken), what was your reaction to her determination? Did you cheer for her—or cringe for her? How did her character change as she came to see that brokenness was what God was trying to achieve in her heart all along? How does that lesson change our perspectives in our own lives?

12. McKenna has to learn how to love her brother, Robert, with a "tough love," something Wyatt Caradon's father taught him long ago. Have you ever had to love someone with "tough love?" A love that literally hurt you inside as you made choices that you knew were best for that person but that were extremely difficult to make and to carry out. How did you find the strength to make those choices? And what were they?

13. In Chapter Twenty-Six, Wyatt reflects on his own life and on what McKenna has told him about her and Robert's parents and their background. In a paragraph that begins with, "Knowing about their parents shed some light for him on Robert's poor choices . . ." he likens the varying situations that people are born into to a game a poker. He concludes,

"It wasn't the hand a person was dealt that determined the outcome—it was the person holding the cards that made the difference." What choice had he made with the life he'd been dealt? What choice have you made?

14. McKenna wants so badly for Robert to succeed that she steps in to shield him from failure, again and again. Casey Trenton, the livery owner, finally calls her hand on this (in Chapter Twenty-Seven) when he says, "I means that's a tall order . . . guaranteeing another person's word. I have a hard enough time keeping my own, much less somebody's else's." This is a turning point in McKenna's perspective. Have you ever struggled, perhaps with your own children, in wanting to shield them from life? How did you learn this lesson and learn to "let go?"

15. Wyatt recognizes a pride in McKenna, one that he's seen in himself. In Chapter Twenty-Nine, in the paragraph that begins with, "She had a streak of pride in her, but it wasn't one of vanity," he reflects on "good pride" and "bad pride." Do you agree with his assessment? Is there a "good" kind of pride? And how has pride impacted choices in your life?

16. In Chapter Thirty-Two, Robert inadvertently "confesses" to Wyatt about events that happened in St. Joseph. It's clear to Wyatt that guilt still weighs Robert down. And rightly so, because Robert hasn't faced his own issues yet. He's been denying them, running from them. In light of 2 Corinthians 7:10, what's the purpose of guilt? And how can guilt be "right" and "wrong?" What's the outcome of "good guilt" and "bad guilt?"

17. Security—both financial and emotional—is something McKenna is searching for during the course of her journey in *The Inheritance*. Yet in Chapter Thirty-Three, she has this thought, "But as it turned out, security was a fickle mistress. And was, at best, an illusion." Do you agree with her? Have

you ever pursued "security" above all else? What does Matthew 6:33 say about doing this?

18. In a final pivotal moment in McKenna's journey, she reflects in a paragraph (in Chapter Forty-Five) that begins with, "She'd once thought God would never intentionally hurt her. But looking back over her life, she'd had cause to rethink that." In reading the remainder of that paragraph, and in dwelling on Job 5:18, do you agree with McKenna's conclusion about how God works in our lives? Do you see evidence of Job 5:18 in your own life? And if yes, how?

19. In the final pages of *The Inheritance*, we get a glimpse of the lives of the characters some months later. As McKenna watches Robert "coming home," she stays exactly where she is. She doesn't step toward him. But it's so hard to keep her feet planted "when her mother's heart wants to ease his journey home." Have you ever experienced this type of angst for someone you've loved? You wanted them to "come home" so badly and yet you've (finally) realized that we can't take those first steps for each other. We can only take them for ourselves. What are those times in your own life and what did you learn that you could share with someone else who's in this situation?

Tamera is available for "Book Club Conference Calls" where she joins your book club for a 15–20 minute conversation via speakerphone. She also has a packet with some goodies for your group that she'll send beforehand, time allowing. For more information, please contact tamera@tameraalexander.com and request information on "Book Club Conference Calls."

ACKNOWLEDGMENTS

When Thomas Nelson approached me about writing the first historical novel for their Women of Faith fiction line, I was thrilled to have the opportunity to pen this story—for a second time. This novel is actually a revised version of the first story I ever wrote. The original version was rejected by a publisher several years ago, so I set it aside and determined to better learn this craft of writing.

After two subsequent years of study and practice, I was ready to submit my next manuscript for review. That second story blossomed into a novel entitled *Rekindled*, and the Fountain Creek Chronicles were born. But there was part of me that continued hoping that my very first characters would someday find their way onto the written page. *The Inheritance* is a complete new write of that first manuscript, with some changes in location and secondary characters. However, Wyatt and McKenna, have "lived within me" for years, and I'm thrilled for the chance to finally tell their stories.

My thanks to my editors at Thomas Nelson—Ami McConnell,

Natalie Hanemann, Becky Monds, and Jennifer Stair—and to freelance editor, Carol Craig, for helping me bring *The Inheritance* to fruition. My thanks also to Deborah Raney, my writing critique partner. I'm so glad God brought us together, Deb. Here's to twelve books and counting, friend . . .

To my agent, Natasha Kern, who's so much more than an agent. Thank you for providing sage counsel and a listening ear.

To my "favorite" father-in-law, Dr. Fred Alexander, for sharing your excellent proofreading skills with me, yet again.

To Joe, Kelsey, and Kurt—without you guys, none of this would be worth doing. Simply put—you are my life, and I love you.

To my Lord and Savior—continue to break me, Jesus, until I'm wholly Yours.

And to my readers, who knew that the connections we share would be the best part about writing? Your kind notes of encouragement are such gifts. I enjoy hearing from you at tamera@tameraalexander.com, and invite you to visit my website at www.tameraalexander.com for the latest news and book giveaways.

Dear Friend,

Stories are journeys, and each story I write is a journey for me. The greatest thrill of these writing journeys is when Christ reveals Himself in some new way, and I take a step closer to Him. My deepest desire is that readers of my books will do that as well—take steps closer to Him as they read. After all, it's all about Him.

As stories are journeys, so is life. And none of us were intended to travel this road alone. We need friends. Sisters. Confidants. We need women of faith alongside us.

I've attended numerous Women of Faith Conferences, and whether I attend with just one other woman or a group of a hundred women, I leave richer, fuller, and more fully focused on what God is doing in my life. I also leave with a greater appreciation of the "togetherness" of our walk here, and of just how very much alike we are—no matter our differences. Plus, the conferences are just flat out fun!

Get ready to do *a lot* of laughing, shed a tear . . . or ten, be uplifted by phenomenal worship music, and, best of all, take a step closer to Christ.

Thank you for sharing Wyatt and McKenna's journey in *The Inheritance*, and here's wishing you joy in your own.

Tamera